HAYDEN AND THE KNIGHTS

# THE MAGIC HOLLOW

# THE MAGIC HOLLOW

BY

## STEPHEN CLARKE

WITH ILLUSTRATION BY NICOLE RASKIN

MAGIC HOLLOW PUBLISHING
OGDEN, UTAH

*For Augustine*

❦

Text © 2021 by Stephen Clarke
Jacket art by Stephen J. Clarke © 2021 by Magic Hollow Publishing.
Illustration by Nicole Raskin © 2021 by Magic Hollow Publishing.



ISBN 978-1-7371565-0-5

Printed in the USA

This edition was edited by Gaven Wood and Iulia M.

# CONTENTS


**ONE** • The Lady in the Water • 1

**TWO** • Bullies and a Hoard • 11

**THREE** • A Strange Conversation • 22

**FOUR** • A Mysterious Threat • 31

**FIVE** • An Unexpected Guest • 39

**SIX** • Crashing the Party • 57

**SEVEN** • Somewhere in Between • 68

**EIGHT** • Siege Perilous • 89

**NINE** • New Camelot • 107

**TEN** • One Really Old Sword • 127

**ELEVEN** • The Other History • 140

**TWELVE** • Life of a Squire • 159

**THIRTEEN** • Lance and a Lance • 176

**FOURTEEN** • An Apparition of Mist • 187

**FIFTEEN** • The Tournament • 198

**SIXTEEN** • The Joust • 214

**SEVENTEEN** • Crossroads • 225

**EIGHTEEN** • Ready the Defenses • 234

**NINETEEN** • The Battle of the Hollow • 251

**TWENTY** • Unlikely Allies • 262

**TWENTY-ONE** • The Sword in the Stone • 269

**TWENTY-TWO** • The Lady of the Lake • 281

**TWENTY-THREE** • The Hall of Kings • 292

# THE MAGIC HOLLOW

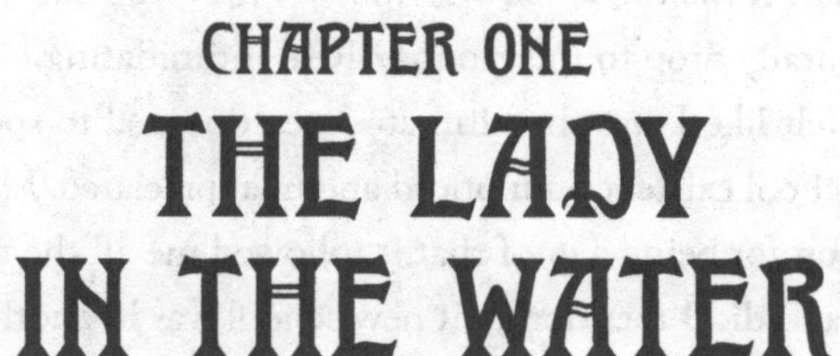

# CHAPTER ONE
# THE LADY
# IN THE WATER

**M**y name is Hayden. Nice to meet you. Normally I don't tell this story to someone I just met, but I have a good feeling about you. Who knows, you might even believe me. First, let me tell you a little about myself.

I've done a lot of embarrassing things growing up. One time, while I was cleaning my room, I tripped on a clothes hanger. Another time, I was in the mall wearing pants that were way too big. Halfway through the food court, they dropped to my ankles.

And then there was the time in a store with my foster mom. I wasn't paying attention, so thinking some stranger was my mom, I grabbed onto her cart and followed her for like ten minutes. I guess she was really weirded out but didn't know what to say, so she flagged down some confused employee to escort me back to my actual mom.

You probably get the point. But as embarrassing and funny as all those stories sound, none of them were the end of the world for me because at least my entire class wasn't there to watch.

If you had known me back then, I wouldn't blame you for thinking I didn't have what it took to be a hero. Even I doubted

# CHAPTER ONE

myself. I mean come on, when was the last time you saw a valiant hero's pants accidentally drop to the ground? Real intimidating.

I always felt like I was the ultimate loser, doomed to spend the rest of my middle school existence unnoticed and unappreciated. I had such a massive reputation for being a goof that it followed me all the way to my new school. Oh, and did I mention that new school was in another dimension?

Let me explain from the beginning.

I sat at my desk, enjoying my English teacher's lecture about this old book called *Le Morte d'Arthur*, which is all about King Arthur and the Knights of the Round Table. I had already read the entire book several times before, but that didn't make me any less interested in what my teacher had to say.

Mr. Bianco was a wizard at medieval literature and all things knights and adventure. Not only that, he knew all these cool facts about the English language, like how to speak Old English and the roots of almost every word and where it comes from. Well, except for the word *sheep*. Mr. Bianco says there's no known explanation for the word *sheep*.

Mr. Bianco made learning fun. He made the material come alive for me. And no matter what the other kids said about his lectures, I loved them. For a so-called geek like me, his class was even better than comic-con. Every class period was a new adventure. By the end of each class, I could *almost* believe that legends like King Arthur were real.

Something strange happened to me while I was sitting in Mr. Bianco's class the day before Halloween as Mr. Bianco was explaining the finer points of what a squire is. I would say it was the weirdest thing that has ever happened to me, but a lot of even weirder things have happened since.

I stared at my desk, trying not to look too interested in what he was saying—because, you know, other kids tend to pick on teacher's pets—but really, I was listening to every single word, taking it all in. I took a quick swig from my thermal water bottle. Before I could screw the cap back on, I heard someone whisper: "Hello, Hayden." Or maybe even, "hello, hero?" I can't remember.

I jumped with fright. Who would be whispering to me in class? Not to be a downer on myself, but nobody had whispered to me during class since like the fifth grade. Nowadays, I wasn't exactly what you would call popular. I guess you could say most kids avoided talking to me for fear of catching geek by association.

That is why I miss the fifth grade. Life was easier then. I don't know why so many kids look forward to becoming a teenager. By this point, I had been thirteen for nearly two whole months and being a teenager seemed entirely overrated. Long gone were the days when I could pick up a stick and start spontaneously sword fighting a bush or something. I mean, I could do that I guess, but I would probably get some funny looks while I was at it.

That right there is what's wrong with growing up. Suddenly, you start worrying about what other people think. Looking back, I know I had it all wrong. By all means, pick up that stick. Sword fight that bush. You owe it to yourself. Plus, maybe sword fighting will come in handy someday. It did for me.

Anyway, I looked around the class but didn't see anyone looking back at me. The girl sitting in the desk in front of me was slumped over in a daze, which made me wonder if we should move her onto life support. The boy in the next desk was spacing out as well, drawing on his arm so vigorously you'd think he was trying to give himself a permanent tattoo.

"Hayden," said the voice again, a little more urgently.

# CHAPTER ONE

This time, I was fairly sure I heard my name. I looked behind me, but no one was there. Just the pencil sharpener and the closed door, with a large purple poster taped haphazardly to it that read:

**BOOKS ARE MAGIC!**

I always sat in the back of the room in the corner closest to the door. If people didn't notice me, they didn't laugh at me when I did something embarrassing, or bully me with annoying questions that I didn't have answers to, like "Why are your eyes two different colors?" or "What happened to your real parents?"

I decided the whisper must have been in my head, when suddenly I heard it again. "Hayden! I'm in here."

I don't know what possessed me to do this next part, but I did it anyway. The voice sounded like it was coming right out of my water bottle. So, naturally, I picked it up, peered inside, and whispered, "How may I help you?"

Inside, I saw the last thing I ever expected to see. A tiny woman floating above the waterline was looking up at me with electric blue eyes, brighter than the ocean around the Bahamas.

I heard myself shout as I jumped back in my chair, sending my water bottle flying. I don't know what crashed first, my water bottle or my desk, but as I fell onto the cold hard floor both came falling on top of me with an earth-shattering *bang*.

My head was spinning in circles, but I didn't need to think straight to know everyone in the room was staring right at me. My water bottle spilled all over the floor and I could feel my pants soaking through. My classmates erupted with laughter. Mr. Bianco must have installed surround-sound speakers because I felt like I could hear everything my classmates said.

"Did you see that?"

"I saw him talking into his water bottle!"

"What a klutz, can you believe he signed up for basketball tryouts?"

"I hope no one invited him to the Halloween party."

Trying to ignore them, I focused on the throbbing pain in my forehead instead. Apparently, I hit my head on my desk as it squashed me like a bug. I didn't need to take a selfie to know my face was beet red with embarrassment.

Everyone was looking at me, but not because I was cool. Not because I had done something impressive, either. I wished just once I could be the center of attention for something awesome, like scoring the final point of a basketball game or making some funny joke in class. At this point, that dream seemed even more fantastical than the stories of King Arthur we were reading about.

The reality was they were staring and laughing at me for only one reason: because I was the *ultimate* geek.

I completely forgot any thought about what I heard and saw in my water bottle. I've never been more embarrassed in my life. My pants were soaking like I had wet the bed, and every giggle and every snicker felt like a sucker punch straight to my gut.

I wanted to disappear, run away, escape. Anywhere would be better than there. But I couldn't move. I was frozen with embarrassment.

I've never wanted to cry at school before. Except for that moment. The second lowest moment of my life. Honestly, I probably wouldn't have been able to hold back the tears any longer if it weren't for Mr. Bianco coming to my rescue. In my eyes, Mr. Bianco was a true hero that day.

"Everyone—*quiet*," Mr. Bianco said in his kind yet commanding tone.

The class stopped laughing, though they continued to murmur with excitement, no doubt retelling what they had seen. Mr. Bianco came to my side. Kneeling beside me, he shielded me from the class's view.

"Hayden—are you okay," he asked. "What happened?"

I made another glance at the pool of water gathered around me, but still, I saw no sign of the little water lady. "I—I don't know. I was leaning back in my chair and tipped over," I lied.

Mr. Bianco watched me closely. He must have noticed the odd way I looked at the water, because he looked down then back at me strangely. Just for a moment, his eyes narrowed, and I thought I saw realization on his face. Did he know what had happened—what I had seen in the water? But then the look was gone, and it was just his normal smiling expression again.

His gray eyes twinkled beneath his glasses. "Come on then, let's get you up." He grabbed my arm and gently, but with great strength, lifted me to my feet. He handed me my empty water bottle and copy of *Le Morte d'Arthur*, which thankfully hadn't gotten wet.

My head was still spinning from the impact, making it difficult to focus. "You hit your head pretty hard, Hayden. You better go see the nurse."

"Yeah," was all I said.

I didn't need to be told twice. Happy to escape that classroom and the peering eyes of all my classmates, I scooped up my bag and practically ran out the door. The worst part was hearing them burst with laughter for a second time the moment I left.

Their laughter ringing in my ears, I decided not to go to the nurse's office. My head started to feel better as soon as I was out the door and up on my feet. My pants were still soaked, though, and I still felt shocked from embarrassment. I was already dreading the next time I would have to face my class.

The halls were empty except for one or two students I didn't recognize.

# THE LADY IN THE WATER

They were on their way to the bathroom, holding bizarre bathroom passes like a red-painted toilet seat or a bright blue lanyard bearing our school logo, a knight in silver armor. The lanyard dangled dozens of obnoxious key chains that clinked and clanged with each step.

I never really understood teachers' fascination with hall passes. It's like they put as much energy into coming up with embarrassing bathroom passes as they do planning a lesson. Sometimes they are funny, true, but most of the time they make timid kids like me hold it until lunch recess.

For the record, Mr. Bianco never made us wait if we had to go to the bathroom. It's a little thing, but I felt like he trusted us. If we said we didn't feel good or had to pee, the good man let us out of the classroom to take care of our business, minimal questions asked.

I did feel guilty for taking advantage of his trust by not actually visiting the school nurse, but at the time all I wanted was to escape. I needed a place to hide where I couldn't be seen. Somewhere where I could try to process everything that had happened. See, I knew this feeling so well by then, I was certain I was experiencing anxiety. In my case, only being outside and alone seemed to calm me down and help me focus.

I exited the school from one of the side doors near the cafeteria, which led me to a large blacktop. It was a cool, crisp day, but not too cold to deter PE class.

I could see Ms. Wallace, our PE teacher, in the field blowing her whistle and barking orders as her class played soccer. Fortunately, they were too far away and too distracted by Ms. Wallace's commands ("PASS THE BALL! SHOOT THE BALL! DEFENDERS STAY IN POSITION!") to ever notice me sneaking off to my favorite hiding place.

A row of large evergreen trees and a tall silver-wire fence lined the perimeter of our school grounds. A large school sign like you'd see at old movie theaters and gas stations stood by a cluster of trees. In big black letters the sign read:

**LAKESHORE MIDDLE SCHOOL: WHERE KIDS MEET THEIR DEMISE BY SUFFERING SLOW AND PAINFUL SOCIAL DEATHS.**

Okay, maybe I made up that last part, but that's exactly the way I felt as I strode across the grass then concealed myself behind the sign.

Once I was sitting still, all my feelings were able to sink in. I felt worse than I ever had in my pint-sized life. Part of me wanted to be angry. Angry at my class for laughing at me, angry at my foster parents for, well, adopting me, angry at myself for being so useless . . . but I couldn't. After everything that had happened, I still didn't have an ounce of anger inside me.

All I felt was disappointment. I felt foolish for thinking I could make the basketball team and even more foolish for thinking I would get invited to the big Halloween party all the other kids had been talking about for weeks. I dreamed of making the team and proving to my classmates once and for all I demanded their respect. I imagined scoring the winning shot with seconds left on the clock . . . all the kids rushing onto the court, lifting me above their heads, cheering my name.

My daydream was interrupted by the memory of what I had seen in my water bottle: the water lady. Her blue eyes flashed before my mind, giving me the chills. It seemed so real. I was certain I had seen her floating above the waterline. But now, sitting outside, trying to recall the details, it all seemed impossible. I had to have imagined it. There was a story in *Le Morte d'Arthur* where King Arthur saw a woman appear to him on a lake. She, too, stood on the water. What was her name? I racked my brain trying to remember . . . ah, of course, I thought, *The Lady of the Lake.*

# THE LADY IN THE WATER

But that was just a story. Nothing more than a myth told by Englishmen who were trying to strengthen national pride after they had been conquered by the Normans. At least, that's what my textbook said. The imaginative part of my brain wanted to entertain the idea further: What if the stories really were true? But I knew that was insane. Even if the Lady of the Lake were real, what would she be doing in my water bottle? Beyond that, what would she be doing in the United States of America appearing to some teenage kid? King Arthur had ruled in Camelot, a made-up kingdom all the way in England, thousands of miles away, and like a thousand years ago.

I had almost convinced myself to forget about everything I saw when I noticed a large puddle of water near the base of one of the evergreens. I'll admit, I felt a tingle of excitement as I considered what might happen if I looked into it. What if I saw the water lady again? What would she say? Then I would know for sure if I had imagined it all or not.

My curiosity got the best of me. I inched slowly toward the water, moving cautiously, forgetting that I was leaving the cover of the sign behind me. I was both excited and nervous to approach it.

When I reached the edge of the water, murky brown from the mud and speckled with pebbles and leaves, I peered inside. All I saw was my reflection looking back at me.

I was disappointed, but I wasn't ready to give up hope. Maybe it worked like a phone call. I needed to let her know I was calling. She had whispered my name, hadn't she? Maybe I needed to say hers.

"Um, water lady?" I said timidly, "Are you there?"

No response. I felt my anticipation dissipate like the air from a leaking balloon. But wait, I realized, maybe I needed to say her name right. Of course, she wouldn't be called *water lady*.

I took a deep breath, then said, "Lady of the Lake?"

# CHAPTER ONE

I waited eagerly, but nothing happened.

Confused, I convinced myself to close the matter. I told myself the whole thing had been my imagination. Thinking about it would just lead to more trouble and more embarrassment.

"Thanks for nothing," I muttered to the puddle, kicking its surface, sending little waves and ripples across its surface.

"Well, well, well. The rumors are true. Cat Eyes really is talking to water!" said a voice from over by the school doors.

Startled, my heart dropped. I knew that voice anywhere. It was the voice of my biggest enemy: Jared Phinkle. And he wasn't alone, either. He was flanked by two cronies, each even bigger than he was. Eighth graders.

Great, I thought. Bullies. Can this day get any worse?

# CHAPTER TWO
# BULLIES AND A HOARD

Every school has a stinky bathroom everyone tries to avoid if they can help it. Now imagine one of those grimy stalls and multiply the smell by at least a million. Jared Phinkle smells worse. Guaranteed. Plus, he's the biggest bully in the whole school.

Jared Phinkle had been my worst enemy since the fifth grade. As we got older, he only got nastier. I don't know what he had against me, but for whatever reason I was his favorite verbal punching bag. Jared had been held back one year, so he was older than me, and he still liked to hang out with the eighth graders because technically, he should be one.

I will never forget the fateful day in science class when we started learning about genetics and my teacher mentioned heterochromia, the technical term for what I have: two different colored eyes. For me, one is bright blue, and the other is stormy gray. Well, forgetting that a student in the class had heterochromia, my teacher put up a picture of a cat with it as well. Imagine a fat white ball of fluff with stout whiskers and big beady eyes, each a different color. Almost immediately, Jared piped up in the background, "Look, Hayden, it's your long-lost mom!"

I never forgave him for that comment. And he never let the joke go either. From then on, to him I was Cat-Eyes or Wussy-Cat or every other cat related name his troglodyte-sized brain could think of.

Now you can understand why Jared Phinkle of all people, was the *last* person I wanted to see right then.

"What do you want?" I asked defiantly.

"I just wanted to see for myself. I got a text saying you were talking to water, and then you fell out of your chair and wet yourself." Jared laughed, shortly followed by the laughter of his two cronies behind him. I realized I didn't recognize them. New students maybe?

My face flushed with anger. "That's not true! Well, some of it . . . my water bottle spilled on me!"

"Is there a madhouse for cats?" Jared asked. "Or do kitties who won't potty train just get sent back to the pound?" He slammed his fist into his palm as he said the last word.

His two new goons seemed interested in the last word. "Pound!" one of them repeated sluggishly, flexing muscles that looked like pythons.

"Different kind of pound," I said nervously, taking a few steps backward. The school bell rang loudly in the distance. Even from outside I could hear the shuffling of students all around the school getting up to change classes. But none of them would ever come out here . . . no one would see me get beat up, if that's what this was going to come to.

"Look, this has been fun, but I better get going," I said with a grin, trying to sound as confident as a lion, but squeaking like a mouse.

I tried to walk past them, but one of the big-uglies I didn't recognize grabbed my arm. He had an insanely tight grip. I thought Jared had smelled bad, but this mammoth of a kid—he smelled like old trash and wet dog fur—a very nasty combination.

The strange thing was, he sniffed at the air above me, then looked at the other guy and said, "he smells."

Could those guys smell fear, or something? Because I didn't know what else they could be talking about. Unlike their leader, Phinkle, I actually practice good hygiene.

"Hey! What is going on out here?" Mr. Bianco stepped through the school's front doors, approaching us in quick strides.

Jared Phinkle backed off quickly, but his two goons stayed behind, the one still holding my arm.

"Let go of him, numskull!" Jared whispered angrily.

Begrudgingly, the big kid let go of my arm, and both of them shuffled back into position behind Jared. I couldn't help but feel relieved. Something was weird about those two, but I couldn't quite place it.

"Get back to class before I put you all in detention!" Mr. Bianco said firmly. He may be a middle school English teacher, but he could easily pass for a bespectacled UFC fighter as well. As big as those kids were, Mr. Bianco towered over them. "Not you, Hayden. Come here."

Jared gave me an angry look, but knowing he was cornered, said, "Come on, let's go." He and his cronies stomped off past us.

One of them, the one who had nearly squished the life out of my arm, whispered to me as they passed: "We'll get you later, *human*."

I wondered if I had heard what he said correctly. I looked at Mr. Bianco, but if he had heard what the kid had said, he didn't show it. He did put his arm around my shoulder, which helped me feel relieved. He was watching the eighth graders intensely, but I couldn't read the look on his face.

"Let's go," he finally said when they were out of sight.

We walked in silence for a minute, Mr. Bianco leading me back inside and down the hallway to my next class.

I broke the silence, however, saying, "I'm sorry I didn't come back to class . . . I just needed some time."

Mr. Bianco stopped and looked down at me again, smiling warmly. "I understand. You missed a thrilling lecture, though. Not that you need it. I bet you read more than the entire class combined."

"I always read what you recommend to me," I said matter-of-factly. And it was true. I loved Mr. Bianco's recommendations.

"Did you finish Howard Pyle's *The Story of King Arthur and His Knights*?" Mr. Bianco asked as we started to walk again.

"Of course," I said. "I loved it, obviously. But I did notice there were a lot of differences from Sir Mallory's *Le Morte d'Arthur*."

"Which do you think was more accurate?" Mr. Bianco asked.

"What do you mean, sir?"

"Both writers were from very different time periods," Mr. Bianco explained, "but each attempted to categorize many of the myths about King Arthur in one place. Do you think one writer did better than the other?"

"They are just retellings of old myths, right? So, can one really be more accurate than the other?"

"I suppose. Which did you find more believable then?"

"Well, I guess, I would have to say Mallory's *Le Morte d'Arthur*. Hypothetically, that is."

"Yes, of course. Hypothetically," Mr. Bianco said.

"Mr. Bianco?"

"Yes, Hayden?"

"I think . . . I think I've been reading too much King Arthur stuff lately. This is going to sound crazy, but I . . . I thought I saw the Lady of the Lake. In my water bottle."

It sounded even crazier to me as I said it out loud, which I regretted almost immediately. I didn't want my favorite teacher to think I was nuts. But Mr. Bianco handled it well. He looked at me curiously, and said, "I don't think that is crazy, Hayden. The imagination is a really powerful thing. It never ceases to amaze me."

I smiled, but inside, I felt embarrassed. He was right, it must have been my imagination.

Mr. Bianco must have been able to discern some of my hidden emotion because he said, "Don't be afraid to dream and imagine, Hayden. I know how hard you've been preparing for basketball tryouts. You have so much potential. I can't wait to see what you'll accomplish, whether it's on the basketball court or not."

Mr. Bianco had a way of making me feel better. I wanted to give him a hug right then, but I held back the desire. The disappointment I felt didn't go away entirely, but at least I felt a little better.

"Well, I better get going to my next class," I said. "Thank you, Mr. Bianco."

"Of course. Oh, and Hayden. Be careful this week. With Halloween coming up and everything, just try not to wander off alone. And keep away from those bullies. I'll take care of them if I can . . ."

The way Mr. Bianco said that, I didn't know if I should be filled with glee or be afraid for their safety. Mr. Bianco was the nicest person I knew, but sometimes he seemed so strong, it was almost frightening. I wondered if he was an ex-marine or something equally hardcore.

The rest of the school day passed by in a blur. Fortunately, my pants dried and the lump on my forehead stopped hurting. Despite my physical recovery, however, it still wasn't easy to pay attention to my teachers. Everything that happened left a lot on my mind. I kept thinking about the water lady, and how real she had seemed. And yet, even Mr. Bianco, who I've always known I could trust, didn't believe it was real, so why should I?

I was grateful for Mr. Bianco stepping in and saving me from Jared Phinkle and his goons. I was equally grateful for his kind words of encouragement. But even after that, I still felt a strange disappointment about our conversation. Part of me felt a little ashamed for not being able to fight my own battles. Not only that, I kept thinking if what he said was true, everything I had seen was just my imagination. And what did that say about my state of mind? Mr. Bianco called it my imagination, but if my class really knew what I thought I saw, they would call it a hallucination.

Fortunately, nobody confronted me the rest of the day, but I heard their giggles and whispers as I passed in the hallways. When the final bell rang, I was the first to reach the school bus.

A few minutes later, the seats were full, though no one sat next to me, the bus rattled with power, the driver gave her usual spiel about safety to a couple kids who were climbing around on the chairs, and the constant chatter of two dozen children laughing and joking and talking about what they were going to do when they finished their homework filled the bus as we made our way along the route to our homes.

Unlike many of my schoolmates, I wasn't particularly excited to go home. Home was difficult for me. See, I was adopted by a couple named Winston and Arabella Keyes when I was just a baby. I never knew my real parents because it was a closed case. Apparently, I will never know them. But that's not the problem. I know lots of kids get adopted, and it's great. They get a home. But I haven't had a home for over nine years. Well, we do have a house, but … my foster parents are hoarders.

A hoard can mean a lot of things. In some of the books I've read, or games I've played, a horde is a massive army of aliens, orcs, or something cool like that. As for us, our hoard is just stuff. Junk. Toys, supplies—you name it. We have it all. I don't know where it all came from, but as I grew up, so did the hoard, like some evil step-twin. It had gotten so bad over the years, there was hardly any space left in the house. Tight paths had been maintained amidst the piles and piles of items, allowing us to walk from room to room, but that was it.

The only truly clean room in the house was my bedroom. I had simply forbidden my foster parents from allowing their hoard to enter my space. This turned out to be my only lifeline. My bedroom was a golden cave deep within a labyrinth of stuff; a treasure I had to fight to defend every day.

With each bus stop, I watched more and more kids get off the bus and run off toward their homes. I imagined them running into the house, to find their mom or dad had made them a delicious after school snack. I imagined them doing their homework on the dining room table, and then, when they were finished, inviting their friends over to play at their house. I was jealous of these children. I was jealous because I didn't have friends. I was also jealous because even if I had friends, I could never invite them to our house.

From a young age, I was too afraid of what people would say if they saw the inside of our house. So, I kept to myself, and I never invited anyone over to play. As I got older, my unavoidable awkwardness and clumsiness repelled enough kids away from me that I could stop *trying* to keep kids from seeing the inside of my house. They simply stopped asking if they could.

I was thirteen years old, and the closest thing I had to a friend was Mr. Bianco. I didn't know what I would do without him. He took me out for lunch sometimes or let me hang out with him in the teachers' lounge during recess. Mr. Bianco loved to read just as much as me, and he was always lending me books and making fantastic recommendations.

I was on good terms with my foster parents, too, of course. I didn't hate them, not by a long shot. Besides the lack-of-space issue in our house, they were great to me. They never yelled at me, and always treated me kindly. The thing is, my foster parents just did things a little differently than most parents. I was never allowed to call them mom or dad for example, only by their names Winston and Arabella. I didn't know why, but I thought something traumatic happened in their past, shortly after they adopted me. I was sure it had something to do with Winston's only brother's death, but we never spoke about that. Whatever happened, I was certain it was the root of their hoarding problem.

In their grief, they turned to shopping. Next thing they knew, there wasn't enough closet space for everything, and so it started stacking up. First, it filled the attic, and then the living room. Not long after we lost the den, the kitchen, and then the spare bedroom. As I grew up, so did the mounds of stuff, room after room falling casualty to the hoard.

To me, our home looked like a tornado in a department store. To Winston and Arabella, the place was a sanctuary. I should mention, unlike many hoarders I've seen on TV, our hoard was surprisingly organized. Arabella categorized almost every pile of stuff she could, and even organized a lot of it. Because of this, they knew where almost everything was. Each important item had a place, a pile, or a stack of boxes. If we wanted to watch a movie, for example, even if we hadn't viewed it in years, one of them could find it in no time flat. They only had to consult the directory first, a heavy three-ring binder hanging from a nail and string on the wall. "Living room, pile three, by the bookcase, green container."

A couple years ago, after a lot of begging and coercing, I convinced Winston and Arabella to start getting rid of things. It was a slow process and seemed like it would never end, but, surprisingly, they had remained faithfully cooperative. Almost every evening since, we spent our time together rifling through the junk, cross checking the directory, and making decisions about what we could throw away.

I wasn't surprised to find Arabella in the kitchen, sorting through boxes, when I finally made it home from school. I weaved my way through the maze of stuff, reaching the pantry door. With a little struggle, I managed to open it, procuring some after-school snacks from inside. After clearing some space at the table, I sat down and sighed, chomping away on my snacks.

"Hey, buddy," Arabella said, ruffling my hair as she passed, chucking some old silverware into a cardboard box. "I can't believe it," she muttered, consulting the directory. "That makes over three dozen forks!"

"Well, there are three of us, right?" I said, playing a game we always played while organizing. It was a sort of numbers game. "Three of us, and three meals a day. That makes nine forks. But, if we ever have visitors—" we *never* had visitors, but I knew from experience Arabella would never let me not count potential visitors, "we'll want at least four extra forks."

"That sounds accurate . . ." Arabella said, rummaging through the box of forks she had amassed.

"So at least twenty-three forks have got to go."

Arabella bit her lip. "Well . . . I can't argue with the numbers . . ." she said hesitantly. "Hmm… but which ones should I keep? I always liked the design on these . . ."

Arabella was younger than most kids mom's my age, which made me wonder exactly how old she had been when she adopted me—nineteen, maybe? She had long brown hair with hints of gold, and a big smile, too. Arabella was the nicest person I knew. And, judging by the countless times guys hit on her at the supermarket, I guess she was beautiful, too. It confused me that someone like her could let her house slip away into such a mess. She was the last person you would ever expect to be battling a hoarding problem.

Arabella continued to rummage through the forks, comparing the sizes, shapes, and designs, trying to decide which she liked best. I knew it was a trifle decision, one that didn't really matter. Compared to the massive pile of stuff, twenty-three forks were nothing. But still, it was better than nothing. Arabella was willing to depart with stuff, she just didn't seem to be in any rush to do it.

"How was school?" she asked, amidst more clinks of silverware.

"Okay," I said, looking out the window through a hole in the junk pile.

"That doesn't sound very convincing. Is everything all right, sweetheart?"

"I . . . spilled my water bottle in class by accident," I said. And I think I'm going crazy. Not to mention I made a total fool of myself at school. I couldn't bring myself to tell her the full truth.

Arabella wrapped her arms around me and gave me a tight hug. "I'm sorry you had a rough day, Hayden."

I wiped my place at the table and washed my plate in the barely exposed sink. "Arabella," I said solemnly, "I'm not going to try out for the basketball team. Just do me a favor, and don't say anything to Winston. I don't want him to be disappointed."

Arabella frowned sadly. "Hayden, I have watched you practice every morning and every night for months. I don't know much about throwing balls in baskets to score goals, but I do know hard work pays off. And you have worked harder than anyone."

I shook my head and laughed, "They aren't called goals in basketball, Ari!"

"Well, whatever they are called, I have seen you get that ball in the hoop more times than you miss lately," Arabella said, pointing at the hoop in the backyard, visible through the fraction of the window not covered by boxes. "So, what do you say, will you still at least try?"

I smiled. "We'll see."

Arabella gave me a warm hug. "You know what, Hayden? Why don't we take a break from the kitchen and go work in the den instead?"

"Really?" I asked, smiling. Maybe this day wasn't going to be the worst after all.

"Of course," Arabella said. "And you know the rule! Every game we uncover has to be played at least once, to make sure it has all the pieces."

"And to decide if it's worth keeping or not," I added with a grin.

"You always keep me in line."

The both of us laughed. We left the kitchen, and I couldn't help but wonder if that was what it felt like to be a normal thirteen-year-old kid.

# CHAPTER THREE
# A STRANGE CONVERSATION

The next morning, I awoke to my alarm, which chirped annoyingly, but for once, it didn't bother me all that much. I hopped out of bed eagerly. Within minutes, I was outside practicing basketball. Even though I had felt discouraged yesterday, today, I felt determined. Mr. Bianco and Arabella were right. I had worked too hard to quit now.

My focus on practicing basketball cleared my head. It also made me cope with a lot of my troubles, like my hallucinations from the day before. That still didn't stop me from wincing every time I approached any water, though. I even went to the bathroom with my eyes shut for fear of seeing the apparition of the woman again in my toilet bowl.

From my bedroom window, I could see the backyards that touched ours, and the yard that touched the corner of mine was the yard of none other than Tiffany Stokes. She was nothing special . . . besides being the head cheerleader, debate team captain, extremely blonde and attractive, and the host of the huge Halloween party everyone was talking about at school. The party that I had not been invited to.

# A STRANGE CONVERSATION

Her voice carried across the crisp morning air, "Let's blow up the giant bounce house over there," and, "Mom, can we put up more lights above the patio?"

To be honest, I was surprised to see them setting up for the party because I had totally forgotten that today was Halloween. I remembered the good old days when Halloween was still fun. Dressing up with friends, going around the neighborhood getting candy. Those days were gone now. Arabella and Winston hadn't let me go trick-or-treating for years. This year would be no different. They said I was too old, and that Halloween was for children.

I shot one more basket, a swish. If only I could shoot that well when people were watching. I wanted to keep playing, but my heart just wasn't in it. Besides, thinking about the party made it hard to stay out there and practice, as well.

When I came inside, Winston was sitting at the table, perusing a magazine he had taken from the small library of them that sat in the corner. Honestly, I was surprised that Winston was my foster dad, and not my biological one. For all our differences in personality, we looked a lot alike. Winston had dark brown hair, like me, and it even poked up in the front kind of like mine did. We each had a scrawny build, and were not too tall, or too short. Winston had stormy gray eyes, almost the same color as my one gray eye.

"Morning, sport," Winston said, taking a sip from a cup of coffee. "You and Ari have done a great job organizing the kitchen. I can't remember how long it's been since I actually sat at the table."

I laughed. "We still have a long way to go before *all* of us can sit at the table." We usually sat in the living room to eat because fortunately, the couch wasn't buried in a pile of stuff.

"We'll get there soon enough," Winston said, eyes returning to the magazine. "How's the basketball practice? Are you ready for tryouts next week?"

"I think so," I said optimistically. "I've practiced everything you showed me."

"That's my boy!" Winston said. "Oh, by the way, I forgot to tell you last night, I found this stuck to the door when I came home."

Winston reached into his pocket and drew out a small, orange envelope, which he handed to me.

I grasped it gingerly. I never got mail . . . but this one wasn't stamped or addressed. It simply had my name on it printed in extremely fine and articulate handwriting, using a gold pen. I tore the envelope open eagerly, drawing out the card inside. My heart started to race as I guessed what it could be . . .

A jack-o-lantern was painted on the front with watercolors. On the inside were the greatest words I had ever read:

Hayden, please join us for an awesome Halloween bash at my place. The party starts at 7 pm. Don't forget your costume! See you there! Best, Tiffany Stokes.

I couldn't believe my eyes. Standing there holding that orange envelope, I finally understood how Charlie Bucket must have felt when he found a golden ticket with his chocolate bar. I almost thought I was hallucinating, but there it was. The invitation was real!

I handed the invite to Winston. "Can I go? Please, please, please! Everyone from school will be there! And it's just over there, you can practically see their yard from ours!"

Winston read over the invite and smiled, "I'll talk to Arabella today, but I'm sure we can work something out. But you know how we feel about Halloween. All these monsters in the neighborhood . . . it's not, er, proper. Yes, proper."

I felt a tinge of worry as I considered the possibility that my foster parents wouldn't let me go to the party—and all because it was a costume party. It's not that they were strictly religious, or anything like that. For reasons I never understood, they always hated Halloween and dressing up in costumes. Well, some costumes were okay—it was anything that remotely resembled a monster that they didn't like. And even if I didn't dress up as a monster, if they knew there would be monster costumes around me, they always got really weird about it.

I couldn't help but remember one Halloween, back when I was six or seven, when they still let me trick-or-treat, Winston and Arabella had gone so far as making me skip every house where someone dressed up like any kind of monster had answered the door.

My heart sank. At a party like this, there were bound to be people dressed up as monsters. After all this, would they stop me from going to the party? That question weighed heavily on my mind the rest of the morning, so I was determined to do everything I could to hide from them the fact that this was a costume party.

I trudged up the stairs with heavy feet. I cleaned myself up, got dressed, and left for the school bus without saying another word to my foster parents.

I had a hard time paying attention in school. All I could think about was the party, what I should wear for my costume, and how I was going to pull it off without my foster parents seeing me change into it. I was so close to getting what I wanted, I couldn't believe I might lose it now over something so silly.

Just before lunch, a cold breeze blew in heavy storm clouds. Halfway through my fourth period class, the pitter-patter of rain started against the window. I couldn't help but hope that Tiffany Stokes's giant bounce house was holding up all right. When the lunch bell finally rang, I collected my lunch sack from my locker. While everyone else was noisily chatting and eating away in the lunchroom, I found a place to sit outside in the courtyard by the school's playground. Large awnings protected my seat from rain, and I was wearing a jacket, so I didn't mind the October chill.

*"Hayden Keyes . . ."*

I froze in my seat. The voice. I heard it again. I looked around, but saw no one, like I had expected. I didn't have a water bottle today, so where was the voice coming from this time?

*"Hayden Keyes . . ."*

A small puddle was forming in the cement not far from my seat. I approached it cautiously, then knelt beside it.

Almost immediately, the face of the water lady formed on the surface of the water, the image appearing like on a clouded mirror, rough from the texture of the cement, and constantly moving with each rain drop that speckled its surface. But there was no question about it, she was there, in the water.

My jaw dropped to the floor. I pinched my arm, closed my eyes and shook my head, but when I opened them, she was still there, staring at me with those bright blue eyes. I was never very good around girls, and this girl's attractiveness level was off the charts. So, like an idiot, I said, "What's up?"

The water lady's eyes glanced up toward the sky. "Hayden Keyes . . . listen to me closely. I don't have much time. Danger is coming. The time for you to make a choice is at hand."

"A choice? Danger—?"

"The choice will not be easy, Hero. I worry an excruciatingly painful fate awaits you. Will you run from it, or will you face it? If you dare, will you change it? The choice is yours."

I froze, an icy chill running up my spine.

"But I'm—I'm no hero," I stammered, trying to process what she had said.

I could never be a hero. I'm just a kid. The most heroic thing I had done by that point was probably the time I stopped Winston from eating three-day old sushi. Besides, anything that had excruciatingly painful in it, was not something I was going to get excited about.

"The knights believe you'll be the hero they once had. Your father cannot return, so they come to you instead . . ."

"Knights? I don't understand . . ."

"I can't keep the connection open any longer," the water lady said. Suddenly I noticed that she looked like she was under a lot of strain. Like she was trying to lift hundreds of pounds. "The choice is yours, Hero . . ." she said as her image faded from sight.

Okay. That was insane.

I threw my sack lunch and book into my bag and practically sprinted to Mr. Bianco's classroom. When I got there, I threw open the door, but the class was empty. Instead, I headed for the teachers' lounge down the hall. When I got there, I could see through the crack under the door that the lights were off in there as well. Before I turned away, I heard voices coming from behind the door.

I inched forward quietly, then pressed my ear against the door.

"I can't believe it's really you, Jack. It's been nearly thirteen years."

I recognized the voice immediately. It was Mr. Bianco's voice.

"Times are not what they were when we last parted," a second voice said, though I didn't recognize it. "We parted as victors, but today, we meet under the possibility of a new threat."

"Could it be Marzon? He was defeated by Hal himself!"

"No, not Marzon. Hal isn't sure what's going on either, though. There have been several disappearances among nobility."

That was followed by silence. I pressed my ear harder against the wooden door. Who was Mr. Bianco talking to?

"Sir Ector, we have come to find William. We need him back, now more than ever."

I wondered if I had heard correctly. I didn't know who Sir Ector was, so I figured there must be more people in the room.

"You have no idea what we went through to open a rift large enough for us to cross over," a third, squeaky little voice said.

"Then you have traversed here in vain," Mr. Bianco's familiar voice said. "William tasked me with staying here to watch over his son. That was the only instruction I received. Will isn't here."

"He had a son?" the squeaky voice of Sir Ector said. "That can't be!"

"The Hollow is afraid," the other man said. "They won't be happy if I return empty handed. Not after everything we sacrificed to open this portal. If Sir William can't come back with us, then at least come yourself, Ector. We need you. *Home.* In the Hollow. That is where you belong. At the Round Table."

"I can't go back," Mr. Bianco said. Wait? The man named Jack had said he wanted Sir Ector to come with him, hadn't he? Slowly, realization dawned on me. I didn't know Mr. Bianco's first name. Was it possible that this Sir Ector was actually my English teacher?

Mr. Bianco continued, "My duty is to stay here and to watch over the boy. He isn't like his father . . . he needs me. Here."

"And when will you tell him the truth?" Jack said. "When will you tell him who he really is? Who his parents are?"

Right then, I had an itching feeling, and an overwhelming anxiety. Were they talking about me?

"He must discover the truth for himself," Mr. Bianco said. "That is how it has to be. The choice will be the boy's and his alone. I could never willingly thrust this fate upon him. He's just a child—"

A choice. Was that the choice the water lady had spoken of? I felt my heart quicken.

"That's real noble of you, Ector," the squeaky voice said, "but what will you do when I tell you that trouble has finally found him here in the Other Realm?"

"What do you mean?" Mr. Bianco asked, sounding nervous.

"Thirteen years on this side has dulled your senses," the squeaky voice said. "Shortly after we arrived here this morning, we picked up the scent of trolls."

"That's not possible—the gate has been sealed for a thousand years. William and I are the only ones who have crossed through in thirteen years!"

"Well, here we are, are we not?" Jack said. "I don't know how the enemy could have known what we were planning. But they seem to have piggy-backed on the rift we opened, and sent a few agents of their own—"

"Trolls? They are the stupidest lot in all of Between!" Mr. Bianco said. "Why would the enemy send trolls? If the shadows really are stirring, I can think of a dozen more suitable choices!"

"I don't know, Sir Ector," Jack said. "Perhaps because magic still doesn't function on this side. And we all know that trolls are nothing but brute strength. No magic necessary."

"That would make sense . . . you opened a rift? How?"

# CHAPTER THREE

"You know magic was never my forte. Hal and his new Apprentice Grand—a charming girl, you'd like her—they worked it up somehow. Like placing a mirror in this realm, Hal said. Whatever that means."

"Of course. That would work, I suppose, with the proper tools to maintain the connection. It means you're both here and there."

"We are here, and that's all that matters. So, let's get to work, shall we? We only have three hours before the rift closes."

I couldn't believe my ears. Was this a prank?

"You shouldn't have come here," Mr. Bianco said abruptly. "I came here to escape. I came here to protect him."

Jack sighed. "All I know is as long as there are trolls on the loose in this realm, he isn't safe. I see now that we were wrong to come here. We came looking for the hero that fought for us thirteen years ago. Instead, we've found a washed-up old knight and a child who has no clue who he is."

This remark was followed by silence. When I heard Mr. Bianco speak next, there was no hint of anger in his voice. "Jack, help me search the school. We must find Hayden. Please, help me protect him at all costs."

"Very well," Jack said.

"Let's hunt some trolls!" the squeaky voice said.

I wanted to step through the door right then. Maybe yell, surprise! The kid you were talking about has been listening the whole time. Can someone please explain to me what's going on?

Magic. Trolls. Knights.

These words I had just overheard added to the noise echoing in my brain, like someone had sat on the TV remote, turning the screen to static.

*Will you run from it, or will you face it?*

Right then, I chose to run from it.

# A MYSTERIOUS THREAT

I didn't wait for school to end. I ran straight home. I have never felt more afraid in my life. As I ran through the rain, tromping through the puddles, every noise startled me.

I didn't know what these so-called trolls would look like, and frankly, I didn't want to know. Trolls belonged in stories, and according to Mr. Bianco's mysterious visitors, trolls were here in my boring hometown, where nothing crazy ever happens.

I didn't even know if what they had said was really true, and yet, inside I knew I believed it. Mr. Bianco had said *my* name at the end. That meant that I was the son of a hero. A knight that Mr. Bianco had fought alongside in some war.

It all sounded so insane. Sure, people still got knighted all the time, but it was just a formality. They weren't expected to actually take fight anyone. Then again, one of the guys had mentioned something about another dimension . . . Something about a gate being closed for a thousand years.

I felt goose skin on my arms, and not from the cold rain. I had an ominous feeling about all of this. If I was the son of some hero, where was he? Why was I adopted?

# CHAPTER FOUR

At the time, the only solution I could find to keep myself from going crazy was to block it all out. I couldn't believe it. I was just Hayden. An ordinary kid. I wasn't a hero. I hadn't seen a vision in a puddle of water and spoken to a water lady. Nope. Not me. Sorry trolls, nothing to see here! I guess you can all go home now. It's been fun.

Foolishly, I convinced myself that if I ignored it, everything would go away.

When I reached home, the front door was swinging open, crashing lightly against the wall in the wind. My heart sank. I could feel tears gathering in my eyes. What would I find inside?

Remember how I mentioned sword fighting bushes with a stick when I was younger? Well, this is where all that practice really paid off. I ran around the house and hopped the fence, trying to be as quiet as a mouse. Eyeing the windows, I crept along the fence line until I reached the wide row of bushes that had been my childhood sparring partner. Never taking an eye of the house, I crawled behind the bush, searching frantically.

I reached into the bramble and extracted a thin wooden sword. It was nothing special, but it would have to do. I had half the mind to hurry to the garage and try and knock some nails through it too, something I had seen done on TV once, but I knew I didn't have time. At least I wasn't empty handed.

Mustering what little courage I could, I crept up to the house, and entered through the back door, clutching my wooden sword with trembling hands. All the while, I couldn't help but think that the bushes never fought back.

Our sliding back door led into the kitchen; a large bookcase sat just in front of me, and I had to peer around it to get a better view. Everything looked the same in the kitchen. No sign of a disturbance. As carefully as

I could, I crept along the labyrinth-like path leading through our piles of stuff. I was slow moving, carefully examining around every corner.

Soon, I made it to the living room, and found nothing there. I reached the front door and closed it quietly. I heard something upstairs, which gave me pause. In every TV show or movie that I had ever seen with trolls in it, they were always huge monstrous creatures. I found it unlikely that something that size could have made it through my front door and navigated the paths without knocking things over.

But then again, just a few hours ago, I would have told you that I found it very unlikely that trolls even existed. And now here I was, clutching a wooden sword peeking around the corners like I really expected to see one waiting for me in the other room.

What had me on edge was how the front door had been left open. That wasn't like Arabella. Maybe it wasn't even trolls I should be afraid of. It could be burglars, or something real. With that terrifying thought, I quietly started my ascent up the stairs.

What I found when I reached the top was anything but terrifying.

Arabella had been organizing a bunch of clothes pulled out from Winston's den. She sat amongst the piles, speaking to someone on her cell phone. Sure, she looked concerned, but she also looked safe. No trolls, no burglars.

When she saw me at the top of the stairs, she let out a sigh of relief. "Don't worry, he's home. He just walked in," she said into her phone. She hung up the phone, and then stood up and grabbed my shoulders. I noticed that she was shaking. "Hayden Keyes, what on earth are you doing home? Why did you leave school?"

"I—I was afraid—"

Arabella's expression softened immediately. She squeezed me tighter.

"Oh, Hayden. I just got off the phone with Mr. Bianco. He told me about the safety threat someone called in. He said he couldn't find you anywhere and I was so worried!"

If my face gave away my confusion, I tried hard to hide it. I had no idea what she was talking about.

"He said the whole school went on lockdown, but they couldn't find you anywhere. Hayden, you never should have run home alone! You could have at least called me—something! I was worried sick about you!"

I had never seen Arabella like this before. She was still shaking nervously and kept glancing over my shoulders at the stairs, too.

"Why was the front door open?" I asked. "I was afraid for you when I got home." I realized I was still holding my wooden sword, which thankfully, I hadn't needed because let's be honest—it wouldn't have done me any good.

Arabella palmed her forehead, then started to hurry down the stairs. "The front door? Oh! Silly me. I just wanted to listen to the sound of the rain while I worked . . . and then Mr. Bianco called, and I got so worried—"

"It's okay, Ari," I said, following her down the stairs. She was moving so fast I could hardly keep up. "I closed the door when I came in."

Arabella reached the door and dead bolted it. She was really shaken up.

"Is everything okay?" I asked, as Arabella hurried to the back door and locked that one too.

"Of course," she said, feigning calmness. "I-I was just shaken up by Mr. Bianco's call, that's all. I'll feel better when Winston gets home. Why don't you go play in your room for a while?"

"Um, yeah. Sure," I said. I tried to read her expression, but Arabella was quickly composing herself. I could tell I wasn't going to get any more answers from her now, so I turned and went upstairs to my bedroom.

I threw myself down onto my bed, my head spinning from everything that happened the past two days. First, seeing that strange water lady in my water bottle, again in the rain puddle, then overhearing Mr. Bianco's conversation with those mysterious visitors—it was all just so weird. The story Arabella gave me definitely didn't match what I had overheard outside of the teacher's lounge either. Aching with curiosity, I fired up my computer and googled my school. Sure enough, I found an article that had just been posted minutes prior.

Above a picture of Mr. Bianco taken from the faculty website, I read the headline: Middle School on Lockdown.

I skimmed the article, but I didn't find any new information. Everything collaborated perfectly with the story Arabella seemed to have received from Mr. Bianco. While Mr. Bianco himself seemed to be the article's primary source, thankfully there was no mention of me, the boy who had gone missing shortly before the lockdown.

All the facts were right in front of me, and yet something didn't seem right. Without question, minutes before this so-called threat would have been made over the phone, Mr. Bianco had been talking to two mysterious people about knights and trolls and magic and different dimensions and all kind of weird things that only happen in books and movies and games and never, ever in normal kid's lives like mine.

The other thing that seemed suspicious to me, was how Arabella had acted so afraid here at home, nearly two miles away from the school. According to the story, the threat had been made directly toward the school. And on top of that, there was no clear information about what "threat" had even been made. For all I knew someone had called up Mr. Bianco and said something like, "Give me an A or I'm going to pummel everyone in school with gummy bears" or something crazy like that. I wondered if Mr. Bianco had said something more to Arabella, something that would have made her afraid even way out here in the neighborhood. Could it be that Mr. Bianco had told her something about the trolls?

I shook my head. This had to be an elaborate prank. It couldn't be real. I wasn't the son of a hero. I was an orphan who had been adopted as a baby. It was a closed adoption, so that meant the identity of my real parents would always remain private and secure. I laughed at myself for almost believing all of this. How could I be a hero? I was a class clown, a klutz. I decided I couldn't let this distract me either. I knew what I really wanted and that was to go to the Halloween party tonight. After that, I would make the basketball team and finally prove myself to my classmates.

I turned off my computer and lay back down on my bed. I noticed my copy of *Le Morte d'Arthur* poking out of my backpack, but for the first time ever, I resisted the urge to read it. I had spent too much time reading about King Arthur and his knights. It was addling my brain.

I knew what I wanted, and I wasn't going to let anything stop me.

I tried to take a nap, but my sleep was troubled and riddled with echoes of the voice I had heard coming from the rain puddle. The water lady had warned me that something was coming, but I didn't want to believe it.

*Danger. . . is coming.*

I awoke from my fitful sleep with a start. I glanced at the alarm clock on my dresser and realized several hours had passed. I could hear Winston and Arabella downstairs cooking in the kitchen, the savory smell of roast and potatoes wafting up the stairs into my bedroom. My stomach rumbled and realized I hadn't eaten since my half-finished meal at lunchtime.

"Morning, sport," Winston said with a chuckle as I came down the stairs.

"It smells delicious!" I said eagerly. "I'm starving."

"Arabella told me about your day. We were all a little shaken up by what happened. How are you holding up?"

"Me? I'm fine," I said. "There is something I wanted to ask you two, though."

"Fire away," Winston said as he scooped up steaming bowls of stew for each of us.

We squished together onto the table, shoulder to shoulder with all the junk amassed around us. There was little room for being claustrophobic in a house like ours.

I felt a lump in my throat bigger than a hot dog. I took a deep breath, doing everything I could to hide my nerves. "Well . . . I was wondering if you made a decision about the Halloween party tonight?"

Winston went silent, then turned to Arabella, with a pleading look on his face. Arabella, in turn, looked at him with a saddened, but hard face. She nodded in encouragement. And then Winston spoke the last words I wanted to hear.

"We did talk about it, Hayden. We both know how important this is to you . . . but we feel like it would be best if you stayed home tonight. With everything going on today, we feel like you'll be safest here at home."

"This isn't fair," I shouted, slamming my spoon down, roast beef and carrots splashing out of my bowl, ricocheting off the wall of junk surrounding us.

Winston and Arabella jumped in surprise. I never threw fits. Like ever. But for some reason, I couldn't stop myself now. I could feel all my frustrations boiling inside of me. I felt like a soda can that had been shaken so much one little twist of my lid and I would explode.

I didn't know what I wanted, or what to expect, but seeing their reactions only fueled my desire to fight back even more. For thirteen years I had been quiet. But now, for the first time, it felt good to fight back.

# CHAPTER FOUR

"Let me guess," I continued, relishing in the utter look of horror on their faces, "Mr. Bianco called you and told you about the trolls? Don't tell me you actually believe in that stuff?"

Winston and Arabella were both pale with fear. Arabella made a cutting motion back and forth before her mouth, motioning for me to stop.

But I couldn't stop. I was just getting started!

"That's right! I know all about that. I overhead everything. So, come on, tell me the truth! What is really going on? Or is this just a big Halloween prank because in case you're wondering, it isn't very funny!"

"What's really going on," a familiar voice said from behind me, "is that your house is about to be ambushed by two bridge trolls."

I froze. Then slowly turned. Standing behind me was a man. Sort of. Instead of having a normal head, he had a head made from a pumpkin, with eyes, nose, and mouth carved like a jack-o-lantern, a soft orange glow flickering inside his hollow head.

A little mouse sat atop him, which stood up on its hind legs, wore a tiny little feathered hat and what looked like a miniature battle ax hanging from a tiny belt around its tiny waist. The mouse held out its little paw in a friendly wave. "I'm Strings, and this is Jack. Pleased to meet you."

Arabella yelped quietly, jumping backward and falling onto an orderly pile of cardboard boxes.

# AN UNEXPECTED GUEST

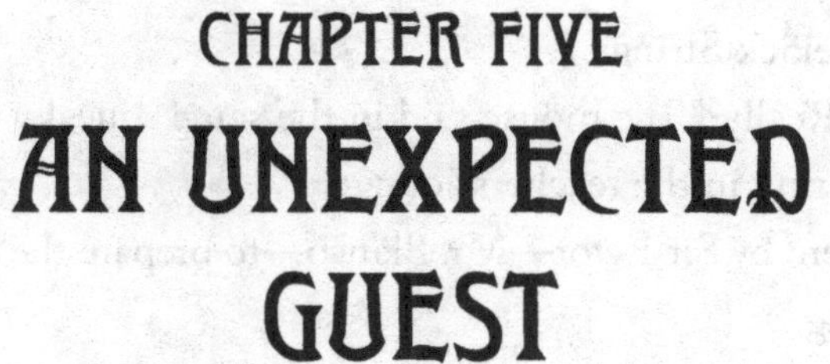

I couldn't believe my eyes. A man with a pumpkin head was standing in our cluttered kitchen with a talking mouse sitting on his head. The pumpkin man, Jack, wore a black leather jerkin known as an arming doublet. This special shirt had steel chain mail woven in large patches near the armpits and arms, as well as along the lower front of the shirt. I knew from study that these special doublets were worn by knights beneath their suits of armor. Jack's pants were of a similar style. He also wore knee high crimson leather boots. At his waist, strapped to his heavy leather belt rested a sword, its fishtail pommel sticking out from its scabbard, the protective sheath that held the sharp blade.

The result was both terrifying and intimidating, especially considering his head looked like a jack-o-lantern, something I had never seen in all my reading about the old knights of history.

But this wasn't something out of history. He was really standing in my kitchen, looking more terrifying than any Halloween costume I had ever seen.

Winston was the first to break the silence. Stammering, he said, "W-who are you and what are you doing in our house?"

"Forgive me, sir, my name is Jack Lantern," he said with a bow so low I thought his pumpkin head might roll right off his shoulders. But it didn't. "This is my sidekick Strings."

"Sidekick? Really?" The mouse said in the same squeaky voice I remembered overhearing in the teachers' lounge.

"We were sent by Sir Ector—Mr. Bianco—to prepare the house for what may be coming."

Winston's face looked pale. "So, you're with him, are you? After all these years, your lot has finally found us! Tell me, Jack, who do you work for? Are you with the government, or are you with someone overseas? Or maybe Canada? Hmm? And what does troll stand for, anyway, some codeword we suspect? For the enemy, right?"

Even for having a pumpkin for a head, Jack looked confused. "I don't understand what you're asking."

"You're international spies, are you not? Just like my brother, William?"

"Spies?" Strings the mouse fell over laughing, clutching his little gut. "That's a good one. You hear that, Jack? Spies!"

I was speechless. For the second time today, I heard that name. William. A brother I had never known Winston had.

Winston didn't back down. He began to speak quickly, growing redder and redder in the face. "William turned up after not hearing a word from him for nearly three years. He handed us Hayden—frantically telling us he has been to this place called *Inbetween* or something like that. He mentioned a magic valley and something about an army of monsters, and then just like that—he's gone again. And here we are. With you, Hayden. We raised you as our own. But we always feared that whatever government was coming after William would finally come after us and his son!"

"I understand your frustration—and concern given the circumstances,"

Jack said. "But I need you all to listen to me. We are not international spies. We are knights. Knights of an ancient order known as the Round Table. Those weren't codewords. William was telling you the truth. Plain and simple."

"Um, technically you ain't a knight, boss," the mouse said. "But other than that, he's got it all right."

Winston fell back onto his seat, clutching Arabella, who looked too afraid to speak herself. I remained standing, shell-shocked by everything I had just heard. I thought I would have so many questions to ask, things to demand to be explained, but at the time, I couldn't think of where to even begin.

"And that isn't a mask?" Winston asked, nodding at Jack's orange jack-o-lantern head.

"Unfortunately, not," Jack said, tugging at his head, which held fast to his shoulders.

The pieces were coming together in my mind. My father was a knight named William Keyes. My father was my foster dad's brother. That meant Winston and Arabella were my aunt and uncle. "Please, tell me more. Tell me about my father, my mother. Tell me everything."

Winston and Ari looked at each other sadly. Winston spoke first. "Hayden, some things are better off left in the past. I don't know if we are ready—if *you* are ready. . ."

I gathered up all my courage, then pressed harder. "Please. I need to know the truth. I need to know everything you know."

Winston and Ari looked pale. Like I was asking them to recount a horrible terrifying event. I could tell it was hard for them to speak. That made me want to know the truth even more. Finally, after a long pause, Winston spoke, "Well, you should know, your father was always a special person. He was gifted, smart, brilliant actually. He studied archaeology at an academy in Iceland. After that, he began traveling the world studying ancient artifacts and bones and who knows what."

"So, my dad was an archaeologist?" I asked.

"Yes. He was a good one, too," Winston said. "He was also a treasure hunter. The real deal! Not like what you see in the movies. I used to follow along in the newspapers and magazines, whenever something was written about his discoveries. But people started to criticize him for his work. You see, your father became convinced that fairytale creatures once lived on the earth. He spent the rest of his life searching for them, and eventually claimed that he found the bones of some bear eagles or something."

"Griffins," Arabella said, looking like she had just uttered a curse word. "They weren't bear eagles."

Winston looked surprised but continued. "A few weeks after he supposedly found the griffins, your father departed for a new location somewhere off the coast of England . . . and then he just disappeared."

"Disappeared?" I repeated, trying to take in all this new information.

"It was in the papers and everything. Nobody knew what happened to him, or his crew. That's when we started to get suspicious. We wondered if all this magical creature nonsense was just a distraction thought up by the government to cover up what he was really doing overseas. Like spy stuff or something."

"But you saw him again, right? When he brought me to you?"

"Yes," Winston said. Opening up about this seemed as difficult for him as it was for me to take it all in. He took a deep breath. "After three years of not hearing anything from my brother, he showed up at our doorstep with a baby in his arms and a wife beside him."

"My mom?" I asked excitedly. "Who was she?"

"She said her name was Anora," Arabella said. "And she was beautiful. Quiet, too. She hardly spoke a word. Parting with you looked like it destroyed her. It wasn't easy for either of your parents to leave you with us."

"But they told us they had to in order to keep you safe," Winston added. "And that they would be back for you as soon as they could."

"So, we waited and waited," Arabella said.

"And waited," Winston added. "But we never saw or heard anything from either of them again."

Tears were gathering in my eyes as I soaked in every word my aunt and uncle said. Looking them in the eyes, I asked the only question I could think of. "Why didn't you tell me?" Sure, I was excited to learn about my parents. I honestly never really thought about them much. But this. This was huge. I wasn't just adopted, I was taken in by my aunt and uncle and they had pretended I was some random kid from a shelter for thirteen years. Honestly, the excitement wore off quickly. In its place was a deep sinking pit in my stomach. This hurt. No, it was something worse. This ached. Hard.

Arabella spoke, tears streaming down her face. "Hayden, we have always loved you, you were the child we could never have had on our own. And yet, we were afraid. That's why we tried to protect you. We always hoped that your father would return. We told ourselves that we were only watching over you as guardians, but year after year, he never came back. Year after year you grew and grew, and we loved you so much. But we knew you were never ours, that your father could return at any moment and take you away."

Winston started crying as well, "I'm sorry I kept the truth from you, Hayden. We were afraid and confused. We love you, sport."

I nodded, then put my arms around each of them. Their apologies didn't fix everything in that instant, but it helped. There were a million more things I would have to ask, especially the story of how my parents left me with Winston and Arabella. I would need to hear every detail of that encounter, probably multiple times. But now clearly wasn't the time. I hadn't forgotten about the trolls that were apparently headed straight for us.

I turned to Jack, who had remained quiet and polite throughout our whole little family soap opera. "What do we need to do?" I asked him, trying to compose myself. I was shaken up, and had so many questions, but I knew we were in danger.

Jack pulled a thin golden-pommeled dagger from his belt. The handle was innately crafted, and the blade was of cold blue steel. "Take this, lad. Be careful. It's sharp. I guess that's all you need to know. That and don't let the bad guys stick you first."

Arabella acted like she was going to stop me from taking the weapon, but I grabbed it and she remained speechless. I held it carefully in my hands. It was heavier than I expected for such a small dagger. Something about it felt good though, really good.

"We need to find a more defensible position," Jack continued. "No offense, but . . . there isn't really room to swing a sword in here." He motioned towards all the piles of junk.

Winston and Arabella turned red with embarrassment.

"Think of them as defensive perimeters," Strings said laughing.

"My bedroom is clean," I said. "It's not the biggest room in the house, but it could work."

"Good. Go there and hide. Hayden, I promise we'll do everything in our power to stop this threat. I never knew your father, but we fought for the same side. It will be an honor to fight for his heir."

Jack drew his sword from its sheath with a long, glorious sliding sound as the sword slid along the gilded wood. The sword shined with a beautiful golden light.

# AN UNEXPECTED GUEST

I couldn't believe my eyes. A pumpkin headed knight was standing in my kitchen, drawing his sword and preparing for battle.

Suddenly, three knocks sounded at the door. We all jumped, except Jack, who spun into a defensive stance between us and the front door.

"Now, up the stairs," he whispered, inching towards the door.

"Come on!" I said to Winston and Arabella, awakening them from their paralyzed fear.

We were halfway up the stairs when we heard Mr. Bianco's voice shout through the door, "You can open up, it's me, Jack. No sign of the enemy."

Jack opened the door, and Mr. Bianco stepped in.

But he didn't look like the same Mr. Bianco who taught my English class. This Mr. Bianco was a knight. He wore a polished silver breastplate over chain mail, a shirt woven entirely from tight metal rings. His pants were thick black hide, and he wore knee-high boots like Jack's, only these were a deep forest green. At his belt hung a two-handed sword with a plain and unadorned handle.

Jack closed the door and locked it behind him. As the door closed, I noticed trick-or-treaters already starting their pilgrimage for candy along the streets.

"Will the trolls really tromp around unnoticed with the streets so busy with parents and kids?" I asked, heading down the stairs toward Mr. Bianco. I felt much more confident now that he was here.

Mr. Bianco clasped his arm around me. "Nice dagger, Hayden. It suits you."

"I know about my father," I said. "Well sort of. So, you fought beside him as well?"

Mr. Bianco nodded gravely. "I did. And I promised him I would watch over you. I know you must have so many questions, and I will answer them,

I promise. But not until I know you and your family are safe."

"I understand. Mr. Bianco . . . thank you."

He nodded. "Jack—about the trolls. There shouldn't be any magic in this realm, and yet, somehow, the trolls are able to camouflage their true nature. These ones are young, not fully-grown. But even though they should be bigger than me, they look like . . . kids."

"Like eighth-graders?" I asked, a realization dawning on me.

"I guess so," Mr. Bianco said. "I didn't get a good look at them from the front, but they were definitely sniffing around the school before I tracked them to this neighborhood. The weird thing is, they seemed to be following around a human kid."

"Jared Phinkle," I whispered like a curse. My worst enemy had found himself a couple of trolls for lackeys.

"You know who they are with?" Mr. Bianco asked readily.

"Yeah. And I think I know where they are going as well. Come with me," I said, hurrying up the stairs.

I led Mr. Bianco and Jack into my bedroom. I took them to my window and pointed toward Tiffany Stoke's backyard. Dozens of kids in costumes were already amassing in between the lights and decorations and the giant blowup bounce castle. I could hear the music from here as kids danced and laughed and mingled.

I scanned the backyard with my eyes, trying to identify all the faces I could see over there, but there were just too many of them. And with so many of them in costumes it was hard to tell who was who. One thing was certain, everyone from my middle school seemed to be going to this party.

I felt a pang of longing as I watched my classmates having fun. But now that I knew who I was, the son of a knight, I had to know more. I needed answers about my parents. Going to a party felt like a silly dream now.

I saw Jared Phinkle and his two sluggish cronies hopping over the fence into the yard, and pointed excitedly.

"There I can see them!"

Even from here, it was easy to tell that they were looking for someone. Me.

"There. There they are," I said, pointing at the trio through the window pane.

"What are they doing following around a human boy?" Strings asked curiously.

"Ah, of course," Mr. Bianco said. "I always thought trolls had an unusually strong sense of smell for something so impeccably stinky themselves. In Between—where the knights are—a troll can track something from miles away by scent alone, but that must be a magical ability."

"One that doesn't work the same in this realm," Jack said, nodding in agreement. "That means the human kid . . ."

"Was supposed to lead them right to me," I said. "Jared thought I was going to be at the party. But he couldn't possibly know what they really are, could he?" That seemed low, even for Jared Phinkle. I was positive he didn't know what they really were.

"I knew I should have put Jared Phinkle in detention," Mr. Bianco said gravely. "I should have done it yesterday. I can't believe I didn't notice those kids were trolls in disguise."

I looked back down at the yard, but I had lost sight of them. So many kids had come by now, the place looked like a concert with standing room only.

It looked like so much fun. But now I knew I would never belong there.

"What can we do?" I asked. "What if they hurt somebody?"

"That is very well possible. But these trolls are oddly restrained for their kind. The fact that they even followed us here shows a determination that is rare for trolls," Jack said.

"You don't mean that they were sent here on a mission, do you?" Mr. Bianco asked, not taking his eyes away from the party. I could see them moving, searching. Many of the kids down there were his students. He may not have sworn an oath to their parents to protect them, but he still had a duty to them, nonetheless. His gray eyes looked as cold as steel. I felt very grateful he was on our side, and not our enemy.

"Sir Ector—you remember what I said. Why I came here. The shadows are stirring. The enemy is on the move."

"What enemy?" Mr. Bianco said sternly. "We defeated Marzon thirteen years ago. You watched him die. You and I both know trolls are too stupid to organize an army. They are also too stupid to take orders."

"Yet here they are, looking for this boy. They knew our plans to try and bring back Sir William. Somehow, they caught on that William wasn't here, but his only heir was. I know it sounds crazy, but even Hal is worried. We don't know who or what is stirring the shadows. But it's happening."

Mr. Bianco nodded gravely. "I hoped this day would never come. All I wanted was to protect you, Hayden. Your father made me promise I wouldn't show you this unless I absolutely had to. And even then, he always wanted it to be your choice."

Mr. Bianco turned to Winston and Arabella, who stood petrified in the corner. I had forgotten they were even here. "Winston left a bag here the night he gave you Hayden, correct?"

Arabella nodded her head vigorously, still too stunned to form words.

"Well, where is it?" Mr. Bianco asked.

Arabella hurried out of the room, towing Winston along behind her.

My heart started to race, and I felt an anxious feeling rising in my chest.

All this time, something of my father's had been here in this house, hidden by our hoard . . .

Arabella led us into Winston's den, which was full of his old stuff. After navigating the room, a trek which had felt a little like climbing Mt. Everest, we reached the ceiling trap door that led to the attic. With a little difficulty, Arabella pulled the line that brought the fold out ladder down.

I quickly realized Arabella hadn't even consulted her directory. She had known all along exactly where this was.

"I'll be right back," she whispered, then scampered up the ladder.

Less than a minute later she returned, clutching a large brown leather briefcase. Between her arm I saw a name gilded in gold on the front of it: William Keyes.

I couldn't believe my eyes. This was proof that my father really had been here before, that he existed . . . And that maybe, I really was who Mr. Bianco said.

"I don't know what you need this for, though," Arabella said, brushing dust off the bag. "It's empty."

"Not in the secret compartment," Mr. Bianco said, taking the bag from her, then handing it to me.

I held that bag like it was an ancient relic. I couldn't believe it. This bag was my dad's.

"Open the main pouch," Mr. Bianco instructed.

I did.

"Feel along the side, do you feel a groove?"

I did.

"Find the tassel and pull."

I pulled.

"Reach inside."

I reached inside. At first, I thought the secret compartment was empty, and then my fingers closed around a single cold medallion. I realized everyone was watching me intently as I withdrew my hand from the bag, clutching my prize.

It was a silver medallion, larger than a quarter, and thicker too. I turned it over in my hands, examining the images and words engraved on each side.

"Admit one, Other World Express" I read from the first side, written below a picture of a griffin rearing on its hind legs. On the other side, I saw a sword and shield encircled by a laurel of leaves. "New Camelot, The Magic Hollow of Between." I read. "What does it mean?"

"That is your true home," Jack said quietly. "That is where you belong."

"And this coin will take me there?" I asked incredulously.

"Yes. It should," Mr. Bianco said. "I watched your father use a coin just like it when he brought you and I here twelve years ago."

I looked up at Mr. Bianco, completely speechless. Great, more secrets. Is that what all adults do these days? Keep secrets from Hayden?

"Hayden, there is something you need to know about your father. We don't know if he's alive. But if he is alive, he's somewhere in the world we call Between. But your father wasn't originally from Between. He was from this world, the one we are in right now. Somehow, he came there, though. He came to us when we needed him most, and he fought for us. But not only that . . . somehow your father became a sort of Gatekeeper between our realms."

"Gatekeeper?" I asked.

"Long ago this world and Between were the same. But King Arthur had to make a difficult decision to end a war . . . well, that decision involved retreating all of magic, and all of his kingdom into a sort of limbo-world."

"The place you call Between," I said.

"Exactly. The two worlds have always been kept separate ever since," Jack added. "But somehow, your father figured out how to travel between them. Something nobody else has ever discovered—not even the evil wizard Marzon."

"The evil-nasty my father helped you defeat in that war you mentioned," I said, to show that I was at least kind of following along.

"Exactly. Wherever your father is—if he's still alive—he holds a powerful secret. And, to be clear, I do believe that he is."

"And this medallion?" I asked.

Mr. Bianco spoke next, "Your father will have enchanted it to take you to Between, if that is what you wish."

"To take you home," Jack said.

"He is *not* going to that place!" Arabella shouted suddenly. "This. Is. His. Home!"

She was crying again. "I've already lost my brother-in-law to that place. Please don't take away my son."

At that moment, I felt so much love for Arabella. Despite all I had been through, and never being allowed to call her mom, right then in that moment I knew that she was my mom. Sure, not directly, but in a special way. Because being a mom is about more than genetics. It's about even more than being called by the title "mom."

"You can't tell him what to do!" Jack said angrily. "Hayden is the son of a hero. He belongs in Between with the rest of us! Right, Sir Ector?"

Mr. Bianco looked grave, looking back and forth between Arabella, who was sobbing, and Jack, whose orange glow had taken on a new intensity to reflect his mood. Mr. Bianco turned to me. "The choice is yours, Hayden. And yours alone. Just know that if you go to Between, you may possibly never return. I don't know if the medallion works both ways."

I clutched the medallion tightly, staring back and forth between Mr. Bianco, whose expression was placid and unreadable, Jack whose inner lights burned wildly behind his eyes, Arabella who was shaking in tears, and Winston who stared at the ground looking like he was going to hurl. Jack had said I was the son of a hero. Part of me was filled with a longing to experience what that might be like. All my life I had been the exact opposite of that. Could this be my chance to finally become something greater?

This was my choice. I remembered the words of the water lady. She had told me I would have to make a choice and that painful things awaited me. I knew what I had to do.

"If I return with you to this Hollow—to Between—will the trolls follow us back?"

"It is possible," Mr. Bianco said. "Seeing as they have yet to harm any other children and are only searching for you, it is likely that they would return back to Between as well."

"But, Hayden, that medallion likely only works for you," Jack said. Travel between this world and ours is rare, and not easily accomplished. The portal we managed to open only has room for myself, Strings, and one other. Which would be you, old friend." He nodded towards Mr. Bianco. "If you'll come. The Hollow needs you. Hal needs you."

Mr. Bianco crossed his arms. "I will only come if Hayden decides to come. I have sworn an oath to protect him."

"Let me remind you—you also swore an oath to the Knights of the Round Table," Jack said threateningly.

Mr. Bianco stared at him coldly. "I have not forgotten my oaths, Jack."

I stepped in between them. "Look, I will go with you. But only if we can guarantee everyone is safe here."

Mr. Bianco and Jack relaxed and stepped back from each other. "These two trolls may not be fully mature, but they are smarter than the others. More aware. I have never heard of a troll taking orders, or at least, carrying out orders, for that matter. This will be dangerous, and it is possible they will have set a trap for us," Mr. Bianco said. "It is too dangerous for you, Hayden. Perhaps, with training, you'll be ready to face more perilous dangers, but now is not the time."

"Then what will you have me do?" I shouted. "Sit here and wait and hope you don't get killed?"

"There is something," Jack said, eyeing Mr. Bianco carefully. "There is no way we can engage two trolls in combat while they are sniffing around all those kids. We'll need to lure them away to a remote location."

Arabella grabbed my arm. "Hayden, please . . ."

Winston rested his hand on her shoulder. "It's okay, darling. Hayden must do this. Don't you see? Like it or not, this is who he is. This is who my brother was." Winston turned toward me. "Hayden, please, be safe. But, if you can, find my brother, and bring him home."

I nodded, then clasped Winston in a tight hug. I turned to Arabella, who looked like she wanted to resist further, but gave in, then embraced me in a tight hug.

That was enough for me. I knew I had their support, which meant I could leave on good terms. For the first time in my life, I wasn't running away. I was making a choice. Probably a reckless and dangerous choice that could very well end in me getting squashed flat by a troll, but at least it was my choice.

"Let me do it," I said to Mr. Bianco. "I can go into the party and try to lure them out. As soon as they see me, I'm sure they will follow me. Just tell me where you want me to lead them."

"Very well," Mr. Bianco said sternly. "Lead them to that park just south of here two blocks. Do you know the one?"

"Yes," I said, feeling a twist in my stomach. I would have to lure two trolls down two whole blocks. I can do this, I thought.

"I will be close by, Hayden, keeping watch in case anything goes wrong. Jack, I want you to hide in the pavilion near the park entrance. As soon as they are inside, I will close the gates behind them."

"And then we engage," Strings the mouse said.

"Yes, then we engage," Mr. Bianco repeated.

"There's just one problem," I said. "Jared Phinkle. He will try to follow me as well. I don't know if I can outrun him."

"Leave Jared to me," Mr. Bianco said. "If there is one thing all kids fear, even if they don't know it yet, it's being embarrassed by their parents in public. Please excuse me for a moment . . . I have a phone call to make. Ms. Phinkle is about to have a change of plans this evening."

"You're going to call his mom?" I asked with a sardonic smile. "Ooh, that's low."

Mr. Bianco instructed me to get ready and then say my goodbyes, while he stepped out into the hall to make his phone call to Jared's mom. Perks of being friends with the coolest teacher in the school, I guess.

I realized part of me was excited to leave, though I would never tell Winston and Arabella that. I couldn't help but think about how I was finally escaping the hoard. I understood now a little better about why they had built the hoard in the first place, though. It lined up with my father's disappearance and my arrival as a baby. I wondered if the hoard had been a subconscious protection they built up, like castle walls, a mote, and fortifications, always surrounding us, protecting and shielding us.

Despite their best intentions to protect me, however, they had shielded me from the truth and tried to stop me from becoming who I really was. I could hardly believe that all along my father's bag had been sitting up in the attic holding the key to finding him: this little silver medallion. It was stowed safely in my pocket, something I checked continually. I had never possessed anything more valuable, and I wasn't going to let it slip away.

After packing a few of my things into my father's leather briefcase, I headed back downstairs to say my goodbyes to Winston and Arabella. The air seemed a million times thicker when I stepped into the living room. The two of them were sitting on the couch, crowded by piles of stuff. I sat down beside them, and for a moment we just sat in silence.

"So, you've made up your mind?" Arabella asked.

"I have," I said. "I have to do this. I have to go with them and try to find my father."

"And there's nothing I can say to change your mind?" she asked.

I shook my head.

"Well, in that case . . . did you pack any underwear? What about a toothbrush? A jacket? Do you know how cold it gets in this Hollow place? Will you be able to contact us when you get there somehow, to let us know you made it safe?"

She started rattling off a million more questions, most of which I couldn't answer, even if she had given me enough time to answer them.

I just smiled, cutting her off, and said, "I love you both."

They seemed caught off guard for a second, but then they gave me a tight hug. They were both crying, and I may have teared up a little, too. "We love you too," they whispered in my ear. "We are so proud of you." Suddenly, I had a deep pit forming in my chest. Leaving them was going to be the hardest thing I had ever done.

"Whether you're becoming an international spy or a knight—whatever it is you'll be doing," Winston said, "Just know that we believe in you. You can do it. Never give up, Hayden, and you'll amaze even yourself at what you can accomplish."

Mr. Bianco stepped back into the room. "I just got off the phone with Jared's mother. She's on her way to the party right now."

"What did you say to her?" I asked.

"Oh, I just told her the truth. I didn't have to dig very far to come up with a thing or two to say about Jared Phinkle."

"Let's hurry to the party then. I don't want to miss this!"

# CHAPTER SIX
# CRASHING THE PARTY

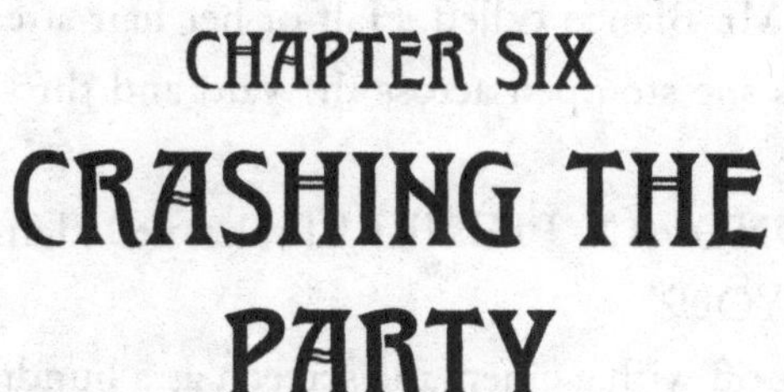

I hid myself from sight behind some hedges in a spot with a perfect vantage point of the party. It looked awesome. Tiffany Stokes had really outdone herself this year. Kids were jumping wildly on the massive blow-up bounce castle, music was blaring, and everyone was dancing, laughing, and having a great time. All the costumes looked awesome, too.

I saw everything from superheroes, monsters, and even a hot dog. It looked like so much fun. Everything I had hoped and imagined it would be. I couldn't help but wonder what it would be like to be out there with friends, just enjoying the party and being normal.

At least I finally knew the truth, though. I had undeniable proof that I *wasn't* normal. I wished the water lady could see me now. I had made my choice. So hopefully it hadn't been the wrong one that was going to end in an excruciatingly painful fate.

"Here she comes now," Mr. Bianco said, nudging my shoulder.

I watched Mrs. Phinkle strut across the lawn. She was a big lady, beefy like her son. She wore tight aerobic pants and a flannel shirt with bright red and green stripes. Her hair was filled with old fashioned rollers, which by the looks of it, she had been halfway through removing when Mr. Bianco called. Half of her hair streamed behind her in curly waves as she stomped across the yard and through the gate into the backyard.

"JARED DONOVAN PHINKLE!" she yelled in a hoarse voice. "WHERE ARE YOU?"

The music cut off with a cinematic screech as a hundred eyes turned to look at Ms. Phinkle.

After a moment of silence, a hesitant voice sounded out from the crowd. "Mom?"

"GET OVER HERE RIGHT NOW!" she screamed, stomping her foot.

Reluctantly, Jared Phinkle emerged from the crowd, approaching his mother.

"I JUST GOT OFF THE PHONE WITH YOUR TEACHER! I CAN'T BELIEVE YOU—YOU INSUFFERABLE TEEN!" She grabbed him by the ear and started pulling him with her towards the gate.

"Mom, stop it. You're embarrassing me," Jared whined, wincing from the pain as his mom practically dragged him across the lawn.

"YOU THINK THIS IS EMBARRASSING? WHAT ABOUT ME? I'M GONNA BE LATE FOR MY HOT DATE!"

Basically, everyone started laughing. And right then, I knew ten years from now nobody was going to remember the kid who always sat in the back of the room and fell out of his chair after talking to his water bottle. But they were going to remember this.

"Let's do this," I said, standing up from behind my bush. I tried to give Mr. Bianco a fist bump, but I accidentally bumped my knuckles against his kneecap, not his fist.

"Make sure they see you, but don't get too close. Head straight for the park. I'll be following you in case things get bad."

I swallowed, and then made my way toward the crowd.

"Nice knife," someone said, pointing at the gilded dagger hanging from my belt. Just as I hoped, they assumed it was some cool costume prop.

I scanned the crowd, trying to spot the trolls. There were so many people it was hard to see. And quite frankly, I just wasn't tall enough. I made my way over to the drink table, careful not to bump into them by accident. After seeing no sign of them there, I decided to try and get a better view of the crowd, so I made my way to the bounce castle and climbed up the side. I was scanning the crowd when I heard two familiar voices coming from inside the bounce castle.

"This isn't a real castle!" the big ugly who had grabbed my arm the other day said.

"A stupid squishy one," his companion said. "Can we just eat now? Me hungry."

"No! Only one tonight. You know the one."

"Yeah, I know the one."

I didn't need to ask to know that I was the "one" they were talking about. It had been so much easier to face them when I thought they were just mindless eighth graders. Now that I knew the truth, it was another story. But what better way to lure them to the park than this.

I jumped down to the entrance of the bounce castle and tore open the doors.

"Don't you think you two are a little big for bouncy castles?" I asked.

The two trolls turned wildly, glaring at me. Then they charged, baring their teeth and snarling. I closed the doors and hopped down from the castle. I kicked the air blower which kept the thing inflated, sending it flying aside. The air shrieked as it started leaking out of the castle, sounding like a giant whoopee cushion. The trolls struggled to exit the bounce castle as it fell on them.

I turned and ran, pushing my way through the crowd who had turned to see the giant farting plastic castle. This really was turning out to be an eventful party. I had nearly reached the gate, when the trolls finally extracted themselves from the jumbled heap. I stopped and made sure they saw me, before continuing to jog through the gate and into the front yard.

"GET BACK HERE!" One of the trolls yelled from behind me.

"WE CRUSH YOU!" The other shouted next.

I ran as fast as I could. It was dark now and the streets were almost empty. Each of my echoing footfalls was followed by the heavy thuds of their massive feet chasing after me. They were surprisingly quick for their size, but not as quick as I was. I could stay well ahead of them, the only problem I foresaw was how long I could keep up this pace.

Halfway to the park and I could already feel my body groaning in protest. A painful stitch was erupting in my side, and my chest was heaving for air. But I knew I couldn't stop. Just as I was feeling myself slow down, I saw the entrance to the park. With what little energy and determination I could muster, I urged my self forward, until I flew through the gates.

I didn't stop running until I couldn't go another step. I fell onto my knees, heaving for breath. I felt cold sweat drip down my face. I hadn't pushed myself this hard since we ran two miles in Ms. Wallace's PE class. I could feel my heartbeat in my skull, and my thoughts were slow and sluggish as I rolled over to look at the park entrance.

I watched the two trolls come running in, not all that far behind me. As they crossed the threshold, both stopped, then turned about trying to spot me.

Suddenly, the gates slammed closed behind them with a rattling clang, as Mr. Bianco and Jack emerged from behind a large tree, each with sword in hand. The trolls crouched into defensive postures and snarled.

"This not fast food, brother," one of the trolls said.

"This full course meal now!" the other said, baring his teeth.

Jack and Mr. Bianco circled the trolls, slowly moving in on the enemy, pressing them closer together. I couldn't believe my eyes. Two knights were fighting trolls in my neighborhood park! They looked so valiant. So cool. I wondered if my dad had looked like that when he fought.

"Who sent you?" Jack asked. "How did you know about the portal we opened?"

The trolls laughed. "It rude to talk to food," one of them said.

"We have you trapped," Mr. Bianco said. "You won't be eating any of us tonight."

"We not trapped!" The troll said, laughing sardonically. "Papa troll is here, too! He crush you, too!"

I heard a crash at the gate, but I couldn't see what the source of the sound was in the dark. The two young trolls laughed maniacally as the second crash broke open the gates. What I saw stride through was absolutely terrifying.

The two younger trolls were big and were so ugly I'm surprised I didn't recognize them as not being human. But what walked through that gate on the other hand—there was no questioning the fact that it was a full-blown troll. It stood about ten feet tall and was fat and thick. Its legs looked as rough as tree bark, and just as thick as a tree trunk. Its skin was leathery and tanned and looked as cold as rock. Its head was pudgy and thick, making its eyes look beady and small like a snake's. A giant wooden club was strapped to a belt that hung from its waist. It wore tattered rags that hung from its body like seaweed.

Mr. Bianco and Jack didn't back down, but they didn't look pleased either. All I heard was Mr. Bianco yell, "Hayden, run!" As the trolls attacked, rallying behind the massive newcomer.

I wanted to run, but I couldn't. I had never been more afraid in my life. Jack was fighting the big troll and Mr. Bianco was single handedly fighting the two younger trolls. I had to help. I had to do something . . .

I reached for the knife at my belt, drawing it from its sheath. Even in the dark of the night the blade glowed beautifully. I realized there was something different about this knife from any other knife I had held and handled before. I didn't know what it was, but I was certain it was far more precious than stainless steel.

I took a deep breath, gripped the weapon tightly, and then charged after the troll fighting Mr. Bianco. They didn't see me coming. I jumped into the air, almost as if I were shooting a layup in basketball.

The knife pierced the troll in the back all the way to the hilt. I heard something shatter like glass, and then the troll was gone, exploding into a puff of ash that blew away in the wind.

A lot of things happened next, and to be honest, a lot of it was nothing but a blur to me. I dropped the knife, surprised by the sound of the defeated troll. The other two trolls bellowed in rage and turned on me, throwing Jack and Mr. Bianco aside, who had also been caught off guard by my sudden attack.

The two trolls sprinted straight for me, heads down like charging bulls. I reached into my pocket and pulled free my father's medallion. I clutched it tightly in my hand. In a flash, the coin felt warm in my hand, then vibrated rapidly like a cell phone stuck on vibrate. I heard a rush of wind like a tornado. The trolls had almost reached me when a massive black shadow eclipsed the moon above us.

"Huh?" they said stupidly, looking up at the sky.

I looked up as well, and just in time to see the most unbelievable thing I have ever seen. A colossal griffin, nearly as tall as a house, a streak of silver claws and red and gold feather plumage, swooped down from the clouds.

SLAM! The griffin let out a loud caw, then bashed right into the trolls, talons first, which sent them flying and toppling over themselves wildly.

"*Ow,*" I said.

"They'll feel that in the morning!" Strings the Mouse squeaked triumphantly.

"I hope so, but that's not what I meant," I said, pointing to the Griffin that landed in the street with a ground shaking thud. "O. W. E," I read. "Oh, Other World Express, like it said on the Medallion."

The Griffin, a cross between a massive lion and an eagle, was huge. Now that it was holding still, I could really take it all in. It stood at least twenty feet high, and when it spread its wings, they completely covered us all in shadow. It stood regally, bowing its head toward me, revealing a wooden step ladder that led to a huge wooden platform secured to its back with massive leather straps. The letters O. W. E. were painted in bright gold across the side of the platform.

Basically, this was the coolest thing that I had ever seen. The griffin gave me a reassuring look with enormous yellow eyes, nodding its large beak toward the ladder, gesturing for me to climb aboard.

"Hayden!" I heard Mr. Bianco yelling. "This is your path to the Magic Hollow! Find Principal Hal there right away!"

I ran forward, past the griffin's colossal beak that was big enough to swallow me whole, then leaped onto the ladder, dodging a giant troll's swinging club by inches. The trolls yelled in anger. I saw one of them try to climb onto the platform after me, but the griffin lurched forward the moment I reached the top of the platform. Its airplane-sized wings beat against the ground creating enough wind to knock the trolls, Mr. Bianco, and Jack to the ground.

"Hurry!" I yelled to Mr. Bianco, looking over the side of the platform and holding on tightly to the wooden railing. Each powerful beat of the wings threatened to knock me over the edge and raised us a little higher into the air. "I can't do this alone!"

"It's all right, Hayden! We'll meet you at the Hollow!"

I felt like I was going to be sick, and not from airsickness. I would have felt a lot better if I didn't have to make this journey alone. I suppose I didn't have much of a choice given the circumstances.

I carefully waded my way across the platform to the first row of benches. Thankfully, leather straps like seat belts lined the rows. I sat down and strapped myself in. We were reaching the clouds and gaining quite a lot of speed.

I'm no weatherman, but I do understand that clouds are made up of water vapor. In that moment, the joy (and fear) of riding on the back of a massive magical creature aside, I remember being weirdly aware of the fact that I was about to get soaked. I closed my eyes right before we hit the clouds, shielding my face, but the cold wet I had anticipated never came.

I opened my eyes cautiously and saw that we were hurtling through a dark expanse, an ocean of a water-like substance below and a sky of stars above. The griffin soared above the water. I peered over the edge and saw the earth, but it was like looking at a reflection of the earth.

"Wow," was all I could say as I looked out at the wide expanse around me. It turns out inter-dimensional travel is quite the breathtaking experience.

It's not easy living a fantasy, you know. We all grow up reading about them, but never believing anything will ever happen, until something amazing really does. Something wild, something beyond our greatest imagination. Suddenly, the greatest challenge isn't believing in the fantasy, but remembering what it was like before.

Just yesterday I was worried about going to a party and making the basketball team. Today, I encountered trolls and uncovered a strange mystery about my family. Not only that, I said goodbye to the two people who raised me and cared for me all my life.

The platform jostled as if we had hit turbulence in an airplane, nearly knocking me out of my seat.

I heard a sinister laugh behind me. I whirled around to find the second eighth-grade posing troll staring down at me.

"Nowhere to run. You destroyed brother. Now you're dinner."

"You know, has anyone told you how eloquent you are with words? Just phenomenal. First class."

The troll chuckled, seeming pleased with himself. I guess trolls don't understand sarcasm.

I was only stalling, of course. The big-ugly was right. I was completely cornered, alone, and weaponless. I had dropped the knife in the park after I attacked the first troll. Gulp. No, mega-gulp.

I looked around, trying to find something I could use to defend myself, but, unfortunately, the griffin's platform was completely empty of pointy sword-like objects. My mind raced, but I was struggling to come up with a solution. What would King Arthur do? I knew the answer was essentially: be a total boss, but that wasn't much help to me here.

The troll laughed maniacally as he walked toward me struggling to keep his balance with the rise and fall of the platform as the griffin beat its wings.

"Me Garl-Oonga," he said, "Prince of all Bridge Trolls and son of King Garl-Oonga-Oonga's! You poked my brother! So now I smash!"

"That's one way of putting it. You could also say I killed him," I said mockingly. "Let me guess, your brother's name was Oonga-Oonga-Oonga what was it again? Oh yeah . . . *Oonga?*"

"No," the troll said. "His name Jon. Me Prince! Only me get Oonga name!"

"Well, I'm sorry about your loss, I really am," I said, unfastening my seat belt so I could slowly back up toward the front of the platform. "I didn't expect him to, you know, puff into ash . . . I just didn't want him to hurt my friends."

"No more friends now, human," the troll spat. "Papa catch them. Me squash you. Me take you to the pound." He laughed at his own joke, which sounded a lot like a wheezing cow.

"Very funny," I said. I only needed a few more steps. "So, you picked up a few things from your time with Jared Phinkle, huh? Well, here's a little advice—"

I turned around and leaped onto the griffin's massive neck, grabbing onto its feathers to hold on. The troll bellowed in anger, shouting "No escaping!" as he started charging toward me. But I didn't try to escape.

"—Phinkle's jokes were never funny!" I lunged to the side and grabbed onto one of the big leather straps securing the platform onto the griffin's back. With all my strength, I yanked the strap loose. The griffin let out a loud squawk of surprise as the platform slid to the side, now only being secured by one strap.

The troll howled in fury, but had to grab onto one of the benches to keep his balance. The griffin looked back annoyingly, struggling to fly straight with the shift of the platform. Thankfully, it kept flying.

"I'm sorry," I said, grabbing onto the other strap. "I really liked your platform, but I kinda want to live."

# CRASHING THE PARTY

I tugged at the strap with all my strength. It broke free and the weight of the platform slipped backward, right off the griffin's back. I clung onto the griffin tightly to keep myself from falling with the platform.

I heard the troll shouting in anger behind me. Understandable considering how I just made the platform fall from under his feet. I was certain my plan had worked and I was safe when a split second later I felt something grip tightly around my ankles, pulling me backward. I scrambled to cling onto the griffin's feathers, the troll grasping my ankle tightly. With a fist full of feathers, much to the griffin's chagrin, the troll and I slid off its back.

I heard a rush of wind like a whip and watched a leather strap from the platform slap the troll across the face with a crack. He howled in pain and let go of my ankle as we both fell into the swirling mist below.

# CHAPTER SEVEN
# SOMEWHERE IN BETWEEN

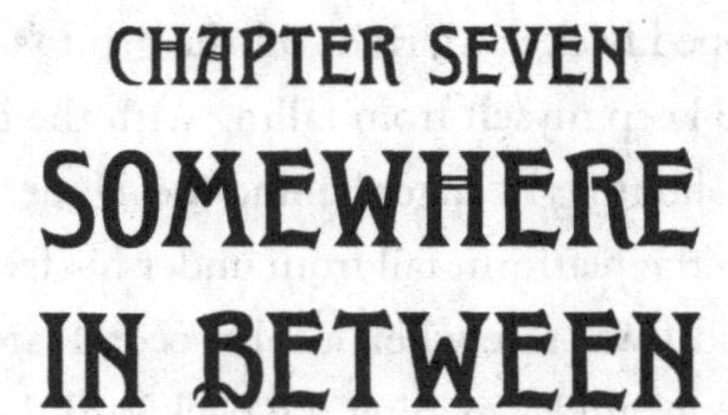

**M**y entire body ached as I woke up. I wondered if I had fallen out of my bed in the middle of the night because I definitely wasn't in my soft comfortable one. The ground was hard. Really hard. And cold. Way too cold.

I opened my eyes, realizing I wasn't in my bedroom. I was sitting in a slump in a dark alley, completely alone. The first thing I noticed was the grimy cobblestone beneath me. The alley was dark, but I could make out barrels and large wooden boxes, and the smell of fish and ocean. Tall brick buildings walled in the alley on both sides of me. Down the alleyway I could make out a dimly lit street.

My head ached, and I could feel a small lump on my head.

The griffin!

It all started coming back to me in a flash. Learning the truth about my dad, Mr. Bianco, meeting Jack Lantern the pumpkin head and his talking pet mouse. Leading the trolls out of the Halloween party, and then battling them in the park. I had managed to defeat one with Mr. Bianco's dagger, and then I escaped on the magical Griffin-airline summoned by my dad's enchanted medallion.

But what happened to Garl-Oonga or whatever his name was? We both fell off the griffin. I remembered it clearly now, falling into the stars and the swirling mists of light. I quickly tested my legs and all my body. I was sore, but nothing was broken. So how did I get here?

I was about to stand up when something scraped along one of the boxes. I turned toward the sound, squinting into the darkness. "Hello?"

Suddenly, a figure emerged from the shadows wearing a black cloak with a hood up that hid his face in blackness. It was probably the freakiest thing I had ever seen, and I had just seen and experienced a lot of freaky things.

"Shh!" a young person's voice said from within the black cloak. "You sure picked an interesting place to take a nap. Have you never been to Centerra before?"

"What?" Was all I could respond with. I was certain he was probably around my age, but I still didn't know if I could trust him.

"You. Napping here. As in this alleyway. Do you know where you are?"

"I have no idea. But if you're concerned for my safety, that means you're not going to mug me, right?"

"Mug you? No, of course not." The cloaked person stepped closer to me, then spoke in the softest whisper, "Hal told me to meet you here and escort you back to the Hollow."

"Wait, you're from the Magic Hollow?"

"Shh! Not so loud. Don't go bellowing stuff like that around here. Okay?"

"I'm sorry. It's just, I don't even know where here is. Are we . . . in Between?"

The boy was silent for a moment. "Yes. We are. But you've heard about the Magic Hollow before?"

"Mr. Bianco—Sir Ector to you—told me about it. That's where he wanted me to go. But I don't even know if he's safe!"

"Okay," the boy said. "Listen. I don't know how you managed to get this deep into Quay, but this is one of the roughest districts in Centerra, okay?" He lifted his sleeve and glanced at a gold wristwatch. "The ghosts will be out in about fifteen minutes. Trust me, you don't want to be around when that happens. Follow me."

The boy grabbed my arm and started pulling me down the alleyway. Not knowing what else to do, I followed along, or I guess got towed along. I didn't know if he meant what I thought he did when he said ghosts, but I didn't want to find out. After seeing two eighth graders turn out to be trolls and a guy with a pumpkin for a head, I was ready to believe just about anything.

When we stepped out onto the street, I couldn't believe my eyes. I felt like I had stepped back in time a few hundred years. It looked like we were on a street in Old London. Except something wasn't quite right, either. The houses and buildings leaned, slanted, and twisted in ways that didn't seem structurally sound. The cobbled street wasn't lit by electric lights, but tall old-fashioned lamps, burning on each street corner. Colored lanterns with burning candles inside of them draped over the streets too.

"This way. Hurry," the boy said, leading me through the winding cramped streets. As we continued along, I noticed how much my surroundings changed. Sometimes it looked like London, other times the surroundings looked Japanese, more medieval, or even like other ancient cultures I didn't recognize. There was no order to it either, it was all just a big random mess.

Fortunately, we didn't run into any ghosts. There were other people out on the streets though. Most of them hooded, like my mysterious companion, though occasionally we did pass some who wore no hoods. Most of them looked like normal people, just dressed like they were ready to go to the renaissance fair. But some of them were different, almost monstrous. We passed one person who stood at least eight feet tall, and had half a face that was nothing but bone. "Don't stare," my companion instructed with a whisper in my ear.

As we went farther, the streets started to widen, the number of lights increased, and so did the people. However, I saw less and less creatures. "This is the market district," my companion whispered.

I liked the market. It was sprawling with booths and vendors all selling interesting wares from livestock to vegetables, sparkling jewels and amulets, armor and weapons, or clothes and boots. They all shouted at the crowds, calling out items and special prices. I overhead people bartering and haggling trying to get a fair price. I had never seen so much excitement in one place.

Everyone here looked just as old-fashioned, wearing medieval clothing like in Quay, but almost none of these people wore hoods to cloak their faces. They went about their business, some even with a courteous smile on their face. I even overheard a mother instructing her five children to behave themselves if they wanted her to get them candy when she was done.

"Come on," my companion said, pulling me along again.

"Is all of Between like this?"

My companion stopped and turned toward me. "You ask strange questions," he said. Then, "You have weird eyes."

Taken aback, I tried to think of a retort, but nothing came to mind. I still hadn't even seen this kid's face. But he seemed trustworthy and was my only hope of reaching the Magic Hollow. I just hoped that Mr. Bianco had been as lucky as I had and escaped the trolls.

"Look, I just haven't seen much of Between, that's all," I said. "Just curious, but what are we *between* anyway? I mean, where are we really?"

"Imagination and reality," he said. "That's what we are in between. Once upon a time this was between England and Ireland."

That was deep. And didn't make much sense. But I accepted it for the time being. Like I said, I had experienced a lot of weird stuff, and now, I would believe almost anything.

"I've got a question for you," my companion said. "Who are you and why did Hal instruct me to meet you in that alley in Quay?"

"I . . . I don't even know who Hal is. Mr. Bianco mentioned him. He told me to find him in the Magic Hollow."

"When you say Mr. Bianco, you mean Sir Ector, right?"

"Yeah, do you know him?"

"No. Not directly. He hasn't been to the Hollow in over twelve years. Rumor has it he was on a mission for an old hero of ours."

"A hero . . ." I said quietly. My real father. "William Keyes."

"That's Sir William Keyes to you!" The boy retorted quickly. "He was a Knight of the Highest Order of the Round Table. He was brave, loyal, and courageous!"

"Did you know him?" I asked quickly.

"No . . . I was just a baby when he disappeared after the war. But I've heard stories. And I've read all of his works!"

"Well," I said nonchalantly, "He's my dad."

My companion stopped and turned to stare at me, causing several people who had been walking behind us to grunt disapprovingly as they nearly walked into us. When they saw my hooded companion, however, they seemed to think twice about saying anything, even though he wasn't much taller than I was.

"You're Sir William's son? I had no idea he had a son."

"Neither did I, until very recently," I said, suddenly feeling very exhausted.

"Where have you been all this time? Why weren't you raised in the Magic Hollow where it's safe?"

"I . . . I'm not from around here, okay," I said. For some reason I felt hesitant to tell him where I really came from. Even here, on the other side, I imagined it probably wasn't usual for someone to talk about traveling between dimensions.

But apparently my companion wasn't fooled. "You came from the Other Realm, didn't you? The real world?"

"What? How did you know that?"

"Well, it's a little obvious. You ask all these weird questions and don't know anything about Centerra, and you're wearing really weird clothes . . . not to mention, Hal just authorized one of our people to travel through a portal we created to the Other Realm and try to bring back Sir William."

Realization dawned on me. "Was your person named Jack, by chance?"

"Yes, do you know him?"

"Hard to miss, considering he has a pumpkin for a head. Nice guy. He saved me from a pack of trolls and helped me get here. With Mr. Bianco—Sir Ector's help, too."

"What? Trolls—he helped you—swords of truth!" He glanced around to make sure no one was overhearing our conversation, then leaned in closer to me, whispering excitedly, "You really are from the Other Realm?"

I knew the cat was out of the bag, so there was no point trying to fake it. I would just have to trust this kid with the truth. "Yes. Yes, I am."

"And you're father. You said you didn't even know he was your father until recently, which means. . . ."

"Which means he wasn't with me . . . in the Other Realm. I've never met him."

"So, Jack. . . ."

"Jack came for my dad and found me instead."

"This is major. We need to get you back to the Hollow right away!"

He grabbed my arm and started pulling me even faster than before.

"So, this Magic Hollow, it's here in the middle of this big city?"

"Yes," he said, "concealed by powerful magic. Only those who are invited can enter. Now be quiet, we are almost there."

The streets seemed like a never-ending maze to me, but luckily, my companion knew exactly where to go. We rounded corners, slipped through alleys, and made turn after turn after turn. There was so much to see, it was hard to take it all in. We passed blacksmiths, cobblers, markets, apothecaries, and more. I felt like I could spend a lifetime exploring this place. It was amazing and terrifying all at the same time.

After a few minutes, we were heading down a long thin alley, when the sound of voices came from around the corner. My companion stopped and signaled for me to be quiet. He inched toward the alley entrance, pressed flat against the wall, hidden in the shadows.

"It's time to pay up, old man," a voice said from around the corner.

"Please," a quavering voice said. "I don't have the money. I need more time. My children will starve if I can't feed them!"

"We've told you before, we can't keep giving you second chances."

"What good is protecting these streets, if you accost the people who live there?" the old man pleaded.

"We have kept these streets clean and safe for nearly three years. That can't happen without money to fund our soldiers. But if we let people get by without paying, then we all lose. Because we won't be able to patrol these streets anymore. Is that what you want? For this district to end up like Quay or Firth?"

"No, no, of course not!" the old man said. "But what am I supposed to do? I don't have the money yet, but if you would step into my shop, I could give you something, anything you like."

"We don't want one of your little creatures, old man. We want your money!"

"But now that you mention it," another voice said, "I heard a rumor that you're keeping some wild creatures in that shop. I would hate to find something dangerous in there that could endanger the neighbors."

"No, no. That's not true. There is nothing dangerous in there, just my babies. These creatures need me, or they'll die!"

"I'll believe it when I see it for myself. Step aside."

"No, please!" the old man begged.

"Step aside by order of the Cerise Guard, or I will make you step aside."

Suddenly, without giving any warning to me, my companion stepped out from the shadows. "Leave that man alone," he said.

I peeked around the corner to watch what was happening. The old man was on his knees, looking terrified. Standing before him were two young men wearing full samurai garb, including long thin swords that hung from their belts. Each had a hand on their sword, ready to draw as they faced my companion, who was unarmed and standing alone.

"One of you!" the first samurai said. "Why don't you mind your own business black cloak? Run along to your hole and hide like the rest of you."

But my companion didn't stand down. "Leave this man alone."

"And why should we listen to you, black cloak? We are members of the Cerise Guard, sworn to protect this district."

"The Cerise Guard is nothing but a band of thugs posing as samurai. You extort this district's citizens for money in exchange for protection they don't want or need."

"You insult our honor," the second samurai said. "Our leader will be pleased when we bring him a black cloak. I don't think he'll mind, though, if we bring you dead or alive."

The two samurai drew their swords.

My companion just stood there, face clouded in shadow. As for me, I was terrified. I wanted to run, but where would I go? My only hope rested in my companion. So, I stayed and watched intently.

"Not backing down? Big Mistake!"

The two Samurai charged with a horrifying battle cry. They moved quickly, but my companion moved quicker. He ducked under the first sword strike, tripping the Samurai off balance as he slid past. Then he rolled, dodging the second attack, causing the Samurai's sword to crash into the stone ground. In a flash of twirling black cloak, my companion flipped around the Samurai, twisting his arms and hands around him in an intricate choke hold. Then, with all his weight he rolled backwards, sending the Samurai crashing to the ground in a heap of red armor.

Before the first Samurai could even recover, my companion had produced a thin gold dagger from under his cloak and held it to the tackled Samurai's throat.

"Sheath your weapon," he commanded the first Samurai.

The second Samurai, who looked terrified because of the knife at his throat, nodded eagerly for his companion to listen.

My cloaked companion reached into a pocket and extracted two small gold coins. "Here is your pay. Now leave here and never bother this nice man again. Or I'll finish what you started today."

He released the Samurai and stepped back, tossing the two coins in front of them. They scrambled to their feet, scooping up the coins. "We may be bound by honor to do as you asked, but don't think that means you aren't our enemy. If we ever meet again on our streets, you won't be as lucky!" They turned and ran down the street, disappearing around a corner.

I ran out from my hiding place and helped the elderly man to his feet.

"Thank you, thank you!" the old man said, trembling with fear and excitement. "How can I ever repay you?"

"Don't worry about it," my companion said. "Protecting others is my duty as a Knight of the Round Table."

My jaw dropped and so did the old man's. He bowed respectfully, "Bless my stars," he said. "I have lived to see the day the knights return. You have done me two kindnesses this day."

My companion reached back into his pocket and pulled out two slightly larger gold coins. "Unfortunately, I must buy your silence. My order is not ready to step out of the shadows just yet. It would only bring you harm to speak of this occurrence." He tossed the coins to the man, who held them gingerly in his hands, looking like he had just won the lottery.

"I—I understand," he said, bowing again.

"Come on, let's get going," my companion said, nodding to me.

"You're a Knight of the Round Table?" I exclaimed as soon as we were alone again.

"Yes," my companion said. "One of twelve. But . . . the knights aren't what they used to be . . ."

"A knight is a knight. It was amazing what you did for that man. You fought so well!"

"Thank you."

"My father was a knight," I said, more to myself than to him.

"Yes, he was. He was a great knight. Brave, chivalrous, everything we knights hope to be."

"I want to be a knight," I said, surprising myself. But I knew it was true. It was the one thing I felt for certain. Whatever happened to me, wherever

I ended up, this is where my father wanted me to be. He must have left that enchanted medallion for me so that I could come here and become a knight. I believed that with all my heart.

"You want to be a knight, huh?" my companion said. "Then you've come to the right place. Come on. We're here."

We stopped at an alley situated behind a dilapidated post signaling we were on the corner of Barrie Road and Carroll Street. My hooded companion led me down an alley that dead-ended at a stone wall with a heavy wooden door. It had no handles or anything, but at about eye level there was a small insignia faintly glowing blue. It looked like a sword encircled in a leaf laurel, with the letters NC, GV, HD beneath it.

My companion touched the glyph and it glowed brighter. Just like that, with no key, password, or anything, the door started to slide open with a low growl as it slid across the stone. I peered inside, but all I saw was blackness. My companion stepped inside, and I followed.

The door slid behind us and closed with a thud. As my eyes adjusted to the darkness, I realized we were standing in a cave, dimly lit by faintly glowing purple crystals scattered about the area. The cave was tall, but not very wide, like a tunnel.

My companion removed his hood, and I immediately realized that he wasn't a he at all.

She had shoulder-length dirty blond hair that spilled out from beneath her hood as she shook her head back and forth. She combed her hair back with slender fingers a few times, though it barely did anything to contain every strand. She stopped and glared at me. Even in the shadow of the cave I noticed how dark and blue her eyes were. Dark like the stormiest parts of the sea.

"What are you staring at?" she said. "Haven't you seen a pretty girl before?"

I fumbled on my words. She was pretty. "I—I'm sorry. I didn't know you were a girl."

"Are you serious? Even in a cloak—look at this figure?" She gestured at her body. I couldn't tell if she was being sarcastic or not, but when she sneered at me with her lip the way she did, she didn't look as pretty as I thought. Just arrogant, and a little terrifying.

"Your voice is kinda deep," I said defensively. "So, it could go either way."

"Oh, that's a great way to win over a girl you just met. Tell her she sounds like a guy."

"No—I mean—I didn't—wait. You're a knight!"

"And what do you mean by that? Because I'm a girl?" She asked, putting her hands on her hips. I knew immediately that I had crossed a line. "That is so fifth century. It's the twenty-first century, dork! There's such a thing as female knights."

"I'm sorry, I'm sorry," I said quickly. "I didn't mean to offend you. I was just mistaken, all right?"

"Well, for what it's worth, I'm Gwenivere Martin, Lady Knight of the Round Table, and First Apprentice to Principal Hal." She held out her hand to shake mine. "But you can just call me Gwen."

I shook it, then said awkwardly, "Ah, I'm Hayden. Hayden Keyes. Nice to meet you, Gwen. And I'm sorry I thought you were a boy. Just because you're a girl, doesn't change the fact that you have awesome fighting moves."

"Thank you," she said grinning. "Now follow me. I'm taking you straight to Principal Hal."

She led me deeper into the cave. The farther we went the more crystals appeared scattered about the walls and ceiling, providing more and more light for us. Not long later, the cave opened into an enormous cavern. Ahead of us stood a giant golden gate ornamented with a giant dragon.

# CHAPTER SEVEN

Its scales were gold and silver, its eyes shining green emeralds. It was so realistic, I almost thought it was real at first. Its body twisted around the sides of the gate, neck forward, above the center of the doors. I noticed the same symbol from the door etched on the dragon's forehead.

Gwen walked straight up to the gate. The dragon looked down at her and nodded. I wondered what it would do if I approached the gate. Hopefully not eat me, or worse, burn me to a crisp.

Gwen didn't walk through. She looked up at the dragon and said, "I, Gwenivere Martin, Lady Knight of the Round Table, and First Apprentice of Principal Hal (I wondered if she really had to go through all that every time) give Hayden Keyes permission to enter the Magic Hollow and here reside as long as he is found worthy of that right."

She turned and gestured for me to come forward. The dragon tilted its head and stared at me as well. Its eyes were only emeralds, but somehow, I felt like it was looking straight through me, seeing all the darkest secrets I didn't even know I had. I stepped forward hesitantly and the dragon looked me over. I winced, waiting for it to open its jaws and take a bite out of me, but it didn't. It nodded, then returned to its original posture, becoming still as a statue again.

The gates slid open smoother than the automatic doors at a grocery store.

On the other side of the gates, I could now see the Magic Hollow clearly, and it was amazing.

Directly after the gate, the cavern ended at a huge canyon, maybe one hundred feet wide and at least two hundred feet deep. The bottom of this second chasm was littered with massive clusters of crystal that looked terrifyingly sharp from up here. A massive stone bridge spanned the chasm to the other side.

Beyond the bridge and the chasm, I saw that the cavern opened entirely, allowing me to see the sky. It was nighttime, but I could see more stars than I had ever seen in my life. The moon and the stars provided so much light, I could see all the Magic Hollow.

And it was huge. The Hollow looked like a giant valley several miles across, surrounded by magnificent snow-peaked mountains all around. In the center of the valley, and directly ahead of us was the most brilliant castle I have ever seen. It had dozens of towers, tiers, battlements, and domes. Smaller towers spouted out of the sides of the larger towers, with even smaller towers spouting out of them in a way that made it seem like the whole structure was held together by magical glue. The windows glowed orange and yellow with light, like hundreds of sparkling Christmas lights.

It was the single most beautiful thing I had ever seen.

To the left of the castle sat a large village sprawling along the base of the mountain. Beyond that, there was a massive stone building rimmed with colorful triangular shaped flags that reminded me of a Roman Coliseum. To the right of the castle, I saw a massive field bigger than ten football fields. In the center of the field, I saw a big mound of stone that jutted up out of the ground. Even from here, I could see a thick steam rising from the rocks. Beyond all of this, I could make out a massive forest stretching all the way back to the farthest snowy mountain.

Gwen noticed me staring, my jaw wide open. She pouted her red lips, giving me that same scary glare from before. "Well, are you finished admiring the view? Can we get going or what? Hal will be waiting for you. Besides, you should have seen it a few years ago. Everything looks pretty dismal these days."

"Sorry," I said. "I didn't mean to hold you up. I just wasn't prepared for this. It's still—"

"Amazing? Yeah, I know," she said, her expression changing. "The Magic

Hollow still takes my breath away. That will never change. I remember the first time I walked through those gates . . ."

"You didn't always live here either?" I asked curiously.

"That's a long story," Gwen said quickly, her face turning cold again. "One that you'll probably never hear. Now come on, let's go."

As we crossed the stone bridge, I was thankful I wasn't afraid of heights. I looked down over the side and saw just how far down it was to the bottom of the chasm.

"This is the Crystal Chasm," Gwen said. "Cool, huh? We like to think of it as our moat in a way."

When the bridge connected to solid ground, we stepped onto a dirt path cut from the grass. It led straight into a beautiful garden and courtyard in front of the castle. Tall white marble pillars circled a grove of weeping willow trees and a garden of flowers.

I noticed that the flowers seemed droopy and colorless, like they were struggling to stay alive in a drought. The dirt path turned to stone and branched off in a circle around the garden. In the very center of it all, there was a huge pool and a fountain. A marble statue of a larger-than-life horse stood inside the fountain, rearing on its hind legs like it was ready to leap straight out of the water.

I tried to take in all my surroundings. It was all so amazing. I couldn't help but think about my father and wonder how he felt when he saw all of this for the first time. What a discovery this must have been for someone who had been researching and chasing after things everyone else believed were legends.

We circled around the garden, then Gwen led me up the marble steps of the castle to the main gate. The doors were massive, solid wood, reinforced with huge steel beams. A small plane could easily fly right through them if they were open. Just above the doors six words were carved into the stone wall, which I read aloud: "Noble chivalry. Gentle virtue. Honest deeds."

"The code of the knights," Gwen said. "We all swear an oath to live by it and uphold it for the rest of our lives."

"I like that," I said. "But what exactly is chivalry anyway? Like being a gentleman—and a *gentlewoman*—I guess?"

"It's so much more than having good manners. Chivalry is the crown of the knight's code. It embodies all the greatest qualities a knight should have, like courage, bravery, honor, courtesy, justice, and most importantly, a constant readiness to help those who are weaker than you. That's what it really means to be a Knight of the Round Table, like me."

I immediately felt sick to my stomach.

I wanted to become a knight like my father had before me. I wanted it even more than I had wanted to go to Tiffany Stoke's party or try to make the basketball team.

For me, it seemed like becoming a knight and following in my father's footsteps was the only way I could get to know him. And obviously, I didn't know him, so this was probably me being hard on myself, but I felt like the only way he would accept me if I found him was by proving myself by becoming a knight.

But the kicker was that all my life I had been the weak one—the weak one that other stronger people protected. I thought of the time Mr. Bianco rescued me from the bullies or shielded me from my class while they laughed at me. Or all the times I ran from my problems rather than face them. I wasn't brave, and I definitely wasn't strong. How could someone who is weak and always needs help, be able to turn around and help others?

It wouldn't work. I would have to learn how to be strong.

Gwen pushed open the heavy doors and led me into the castle. Crossing the threshold, I repeated the knight's code in my mind again and again. Noble chivalry. Gentle virtue. Honest deeds.

"Welcome to New Camelot," Gwen said, gesturing to the entrance hall of the castle.

My mouth dropped open in awe for like the gazillienth time tonight. The castle foyer was huge. The arched ceiling seemed miles away, and its ceiling was covered in paintings depicting scenes of nature and knighthood. There were dozens of doors on all sides, and large torches along the walls providing light. A crimson-colored carpet led from the door ahead to a magnificent staircase nearly as wide as the room was. The staircase led up to a higher platform, where I could see even more doors and smaller staircases going in every other direction possible.

"New Camelot? This isn't the original?"

"Of course not. Camelot was destroyed over a thousand years ago. The original knights rebuilt this castle shortly after we came to this realm."

"Huh," I said. "I guess there is a lot I have to learn about the history of this place."

"Good luck trying to learn it all. I spend four to five hours in the library a day trying to read all the books we have on the history of Between, and I have hardly made a dent in the castle's collection. And I'm a really fast reader."

"There's a library? Can I see it?"

"Not now. I need to take you to Principal Hal, remember?"

"Oh, yeah. Right." I had been here for three minutes and I was already being taken to the principal's office, I thought.

As Gwen led me up several more staircases and deeper into the castle, I was bewildered by how big this castle really was. I was so busy gawking at all the paintings, tapestries, statues, stained-glass windows, weapons, artifacts, and full suits of armor decorating the halls, that I wasn't paying any attention to where we were going. I knew I would get lost if I ever tried to retrace our steps. I bet museums in my world would pay a fortune for even one of these items.

At one point, we passed a fully-grown oak tree with massive twisting roots that spouted straight out of the wall and floor. Some of the tree's longest branches stuck straight out of a nearby window.

Even crazier than the tree, however, was the snowy white leopard resting in the roots. It perked its eyes and looked at us lazily, as if it were just another domestic pet. Gwen must have seen the look of terror on my face as we passed it because she just shrugged her shoulders and said, "That's Spots. Don't worry, he's house trained. There are several magical creatures who have taken refuge in the castle, and hundreds more who live in the Enchanted Forest north here."

"Oh, okay," I said, reminding myself that chivalry included bravery. A real knight wouldn't be afraid of a leopard, no matter how sharp its teeth look.

"The castle can be tricky to navigate. I bet it will take you ages to figure it out, even if you're the son of Sir William."

I'll admit, that comment stung a little. I was quickly realizing, here in New Camelot, my dad seemed to be something of a legend, their missing hero. The worst part was, I suspected Gwen was right. I was going to turn out to be nothing like my dad.

"The castle has eight floors, not counting the basements," Gwen kept going, like she was my private tour guide. "There are hundreds of staircases, and four main wings: North, South, East, and West. But every wing has its own wings as well, like the East-East Wing, and the East-East-East wing."

I couldn't tell if she was trying to brag about how much she knew about the castle or make me feel like a total moron. Whatever her goal, though, she was succeeding at both. I cursed myself for thinking she was pretty when I first saw her face. I immediately made a mental note to myself to be more careful with my judgment. This girl was a total nightmare.

After a few minutes, we reached Hal's private office. The door looked like any others we had seen on our trek into the castle, except this one had a large golden plaque hanging by it that read: "Principal Hal."

"Hmm. No crazy long title?" I asked, sarcastically.

"Shut up," Gwen said. She knocked on the door.

I didn't know why I felt so nervous. Maybe it was because this guy called himself a principal. It made it seem like the Magic Hollow was some kind of school. Then I realized, maybe it was. They were technically training new Knights of the Round Table here.

Gwen knocked again, but no one answered.

"Strange," she said to herself. "He told me to bring you straight to him."

After a third knock with no response, Gwen grew impatient. She checked the door and found that it was unlocked. I gave her a questioning look as she pushed open the door.

"I'm Hal's First Apprentice," Gwen said. "I can do whatever I want."

"That's really humble of you," I muttered under my breath. I didn't know what kind of principal Hal was, but in my experience, breaking and entering a principal's office was never a good idea.

"Hal?" Gwen asked, as she stepped into the room.

I followed her in. The room was cozy. There was a large fireplace with a comfy looking chair close to the hearth, though the fire had all but died out. There were windows on three of the walls, and I quickly realized we were in one of the tallest towers because I could see most of the Magic Hollow through the glass panes. Almost all the walls were covered in bookcases and filled with old books. In the center of the room was a large wooden desk and a tall high-backed wooden chair, ornately carved with what looked like trees and animals, like wolves, stags, bears, and more.

But there was no principal to be found.

"Where could he be?" Gwen asked, probably speaking to herself again, though I took it upon myself to answer:

"Maybe he had to go to the bathroom?"

"Shut up," was all she said in return.

"You're great at first impressions," I retorted.

Gwen ignored me, inspecting a single white envelope that was resting on Hal's desk.

"It's addressed to me," Gwen said, tearing open the envelope's seal.

I watched impatiently as her eyes zoomed back and forth across the page, reading the letter. Her eyes grew alarmingly larger the longer she read. I remembered reading once that the Vampire Squid had the largest eye to body ratio in the world, but after seeing the look on Gwen's face just then, I thought it was time we submitted a petition for that world record.

When she was finished, she slumped into Principal Hal's chair, pale faced and looking terrified.

"What is it?" I asked.

"I can't believe it," she said. She closed her eyes, took a deep breath, probably trying to compose herself. Unexpectedly, her eyes popped open and she grabbed my arm, yanking me back out of the office.

"What is going on?" I blurted out, trying to keep myself from tripping over my own two feet as we hurtled down the hall.

"Hal and some of our knights might be in trouble," she said. "I have to call an emergency council meeting."

"And what about me?" I asked. "What exactly am I doing?"

"You're a part of what we have to counsel about," she said.

Shortly after that, the sound of bellowing horns filled the halls. I wondered if it was some sort of medieval school bell, but then again, it was the middle of the night so that seemed unlikely.

"They're back!" Gwen shouted. "This way!"

She yanked me in a completely new direction as we hurtled down a spiraling staircase. As we ran, I began to see other kids stepping out of rooms and starting to make their way down the stairs, too. Most of them were still wearing their pajamas.

When we reached the main entrance of the castle again, at least two dozen kids had gathered there, as well as a handful of adults, too. The castle doors flew open. Three people walked in, all of them looking injured. I stood on my toes, trying to look over the crowd. I didn't see Jack Lantern or Mr. Bianco.

Gwen shouted someone's name and ran forward without me, but I wasn't listening or paying much attention. My heart fell in my chest. For the first time I considered the possibility that Jack and Mr. Bianco had lost the battle against the troll. I hated thinking that Mr. Bianco could be hurt because of me.

Gwen, who was now supporting one of the injured guys and helping him walk, turned to the crowd and said, "Knights, I've got bad news." She held up the envelope in her spare hand. "It's a letter from Principal Hal, and I think the Round Table needs to hear what it says."

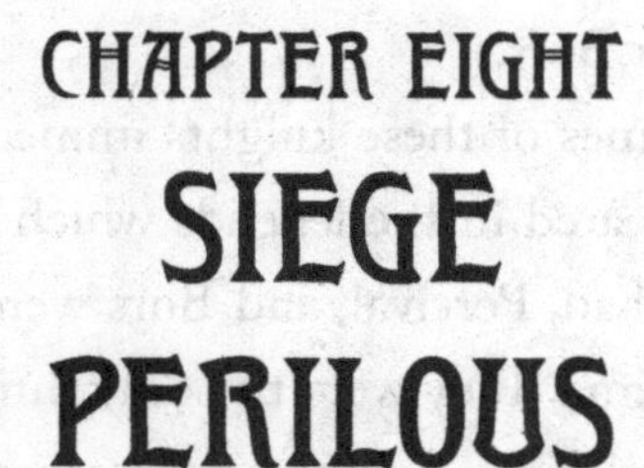

# CHAPTER EIGHT
# SIEGE PERILOUS

The Round Table, as Gwen called it, met in a special room called the Round Hall, deep within the castle keep, which was the most central and protected part of the castle. This was by far the coolest room I had seen in my short visit to New Camelot.

A magnificent round table of beautifully stained wood took up most of the round room. The table was surrounded by chairs plated with gold. I quickly examined the rest of the room and saw that there were only four decorations on the wall: four oil paintings, organized next to each other. The first painting was of a tall, proud looking man in green and gold ornamented armor, wearing a crown of blue crystals. A gold plaque beneath him identified the man as King Arthur.

The painting beside King Arthur's depicted a young knight walking on foot leading his horse behind him. This painting was labeled Sir Galahad. Besides that, was a gorgeous, yet sorrowful, painting of a knight weeping over a dying young lady. This painting was labeled Sir Percival.

Finally, the fourth painting depicted a broad-shouldered knight in bright silver armor holding a beautiful golden chalice. The man had long thin brown hair and a very distinct, wide scar on his forehead. This painting was labeled Sir Bors.

I recognized the names of these knights immediately. They were written exactly as they appeared in the legends which I read in Mr. Bianco's English class. Sir Galahad, Percival, and Bors were considered the three greatest knights of all time. They were the only three, according to legend, to achieve the Holy Grail. King Arthur, on the other hand, never found the grail, but was still honored above all other kings and knights for uniting so many countries and forming the Round Table.

Gwen and the limping boy sat beside each other on the far end of the table, but I stood in a corner out of the way, while the rest of the knights filed into the room and took their seats at the Round Table. A lot of them noticed me and gave me weird looks when they realized they didn't recognize me, but nobody said anything. I was surprised to see that the majority of the knights appeared to be teenagers, or at best very young adults. They all looked extremely nervous.

All the seats but three were filled when a tall scrawny man entered the room. He stood out like a sore thumb, surrounded by such younger people. He was at least twenty years Mr. Bianco's senior. His hair was spotted with gray and his clothes looked just as shabby. He wore an old greasy fur scarf wrapped around his shoulders like some kind of wacky cape. His black beady eyes glared around the room from under a bushy unibrow. This guy looked like a cross between a reptile and a weasel. I didn't know if he was terrifying or just funny looking.

"Did you call this emergency meeting, Gwenivere?" he asked with a raspy voice.

I could tell by the way Gwen looked at him, that he definitely wasn't Principal Hal. "Yes, I did, Baron," she said coldly. "Hal left a letter for me.

And we have important matters to discuss."

This guy, Baron, looked around the room pryingly, like he was only just taking it all in for the first time. A look of realization seemed to dawn on him, and his lips curled into a nasty snarl. "Where's Hal?" he asked.

"Yeah. We can't start without Principal Hal," a tall black-haired girl chirped up from the table with a heavy accent.

"He isn't here," Gwen said. "That is part of the reason why I called this meeting. So, can we begin?"

"Of course," Baron said coolly. "Please proceed." He nodded towards Gwen then took a seat at the Round Table.

Gwen turned towards me and said, "Are you going to stand there like a vulture or are you going to sit down?" She gestured toward the empty chair beside that Baron guy.

I wasn't exactly thrilled to sit by him, so I just sat down in the other empty seat furthest away from him.

The entire room gasped. I think someone even screamed a little and almost fell out of their own chair. I looked around frantically, trying to see what I had missed, but everyone was staring at me.

"Holy swords," a boy sitting one spot over from me said. "We're *doomed*."

"What's going on?" I asked. "I just sat down—"

"He doesn't know?" The boy said, panicking. "He doesn't know what he's done!"

"Oh, shut up, Tristan," the boy Gwen had helped said. "It's just a silly superstition."

"Silly superstition?" Tristan said. "You're the Defender of New Camelot, Lance."

"Acting Defender," the black-haired girl said. "We haven't had a true

Defender in hundreds of years." Gwen's friend glared at the girl, but he didn't respond to her comment.

The boy, who I heard was named Tristan, continued, "Call him what you want, we elected him as our leader. And you should know better, man. Nobody has sat in Siege Perilous since Sir Galahad!"

Gwen must have seen my confusion and decided she had seen me squirm enough because she finally spoke up and explained to me what was going on. "Hayden, that seat is supposedly forbidden. It's called Siege Perilous: the empty seat. It's an old tradition from King Arthur's time. One of the thirteen chairs at the table was always to be left empty because they believed that only a knight destined to achieve greatness could complete the circle. Everyone else who sat in it burned to a crisp, or got really bad luck, depending on which story you want to believe."

My face went pale. I didn't know what to be more afraid of, the 'destined for greatness' part, or spontaneously erupting in flames.

"It's not a superstition," Tristan said angrily, glaring at Gwen. "It's tradition. And it's real."

"Seeing as you haven't caught on fire yet," Gwen said to me, "I think we can all assume that the tradition is moot."

"Sir Galahad could sit in the chair because he had the Grail," a blonde-haired boy argued, joining the conversation. He turned to me. "You wouldn't happen to have a Holy Grail on you, would you?"

I shook my head. "I'm sorry I sat here. I can move to the other seat—"

"It's fine, Hayden. Sir Tristan's just being annoying," Gwen said, staring daggers at Tristan.

"What? All I'm saying is this kid is lucky he didn't burn on the spot, get struck by lightning, or fall over dead!"

Baron pounded his fist on the table. "Pull it together, you lot! It's late, and I'm tired. We don't have time for this nonsense. Seeing as the kid doesn't have a grail and he hasn't burnt to a crisp, I think we can all assume that Siege Perilous is pure hokum. Now please, Lady Gwen—let's get this meeting going, shall we?"

Tristan didn't look pleased, but everyone in the room turned toward Gwen to hear what she had to say. I could tell nobody particularly liked this Baron guy, but they weren't going to question him either. Gwen cleared her throat. "Right. Thank you, Baron. As you know, Principal Hal sent some of us outside of the Magic Hollow on two covert missions. Jack and Lance," she nodded to the older boy beside her, who had been limping, "led a small party who were sent to open a temporary gate to the Other Realm in search of Sir William and Sir Ector. I was sent to Quay, after helping Hal open the rift of course, to pick up a newcomer on Hal's direct orders."

I remembered how Gwen had told me how dangerous Quay was. The way she spoke about her mission made it seem like she was trying to brag to her peers as well. Judging by their reactions, I wondered how often they were given assignments that let them leave the Magic Hollow.

"First things first, Lance—can you report on what happened to your squad?" Gwen asked.

Lance winced as he sat up in his chair, clutching his side. "Like you said, Hal sent us to go through the rift. Jack was to pass through, while I was meant to stand guard to protect the way in. Sure enough, it worked. Jack and the mouse passed through it into the Other Realm. But . . ." Lance faltered, like he was struggling to say the rest. "We were attacked shortly after Jack entered the rift."

"Attacked? By whom?" Someone at the table interjected.

"Three bridge trolls," Lance said sheepishly. "We tried to stop them, but they outnumbered us. There was nothing we could do . . ." I noticed how embarrassed he looked by his failure.

Gwen must have too because she said quickly, "Three full-grown trolls, though. The fact that all of you're still alive shows that you fought bravely and defended your squad!"

I made eye contact with Lance. He seemed to know that I knew the truth. Only one of the trolls had been fully grown. The other two were juveniles. I could tell that Lance seemed beat up about his loss, and I didn't want to make it worse. Besides, we didn't even know each other yet. He seemed grateful that I kept quiet.

"Do you know what they were doing?" Gwen asked. "Trolls coordinating an attack? I've never heard anything like it!"

"It's possible that they just found us by accident," Lance said. "Maybe they didn't know what they were doing when they stepped through the gate."

"No," I said, surprising myself. With all my nerves, I spoke louder than I intended.

The room went quiet as everyone turned to look at me. "Do you know something more about this?" Lance asked.

"Yes, I do," I said. "The trolls were looking for my father, William Keyes, too."

Everyone gasped, then started whispering excitedly.

"Holy swords," Tristan whispered. "No wonder he didn't burn to a crisp. He's the son of a legend!"

That made me wince. The way everyone was looking at me, like they expected me to be something amazing. How could I tell them that I didn't even know my dad? And, from what I had heard, I was nothing like him.

"Wait—Sir William? The Sir William?" One girl asked. "The hero of the Shadow Wars who helped defeat Marzon at the Battle of Nocturnus?"

"That's the one," Tristan said, smiling at me like I was a god.

"Where is Sir William?" someone else asked excitedly. "Where is your father? Is he coming here?"

"No, no," I said. "You don't understand. I don't even know my father. He left me with my aunt and uncle when I was just a baby. The trolls came looking for him, but they realized he wasn't there. Just me, his son."

"But that means you're from the Other Realm," someone said excitedly as it finally dawned on them. This was followed by more excited whispers that made my stomach squirm even more. I was starting to get nervous.

"What happened, Hayden?" Gwen asked, gesturing for silence.

"The trolls attacked us. But Mr. Bianco—I mean, Sir Ector—and Jack Lantern helped me fight the trolls. We managed to get one—maybe two— but we got separated. I used a magic medallion my father had left for me, and it brought me here. Well, sort of." I looked at Gwen, and she nodded, understanding.

"A few hours ago," she said, "Hal called me into his office and gave me special instructions. He told me to go to the north alleyway between Wharf and Fishtail Streets in Quay. He told me I would find a young man there, and I was to escort him back to the Hollow immediately."

I felt a weird, cold feeling in my stomach. How did this Hal guy know exactly where I was going to be? Especially because I didn't even know how I got there. I fell off the griffin and then blacked out. Next thing I knew, I was in the alleyway, and Gwen was there annoying my socks off all the way back to the Magic Hollow. Could this Hal guy see the future?

Gwen continued her story. "I did exactly as he instructed and found Hayden. I brought him back and went straight to Hal's office. Well, we did have a quick run in with the Cerise Guard," there were a few gasps around the room, "But I took care of them no problem." Gwen smiled proudly. I could tell she loved every minute of this. "Anyway, when we reached Hal's office, I found it empty. All he left behind was this letter."

"What does it say?" A young man asked from across the table.

"Yeah, read it!" Another girl said.

Gwen cleared her throat and read the letter. "Gwen, if you're reading this letter then I assume you have returned from the mission I gave you. You have done a noble deed by bringing this young man to the Hollow and protecting him from the dangers beyond our walls. However, as you have probably since surmised, I also gave this mission to you as a distraction. I am truly sorry, but I knew you would never let me leave alone. I couldn't risk you following me."

Gwen paused, and rubbed her eyes. It looked like she was fighting back tears. In that moment, she looked like a normal teenage girl and not quite as terrifying as she usually appeared. She composed herself and continued reading. "The shadows are stirring again. This is not a good sign. There is something I need to check on, just to be certain. I expressly forbid anyone from leaving the Magic Hollow before I return. Under absolutely no circumstances is anyone to come and look for me. I may be getting old, but I can look after myself. Best wishes, Hal."

"Aha!" Baron said, smiling stupidly. "You runts hear that, Hal said nobody is leaving until he returns. As seniority here, I should be Castellan. Nobody is more fit to run this castle than me."

"Never mind, we are doomed," Tristan whispered to his neighbor.

"But what does Hal mean by the shadows are stirring?" Someone asked.

"This is how it happened, all those years ago," Baron said, suddenly growing grim, "when the Shadow War began. The evil wizard Marzon unlocked an ancient shadow magic that reshaped the entire face of Between, and almost swallowed up the Magic Hollow entirely."

"But Marzon is dead," the blonde haired boy said quickly. "My father was there. He fought alongside Hal in the final battle. He watched Marzon fall!"

"He is one of many witnesses to Marzon's defeat," Baron said. "I was there as well. I fought alongside your father, too, Gale. Believe it or not. He was a good man, rest his sword."

I started to understand better why all these knights were so young. The way Mr. Bianco and Jack had spoken about the Shadow War, I was certain it had been a horrible war that had taken many lives.

The tall black-haired girl spoke up next, "I think we can all agree that Marzon isn't the issue here. But Between is a massive place. There could be any lord or wizard or witch or monster who could have dabbled into some dark magic that is now helping them rise in power."

"So basically, you're saying it's impossible to know who our enemy could be," Tristan said, crossing his arms.

"My point," the black-haired girl said, "is that there is no use debating this right now. Hal said he needed to check on something. We need to trust Hal and stay in the Hollow. All we can do is continue to train and prepare."

"I agree with you perfectly, Isabelle," Tristan said.

A tall handsome boy with dark brown skin, and neatly coiffed black hair pounded his fist on the table. "If Hal says trouble is stirring out there, why should we stay in the Hollow and keep playing pretend war? If my family knew what has become of the Round Table, they would be furious. There are still houses outside of the Hollow that are loyal to the Table. We need to be out there finding them and rallying them to our cause. Not sitting here, prancing around in our little tournaments in the Arena."

"If you want to run back to your precious parents," the black-haired girl, Isabelle, said, "then be our guest. Nobody is stopping you, Percy. But none of us are Igthams—*thankfully*. Our parents actually fought in the Shadow

War, instead of hiding in their mansion and waiting to see which side won."

The boy, Percy, was furious. He stood up, sending his chair flying behind him, his hand reaching to his side, perhaps for a sword, though there wasn't one there. "I'm Percy Igtham, heir of House Igtham. Our family has sacrificed more for the cause than you could ever know! And you sit here and insult my name?"

"What are you going to do? Run back to your parent's castle and cry about it?" Isabelle said, not backing down.

"All right, all right. Shut up!" Baron interjected. "Sit down and shut your whining traps!"

Percy scowled, but he did as he was told.

"There is nothing else to discuss here," Baron said, seeming to relish in the authority he had received from Hal's letter. "Nobody is leaving the Hollow. *Nobody*. Which means all of you need to get back into your beds. We will proceed with business-as-usual tomorrow morning."

"No," Lance said fervently. He kicked back his chair and stood up quickly, making several people jump in surprise. "I for one am not going to just sit back and let you seize control of New Camelot, Baron. Percy is right. We shouldn't be playing war. The Cerise guard is rampaging in the streets just outside our door. And what do we do about it? Nothing?"

Several of the knights pounded their fists on the table in agreement. This seemed to encourage Lance to keep going.

"I say, we call the banners. Each and every one of us are ready for this. We have the Captain's Guard as well. Together, the Cerise Guard wouldn't stand a chance. We'll be rid of them before sunrise!"

"The Captain's Guard without their captain?" Baron spat. "Who do you think you are, boy! Telling me what to do. Hal said nobody leaves. If you break his order, you are breaking a direct order from your principal."

"Hal didn't want anyone to try and follow him. But after what Gwen has told us, how can we not take action. People are suffering. We swore oaths to protect the weak! How can we protect them from inside these walls?"

"Sit down, boy," Baron said coldly, "or I will have you locked in the dungeons."

"My friends, by your honor as sworn Knights of the Round Table," Lance said confidently. "I'm Defender of New Camelot, chosen by each one of you. Stand beside me. Stand together. Defend the weak. Arrest this pretender."

Most of the room looked shocked, but several knights, including Percy rose to Lance's call.

Isabelle stood up quickly, drawing a hidden dagger. "Don't take another step, Igtham," she grunted, standing between him and Baron.

Baron smiled smugly. "Now, now, children. None of this. Guards, enter!"

The doors burst open and several armored guards entered the room carrying shields and spears. I quickly realized these must be the Captain's Guard I had heard mentioned—the ones that Jack Lantern was in charge of.

Lance looked shocked as the guards entered the room, leveling their long steel spears.

"I am willing to be a benevolent leader," Baron said. "I hope you will see reason and stand down. The Captain's Guard is loyal to this castle. But more importantly, they are loyal to me. They will arrest you if I command. They will fight you if you resist. Stand down and accept me as Castellan."

Lance looked like he wanted to argue. He glanced around the room, possibly sizing up the guards. Even I knew it was a hopeless battle. After a long, tense moment, Lance sighed and put away his sword. He nodded to the others who had risen to his call to do the same.

"Smart children," Baron said mockingly. He nodded toward the guards and they lowered their spears. "Now, do we have anything else to discuss?

I'm tired and would very much like to go to bed!"

"What about Captain Lantern?" someone asked. "And Sir Ector? They never came back. What if they are injured . . . or worse?"

Baron slammed his fist on the table. "Sir Ector is a deserter and a coward. Most of you don't even know who he is because he hasn't been here for thirteen years. Now, he turns up out of nowhere and you want to risk your life to save him? Sounds like he's up to no good if you ask me."

"Liar!" I said, standing up. At that moment, I felt a surge of anger toward Baron. He was wrong, and everyone needed to know it. "Sir Ector has spent the last thirteen years watching over me. He swore an oath to my father that he would protect me, and he has kept that oath. He's an honorable man. I wouldn't be here if it weren't for him. We have to do something if they are in danger!"

"You have no right to speak in this room, boy," the Baron said roughly. "You aren't a knight. You aren't even a squire."

"Well, I am a knight," Lance said angrily, staring down Baron. "And Hayden speaks truthfully. Besides, setting aside your apparent dislike for Sir Ector, Captain Lantern is out there somewhere as well. They may be held hostage by the trolls—who knows. But Hal said—"

"Hal said," Baron pantomimed. "Hal said the shadows stirring—absurd. Anyone who thinks they've seen shadows stirring needs to get their eyes checked. It's all a bunch of nonsense."

"Are you questioning Hal?" Gwen asked threateningly. "I thought you were loyal to him? Or are you only loyal when it means you get to be Castellan?"

"So, what if I am? Trolls are stupid. Even if they did capture them, they won't be able to keep them contained for long. They'll escape, gut the trolls, and be on their merry way home in no time. Mark my words."

"We should vote on an action," Gwen said confidently. "We outnumber you nine to one."

Baron laughed. "Foolish girl. If you try to override my commands, then I will have you tried as a traitor and an enemy of New Camelot as well. You heard the letter. Hal said no one leaves, and I am in charge while he is away. Is that clear?"

"Yes, Baron," she muttered.

"What was that? All of you, let me hear you. Is that clear?"

"Yes, Baron," everyone said in unison.

"Clear as mud," Tristan added under his breath.

"But what about Hayden?" Lance said defiantly, still staring at Baron.

"Hmm? Oh, yes, the boy," Baron said. "Well, if Hal wanted him to come here, then I guess we have no choice but to let him stay."

"The law of the Hollow states that no one in need can be turned away," Gwen said. "But I'm sure a ruler as wise as you didn't need to be reminded of that."

"Forget the law," Baron said angrily. "I'm in charge, and I say he can stay, if he earns his room and board. I'm sure we can find him a bed in the old servant chambers."

"Let him be my squire," Lance said, giving me an encouraging smile. "We have an extra bunk in our dormitory. I will train him and prepare him for the trials if he wishes to become a knight. If you want to, of course," he added, looking at me kindly. "You're the son of Sir William Keyes, hero of our realm. You deserve this by right of birth."

I couldn't believe what I was hearing. Lance, apparently the lead knight, wanted me to be his squire. If I was going to become a knight like my father, this was my chance. I couldn't mess this up. I realized that everyone was watching me, waiting to hear my answer to Lance's proposal.

"Lance, I would be honored to train as your squire. I want to become a knight like my father. At least, I'll try."

"This is ridiculous," Isabelle said, getting red in the face. "We don't even know anything about him. He has to be what, twelve, thirteen years old? He hasn't even been a page! How can he be a squire?"

"That's just a tradition," Lance argued. "There is no rule that says a squire can only be chosen from the pages."

"It's true," Baron said. "A squire doesn't technically have to be a page. But it will be a major setback. You will have a lot of catching up to do in his training Lance. Are you sure you really want to take on that responsibility?"

"Of course, I do. I wouldn't have volunteered if I didn't. Besides, he's the son of Sir William Keyes. It's an honor to train you, Hayden."

I saw Isabelle roll her eyes, and look away, like I was something really obnoxious or smelly.

"Then it's decided," Baron said in his rough voice. "The boy will squire for Lance. He can prove his worth or die trying. Now get to bed, you little ruffians! And no funny business, understood? I'll be posting guards around the clock. Nobody leaves the Hollow!"

Baron stood up and was escorted out of the room by the Captain's Guards. Everybody seemed to be in a much better mood as soon as he left, despite the bad news that had been delivered during the meeting, and the tense moment when Lance stood up against Baron.

"I don't think becoming a knight will be a problem for you," a girl who hadn't spoken at all during the meeting said. She was petite, but taller than me, and wore a flowing white tunic tucked into high-waisted trousers, tied off with a thin gold rope. Her long auburn hair was tied in a thick braid, slung over her shoulder, with a few wayward strands falling down the side of her cheeks. "You're the son of Sir William, the hero of the Shadow War!"

"Thanks," I said, feeling like I was going to pass out. I wanted to say something, but I didn't know what to say. They didn't even know me yet, and everyone seemed to expect great things from me because of who my father was. Somehow, I knew they were going to be greatly disappointed.

"I'm Lady Elibora, by the way," she said, curtsying to me. "Knight-junior of the Round Table. If you ever want to go on a hunt, I'm your girl."

"Thanks," I said, forcing a smile. "I'll remember that."

"If you do go on a hunt with Elibora," Lance said, "you'll be lucky if you even get in a single arrow. Elibora is the best archer in the Magic Hollow."

Her dimpled cheeks blushed as she smiled admirably at Lance. "Well, goodnight." She curtsied again and left the Round Hall.

"We expect great things from you," another girl said, shaking my hand. She had thick golden blonde hair, tied back with a dozen ornate little braids. She had an infectious smile with one crooked tooth, which I found surprisingly adorable. "Welcome to the Magic Hollow. You're going to love it here. My name is Lady Kaylinelle, Knight-junior of the Round Table, Lady of House Trent, *blah*, *blah*, *blah*. All that title stuff." She curtsied to me as well, and I attempted a bow in return.

"Wow," she said, leaning really close to my face and looking at my eyes. "You have beautiful eyes!"

I had never had a girl that close to my face before, so naturally, I panicked and said something smart like, "Thanks, you do, too!"

I shook several more hands and met the rest of the knights. There was Tristan, who formally introduced himself as "Tristan, son of Tristan, son of Tristan," then clapped me on the back and thanked me for standing up to Baron and calling him a liar. He was followed by Sir Gale, a friendly blonde-haired boy who was a few years older than me. After him, I was introduced to Lucas, who said he was the butler ("I'll explain later," Lance whispered), and Percy, the proud looking one, who introduced himself as "the heir to House Igtham."

Finally, the tall girl Isabelle, who looked like she could out wrestle a water buffalo approached me. She towered over me and was even a little taller than Lance. To be honest, I wondered if she was part-troll. "I'm Isabelle," she said. "My father fought alongside yours in the Shadow War. Not that our dad's accomplishments guarantee our own. I guess we'll have to see what you're really made of."

I nodded, trying not to be intimidated by her threatening demeanor. Isabelle would have seemed more like a Viking than a knight, if it weren't for her tawny beige skin, and accent that reminded me of Italian.

"That was tense, Lance," Gwen said. "I would fight for you any day. But I think you made the right decision standing down. At least for now."

"As long as that coward is in charge, things are never going to get better around here. We have to do something," Lance said.

"But you heard Baron," Gwen argued. He will be posting guards. We would never make it out the front gate. At least not without a fight."

"I know," Lance sighed. "For now we just have to keep playing these games."

Gwen turned to me. "I don't think you realize what an honor it is to squire under Lance. He's the best knight we've got. Well, he's lousy at spells and potion work, but I guess, you can't have everything."

"That's why I have you, Gwen," Lance said. Gwen smiled at him, and I could tell there was a strong friendship there.

"Well, I'm off to bed. We can talk more in the morning," she said heading for the door.

"Goodnight," Lance said, as I waved.

Lance turned to me. He was tall and muscular with brown eyes and dark brown hair that fell to his shoulders. To me, Lance was everything a true knight should look like, which meant he was everything I wasn't.

"I guess I should formally introduce myself. I'm Lance, Lord of House Hawkwood, Knight-junior of the Round Table, and Defender of New Camelot."

I bowed. "Thank you, Lance. Thank you for taking me on as your squire."

"It's an honor to train the son of Sir William," Lance said. "Besides, it was worth it just to stand up to Baron. He's a jerk to think the son of our hero would sleep in the old servant chambers."

I felt my stomach squirm again at the thought of my father, the hero. "Look, there is something you need to know. I never knew my father. Where I grew up . . . this is all so foreign. I have no clue what I'm doing . . ."

"That is why you'll be training with me," Lance said. "Don't worry, I'll teach you everything you need to know."

"And I appreciate it, I really do, but—"

"But what?" Lance interrupted.

I wanted to tell him the truth about what I was thinking: What if I fail? What if everyone finds out that I'm nothing like my father? But I couldn't say it. Not in front of Lance Hawkwood, Defender of New Camelot. "Nothing," I said. "I will do my best to make everyone proud."

"Make your father proud," Lance said. "Come on. Let's get to bed."

As he turned and left, I took one last look at the Round Hall. My eyes lingered on the chair, Siege Perilous, and I wondered if the legend about the chair was real or not. The words of the Lady of the Lake came to my mind, "The choice is yours."

That morning, I was like any other kid trying to make it through middle school. Now, I was still afraid and doubted myself, that hadn't changed,

# CHAPTER EIGHT

but when I left the Round Hall, I left as a squire. For good or for worse, things were about to change, and I was one step closer to finding out what happened to my parents.

I took a deep breath, then followed Lance to the dorms.

# CHAPTER NINE
# NEW CAMELOT

I had a hard time sleeping my first night in the Hollow. I tossed and turned all night long, my dreams filled with gigantic trolls swinging clubs and trying to bash me in. I also dreamed of the water lady. In my dream, I was standing in a dark cave, and the water lady was there, too, standing on clear blue water. She tried to say something to me, but I couldn't hear her. "What?" I asked, "What?" But no matter how many times she spoke, I could hear no words.

When I finally stirred in the morning, the feeling of warm sunlight on my face and the sound of my roommates bustling around and chatting, I felt like this was something I could get used to. Then something heavy landed on my chest with a thud.

"What gives?" I shouted, opening my eyes as I gasped for air.

I nearly screamed. A little dragon was sitting on my chest, staring right at me with fiery red eyes. The creature had a small head with a long pointy snout and long flowing white whiskers that reminded me of a wizard. Thick blue scales covered its whole body like armor except for its long leathery black wings that flexed and flapped as it twisted its head and looked at me curiously.

"*Wreee!*" the little dragon hissed as it bit at my blanket.

# CHAPTER NINE

"You want me out of bed?" I asked, as everyone in the room laughed. "Okay, okay! I'm awake! A simple alarm clock would suffice."

"A what clock?" Lance asked. "This is my pet drake, Goliath. Sorry, he can be a little compulsive sometimes."

"He's magnificent," I said, as Goliath leaped off the bed, soared around the room and landed on Lance's shoulder. Goliath was only about two feet tall, but his wingspan was at least five.

"He's really smart," Lance said. "He sleeps up in the rafters, but he likes to keep Room Three in line, so keep that in mind. Make too big of a mess and he will probably be nipping at your fingers until you clean it up."

"That's handy. I wish my aunt and uncle had a drake. They're house is a mess."

Two boys approached me and shook my hand. They looked like perfectly identical twins. Each had shoulder length brown hair, sharp features, and Adam's apples the size of small apples.

"I'm Alex," the first one said.

"I guess that makes me Eric," the second boy said. He turned to his brother and said, "But I thought you were Eric."

"Hmm, I don't think so. I'm passing sure I'm Alex. I was born first."

"Then that would make you Eric. Eric was born first. So, I'm Alex."

"Er, I'm sorry if I have a hard time telling you guys apart," I said, laughing at their feigned identity crisis.

"Don't worry, we do too," they said at the same time, laughing. "We actually have a third brother," Alex said. Or was he Eric? I was already confused. "We're triplets. But he doesn't look anything like us."

"Poor fool," the other said.

"Well, see you at breakfast. Good luck with your first day!" The two brothers turned and left.

"I'll tell you a secret," a boy I recognized from last night said. It was Sir Lucas, a Knight-junior of the Round Table. "One of them has a freckle on his right ear. Not that I know which one he is, but at least you don't try to continue a conversation with the wrong one."

"Even if you do get it right," another boy, who I hadn't met yet said, "if they don't feel like talking anymore, they usually just pretend you have the wrong brother and they don't know what you're talking about. I'm Cole by the way, nice to meet you. I'm a squire, too. I squire for Sir Lucas, he's the butler."

"I guess you don't have butlers in the Other Realm, do you?" Lance asked, noticing the look on my face.

"Actually we do," I said. "They are different though."

"Well, when we say butler, we mean kind of like a glorified secretary. It's a tradition that traces back to Arthurian times. I'm responsible for recording the history of each meeting, running the royal court—stuff like that," Lucas said. "What's a butler in the Other Realm?"

"Well, basically butlers are paid servants for really rich people. They aren't very common anymore though, I don't think."

"Huh. That's not fair," Lucas said. "I don't even get paid. Well, see you two at breakfast. Come on, Cole. We've got a busy day ahead of us."

"Well, there you have it," Lance said. "Room three. We've got the twins, I mean triplets—well, you get what I mean—Alex and Eric. And then Sir Lucas and his squire Cole." Goliath chirped loudly. "And Goliath of course."

I knew I had stepped backward technologically when I came to Between because I hadn't seen any electricity. What I wasn't surprised about, however, was the food. I should have known I wasn't going to find anything familiar at the breakfast table. This was a separate world, which hadn't openly been connected to our world for over a thousand years. In the Other Realm, my diet consisted of all your stapled processed foods like toaster pastries, fast food, and anything you can heat up in less than two minutes in a microwave. What was set out for breakfast here was completely unfamiliar to me.

"What is that?" I asked Lance as he served himself a slice of what looked like a pie.

"It's a meat pie," Lance said. "It's called *custarde*." (He pronounced it like custard-eh.) "Baked with beef, eggs, dates, prunes, and ginger—maybe some other stuff. It's good."

The custarde didn't look bad, just plain. I had never eaten dates or prunes before, but I didn't want to look too picky, so I took a slice of the meat pie myself. Surprisingly, it wasn't all that bad. I ate the whole thing. I realized I hadn't eaten anything in almost a day.

There were at least thirty knights and squires all gathered in the dining hall, enjoying breakfast, not to mention soldiers in the Captain's Guard, too. Much younger kids, around the age of seven or eight, were busy serving the food and cleaning up after the knights and squires. Lance explained to me that these were the pages. I couldn't help but imagine if I had been made a page instead of a squire. I was suddenly very grateful for Lance speaking up for me, even if it had only been because of who my dad was.

I noticed that most of the squires seemed cheerful and happy, while the Knights of the Round Table seemed much less so. I wondered if the news of what had happened last night had yet to fully spread around the castle.

A young page, probably no older than eight, stopped beside our table and gawked at me. "It's true. You have two colored eyes. You're the hero's son. I read all about your father's victory at the Battle of Greenwater just yesterday!"

"How many battles did my dad fight in?" I asked facetiously.

But the boy answered, "Three, sir. But didn't you know that? You're his son after all!"

Obviously, I hadn't known that. Apparently even little kids here knew more about my dad than I did. I'd gone all my life, never knowing the truth, just believing that I had been given up in a closed adoption. Now, I was realizing that in this alternate world, even little kids grew up hearing stories about my dad's heroics.

"Run along," Lance said. "Don't let Baron see you slacking off from your duties."

The little page's eyes widened as he looked around to make sure nobody had seen him, then hurried off toward the other pages.

"Morning, Gwen," Lance said, as she came and sat beside us, bringing with her a plate of some kind of oatmeal cakes.

"What's that?" I asked, eyeing her food. It looked delicious.

"*Eisand mid otemeale grote*," Gwen said, taking a bite out of one of the cakes. I could tell that was more Old English because she pronounced all the vowels in a rhythmic sort of way that reminded me of Mr. Bianco when he would teach us Old English in his class.

"I don't know what that means, but I know I want some," I said, hurrying over to the serving table to fill up another plate.

When I returned, Lance and Gwen were talking quietly about last night.

"Do you really think we should just stay here and do nothing?" Gwen asked. "Hal could be anywhere. What if he doesn't know Jack is in trouble?"

"Hal always knows when trouble is around. And besides, he can take care of himself. He's the greatest sorcerer in Between, after all."

"Whatcha talking about?" I asked, my mouth stuffed with food.

Gwen looked at me like I was something slimy, slithering, and disgusting. "We should probably warn him about *cursas*. Although it would be funny to watch him turn into a pig."

"What?" I asked. "What's curse-saws?"

"*Cursas*," Gwen said. "It's Old English for curses. You know, like bad things happening to someone? Basically, if you eat too much, you could turn into a pig or something else gluttonous."

"What?" I said, spitting out my mouthful of oatmeal cake back onto my plate.

"Don't worry, Hayden, it's not going to happen to you after just one plate," Lance said, laughing. "Gwen is just trying to scare you."

"So, I'm not going to turn into a pig?"

"Definitely not. You would have to eat a ton, every day. And food would have to be the center of your existence," Lance explained. "Gwen, you should explain it. You're the smart one."

Gwen smiled. "I know. Let me put it this way, Hayden. Do you remember passing by some strange looking people on the way from Quay?"

"Yeah, of course. It was terrifying."

"Well, that is the same problem we are facing across Between."

"If eating too much can turn someone into a pig, what happened to those guys in Quay to make them look like that?" I asked, shoving my plate away from me, remembering the guy I saw whose entire half of his face had been nothing but white bone. It made me shiver just thinking about it.

"Let me explain," Gwen said. "See, according to history, King Arthur and Merlin opened the portal that brought all of Avalon, and all the magic in the world to Between over a thousand years ago. Legend has it, they did it to trap an evil sorceress in the Other Realm, buried deep below ground with no magic to help her escape. But this meant all magic was now trapped in this limbo dimension created by the portal. Lots of historians, like Hal, have studied this phenomenon and believe that magic became far unrulier in Between because it was no longer contained by the same realities that existed in the Other Realm. Basically, magic here is way more powerful than it ever was on the other side."

"But what does magic have to do with eating too much food?" I asked.

"Well, the nature of Between, Hal believes, is that it tries to give you what you desire most. The problem is, sometimes we don't even realize what we want most ourselves. It's our actions and choices that reveal that the most. A lot of those monsters you saw have let themselves become twisted by greed, lust, anger, hatred, or fear. It wouldn't have happened immediately, but slowly over time the magic in Between has changed them into what they are now."

"That's horrifying," I said. "If only one of those curses would turn Baron into a pig. Or something worse, like a naked mole rat."

Gwen laughed, then continued, "Hal says it can even happen to someone who tries to use magic more powerful than what they can handle. It can be really dangerous. I've heard of entire villages or neighborhoods burning down by one kid who got a hold of some magic he couldn't handle," Gwen said. "That's why Hal doesn't just teach anybody magic." She waited to see if I would say anything, but when I didn't, Gwen continued, "That's why I'm Hal's First-Seated Apprentice. He trusts me, and he knows I can handle it."

"But don't look so scared, Hayden. Look at Alex and Eric over there. They stuff their faces all the time, and none of them have turned into pigs. It would take a serious addiction to change your very nature like that. Plus, somehow I think the Magic Hollow protects us from the worst of Between's side effects."

Gwen looked over at Alex and Eric, her lip twitching in disgust as they piled more food onto their plates. "Sometimes I wonder if they are trying to make it happen," Gwen said. "Just because they think it would be funny."

# CHAPTER NINE

I looked over at them, laughing and joking with each other as they ate, and I knew Gwen probably wasn't too far off in her assumption. "I just can't believe how powerful magic can be," I said. "It's hard to comprehend. I grew up learning about physics and scientific laws. And my foster parents tried really hard to squash any concept of magic right out of me. I think they did it because they didn't want to believe this place exists."

"Well, physics exists in Between too," Gwen said. "Most of the laws function almost exactly the same, just with a little spice of magic."

"A little spice?" I spoke. "The magic of Between sounds like the whole pie."

"Don't fear magic," Lance said. "Hal always teaches us that magic is a tool. When properly controlled it can be extremely effective, but when misused, it becomes dangerous, even lethal."

"And it really only affects the weak-minded," Gwen added. "It can bring out the best or the worst in people and show everyone who you really are. Unless of course you're smart enough or strong enough to resist it."

Lance nodded. "Do you remember when we mentioned the Dark Sorcerer Marzon last night?"

"Yeah, of course. I've heard his name a couple times. Something about the Shadow War my dad fought in, right?"

"Exactly. Marzon was the one who started the war. He caused a huge civil war in Between. But the crazy thing is, they say he looked completely normal. He was just a handsome, normal guy. But he rose to power and manipulated enough people to trust him, before his true colors ever really showed."

"So, what about Jack Lantern? He has a pumpkin for a head. That can't be normal?"

"The Lanterns are an interesting story," Gwen said. "Once there was an entire Royal House of them, hundreds, probably. As far as we know, Jack is the only one left though. He was probably born that way. But how his ancestors got that way . . . who knows? Maybe they did it to set their House apart? It's possible that someone could willingly allow Between to change them, I suppose. But it would be dangerous, too. Who knows what you would become? But that's just theoretical of course. I would have to do more research to confirm or deny it."

"Does she always talk this much?" I asked, teasingly.

Gwen punched my shoulder, and Lance laughed. "Gwen is the brains of this whole operation," Lance said. "I just swing the big swords."

At that moment, the doors to the dining hall creaked open and Baron walked in looking like a king, flanked by several guards who looked less than enthusiastic about their new duty of following him around. Everyone went quiet, a sea of heads turning to look at their new leader.

"I'm sure you have all heard the news by now," Baron said. "The castle is mine while Hal is off on important business. That means we do things my way. There will be no more funny business," he looked directly at Alex and Eric, who were pantomiming Baron to much laughter. "If you are late to your duties, it will mean double chores for the rest of the week. Am I clear?"

"Yes, Baron," the sea of young knights and soldiers said unenthusiastically.

"Good. Now where is our newest guest—Hayden Keyes?"

A buzzing murmur filled the crowd as knights started whispering to each other excitedly. I could hear some of the closer conversations:

"Did he say Keyes—like Sir William Keyes?"

"Yeah, you didn't hear? Sir William's son is here!"

"—He arrived last night."

"Where is he? I want to have a look?"

Begrudgingly, I stood up. Dozens of faces turned in unison to stare at me, the son of a hero. Right then, with all those knights staring at me, I didn't feel anything like a hero. In fact, it made me think about the time just a few days ago when my entire classroom had stared at me. Sure, these guys weren't laughing at me, but somehow this feeling was worse. I wondered if this is what anxiety felt like, this hot balloon of nerves rising inside my chest, feeling like it was going to burst right out of my mouth.

Baron saw me standing and smiled, but it was not a friendly smile by any means. "This is Hayden Keyes, son of William Keyes. He has come to the Magic Hollow to become a knight. Please give him your warmest welcome."

This was followed by even more whispers across the room.

"Sir William was the greatest knight of our age—"

"Maybe his son is even better!"

"Shut it," Baron growled. "I'm not finished yet. Hayden—I want you to meet me at my office today at 1 o'clock. Got it?"

"What for?" I asked.

"We've got work to do. Because I've had a change of heart. There are things these kids learn as pages half your age, that Lance and I have to teach you. So, don't be late."

Baron stomped out of the dining hall and slammed the door behind him. Suddenly, the whispers erupted into a roar of noise. Everyone started talking excitedly. Tons of knights started standing up or craning their necks to get a good look at me. At least ten walked over to our table and shook my hand and introduced themselves. While my fear of failing lingered in the background, in the moment, I started to feel better. If I just pretended that I was good enough to be the son of a hero, this moment was thrilling. It was what I always wanted: the praise and respect of others. It felt good. Really good.

When we were all done with breakfast, Gwen gave us one last before she departed to study. "Baron may not think anything is wrong, but if Hal says the shadows are stirring again, that isn't good. We'll have to be prepared. I hope that you're ready when the shadows come. I know I will be."

"Is she always that intense?" I asked Lance as we watched Gwen strut out of the dining hall, her blonde hair bouncing behind her.

"Truthfully, yes," Lance said. "But she's like family to me. Like the little sister I never had. You'll warm up to her, I promise."

"The real question is if she will ever warm up to me," I said. "If she punches my arm one more time, I think I'll bruise."

Lance laughed, then he punched my arm. "You're a squire now, Hayden. Training to be a knight. A little pain is good for you. It'll toughen you up!"

"If you say so. Well, should we start the tour? The sooner we finish that, the sooner we can start training," I said.

"Of course. Just know being a knight isn't all sword fighting and bravado. Like Baron said, you've got a lot to learn to catch up with everyone else."

During the tour, Lance showed me all the most important places he could think of. He showed me the best way to the dorm hall where our room was, the lecture halls, where many training sessions and classes were held, the library, and where all the nicest bathrooms were.

After that, he took me to the undercroft, a large vaulted storage area beneath the castle. There I was issued new sets of clothes, which I was grateful for because in my Other Realm clothes, I stuck out like a sore thumb. I received several pairs of trousers, tunics, woolly socks, and knee-high black leather boots, like the ones all the other knights wore. I also received a black cloak, like the one I saw Gwen wearing when she found me.

Lance let me change. It felt a little weird to wear these old-fashioned clothes, but it was also nice to not stick out so much in my normal clothing.

When I was done dressing, I looked myself over in a faded mirror. I felt like a character from a Shakespeare play. The knee-high boots were no sneakers, but they were surprisingly comfortable. At least I finally looked the part of a squire now.

"Do I get a sword?" I asked, when I returned to Lance.

"When you're ready you'll be issued a sword and a shield. We'll even loan you armor, too."

"Last night, you mentioned trials—to become a knight?"

"Yes, you see because we are so secluded in the Magic Hollow, it is difficult for us to prove ourselves and become knighted. The solution was to create a series of trials to test our squires before knighthood. But that's why we all have the title Knight-junior."

"Oh, yeah, I was wondering about that. Do all of the knights sit at the Round Table?"

"No, only twelve. Well, traditionally there should be thirteen, but you know—that whole siege perilous legend makes it difficult to fill the thirteenth seat. We have a little over thirty Knights-junior in the Hollow right now."

"You know, in the Other Realm, thirteen is considered an unlucky number. I've heard that superstition dates to medieval times."

"Is that what they call it, medieval?" Lance asked. "Interesting. You do mean the time of Arthur, right?"

"It refers to a broad period of time, but Arthur would be included in the beginning of it, yeah."

"As far as I know, there have always been thirteen chairs at the Round Table. Maybe the superstition is related somehow. I'll have to tell Gwen about that. She might find that fascinating." We started to walk back up to the main part of the castle. "This superstition doesn't bother you, does it? That there are thirteen chairs?"

"No," I said, truthfully. "I never cared much for superstitions, and trust me, we have a lot of them in the Other Realm. Like, don't step on a crack, or you'll break your mama's back, it's bad luck to break a mirror indoors, if you don't knock on wood when you say something it will come true, oh, and black cats, they're bad luck if they cross your path."

"Huh, I never would have taken Other Realmers as the superstitious type," Lance said.

"I'm just getting started. There's people who say a rabbit's foot brings good luck, never open an umbrella inside, and definitely don't walk under a ladder."

"I guess that makes Tristan seem a little better after all that Siege Perilous nonsense last night."

"So, you don't believe in Siege Perilous? You don't think it means anything that I was the first person to sit in that chair in over a thousand years?"

"It just means you should check your pants for any stains because that was a really dusty chair."

I laughed, but inside, I felt a surprising twinge of disappointment. Last night, with all of the Knights of the Round Table scrutinizing me, I had been petrified at the thought of being the first person to sit in a chair that meant blessings or curses. But as I lay in bed thinking about it, I couldn't help but entertain the possibility that I was destined to be something special. Because that meant that I could actually obtain my new goal of becoming a knight. The Lady of the Lake herself had appeared to me in the water, twice. Was it just a coincidence that I sat in Siege Perilous? Lance seemed to think so.

"I don't believe in stuff like that," Lance said, "because in my experience the only thing that matters is you, not prophecies, superstitions, curses, or blessings. Becoming a knight is about hard work, talent, and luck. Every knight started with the same thing, two hands, two feet, two eyes, and one brain. Sure, having money helped because they could buy nice armor and a horse, but in the field of battle none of that mattered if they were a coward. Only the truly brave and noble could win themselves glory and prove their worth."

I really thought hard about what Lance said. It made sense to me and helped me feel better about myself. Thinking about superstitions made me wonder if I was good enough to live up to what everyone expected of me, but Lance had a different opinion. In his view, becoming a knight was about hard work. That was something I could do.

"I don't want you to be alarmed," Lance said, "but we employ several Bunyanish Giants to help work in the forges."

"Bunyanish?" I asked, "Like Paul Bunyan?"

"Never heard of him," Lance said. "Who is that?"

"In the Other Realm, we have some old American myths about a giant named Paul Bunyan."

"Interesting. I'm sure all the Bunyanish Giants would have traveled to Between during the Divide, but I guess it makes sense. Your myths would have to come from somewhere."

"The Divide?"

"Oh, yeah, sorry. That's what we call the moment when King Arthur and Merlin made the split, pulling magic into Between."

"I can't imagine that," I said, as we walked down a spiraling staircase into the forges. "Do you think it happened quickly? Like one moment you could be taking a nap and then next thing you know you're ripped out of your house and wake up in Between?"

"You'll have to talk to Baron about it during your history lesson. He knows a lot about it. But to be honest, you probably aren't that far off. King Arthur did what he did to try and protect his kingdom, but he also made a lot of enemies that day, too. Avalon wasn't the only magical kingdom in the world, you know. There were others. Magic from all around the Other Realm was ripped from its home and transplanted here. That's why clans like the Cerise Guard exist here. They descend from a type of knight called samurai. Sound familiar?"

"Yeah, you're right. They were a country called Japan's version of knights. I've read about them before."

Lance nodded. "Gwen knows more about it than me, and Baron knows even more than both of us combined, but I do know that a lot of people weren't happy with King Arthur. There have been tons of wars from the very beginning of Between."

"That's awful," I said. "But didn't everyone realize what King Arthur had done it to save them? From that one lady who tried to take over?"

"Morgana," Lance said gravely. Just hearing the name sent shivers down my spine. Of course. Even that name had survived the tests of time. She was remembered in all the legends, even today, as a great enemy of King Arthur.

"You know about her?" Lance asked.

"She's mentioned in our legends, quite often."

"They call her the Witch Queen. She almost destroyed King Arthur and the entire Round Table. She nearly conquered Avalon and wouldn't have stopped there. They say she was mean and cruel and ruled with fear. But people are fickle, Hayden. Even though King Arthur had saved them from the Witch Queen, many of them were still upset. They felt like they had been locked away in a prison, taken from their homes and lands. There were uprisings, revolts, and wars. King Arthur eventually died trying to keep the peace. The Knights that were left were forced to retreat into the Magic Hollow and go into hiding. The Lady of the Lake is said to protect our borders and keep us hidden. Hal says we'll stay hidden until we are ready to go out into Between again and try to restore peace and honor."

"The Lady of the Lake," I whispered. I wondered if I should tell Lance about the visitations and warnings I had from the Lady, but I decided not to. Lance didn't seem to believe much in visions and visitations anyway, so I doubted he would even believe me.

We reached the bottom of the stairs and stepped out into a large room supported with vaulted arch ceilings and stone pillars wider than redwood tree trunks. Massive forges glowed with fiery heat as the smoke billowed up great big chimney stacks. It looked like they were just starting to get the forges burning for today's labor. At first, I only saw a couple knights lumbering around doing the work, but then, a large door on the far side of the chamber opened, and I gasped. Three superhuman guys shuffled into the chamber. They were at least twelve feet tall and had pale blue skin. Their hair was wild and curly, and they wore rough tunics and furs around their waists.

"Bunyanish are the tamest of the giants," Lance said. "And the smartest. Don't worry, they're good friends of Hal. They won't hurt you."

"Look how big they're hands are," I said. "They're so cool!"

Lance laughed, realizing I wasn't afraid. "They do great work in the forges. Bunyanish are highly impervious to fire. See, watch."

One of the Bunyanish walked over to the forge, reached his hand straight into the opening and pulled out a rod of steel that was molten red. He sauntered over to a big pale of water and dropped the rod inside. The pale hissed with steam.

Lance led me past the Bunyanish over to a strong looking kid who was pounding a sword into shape on a large anvil with a heavy mallet. He looked up from his work and said, "Morning, Lance."

"I didn't see you at breakfast," Lance said.

"I skipped breakfast so I could get a head start on this sword," the boy said. "I think I'm on to something this time. I made the core of the blade with iron to make it more flexible and resilient, and now I'm trying to bond the iron to some Sanctified Silver for the edges. The trouble is, tempering Sanctified Silver seems just as hard as wielding it in a fight. I just can't seem to find the right temperature."

He set down the mallet, and then smiled at me, like he just noticed me for the first time. "Ah, so the rumors are true," he said in a thick accent that sounded Scottish. "Lance has taken on a new squire. My name is Weyland," he said, shaking my hand.

"Hayden," I said. "Nice to meet you. What's Sanctified Silver?" I asked.

Weyland smiled, gesturing at the blade. It wasn't polished or anything, so at the moment, it looked no greater than any steel sword by my eye. "Sanctified Silver is a rare ore that contains magical properties. It was harvested in Avalon and underwent a special purifying process before it could be used. Today, there is only a little amount of it left. We have it here in the castle locked away in a secret chamber."

"So, it's better than steel?"

"Oh, yes. Much better. Sanctified Silver is the most common material used to make Legendary Weapons. That and Avalonian Gold, but we don't have any of that." Weyland looked like he thought that would be a big deal to me, but I just looked at him blankly. "Lance, are you telling me this kid wants to be a knight, and he doesn't know what a legendary weapon is?"

Lance laughed. "He isn't from around here."

"Ah, well, you should have Lance take you to the Hall of Kings. The legendary weapons are the best weapons. They say a single blow from a legendary weapon can disintegrate a monster into powder finer than table salt."

"But unlike normal weapons," Lance said, "Legendary weapons can't be wielded by just anyone. You must win their loyalty by some great act or feat of battle. Otherwise, they won't ever work for you."

"I think that's the problem of trying to forge weapons with this stuff as well," Weyland explains. "With every drop of the mallet, I can feel the Sanctified Silver resisting me. It's like it doesn't want to work right or form the way I try to tell it to. I get winning a sword in battle by some valiant act, but how is a humble blacksmith supposed to win over a blade he hasn't even finished yet? It is so frustrating!"

"You'll get it," Lance said encouragingly. "The fact that legendary weapons exist is proof that it is possible. If they could do it before the Divide, then you can do it now."

"I know, I know," Weyland said. "It was nice to meet you, Hayden. But if you don't mind, I'm going to get back to work."

The Hall of Kings, where Lance took me next, was incredible. I had seen a lot of beautiful things during my short stay in New Camelot, but nothing compared to this. The first thing I noticed was the massive stained glass at the far end of the room. Every shade of the rainbow was included in this work of art that depicted the Magic Hollow and New Camelot, standing gloriously in the shining sun.

Directly in front of the stained glass, a magnificent throne of wood and gold embellishments sat in a raised marble dais, with stairs leading up to it. Both sides of the long rectangular room were flanked with massive marble pillars. A plush red carpet led down the middle of the hall all the way to the throne. Each side of the hall was covered in tapestries, paintings, and old relics as well.

We walked down the hall, Lance letting me look at everything along the way. It was like a glorified museum. I had never seen a collection like it. There were swords, lances, shields, armor, trophies, and finely embroidered tunics. It was impossible to take it all in at once. I was impressed though, at that moment, to realize that this one room contained more history in it than every museum in the Other Realm combined.

We reached one sword, Joyeuse, Lance called it, that caught my attention for at least ten minutes alone. "There's a legendary weapon, if I've ever seen one," Lance said. "They say it belonged to Charlemagne himself. We know it's special because it found its way here, even though Charlemagne was long after the Divide."

Joyeuse was a long, double-edged sword with an ornate handle and pommel. The blade, however, was what caught my attention for so long. Right before my eyes it glowed and changed colors every few seconds, turning every shade of the rainbow and more.

After Lance finally convinced me to move on, it still took us almost an hour to reach the end of the hall. When we reached the end, I looked up at the throne eagerly, and Lance nodded, giving me permission to approach it. "They say that was the same throne that sat in Camelot," Lance said. "And look there, at the case beside it."

I approached the large glass box resting on a table beside the throne. The box contained a single silver blade, simple and unadorned, but beautiful and polished. "Is this Sanctified Silver?" I asked.

"The purest and finest blade ever created," Lance said. "Its name is Clarent."

I didn't want to be rude, but to be honest, compared to Joyeuse, Clarent almost looked like a cheap movie prop. It was nice, don't get me wrong, but I didn't see anything special about it.

"Clarent is a pure blade," Lance said. "It has never tasted blood and never been used in battle, not even in a practice bout. We call it the Sword of the Kings. It can only be touched by a chosen few who use it for ceremonial purposes. If you become a knight, Hayden, this is the blade that will touch your shoulders when you're proclaimed a Knight of the Round Table, just as it was used by Merlin to anoint King Arthur."

"That's amazing," I said, seeing Clarent in a new light. "There's one other sword I hoped I would see here though. It must exist."

"What sword is that?" Lance asked. "We also have Tizona and Colada, Grunwald, and Rhongomiant, well that last one is a spear."

"I'm sure all of those are great, but if there is one legendary weapon I know, it would be Excalibur. The sword of King Arthur!"

Lance winced. For a moment I thought I saw surprise on his face, but then it was gone, and he smiled. "Of course, stories of his legendary blade would survive even after the Divide. Well, Hayden, Excalibur *is* here, in the Magical Hollow. Do you want to see it?"

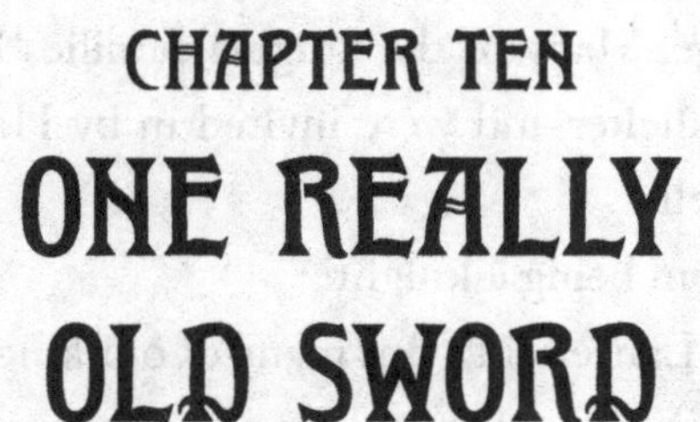

# CHAPTER TEN
# ONE REALLY OLD SWORD

The sun pierced the clouds above, lighting patches of dirt and downtrodden grass across the fields outside of New Camelot as the sounds of clashing swords and clattering horse hooves carried along the Fall breeze.

Lance pointed to the left of the castle, toward the largest open field, and the strange black rock that jutted out of the ground. "We call that Festival Field," Lance explained. "We host special tournaments and festivals there. That rock formation has an entrance that leads down into Crystal Cave, which contains several hot springs. It's a great place to go after a long day of training. Just mind your toes, Henrietta, our pet sea monster, doesn't always know when to stop playing."

"Pet sea monster?" I asked. "I prefer my toes just how they are, thank you, so I think I'll pass."

"I was just teasing you," Lance said. "She's really friendly, I promise."

We walked around the castle and I admired the hundreds of statues and gargoyles that lined its roof. Lance stopped and pointed toward a small gated village off to the right of the castle that stretched up the mountain a little way. "That is Caerleon. The Magic Hollow's only village. Many of the knights' families live there, or others who came seeking shelter and were invited in by Hal. There are several retired knights as well."

"You can retire from being a knight?"

"Not technically," Lance said. "But many of our knights were so brutally injured during the Shadow War, we vowed to protect them, so that they could live out the rest of their days in peace in Caerleon."

"That's honorable," I said, admiring Lance even more.

"It is the most important vow I have ever made. And yet it is so frustrating at the same time. We can only leave the Magic Hollow if we get permission. So, how are we supposed to do something valiant enough to become full-fledged Knights if we can never leave the Hollow? How can I protect them with my life if I'm only a Knight-junior?"

I didn't know what to say. I looked up to Lance so much, it was hard to imagine that even he, Defender of New Camelot, was unhappy with his current station. "At least you're a Knight-junior," I said. "I'm just a squire."

"You just got here, Hayden. Besides, your time will come. You're the son of Sir William Keyes, one of the greatest knight of the modern era."

"Everyone keeps saying that. But I don't even know what he did that was so great," I said, frowning.

Lance eyed me closely, but he didn't say anything else about it. We passed the outskirts of Caerleon and the coliseum looking building, which Lance identified as the Arena. It was from within there that the sounds of clanging swords were ringing. Beside the Arena, there was a large stable, filled with horses. Some of these horses were out of their stalls in a large coral, training with knights and squires, leaping over poles and obstacles.

"That's where we'll train two times a day," Lance said, pointing to the

Arena. "And we'll also work on your horseback riding several times a week as well. You probably won't be ready to compete in the next tournament, but I'm sure we could have you ready by the one after that."

As we neared the river, I noticed it was actually nothing more than a small trickle down the center of the large rocky riverbed. On the opposite bank, the dense forest started. "This used to be the Serpentine River. It flowed down from the Snowy Mountains, so the water was always freezing."

"What happened?" I asked. "To the Hollow? Gwen mentioned it used to look a lot brighter a few years ago."

Lance sighed. "A few years ago, it was full of life. The river was always flowing, and Festival Fields was the greenest most inviting grass you'd ever see. The forest was bright and beautiful, and at night it would glow with the light of a thousand fairies dancing above the trees. But, as you can see, things just aren't like they used to be. Recently, we noticed the river starting to flow less and less, and then just like that everything started dying. The fairies disappeared and the forest started to change."

"That's horrible," I said. "But why? What stopped the river flowing?"

"Hal says the magic of the Hollow comes from the Lady of the Lake. She protects this place and gives it life. But apparently, her power is weakening. At least the protective barrier still keeps everyone safe . . . if that were to fail . . ."

"Hey, I'm sorry for bringing up such a gloomy topic," I said.

Lance grasped my shoulder. "No. Don't worry about it. As long as I'm here, I'm not going to sit back and watch that protective barrier fail. I'll do anything I can to protect this place."

It was easy to cross the riverbed with the water not flowing hardly at all. Lance jumped nimbly from boulder to boulder, crossing in a few quick strides. I tried to follow and, well, kinda fell into a muddy puddle, scraping my hand as I caught my balance on a stone. Lance looked back at me, but thankfully was kind enough not to laugh.

Embarrassed, I scrambled up the bank onto the other side hating myself for being such a klutz and looking like an idiot my first day of being a squire. We were just about to step into the woods when we heard a loud horn bellow from deep within the trees.

"Quick, hide!" Lance said, tugging me with him behind a large oak.

We crouched down as the sound of hooves clattered through the trees.

"Centaurs," Lance whispered. "They share these woods with the wolves, as well. Lately, tensions have been escalating between the two, and they're getting upset with us for not taking a side."

"When you say centaurs, you mean like half person and half horse, right?"

"Exactly. They're brilliant creatures and fierce warriors. Very territorial and protective of their own. They craft the finest bows I've ever seen. But in my opinion, it's the wolves you should be most careful around. They can speak, but they seem to prefer gnashing their teeth over holding a conversation."

"And why are we here exactly?" I asked jokingly.

"To see Excalibur," Lance said with a gleam in his eye. "It's been a while since I've seen it too. Wait, look!"

Lance pointed about fifty yards down the tree line toward a large crowd of knights that was gathering along the dried up banks of the Serpentine, all looking a little apprehensive. Another horn bellowed from deep within the woods, and it was met by a horn ringing from New Camelot.

"This might not be good," Lance said, creeping closer, but staying hidden just within the tree line. "Look there," he whispered, pointing into the thick trees.

I didn't see them at first, and then all at once, I realized there were dozens of centaurs gathering in a large crowd directly opposite the group of knights. I couldn't tell through the trees, but it looked like several centaurs were wrestling with something. When they finally broke the tree line, I realized it was a person. Poking my head around the trees, I got a clear glimpse of who it was: Baron.

A large stallion-sized Centaur with a thick brown mane and beard stepped out of the trees and stood above Baron who was cowering in fear. He had a huge bow and sheath of arrows strapped around his bare chest.

"That's Ixion—their chief," Lance whispered excitedly.

The centaur spoke, and I heard his voice clearly, even from here. "I don't know why you were sneaking around our village, Baron. Perhaps in better times we would have welcomed you as a guest. But you have long denied us aid in our skirmishes with the wolves, who have been trespassing on our hunting lands for many moons. Now we deny you entrance into our lands as well."

Baron stood up, red in the face. He pointed a finger at Ixion, who was nearly twice his size. "You can't ban us from our own forest! I am Castellan of the Magic Hollow. You must obey me!"

Ixion crossed his arms, his bulging muscles flexing threateningly. His front legs scraped at the ground impatiently. "No," he said.

Baron started to yell, but it was lost over the sound of hooves as the centaurs and fauns began retreating back into the woods. After stomping his feet and pulling at his beard in frustration, Baron turned noticing the crowd of knights for the first time. I recognized a few faces, like Gwen, Alex, Eric, Elibora, and a few of the other members of the Round Table. Alex and Eric were looking like they were trying really hard not to laugh.

"Father—what is the meaning of this?" A female centaur asked, pushing through the crowd.

"Stay back, Luna, dear," Ixion said, holding the centaur tightly. "This is no place for my daughter. Go back to the village while I deal with this."

"But I don't want to," she argued.

"Luna," Ixion said threateningly.

She lingered for a moment, surveying Baron and the gathered crowd of knights, then snuffled loudly, turned on her hooves, and galloped away, crying loudly.

"That was Ixion's daughter. She's like a princess to the centaurs. I've never seen her before now," Lance whispered. "I hear Ixion is extremely protective of her."

"What are you staring at?" Baron yelled, turning to the crowd of knights and squires. "Get back to work or I'll have you all thrown in the dungeons! And stay away from here. No one crosses this river, or I'll throw you into the dungeons for that, too!"

"We better go back," I whispered. The last thing I wanted was to experience death by an eternal dungeon sentence, but Lance didn't seem to have the same idea.

"Come on, Hayden. I thought you wanted to see Excalibur."

"Well, that was before I knew it was in a forest with a bunch of angry centaurs who might roast us alive if they catch us. And even if they don't catch us, maybe Baron will."

"That's what makes it fun," Lance said. "Think of it like an adventure—a quest. How are you ever going to become a knight if you don't mind a little danger now and then?"

I gulped, trying to swallow my fear. Lance was right, I really did want to see Excalibur, and I didn't want to look like a coward. I nodded. "Okay, fine. Let's do this."

I was about to start walking when something grabbed my shoulder. I yelped and spun around. Gwen, who had sneaked up behind us, nearly fell over laughing.

"You should have seen your face," she said, leaning against a tree to keep herself from falling over.

"I think you'd be startled, too, considering what we just saw. Centaurs are terrifying!"

"Yeah, yeah, yeah," she said. "Excuses."

"How did you know we were here?" Lance asked.

"A good knight is always aware of her surroundings. I was skimming the forest to see if any wolves were watching. That's when I spotted dork face over here," she nodded at me. "And where there's a squire, there must be his knight as well."

"Did you see any wolves?" I asked cautiously.

"Oh yeah, there were like a ton of them right by you guys."

"Are you serious?" I asked, looking around nervously.

"No," Gwen said, forcing the words through more laughter. "You make this way too easy!"

Lance smiled and shook his head. "Don't let her bother you, Hayden. She doesn't know any other way to interact with human beings."

"Hey!" Gwen said, lightly punching Lance's shoulder.

"I'm still surprised you're here," I said to Gwen. "I didn't hear you coming."

Gwen grinned. "Maybe someday you'll be as skilled as me. So, Lance, what's going on? You heard Baron. He wants us to stay out of the forest."

"I was just about to take Hayden to the spring so he could see Excalibur."

Gwen's eyes lit up with excitement. "Ooh nice," she said. "Then I'm coming with you. It could be dangerous, so we'll have to be extra cautious."

"You want to break the rules?" I asked Gwen. "I thought you were the perfect-type, who never breaks rules?"

"Me? Nah. I never break *Hal's* rules. But I disrespect Baron's authority. Think of it as me stepping up to the man, or something rebellious like that."

"We better get going," Lance said, scanning through the trees ahead of us. "Excalibur is technically in neutral territory, but those lines have started to blur with all the trouble between the wolves and the centaurs."

We moved as quietly as we could, staying low and under cover of trees and brush. The forest was thick, but not thick enough to choke out all the light from above. Fragmented pillars of light broke through the foliage like bolts of lightning frozen in time. There seemed to be traces of a path, but Lance didn't want to stay on it too long, preferring to move under cover of the trees and underbrush. I was happy to agree with him there. The last thing I wanted was to get captured by a band of angry centaurs.

Fortunately, the forest was quiet. Well, except for the natural forest sounds, of course. I quickly realized that forests had lots of those. There was the sound of the wind rushing through the treetops above us, sounding like waves in the ocean. There was the random crack of branches and twigs that made me jump every time and look around expecting to see a centaur or a wolf coming after us. There was the occasional chirp or song of birds, or the clicking of a squirrel as it ran up a tree to get a safe distance from us. All of this proved to me that I loved the forest. I realized, if it weren't for the looming possibility of being captured by centaurs, I might have enjoyed this place.

After almost half an hour, we finally reached a large spring. I could hear the trickle of water before we broke through the trees and saw it. There was a large clearing, mostly filled with a shallow pool of bright blue water. A gentle stream left from the pool and meandered into the woods in the direction we came. Across the water from where we stood was a huge cluster of rocks rising at least twenty feet tall. This mound seemed to be the source of the water, which came spilling from its top, then trickled down in dozens of little waterfalls.

"It's beautiful," I said. And I meant it. This looked like a place right out of one of Arabella's mindful meditation videos.

"Look, up there," Lance said, pointing to the crown of the rocks.

I followed his finger and sure enough, there it was: Excalibur. The sword was sticking out of the rock, at least half of its bright blue polished blade sunk deep into place. Excalibur's hilt was silver and ornamented with dark blue jewels. Its handle was wrapped in fine leather, and its pommel was shaped like a fish tail. The sword glowed in the dim light enchantingly.

"I can't believe it," I said. "The legends are true."

"Do you want to try and pull it out?" Lance said. "You have to, it's tradition."

I gulped. Could I do it? Deep inside, I wanted to pull it and feel the sword slide out of the rock. I wanted to be the one to wield Excalibur again. I had tried to imagine a thousand times before what it must have felt like for King Arthur to pull the sword free from the stone. Now, for the first time, I imagined what it would be like if I pulled the sword from the stone. I imagined holding it above my head as Lance and Gwen bowed before me. I imagined my father being so proud of me when I found him. This could be the moment. And why not, I decided. I had sat in Siege Perilous, and I had been visited by the Lady of the Lake, the very person who gave Excalibur to King Arthur in the first place.

I walked around the pool, then started my careful ascent up the rock formation. The rock was slippery, but I found good enough handholds, and eventually reached the top. Excalibur was even more magnificent in person. I circled around it, taking in all its glory. Suddenly, there was a flash of gold on the stone beside the sword, and fine scripted letters etched onto its surface. I crouched over and read them. This is what they said:

"He who worthily protects the Magic Hollow's Keep, a worthy protector the Magic Hollow keeps." And then, suddenly almost the same words appeared below the first, "She who worthily protects the Magic Hollow's keep, a worthy protector the Magic Hollow Keeps."

"It always changes," Gwen said, startling me. Again, I hadn't heard her behind me. "Whether it's a boy or a girl, the message changes."

"What does it mean?" I asked. "You're the smart one, after all."

"Smarts and solving riddles don't always overlap," she said, biting her lip. "I wish I could decipher it. I don't know why, but I've always felt like Excalibur was the missing link. Between has been at war for as long as Between has existed. And it seems like goodness is losing, slowly, but surely. There is no chivalry left in the land. The time of the knights is failing. We'll fail and be forgotten if we don't fight back."

"But who are you going to fight?" I asked. "All of Centerra?"

"No, of course not. I don't mean fight back with swords and shields. I mean, we need to fight back with goodness and kindness. We need to spread goodness through the world by committing great and noble deeds and serving the people of Between. We need to rekindle chivalry in their hearts and teach them to resist the darkness themselves. That's the war we need to be fighting."

"Noble chivalry, gentle virtue, honest deeds," I recited, remembering the mantra I had seen etched above the doors of New Camelot."

"Exactly," Gwen said. "I trust Hal's judgment. I know he's preparing us for what's out there. He would know better than anyone. But still, it doesn't make me any less anxious about when that time will be."

"What about Lance?" I asked. "Does he feel the same way?"

"Even stronger than I do," Gwen said. "You have a good trainer, Hayden.

Learn from him. Now go ahead and give that sword a pull. That's why we climbed all the way up here right?"

"Uh, yeah, right," I said, turning to look at the sword again. "What about you? Have you pulled it before?"

"Yeah, I tried."

"But it didn't work?"

"Oh, it worked, I just left it here for safekeeping—of course it didn't work!"

"Right, right," I said. As soon as I was feeling like Gwen was starting to warm up to me, she had to go and be a jerk about it. "Well, here goes nothing."

I wrapped my hands around the leather handle, jittery with excitement. I bent my knees, ready to pull with all my strength. I tightened my grip, flexed my muscles, and pulled with everything I could . . . and nothing happened.

Excalibur didn't budge an inch.

Gwen clapped excitedly. "Congratulations, Hayden! You're officially a squire!"

"But I didn't pull it out," I said, collapsing onto a dry spot of rock to catch my breath.

"That's the point," Gwen said. "I didn't actually think you had a shot at pulling it out. But we still try anyway. It gives us hope, and then it teaches us to stay humble."

"What about Lance?" I asked. "Has he tried to pull the sword from the stone?"

"Well, Lance . . . he's a different story. He hasn't pulled it out. Yet."

"As in, you think he can really do it?" I asked. "What's he waiting for?"

"The inscription says 'he who worthily protects the Magic Hollow's keep' right? Well Lance has been nicknamed Defender of New Camelot. He's the best knight of our generation. If anyone has a shot at it, it's him. I don't think he feels 'worthy' yet though. I know his time will come, and he will do it. I believe Lance is the knight who will lead us out of hiding. Lead the fight against the darkness."

Sure, I felt disappointed in myself. Against all my best judgment and prior track record, I knew it couldn't be me to pull out the sword. That just wasn't who I was. But it didn't change the fact that I wanted it so badly. I wanted to be a knight so bad, I could feel it in my gut. Then, a thought came into my mind.

"Gwen, do you know if my father ever tried to pull Excalibur?"

"He did, actually," Gwen said. "It's recorded in the Great History of the Hollow."

"He failed . . . but he was still a great knight?"

"Of course," Gwen said. "Hayden, wielding a legendary weapon isn't a one-way ticket to becoming a great knight. Sure, many of the great knights did wield legendary weapons, but not all of them. Noble chivalry, gentle virtue, and honest deeds. Those are the makings of great knights. So, don't forget it. Lusting after power and legendary weapons is a surefire way to guarantee that you never get one."

I felt the tension in my gut lessen, and a new fire ignite in my chest. Gwen was right. I had allowed myself to be too allured by the glory of Excalibur. I needed to refocus my goals on becoming a knight at least. That alone would be an amazing accomplishment for me.

I saw it as the only logical step in discovering what happened to my parents. He was somewhere here in Between, maybe even in danger, but he trusted me to come to the Magic Hollow. He must have wanted me to train so that I could come and find him, maybe even my mother, too.

"Thank you for saying that, Gwen," I said. "I needed to hear it."

She smiled and clasped my shoulder. "Trust me, you're handling it really well. I've seen grown men cry over not being able to pull Excalibur from the stone. Like I said, it keeps us humble."

"Hayden, Gwen, are you two done?" Lance called. "You've been up there forever. You better not be making out."

"*What? Ew! No!*" Gwen shrieked, putting so much distance between us she almost fell off the rocks.

Lance laughed. "Don't forget, Hayden, you have a history lesson with Baron this afternoon. For both of our sakes, I don't want you to be late."

I groaned. "Do I have to?"

Gwen and I descended the rock, then joined Lance on the trek back to the castle. Sure, Gwen didn't want to kiss me, and I was perfectly okay with that, it's not like I wanted to kiss her either, but somehow, it seemed like she was a little kinder to me after our conversation on the rock. For the first time in a long time, I felt like I was making real friends.

# CHAPTER ELEVEN
# THE OTHER HISTORY

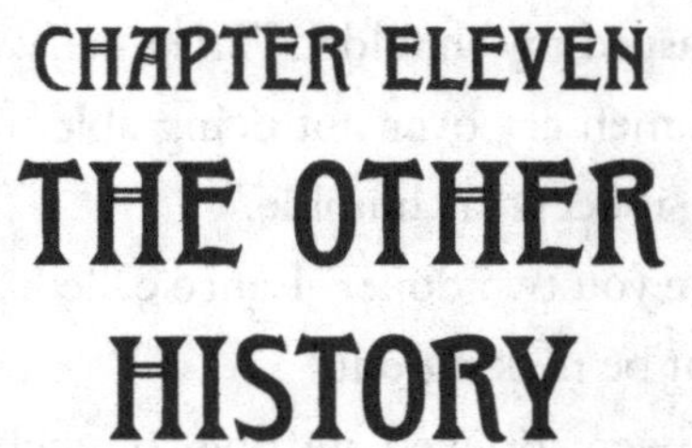

The last place I wanted to be was alone with Baron to talk about history. Lance and Gwen showed me where his office was, before waving goodbye and departing for the Arena to get in some training.

I wished I was going with them, learning something useful like horseback riding, shooting a bow, or wielding a sword. Those were knightly things. Sitting in an office with Baron learning about history on the other hand didn't sound like a great way to spend an afternoon. Maybe if it were Mr. Bianco teaching the lesson I would feel differently. However, I didn't have high hopes for Baron's teaching skills.

I felt worry as I knocked on Baron's office door. We still hadn't heard any news from him or Jack Lantern. I hoped they were okay. That made sitting still for this lesson seem even harder. I wanted to be doing something. If I was training, at least that meant I was getting stronger. Maybe then I would be able to help Mr. Bianco if he needed me.

Baron opened the door, just enough to peek through the crack. "Who is it?" he asked with his deep, rough voice.

"Hayden, sir," I said. "I'm here for my history lesson."

"Come in."

Baron opened the door and stepped aside, gesturing me into his office. A large fire was going, which made the room stifling hot. I saw a giant bookshelf covered in well-worn books and ancient tomes. Beside the bookshelf was a wooden desk and chair littered with paper scraps and ink bottles.

"Sit down," Baron said, nodding toward the chair by the fire, as he started hurriedly cleaning up the papers and shoving them into a drawer of his desk. I caught a glimpse of some of the papers as he stashed them away. It looked like a hand drawn map of the Enchanted Forest, and a letter he was working on. That seemed strange. Who could he be writing to that would want to see a map of the Enchanted Forest?

"I said sit down," he repeated angrily.

I sat down in the chair by the fire, and Baron sat down at his desk, staring at me intently, the long fingers of his hands curling before him into a tightly knit arch. "Knowledge is power, Hayden. In my lifetime, I have acquired a lot of it," he said. "I may not be able to wield a sword, or cast ornate spells, but I know how to outwit and outlast enemies. Swords don't win wars, people do. People like me. I advised Hal and your father during the Shadow Wars. I am remiss to admit that your father showed little care for my advice."

"I'm proud to become a knight, just like my father did. Gwen told me my father left behind a lot of his scholarship in the library here. He was an archaeologist in the Other Realm, someone who didn't just read about history, he discovered it."

Baron sneered. "Your father was a brilliant scholar in his own right, I'll give him that much. His histories on the Other Realm following the Great Divide are quite fascinating. However, I will admit, I don't think his discovery of the gate between our two realms was because he was somehow smarter than the rest of us. I think he was simply in the right place at the right time."

"Jack crossed, and then I did, too," I said. "I used—"

"You used an enchanted medallion," Baron said. "Created by your father. Rumor has it he made a couple of those, in case of emergencies. How many remain, who knows? Our enemy wasn't concerned with one or two medallions, however. That would never have been enough to transport an army."

"Marzon wanted to transport an army to the Other Realm?"

"Ah, so you know the name of the Evil Wizard? Good, that's a start. Yes, that is exactly what he wanted to do. And your father was the key to making that happen. The single most important card we held in a game of war, but that didn't stop your father from being foolish and reckless. He insisted on fighting at the front lines, even though I warned him of the devastation that could happen if he fell into the enemy's hands."

"It sounds like my father was brave and true, like any knight should be. I once read in a book that armies should be led from the front not the back."

"Whoever wrote that was a fool, just like your father. When a battle is lost but the leadership remains, that army survives to fight another day; but if its leadership is slaughtered at the helm of battle, that army not only loses the battle, it loses the war."

I could feel the anger rushing inside me. No matter what I said, Baron was ready to contradict me. It was like he wanted to antagonize me. I didn't know if my face was flushing with rage, or if it was just the heat from his fire.

"You quoted someone though, a war strategist from the Other Realm I reckon. So at least you have some of a mind for scholarship. What about you, Hayden? Tell me about your own research."

"Research? I mean, I don't know, I've read a lot of books."

"Philosophy, history?" Baron pressed.

"Mostly legends and stories," I admitted. "Like *Le Morte d'Arthur*, *Sir Gawain and the Green Knight*, just classic legends for us."

Baron clicked his tongue, shaking his head in disappointment. "That can hardly be classified as real scholarship. Nothing but legends, which you will soon find are not as accurate to what really happened as they say. You have much to learn, Hayden. Unfortunately, the task of teaching you falls on my shoulders. But before I can do that, I imagine you probably have a lot of questions you want to ask me, so go on. Spit them out."

This caught me by surprise. Of course, I had questions, but now that I was here, all flustered by Baron's unenlightening personality, I didn't know where to begin.

"Mr. Bianco and Jack told me that my father met my mother, Anora, in the Magic Hollow. Who was my mother?"

"I don't know where she came from, but she was not from around here. A refugee from the war, I reckon. She was quiet. Kept to herself. She lived in a cottage in Caerleon while your father was at battle."

"What did she look like?" I asked.

"She looked like you. She had blue eyes, just like your blue one, and long black hair. She was . . . a beautiful woman. Kind, too. I can't believe she fell for someone like your father—"

"What happened to her?" I interrupted.

"Unfortunately, I don't know. Your father had departed on a secret mission for Hal, and Anora was in Caerleon, far into her pregnancy by then— pregnant with you, I suppose. The next morning, she was gone. Your father never returned, either. I assumed he had failed whatever mission he had been given. When I asked Hal, he insisted that he would return, but he never did, nor did Anora."

"After I was born, my mom and dad returned to the Other Realm. They visited my aunt and uncle and left me with them. They told them to watch over me and keep me safe until they could come back for me. Apparently, he also charged his friend Ector Bianco to stay in the Other Realm and watch over me, too. Until I was ready to come here and complete my training to become a knight."

"How noble," Baron said, his lip curling when I mentioned Mr. Bianco.

"You don't like Mr. Bianco, do you?"

Baron frowned angrily. "We are not here to discuss personal matters, only facts of history. While the new information you offer about Sir William and Anora's actions before their disappearance are enlightening, the fact remains, no one knows where they are."

"I will find them," I said. "They are still alive. They have to be."

"Thirteen years is a long time, Hayden. All I know is that if your father is alive, we would want to find him before our new enemy does."

"So, you do believe what Hal said—that the shadows are stirring? That something bad is coming?"

"Hearsay and rumors are not enough to frighten me. But I am no fool either. If a new enemy is rising from the shadows, your father falling into their possession would not be good. Imagine, Hayden, if the wall between us and the Other Realm fell. How would your people fare against magical monsters and sword-wielding fiends intent on destroying them and their world to reclaim the lands they believe were stolen from them by King Arthur?"

"That would be horrible," I whispered.

"That was Marzon's very desire. And he was very successful among the great houses beyond the Magic Hollow. Thousands rallied to his side, ready to battle to reclaim their homeland."

"How did we stop them?"

"By killing their leader. The death of Marzon was the only thing that stopped them from razing New Camelot to the ground. Without Marzon, the people became fractured and disorganized like they had been before. They returned to their castle keeps and continued squabbling and warring with each other. And we lived to fight another day.

"Here is your first lesson: there is no honor in war. There is no righteous victory. Every war comes with great cost and sacrifice. A good leader knows that he must do whatever it takes to win. You would do well to remember that. Who cares if we didn't crush our foes in some magnificent onslaught to be praised in song and story? We won. Marzon is dead. That's all that matters."

"And what's left of the Round Table is a bunch of kids, like me. Maybe I should question your battle tactics. From what I've heard, a lot of good knights died fighting in the Shadow War."

Baron's splotchy skin flushed red and pink with rage. "You insolent little child," he spat. "Those men died because they believed in glory. Even when they should have retreated and lived to fight another day, they rushed entire armies practically alone, for what? Glory."

"But the code of the knights—"

"The code of the Knights doesn't say a thing about being a fool for glory's sake. Noble chivalry. Gentle virtue. Honest deeds. Those have nothing to do with fighting. If you want to live long enough to make a difference in this world, you will learn this valuable lesson. It's all for naught if we die on the wayside. We need to live, so that we can keep fighting. Losing one battle, but surviving, is the only way we can continue on to win the next."

I wanted to argue with him, but I couldn't think of any chink in his defense. I didn't like it, but part of me knew that Baron was right in his own way. It seemed wrong to me, like it contradicted everything I had ever read about knights, but on the other hand, it did seem logical.

"Your father was the same way," Baron said, dealing the final blow, "Maybe if he hadn't been so hungry for glory he would be here today, teaching you himself. At least then I wouldn't have to bother."

I clenched my fist, holding back my anger. I wanted to rage against Baron, tell him to shut his filthy trap, before I shut it for him. But I didn't. I bit my tongue to keep myself from responding. I knew he was trying to bait me into a response. I realized this was just a game to him. He could speak circles around me all day. Using his own advice against him, I told myself that this was a battlefield I couldn't win on, but I could survive to fight another day.

I breathed out, and let all my anger melt away, deflating like a sad balloon. "Teach me what I need to know to be a great knight," I said.

Baron looked disappointed that I had resisted his bait. "Very well," he said, standing up and walking over to the bookshelf. He pondered over the spines for a few moments, then pulled out an especially large book. Then, he pulled out another book from a separate shelf. He heaved the two large books over to me and dropped them in my lap.

"*Old English Essentials*, and *A Detailed History of Avalon*," he said. "That will be a good place to start. Many people in Between still speak the old languages—you will be useless without a knowledge of them. Plus, the book on Avalon is written in Old English, so I guess you will need that reference if you are ever going to get through it."

"I'm supposed to just read a book and somehow learn how to speak a new language?"

"New? You already speak English. Now you just need to learn its true form. I want you to come back here in exactly a week to report on your progress. Understood?"

"Yes, sir," I said glumly. Great. Homework.

"What was that? My name is Baron, not sir."

"Yes, Baron," I repeated, wishing I had given him what he deserved for his rude comments about my dad. "May I be excused now? I would like to get training that actually matters."

Baron laughed. "Ho-Ho! Fie on you, Hayden. I will let that one slide because you are new around here. But I will leave you with a little warning. I am not someone you want as an enemy."

"May I be excused then?" I said, standing straight and looking Baron in the eyes. I wasn't about to show him any sign of weakness.

"Yes. Get out of here. I have more important work to be doing."

Without another word, I stood up, heaving the heavy books, and departed straight for the door. On my way out, as I was closing the door behind, I peeked back in for a moment. I saw Baron pulling the papers back out of his drawer. The top paper was certainly a letter, but I couldn't see who it was addressed to, and I didn't want to linger any longer than I needed to. I shut the door behind me and departed for the Arena.

I was almost to the arched entryway of the Arena, when I heard someone call my name. "Hayden, hey, wait up." I turned to see the Knight-junior of the Round Table I had met the night before. It was Gale. Today, he was wearing a full suit of bright silver armor, neatly polished and decorated with red trim. A large two-handed sword hung from his belt, and he had a large shield draped over his back. He was the first person I had seen wearing a full suit of armor. It was even cooler up close and in person than seeing it on TV.

"Hey, it's Gale, right?" I said as we shook hands.

"Yep, that's me. Lance told me you might be coming this way. He wanted me to pass along a message. Something came up that he and Gwen had to do, but they wanted to meet you by the gates at Caerleon. He said to tell you there's something they wanted to show you."

"Huh, thanks, Gale."

"Do you want me to show you to the gate?"

"Nah, it's alright, I know the way. Thanks."

"Well, let me take those books from you. I'm headed up to the dorms anyway, I can set them by your bed."

"Really?" I said, realizing just how much my arms were starting to ache. "You're a lifesaver. Thanks so much!"

"No problem. See you around," he said with a kind smile.

I liked Gale and decided I should spend some more time getting to know him. He was one of those people who just oozes kindness.

When I reached the gates to Caerleon, Lance and Gwen were already there waiting for me.

"What? No reading assignment?" Lance asked. "You got off lucky, Hayden."

"Not quite. He gave me two huge books, but Gale offered to carry them back to the dorms for me. So, what did you want to show me?"

"Well, it was actually Gwen's idea, but we just thought, maybe you would want to see the cottage that your parents lived in?"

"I broke into Hal's office and found the key," Gwen said, holding a large steel key up for me to see. She tossed it to me. "Well, technically, I didn't break in. Hal did give me a key to his office, you know because I'm his First Apprentice and all. I don't think he'd mind."

"This is amazing. I don't know what to say."

"So, you do want to see it?" Lance asked.

I nodded enthusiastically. "Yes, please."

Lance pushed open the gates to the village and gestured for us to follow. "They lived at the top of the village," he said, "so we have a bit of a walk ahead of us."

Caerleon was even cooler up close. The roads were narrow and paved with cobblestones. The streets were lined with homes and apartments above shops and a few pubs and taverns. The window fronts looked old and worn, but they were filled with all kinds of interesting things. There was a blacksmith displaying awesome armor and weapons, a seamstress, whose front was filled with beautiful dresses and tunics, and an apothecary whose windows were crammed from bottom to top with tiny little glass jars containing various medicines and herbs.

The streets were nowhere near as busy as out in Centerra, but we did pass by a lot of people, several of whom stopped to greet Gwen or Lance. We even passed by a few familiar faces from New Camelot. Elibora, who I had first met in the Round Hall, and a girl I didn't recognize were sitting outside of a tavern with a pristinely dressed elderly woman, all of them eating a delicious smelling vegetable stew.

When Elibora noticed us walking by, she stood up and greeted us warmly. "Hayden, do you remember me? We met in the Round Hall. This is my friend Cecily, by the way. She squires for me and is about to take the trials to become a knight-junior." Cecily was a pleasant looking girl with eyes like emeralds.

"Nice to meet you, Hayden," Cecily said. "We were just talking about you. Elibora says you're the son of Sir William." She smiled, flashing perfectly straight white teeth, then curtsied politely, holding the corners of her pale blue dress and dipping her knees slightly.

"And this is my grandmother," Elibora said, gesturing.

"Lady Albreda," the woman said, bowing her head respectfully. "Pardon me for not giving a proper curtsy. I'm getting old, you know." She held up an ornate wooden cane to further prove the point, the top of which was carved like a boar. "It's a pleasure to meet you all. Especially you, lad," she said to me. "I knew your parents. They were darling people."

"Thank you," I said, a little awkwardly.

It was strange hearing people talk about my parents and telling me that they knew them. She meant well, but I was starting to get tired of being reminded that I was the only one around here who hadn't met my parents, or at least grown-up hearing stories about their heroics. Part of me wanted to ask her if she knew anything about where they might be, but there was something about how she said they were darling people that discouraged me, making my heart drop.

"Hayden, if you ever need a new sparring partner, you should ask Cecily," Elibora said, beaming at her squire. "She's the best squire I've seen with double short swords."

Cecily looked down bashfully and smiled. "I guess I'm alright," she said, grabbing Elibora's hand and squeezing it affectionately. "But I had a great teacher."

"We were just showing Hayden the village. It was a pleasure to make your acquaintance, Lady Albreda, but we better continue along our way," Lance said, bowing to Elibora's grandma and gently kissing the top of her hand in respect.

Lady Albreda chuckled. "Now there is a knight if I ever did see one. You're Lance, right? I'm sorry, I'm not familiar with your house?"

Lance fidgeted a little, but if the question made him feel uncomfortable, he masked it well. "I'm from a small house of little import."

"There's nothing wrong with that," she said warmly. "Don't be bashful. What's the name?"

"House Hawkwood," Lance said. "I'm sure you haven't heard of them."

"Lance is too humble," Gwen said, speaking for the first time during the visit. "He's the last living heir of his house, making him *Lord* Hawkwood."

"Oh, I am so sorry, dear. Forgive me for prying. The Shadow War was a terrible time for us all. I'm afraid Elibora is the only heir I have left as well. I lost my son in the war. It was just horrible. But you are such a fine young man, indeed. And a worthy knight from what I've heard. House Albreda would be honored to form an alliance with House Hawkwood, you know. We could revitalize your entire estate. Eli, dear, just think of the strapping babies you two could have."

Lance and Elibora turned bright red, and Gwen looked like she didn't know if she should laugh out loud or panic, her eyes darting nervously between Lance and Elibora. I wondered if Gwen had a crush on Lance.

"*Grandma*," Elibora said, fumbling with her long braid in her fingers. "Please." Elibora looked at Cecily apologetically, but obstinately Cecily was looking the other way. I also wondered if Cecily had a crush on Lance as well, because she didn't seem thrilled by the sudden turn in the conversation.

"I'm not trying to be rude, dear," Lady Albreda said. "Just speaking an old woman's mind, that's all. I've lived far too long to not say what I think when I think it. Lance deserves it, after everything he has been through. And I do too. I would love nothing more than to have little ones running around my home again—sweet little lords and ladies who can carry on our legacy." She sighed, leaning onto her palm.

"Grandma—we've talked about this before. I'm too young to be worrying about having kids. I'm still a teenager!"

"Pish posh," Lady Albreda said. "When I was a girl, young ladies could be wedded by thirteen! In fact, it was the day before my fourteenth birthday that I married your grandfather. Now he was a passingly fair knight! I didn't question my mother at all when she suggested the pairing."

Elibora looked like she wanted to argue the point further, but she turned to us instead. "Please forgive my grandma, she doesn't have a filter. And she's obsessed with trying to marry me off."

"Only so you can have wonderful little babies that can carry on our legacy. Is that too much for a poor old lady to ask for?"

Cecily, who had remained stoic throughout the entire turn of this conversation, continued to stare down at her soup, twirling a few carrots in circles with her wooden spoon.

"I mean no disrespect, milady, and thank you for the offer," Lance said politely. "But I think Lady Elibora will agree, neither of us are in a position to consider such a proposal. No offense," Lance said quickly, to Elibora.

"None taken," Elibora said, as her grandmother shook her head. Gwen and Cecily both let out a sigh of relief, as I watched a tension dissipate that I hadn't even noticed was there. "And no offense," Elibora whispered to Lance so her grandmother couldn't hear, "but you're not really my type. She'd have much better luck if she stopped trying to pair me with guys." Elibora winked and Cecily blushed, though smiling brightly. Lady Albreda cleared her throat, dispelling our whispering conversation. "You are a kind and respectful boy, Lance, but if you change your mind, you know where to find me."

"Grandma!" Elibora said sharply. "I can pick my own partners, thank you very much. And I will when I'm ready. I'm only fifteen, after all. We aren't living in the Middle Ages anymore!"

Lady Albreda huffed. "Are you implying that I was born in the Middle Ages? How old do you think I am?"

Lance laughed uncomfortably. "Well, we better get going. It was nice to see you all. And you, milady." He bowed to Lady Albreda.

As we left, we could hear Elibora continue to argue with her grandmother about watching what she says in front of her friends.

"Are you okay?" I asked Gwen as we continued up the road, which had very suddenly turned into a steep hill.

"Yeah, I'm fine. I just don't get along with Cecily very well," she said.

"Do you get along with anyone?" Lance teased.

"Fair point. I do get along with you though. I guess that doesn't say much about your personality then, huh? I used to be really good friends with Elibora, too," Gwen said to me. "At least before Cecily came around. Ever since they started hanging out, Elibora never seems to have any time for her other friends."

After practically climbing up the steep hill for another fifteen minutes, we finally reached the top. We turned and looked down over Caerleon and all the Magic Hollow. It was a phenomenal view. We were even higher than the tallest tower in New Camelot.

"I love coming up here," Lance said. "It still takes my breath away, every time, just like it did the first time I saw this view."

It was strange thinking of Lance being in a similar position to mine. It was hard to imagine a time when he hadn't been a knight."

"How old were you when you came?" I asked.

"I was just seven years old," Lance said. "Which means I've been in the Magic Hollow for ten years."

"If your family isn't from around here, how did you find your way here—if you don't mind me asking?"

Wandering Centerra for even just an hour had been a terrifying. I couldn't imagine walking those streets alone as a seven-year-old.

"Luckily, I wasn't alone. My grandpa was the only survivor of our house after the war, beside me of course. I was almost too young to remember, but he told me there were dozens of Hawkwoods once, all living in the same castle. I had sisters and brothers and cousins and aunts and uncles and parents. But they're nothing but a blur to me now. I couldn't even tell you what they looked like. And our home is nothing but forgotten ruins. I wandered across the realm with my grandpa for three years trying to find the Magic Hollow. He had heard rumors about the Round Table, and his dying wish was that I train with them to become an anointed knight. He's buried in the cemetery on the other side of the village."

I felt a strange sense of relief and sadness hearing about Lance's past. Somehow it gave me courage, knowing what a great knight Lance had become even though he came from a difficult past, and hadn't been raised in a traditional home setting like me.

"I didn't really know my parents either," Lance said. "I don't want to assume that I know how you feel, but for what it's worth, if you ever need someone to talk to, I'll listen. Maybe I could understand, given my experiences."

"I get it," I said, "I don't really know how to feel yet. I never knew them—so to be honest, it's kind of hard to miss someone when I don't even know what I'm missing. I just wish it had been different for me so that I would be normal like everyone else. That probably sounds horrible, huh?"

Lance was quiet for an excruciatingly long time, staring out over the Hollow. "I don't think that's horrible, Hayden. The only way you'll become a knight is if you come to terms with who you are first."

"Hey, over here," Gwen said from further down the street. "I think I found it. I think it's that cottage down this lane."

I felt like I swallowed a frog because the lump in my throat felt like it wanted to leap right out. Part of me was excited to see the cottage that had belonged to my parents. I hoped it would provide more clues about who they were and where they might be.

"I understand if you don't want to do this," Lance said. "We could turn around right now, and no one would judge you for it."

I took a deep breath. "No, it's okay. I want to do this. I want to see my home."

My parent's cottage was a small little structure surrounded by a yard wildly overgrown from thirteen years of neglect. A small path led from the main road to the front door almost completely hidden by thick bushes and grass. As I walked along the path, I couldn't help but imagine how it might have looked neatly cared for and tended to. I saw a crab apple tree near the side of the house, and imagined my childhood self, climbing its boughs, looking for a snack to eat.

I felt my heart jump as the key slid into the keyhole. I turned it, and the door unlocked. The front door creaked loudly as I pushed it open. The inside of the house was surprisingly tidy, despite thirteen years passing. I saw a little kitchen, with a wooden table, pots and pans hanging on the wall beside it. There was a sitting area with a bench and chairs by a large brick fireplace, black and charred. There was a large bookshelf, but it was almost completely empty. I wondered if many of the books had been relocated to the library in New Camelot. An open door revealed a small room that must have belonged to my parents. There was a bed, a rocking chair, and a large closet filled with moth-eaten clothes that must have belonged to them.

A second door led me into a room that undoubtedly must have been mine. A small wooden crib sat in the middle of the room, under a precariously hanging mobile. There was a dresser and a shelf covered in little wooden toys. Everything was caked with dust, but in my mind's eye, I saw a baby sitting in the crib laughing as two parents leaned over the side giggling and tickling its feet. The image changed as I imagined the crib being replaced with a small bed, and that boy becoming a toddler. The toys were replaced with wooden swords and horses. My parents scooped me up in their arms, spinning around and holding me close.

That was when I noticed a strange, dust-covered orb sitting in a cobwebbed corner of the bookshelf. I picked up and it was cold as ice and solid as glass. It appeared to be filled with liquid inside, swirling purple and blue. I shook it around, watching the colors swirl and blend like a snow globe. Eventually, however, I set the orb aside, unable to find anything special about it. I continued my search of the room, uncovering nothing remotely significant or meaningful. No obvious clues either.

I remembered after a time, that Lance and Gwen were still waiting at the open door. I was grateful they had done this for me, but I was equally grateful they gave me space. I didn't know how to feel in this little house. Part of me felt nothing. I had no memory of this place, which made it seem like even less of a house than the cluttered hoard I had grown up in with Winston and Arabella. Another part of me felt robbed. Robbed of a wonderful life I could have had here with my mom and dad.

I sat down beside the dusty crib and buried my head in my hands. There were no clues in this house, at least as far as I could tell. I felt silly for expecting to find something. As I sat there, thinking about the life that I could have had in that house, I knew it wasn't my parents' fault that the life I could have had in this house was taken from me. They had only done what any parent would do, protect their child at any cost. It was the Shadow War that had done this. The evil sorcerer Marzon was dead. He could never pay for his wrongs, yet I had to suffer. That wasn't fair.

If the shadows really were stirring again, it meant someone just as evil or worse was coming to power. If that happened, I wanted to do everything in my power to stop them, just like my dad had done thirteen years ago. Whether that meant finding my father the hero, or simply becoming a powerful and valiant hero myself, I would do it. I would do anything to be sure that more lives wouldn't be ruined like mine and Lance's had.

"Someday, I'll clean you up," I whispered to the house around me. "Just keep hanging in there a little longer."

I was on my way out of the house when I noticed three colorful embroidered banners hanging from the wall by the front door. Each banner, red, orange, and gold, featured the sigil sword of the Magic Hollow on them. Beneath that they read "Tournament Champion at Arms." Two of the banners were for winning at joust, and one was for winning a sword contest.

I should have been excited to see them. These banners were proof that everything everyone told me about my father was true. He was an exceptional swordsman, knight, and even jouster. Winning three tournaments wouldn't have been an easy feat. Yet seeing those banners there made me feel surprisingly uncertain about myself. How could I ever live up to his legacy? I knew I could try, but would I ever win three tournaments? I had never won anything in my life, let alone a test of martial prowess. Just like Isabelle had said, all the other knights had been training since they were kids, first as pages, then as squires. They had all passed their own tests to become Knights-junior. All I had to say for myself was that my dad was a famous knight. In the end, that would never win me any glory. If I was going to become a knight, I had to figure out how to do it myself.

When I finally left the house, I left with a renewed purpose. Despite the doubt I felt, I knew what I wanted, and now I felt like I had found the determination to make it come true. I had to live up to my dad's legacy. I was going to become a Knight of the Round Table.

# CHAPTER ELEVEN

"Did you find what you needed?" Lance asked, as I stepped out onto the porch, closing the door behind me. I could see the sun setting behind the Snowy Mountains, which made me wonder how much time I had spent inside my parent's cottage.

I nodded. "I'm going to do whatever it takes to become a Knight of the Round Table. When the knights ride out of hiding to face whatever is out there, I want to be one of them."

"Good," Lance said, clasping my shoulder, "because tomorrow the real fun begins. I'm going to teach you how to fight like a proper knight."

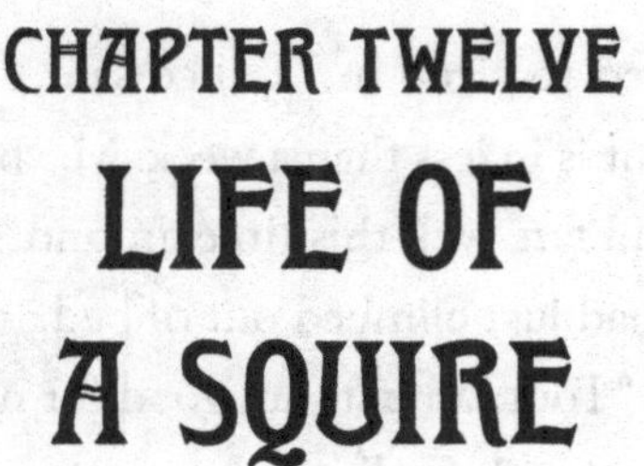

# CHAPTER TWELVE
# LIFE OF A SQUIRE

No amount of practice would ever get me used to the alarm clock that is Goliath the drake. There's nothing like opening your eyes in the morning to the snarling teeth of a pint-sized dragon.

"I'm up, I'm up," I said defensively, letting out a huge yawn. Goliath nuzzled my chest with its head and then flew off to the bed of its next victim.

Lance and Lucas were already awake, sitting by the fire talking quietly. It sounded like they were talking about . . . sports? No, the next tournament. "Depending on the early draw, it could make or break your chances at the joust, though," Lance was saying. "If Isabelle jousts Percy, I think she has the best chance of beating him in the early rounds."

"Aye, that might be true. But Percy has been training hard. He makes up for his lack of brawn with pure skill. He could be a formidable foe this time around."

Alex or Eric, I still couldn't tell which one was which, finished shewing Goliath away, and climbed out of bed sleepily. "How am I supposed to sleep in with that thing harassing me every morning?"

# CHAPTER TWELVE

"You're not supposed to sleep in," Lance said. "We've got work to do. Besides, the tournament is in less than a week. Maybe if you put some effort into training, you could fare well this time around."

His brother, who had just climbed out of bed as well, stood by his side, yawning dramatically. "Tournaments are good for nothing but bruises. We want to stay handsome for the ladies."

"You two are uglier than a bridge troll's backside," Lucas said laughing.

"Hey, watch it!" one of the brothers said. "Or we might actually put some effort into fighting this tournament."

"I would be honored to face either of you, if that's the case," Lance said.

"Duel you? There's no way in this realm or the old that we would face you! We'd lose for sure."

"I can't believe you two passed your trials and become Knights-junior," Cole, Sir Lucas's squire said. "When I pass the trials, I hope I show a little more initiative than you two."

"How noble of you," the brothers said in unison. "Well, we'll be getting some breakfast. See you around!"

"So, they are knights-junior?" I asked Lance when the door had closed behind them.

"Yep, but they haven't obtained the lower order of the Round Table yet. Currently, we only seat thirteen at the table anyway, which means there is only one more open seat, but you know, the whole Siege Perilous myth means we may never fill that seat."

"I already sat in Siege Perilous," I said. "It was an accident, obviously, but I think I was just warming it up for myself. I'm going to be the thirteenth knight on the Round Table."

"That's the right attitude. And if you fare well in the tournament, you just might be able to. But that means we only have one week to prepare you."

"Just tell me where to start," I said excitedly.

I felt a mix of anxiety and excitement as I stepped into the Arena. The floor of it was covered in a soft white sand. It was a large space, with plenty of room to train for everyone. Many knights and squires were already at work, sword fighting, spear throwing, shooting arrows, or jousting targets on horseback.

I was wearing a partial suit of armor, which we picked up from the armory. It wasn't custom built for my body, of course, but it was still a good fit. I wore a steel chest plate, with mail beneath. On my shoulders were the pieces called the pauldrons, and protecting my hands were special gloves called gauntlets. I didn't wear a traditional iron helmet but did put on a padded leather cap that strapped beneath my chin. Altogether, the armor wasn't too heavy to manage, but it was still an adjustment getting used to the added weight. Lance said that after a day or two he would let me start fighting with a full suit of armor on.

"First, we need to decide what kind of sword you prefer to fight with best," Lance said. "There are dozens of designs, but the most popular amongst the knights are longswords, claymores, great swords, and arming swords."

Lance led me over to a rack filled with swords of different sizes, shapes, and lengths. Lance pulled one sword from the row, which looked average in size. "This is a standard weapon we call an arming sword. It's a one-handed sword, but very agile."

I held the sword in my right hand and was surprised by how light it felt. "This must only be like two or three pounds."

"It's a common misconception," Lance said.

Lance replaced the arming sword on the rack, and grabbed a longer weapon, which also had a longer hilt, the spot where you grip it. "This is what we call a long sword. The two-handed grip makes it much better for cutting, but it will be a lot slower."

The longsword was noticeably heavier than the arming sword, but not by much. It felt nicely balanced; however, I could see how the great length would slow me down in a fight.

"Next, we have the great sword," Lance said, handing me a weapon that was as tall as I was. It was a double-edged blade, but a portion of the blade closest to the hilt was unsharpened. It also had two cross guards, the one closest to the grip was the longest, and it had smaller ones at the top of the unsharpened portion. "Nobody carries these around, but they can be very useful in combat. They can hack right through enemy spears, allowing the knight to stay at a safe distance. The claymore is basically a great sword as well, just a Gaelic design. Typically, they don't have the secondary cross guard, but will function in battle about the same. I would suggest sticking to the arming sword, or the long sword, if I were you."

In the end, we decided to practice with each so I could see the difference for myself. We started with Lance instructing me on proper stance and how to hold a sword. He set up a couple straw dummies for me to strike at. Lance proved to be an excellent teacher.

"Good, Hayden, that was perfect. Never forget your stance. Footwork is necessary to always be ready to strike or parry. If your opponent forces you into sloppy footwork, you're done for. Now try again."

Lance had me repeatedly circling the dummies using careful footwork, then striking from every possible direction. After several hours of hard practice with the arming sword and the long sword, I decided I preferred the arming sword's length. It was fast and easy to handle. Part of me wished it had a longer hilt, though, so that I could still use two hands if I wanted.

After a short break for lunch, we returned to the Arena to work some more. This time, Lance exchanged himself for the dummies, and we started to spar each other. Lance would tell me what to do, then I would step and strike. He parried every time of course, and then we would reset and try again. It was all new to me, but it came quickly enough. With Lance's guidance and direction, I was already starting to feel myself simply trusting my gut, and letting the motions happen naturally.

"Good. Reset!" Lance said. "Now, I want you to attack with any maneuver of your choice. Don't worry, these swords are dull, so even if you did manage to get past me, you won't hurt me."

I nodded, taking a deep breath. Stepping as precisely as I could, I circled around him from a safe distance, holding my sword in an offensive posture. When I was ready, I lunged at Lance swinging my sword across, toward his chest. Lance parried it with ease, as I knew he would, but that was only a distraction. Using the momentum from his parry, I let the arming sword swing around in my grip, then stepped under his guard and slashed again. Lance fumbled backward, dropping his guard, just managing to catch my attack with his cross guards. He took two steps back, then reset his posture into a defensive stance.

"Hayden! That was impressive. You're agile!"

Too exhilarated to speak, I lunged in for another attack, trying a different approach than before. Lance parried every attempt, but I remained on the offense, testing his defense, as well as my own abilities. Our swords clanked loudly, catching the attention of the other knights and squires in the Arena. Next thing I knew, a small crowd had gathered around us to watch our swordplay.

"You're a natural, Hayden," Lance said through gritted teeth. "But let's see how you do on defense."

Lance spun around, blocking my move, then placing himself in a position that gave him the upper hand. He swung at me, and I was forced to retreat a step, throwing up my guard to parry. My footwork was sloppy, and that only made it harder to block the next few strikes Lance threw at me. He was fighting with a longsword, so each attack was slower, but came with a crazy amount of force that seemed to knock me back with each parry.

I knew I couldn't keep up with him long, and I had to find a way to break his momentum. I decided not to parry the next strike he sent at me, but rather dodge to the side. I pulled it off, barely, escaping to the side as his longsword crashed into the sand with a muffled thud. I reset my stance, breathing deeply, but not ready to stop. This was easily the most fun I'd ever had.

Lance heaved his sword out of the sand. "You should have attacked first," he said, rushing in at me.

This put me back on the defensive, but I was more careful this time. After a few quick strikes, I tried to use the slower speed of Lance's attacks against him. His sword required a bigger swinging motion in-between each of his attacks, which allowed me to quickly rush in under his guard and launch my own barrage of attacks. Just like that, I had Lance on the defensive again. I could see beads of sweat growing on his forehead as he retreated step after step.

I pressed as hard and fiercely as I could, until at last, Lance made a misstep. I lunged at him quickly. His expression changed from enjoyment to serious concentration. Next thing I knew, Lance had whirled around me, tripping me over his leg. I fell flat onto my back, looking up at the dull point of his sparring sword.

"Not bad, Hayden," he said, helping me back onto my feet. "You have the determination and the drive to be a great fighter. Maybe even some raw talent, but your footwork is sloppy, and your technique will need work. Keep practicing, though, and you'll master all of that."

The crowd that had gathered around us cheered loudly as they stepped forward. At first, I felt embarrassed for losing flat on my back, but I quickly realized they weren't coming to congratulate Lance. Next thing I knew, I was being lifted onto my feet and congratulated by tons of knights and squires.

"That was brilliant sword play," Tristan said, clapping me on the back. "I haven't seen Lance sweat like that in ages. Keep at it, and you just might beat him in a bout!"

"Nicely done, Hayden!" Kaylinelle said, giving me a hug that made me feel dizzy.

Outside the crowd, I saw Percy Igtham standing near the stands, arms crossed. We made eye contact, and he nodded at me, smiling barely.

Elibora and Cecily came and congratulated me as well. "I was right. You'll make a great sparring partner for Cecily," Elibora said. She turned to her squire and said, "If you're not careful, Hayden might pass you up, Ceci!"

Cecily pouted her lip and looked away. "Yeah, not bad for a beginner, I guess."

"All right, all right," Lance said. "Give him space. We've still got work to do."

"Hold on," Isabelle said from the crowd. "Why don't you take a break Lance. Someone else can spar the hero's son. How about . . . me?"

She stepped forward, holding a long spear in her hand.

I gulped. Lance hadn't taught me anything about fighting someone with a spear.

Lance's eyes thinned, and he didn't back down. "He's my squire," Lance said. "I'll train him at a pace I see fit."

"If he really is the son of a hero, and is worthy of sitting in Siege Perilous, I think he'll do just fine in a bout with me."

I heard whispers spreading through the crowd as everyone looked at me. I didn't have to hear what they were saying to know what they were talking about. Hayden, the son of Sir William, their beloved hero—would he back down from a fight?

To be honest, I was terrified. Lance had been teaching me, Isabelle, on the other hand wouldn't likely show me the same level of restraint. She seemed bent on one thing, and that was proving whether I was as good as my father or not.

"Hayden is only a squire; therefore, you can't challenge him without my approval. He's not ready yet, and it wouldn't be a fair bout."

"It's okay, Lance," I said, stepping forward. "I can do this. Let me try."

Isabelle grinned sinisterly. "You heard the boy. He wants to duel! Clear the ring everyone!"

"I hope you know what you're doing," Lance muttered in my ear.

Isabelle spun her spear around her in elegant twisting motions, whirling it around so quickly, I could hear it whistle threateningly as it whipped through the air. "They say Sir William was one of the greatest natural born fighters of our time, a genius in combat, and a wonder to behold. I wonder if his son has the same skill, eh?" She snapped into an offensive position, the spear held tight under her arm, pointed right at me.

"Hayden—you don't have to do this. Even your father needed proper training. You're not ready," Gwen said, grabbing my arm. "Isabelle is too strong. She will pulverize you!"

I looked around at all the knights and squires who had gathered to watch our fight. This should have terrified me, but now, I felt something else entirely. It was exciting. I wanted to fight. I wanted to prove myself to all of them, and this was my chance.

I stepped forward, gripping the arming sword tightly in my right hand. I fell into the offensive stance Lance had just taught me.

Lance shook his head in frustration but didn't stop me. "Fine," he said. "Sir Lucas, I want you to officiate this. Keep it clean. I don't want anyone to get hurt."

He said anyone, but I knew he was only talking about me.

Sir Lucas the Butler retrieved a handful of bright red flags from a container beside the sword rack and stepped forward, looking nervous. "Lady Isabelle of House Isolde has challenged Hayden, squire and son of Sir William, to a duel. The contenders shall fight first to three strikes. If you're unable to fight, or yield, it is an automatic defeat. I'll throw a flag for each successful strike. May you both fight with honor."

Isabelle started circling the ring that had been formed by the gathering crowd, her eyes focused on me and my every movement. I kept my eyes on the tip of her spear, reacting to her moves as if she were just another player on the basketball court I was defending. Only, I knew she was much more dangerous than any basketball player. Her spear was long, and that would give her a lot more reach than I had with my arming sword. But if I could get inside her guard, I realized, she would have a much harder time blocking my sword thrusts. Deciding on my course of action, I rushed in at Isabelle trying to anticipate how she would counter with her spear.

In a flash of wood and steel, Isabelle spun the spear around her like it was a windmill of death. I hesitated for a moment, but I didn't stop my charge. I tried to keep my eye on the point of the spear, which was spinning around wildly. Three steps away. Two. One. I thrust my sword, and Isabelle snapped into defense, knocking my sword away with her spear. She immediately spun it around, sending it right at my head. I ducked, but the spear was already coming around for another attack from a different direction. I tried to use the defensive posture that Lance taught me and blocked the attack. Isabelle attacked fiercely, forcing me to retreat step by step as she pressed my defense.

"What's the matter?" Isabelle said. "Are you going to yield?"

I gritted my teeth, feeling the excitement growing inside me. As terrifying as this was, it was fun, and I was determined to win. I ducked under Isabelle's next attack, then stepped in under her guard. I struck her steel chest plate and it rang loudly.

The crowd erupted in cheers as Sir Lucas tossed a red flag in the air, "First strike!" he shouted.

Isabelle growled in frustration, then rammed me hard with her shoulder. I fell over and had to roll twice to avoid her spear thrusts. I scrambled back onto my feet just in time to knock her spear away. She attacked again and again, with maddening ferocity, and it took all my concentration and strength to knock away her attacks. I was starting to breathe heavily, getting tired from all the training I had done, while Isabelle was fresh. She hadn't just dueled Lance like I had.

Finally, my footwork faltered beyond recovery, and Isabelle scored not one, but two strikes as she knocked my chest, then brought the spear down on my head, which thankfully, was padded from my sparring helmet. It still hurt, though. I fell to my knees as my vision went blurry. "Two strikes to Isabelle," I heard Sir Lucas say.

I knew I had to get up. I had to keep fighting, but it was becoming extremely hard to focus. I saw Isabelle swooping in, spinning her spear over her head like a helicopter. Then I heard Lance's voice, "Stop! He's on his knees. Let him yield!"

Yield? That meant surrendering the fight. I couldn't yield.

Isabelle, ignoring Lance's call for mercy, swooped in to deal the winning blow. I gripped my sword tightly and threw it up. Blocking her strike just in time. The crowd cheered, and I let their excitement drive me. It lifted me up and gave me courage. This was what I had always dreamed of. Sure, I wasn't going to score the last basket in a basketball game like I used to pretend shooting hoops in the backyard, but this was even better. I was going to beat a Knight of the Round Table in a duel!

Isabelle was so surprised that I had countered her attack, I was able to slip under her guard a second time, and even score another hit.

"Second strike for Hayden," Lucas shouted, sounding just as surprised as Isabelle.

Isabelle cursed under her breath and spun around attacking me again and again. I pressed back with all my strength, doing everything I could to try and counter her attacks and score the final hit.

We were each starting to get reckless now, eager to score the winning point. But strike for strike, we blocked each other. The sound of our weapons clashing rang through the Arena, which was completely silent as everyone watched intently.

Desperate, I swung my sword wildly, as Isabelle did the same with her spear coming from the other direction.

"STOP!" Gwen shouted unexpectedly. I felt a force hit my body like a tremendous gust of wind. When the wind passed, I was frozen in place, mid-swing, and completely paralyzed from head to foot, the tip of my sword, just inches away from Isabelle's chest plate. The same thing had happened to Isabelle, whose spear was just inches away from my chest.

"What's the meaning of this?" Sir Lucas said. "Why did you stop them?"

I swiftly concluded that Gwen must have used a magic spell to freeze us in place. For the record, it was extremely uncomfortable.

# CHAPTER TWELVE

Gwen rushed forward, scooping up a bird in her hands. From the corner of my eye, I saw that it had a little scroll tied to its leg. "It's a message," Gwen said, pulling the scroll from the bird, which flew away immediately. "It's a message from Principal Hal! Knights—Round Hall. Now!"

"But what about the match? Can we at least get out some rope and measure who was closest to striking the other?" Tristan asked, walking up to our frozen bodies and inspecting each other's weapons. "I can't tell who would have hit first."

"Lucas—end this fight," Lance said seriously.

Sir Lucas nodded, then threw up the flags. "I hereby declare this duel a draw. The match is over. Knights of the Round Table, let's go."

Isabelle, who like me, couldn't move or speak, was staring daggers with her eyes.

"Gwen, will you reverse your spell?" Lance asked, grabbing our immobilized weapons and pointing them into the sand.

"Ah, I was really starting to like them that way. Much quieter. Besides, the spell would have worn off in an hour or so anyway." She snapped her fingers, and I felt a tingling chill pass over my body like someone had just dumped a bucket of ice water on me. I let out a big breath of air, grateful to have the pressure of being frozen taken off my lungs.

"HOW DARE YOU STOP OUR MATCH!" Isabelle yelled, grabbing Lucas by the collar of his shirt. "We weren't finished yet!"

"Isabelle. Stop," Lance said forcefully, grabbing her arm. He didn't yell, but he spoke with commanding confidence. So much so, it worked. Isabelle let go of Lucas, who quickly stepped back, smoothing at the ruffles in his shirt, looking rather peeved.

"Listen to Gwen," Lance continued. "We need an emergency meeting in the Round Hall. Percy, can you find the others and let them know?"

Percy, who had remained on the outside of the crowd, watching over the battle like a hawk, nodded his head, then departed, a hand on the hilt of his sword which swung from his heavy leather belt. He had such a stoic personality, like a statue, it was almost unnerving when he moved.

"Don't think I'm done with you," Isabelle whispered to me. "We'll face off again sooner or later in a Tournament."

"I'll be ready for you," I said, trying to sound as confident as I could.

Close by, Elibora said goodbye to Cecily. "I'll meet you in the dining hall, okay?"

Cecily looked disappointed, but agreed, and gave Elibora a halfhearted hug goodbye.

That was also when I realized, I probably wasn't invited to this meeting either. There hadn't been any squires present last time, and almost all the Round Table did have squires currently.

"Lance? Can I sit in on this one too?" I asked hopefully. "What if it's about Jack and Mr. Bianco? I've got to know if they are okay."

Lance frowned. "Hayden, I'm sorry, but rules are rules. I won't be able to budge on this one. I can't make it seem like I'm giving my squire special treatment. But I promise, I will tell you everything I can right away."

As Lance, Gwen, Elibora, and Tristan hurried off toward the castle, I couldn't help but feel jealous. Mr. Bianco meant more to me than anybody else here, and it had been three days since we had been split apart and I had stepped aboard the griffin.

"You get used to it," Cecily said, watching Elibora depart.

I nodded, trying not to show how disappointed I was about not being able to join the meeting.

"That was amazing what you did against Lance and Isabelle, by the way." Cecily said, as we walked toward the dining hall. "I mean, sure, your technique will need some work, but who could expect someone to fight perfectly on their first day? You've got talent, Hayden."

"Do you mean it?" I said, beaming. That helped me feel a little better.

"Just watch out for Isabelle," Cecily continued. "She has a fiery temper and won't forget today easily. Next time you battle her, be prepared for the wrath of a full-fledged knight."

I gulped. "She's very intense."

After what felt like at least a million years, the Knights finally came down from the Round Hall. Everyone else had already started dinner by then. Gwen saw us first, and her eyes immediately narrowed when she saw me sitting by Cecily. Gwen had been chatting with Elibora, who rushed forward to speak with Cecily.

I smiled at Cecily as she got up to leave with Elibora, and we exchanged goodbyes. To be honest, I didn't get what Gwen's problem with Cecily was. After our conversation today, I thought she was really nice.

Gwen sat down across from me, and then Lance beside her.

"What were you doing with her?" Gwen asked, eyeing Cecily as she departed.

"We were just talking," I said defensively. "She's actually really friendly. Besides, it's not like I could come into the meeting with you. So, come on, spill the beans."

"Spill the beans?" Gwen asked.

"It's an expression in the Other Realm. It means, tell me everything."

"Oh, okay. Beans? Whatever. Well . . . good news and bad news," Gwen said. "The good news is Hal is fine, and he seems to have found whatever he was looking for. All he said was 'the greatest avenue for darkness remains sealed.' So, I guess we can all rest easy knowing that the next Shadow War isn't going to start, yet."

"And what's the bad news?"

"Well . . . it's Jack and Sir Ector. They've been captured by a tribe of bridge trolls, and they are holding them for ransom."

"What?" I said, a little too loudly. "They've been prisoners this whole time, and we've just been sitting here eating meat pies and sparring with dull swords?"

"Like we always have," Lance said roughly. "Hayden, I know how frustrating this must be for you, trust me. I feel the same way. We may be young, but we are still knights. We should be out there. But we aren't. That's the way it is for now."

"But what about Mr. Bianco—Sir Ector? He needs us!"

"Hal was very clear in his letter," Gwen said, "that he doesn't want any of us to try and look for them. He said he will handle it himself."

I wanted to argue, but Gwen shushed me. "Principal Hal is the most powerful sorcerer in Between. They will be okay. He will rescue them and bring them back here. We just have to trust him and be patient."

"I hate being patient," I said, rubbing my face with my hands. "It's so hard."

"The best thing we can do is continue our training," Lance said. "Redouble our efforts. Work as hard as we can. Sure, whatever Hal was worried about doesn't seem to be a problem right now, but I've still got a bad feeling about all of this. Trolls holding hostages? They are supposed to be too dumb to work out something like that on their own. Someone must be pulling the strings. Whatever is coming, we have to be ready for it."

I knew Lance was right. Compared to Hal, what use would I be to Mr. Bianco and Jack? Plus, we didn't even know where they were anyway. The best thing I could do was keep training and preparing to become a knight.

# CHAPTER TWELVE

I hated doing nothing when I knew a friend was in danger, but it was the only real choice I had.

"Oh, and Hayden, one more thing. The tournament is still happening next week. And, well, there is going to be an exhibition match. I tried to stop it, but I was outvoted."

"What do you mean?" I asked nervously. "What's an exhibition match?"

"It means there is going to be a match before the actual tournament starts. I tried to stop it, but Isabelle pushed really hard. She said it wasn't fair we ended her match the way we did, and that it was an insult to her honor. Enough people gave in and decided to give her what she wanted. A rematch against you."

"Another sword fight?"

Lance shook his head. "No . . . a joust."

"Looks like I have a week to learn how to joust," I said. "You seem upset, Lance. Is that the only thing bothering you?"

Lance sighed. "I don't know. The Round Table got into another argument today . . . it seems like all we do is argue nowadays. Nobody can agree on anything. Especially with Hal gone, it seems like tensions are reaching an all high."

"Things aren't looking good for the Magic Hollow," Gwen said seriously. "The Enchanted Forest is on the verge of war, and the Round Table probably isn't far behind either."

Lance sighed loudly, slouching in his seat. "I wish there was something more I could do. There must be something that would give us the push we need in the right direction . . ."

"How is your studying going with Baron by the way?" Gwen asked me.

"Horrible," I said. "I can't stand him. Why does he have to be so rude? And so . . . so—"

"Mean? Nasty? Stinky?" Gwen offered. "All of the above?"

We laughed. "Yeah, I'll go with all of the above," I said. "I haven't made any progress because he wants me to read this history book written in Old English. It's like gibberish to me."

"Baron is mad. My Old English is horrible," Lance said. "So, don't feel too bad."

Gwen frowned. "Anglo-Saxon is the language of the kings. It's our history and tradition. Plus, if we ever start traveling outside the Hollow, we'll have to use it to converse with a lot of the locals."

"It's hard to learn a new language when I'm just trying to stay alive in the sword ring," I said. "Besides, I just want to make sure Isabelle doesn't pulverize me during the exhibition match."

"You're the one who accepted her challenge in the first place," Gwen said. "I could have guessed that she wouldn't be satisfied with a draw. For her, it's win, or die."

I gulped. "I'm okay with losing. If it means, well, living."

"Nobody is going to die. Especially not my squire," Lance said seriously. "We'll start training in the morning. I'll have you ready for this joust if it's the last thing I do."

# LANCE AND A LANCE

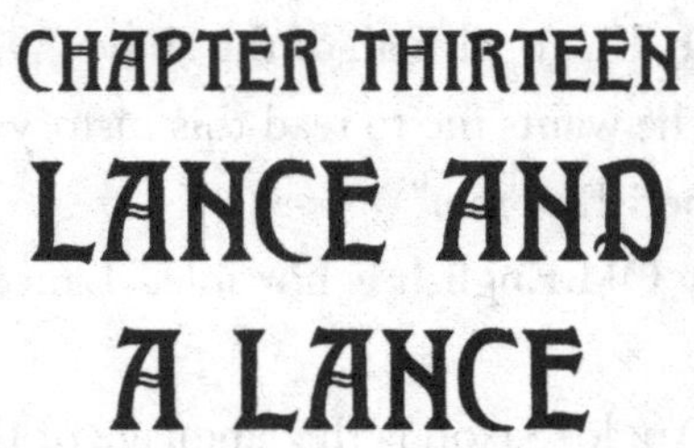

I had one week to prepare for the tournament. Fortunately, Lance was a dedicated teacher. We woke up every morning long before any of the other members of Room Three ever did, with the help of Goliath of course. Nothing says time to wake up better than a drake nipping at your toes. Forget alarm clocks. Drakes are way cooler.

A big portion of my training for the joust was learning how to ride a horse. The rules of the game were simple enough, it was executing them that was going to be the real challenge. The way a joust works is that a single fence, known as the tilt barrier, is set up in the center of the Arena. Then, on each side of the tilt barrier, is a shorter fence, called the counter tilt, which forms a straight lane just wide enough for a horse on each side.

"A match," Lance explained the first morning of our training as we walked around the jousting area, "consists of three passes. You score by breaking your lance on your opponent's shield, upper body, or helm. Illegal strikes include hitting the horse or barricading your opponent by hitting them with the side of the lance, rather than its tip."

"We call that clotheslining someone in the Other Realm," I explained.

"Hmm. Walking into a clothesline would be similar, I guess. Except a lance is made of wood, so it is going to hurt a lot more I imagine."

"But I will be wearing a full suit of armor, right?"

"Yes, of course. Jousting isn't without its dangers, but we do what we can to keep it fun and keep our knights safe. Isabelle is going to try and beat you as badly as she can, but she would never *intentionally* kill you."

"Which implies that people unintentionally get killed in the joust?"

"It has happened. But not in a long time. Like I said, we do everything we can to keep our knights safe. In the end, it's just a game, and your lives are too precious to waste. Every lance will be inspected before the match by Sir Lucas, the Knight Marshal for the event."

"The Knight Marshal is like a judge then?"

"Exactly. Sir Lucas is honest and fair, he won't favor Isabelle over you, but that means he isn't going to be lenient on you either, so don't try and pull any tricks. Also, if you get knocked off your horse, then you automatically lose the match no matter what the score was. Whatever you do, try not to fall off your horse."

"Make a horse run down a straight-line charging at a monstrosity of a girl who wants to brutally humiliate me in front of everyone. Then strike her with the tip of a ten-foot-long piece of wood before she strikes me. Got it. Did I miss anything?"

"You were quite accurate, actually," Lance said. "Come on, let's get you onto a horse."

I had never ridden a horse before in my life, so that was a big obstacle to overcome. Once I was on top of the horse, and sitting on the saddle, I felt comfortable enough. It was a little jarring being so high up and trying to control a beast that was way bigger and stronger than me though.

# CHAPTER THIRTEEN

"What's her name?" I asked, sitting atop a gorgeous tawny brown horse.

"This girl's named Arion," Lance said. "After the mythical horse. She's very fast and very loyal. I have ridden her in three jousts, and she has never failed me. I think it will be best if we get her used to you as well."

Lance showed me how to use the reins and how to guide and command Arion. Luckily, all the horses in New Camelot's stables were extremely well trained and taken care of. I just needed to tell it where to go and what to do and make sure that she trusted me and knew that I was in charge.

After a few laps around the Arena at a slow trot, Lance stopped Arion and said, "Okay, now I want you to start galloping."

I led Arion to one end of the Arena and lined it up with the lane between the tilt barrier and counter tilt. My heart was racing, but I knew I couldn't be afraid. All I had to do was get the horse to gallop in a straight line. I would need enough momentum from my horse to get a good strike on Isabelle, especially because she was so much bigger than me.

"You can do it, Hayden," Lance said encouragingly from behind me.

"Yah!" I shouted, urging Arion into a quick gallop. She responded to my command and took off straight down the jousting lane. The roar of her hooves and the fierce bouncing of her steps was so jarring I almost fell off, but I squeezed my thighs tightly against the saddle and managed to stay on. I wasn't even holding a lance or anything, though it still felt thrilling to ride like that.

When we reached the end of the tilt barrier I shouted, "How do I stop this thing?"

"Pull on the reins!" Lance shouted.

I pulled on the reins, slowing her down, then spun her around, ready to run down the opposite lane.

"Go for it," Lance shouted.

# LANCE AND A LANCE

This continued every morning of our training. Lance always wanted me to start the day by simply riding Arion and becoming more confident on her back. As the week progressed, he started having us ride through obstacles, like hopping over little fences and weaving through poles, like you would see in rodeos and horse racing. Even though I only needed to gallop in a straight line during the joust, it helped me feel confident riding Arion. By the end of the week, I felt like it was easy to guide her and tell her what to do. Hopefully Arion was also learning to trust me, too.

Besides the fundamentals of horseback riding, Lance also had to teach me how to hold a lance and how to strike. I was grateful we woke up early to do this stuff when nobody else was around because my first few attempts using the lance were embarrassing. The thing is, it's not easy to balance this big long pole out in front of you, let alone be able to aim it, all while hurtling down a lane on a galloping horse. But with practice, I got better.

Lance set up targets of hay, about the same height as Isabelle would be mounted on her horse. He also fastened a wooden shield to it. My primary goal was to try and strike the shield with my practice lance. It seemed easy enough, but in practice, it was extremely difficult. It took me three passes just to touch the shield. And another two passes to finally score a hit strong enough to get a point if it were a real joust. In the back of my mind, I tried not to dwell on the fact that the hay bale wasn't fighting back, galloping toward me with a lance of its own.

After a few days running the hay bale through with my lance, I started an even more difficult task of trying to get my lance through a little ring about the diameter of a person's head. This was so hard, it seemed almost impossible.

"If you can break a lance on your opponents' helmet, you'll score double points," Lance explained. "Isabelle is most likely going to try and knock you off your horse, so it is unlikely she will be going for a head strike. If you can stay mounted and not fall off when she strikes your body and land at least one head strike, in addition to two body strikes, you'll win."

"But if I miss the head strike, I will lose by one point," I added.

"True. So don't miss."

After much more practice, on the third day of jousting, I finally got my lance through the ring. As we continued to practice, I did it again, and again, and again. By the end of the week, I was confident that I could get the head strike I would need to win the match.

Training with Lance made for some of the best times of my life. In fact, I didn't even care that Baron still wanted me to meet with him to learn Anglo-Saxon and study old history books. Sure, if I had to read about one more king who lost or won some battle over this or that, I thought I would go crazy, but at least I had training with Lance to look forward to every day. Plus, deep down, I knew I found the history fascinating, it was just when Baron taught me, it was so different from Mr. Bianco. Mr. Bianco made literature and history come alive and seem real. Baron just droned on and on, forcing me to spew out dates and details of events from memorization. It took away all the fun about history and turned it into a big memory test.

We decided not to enter me into the squires' tournament for any sword fighting, even though that was clearly my best skill. "The sword fighting will come before the jousting events," Lance explained. "Even though it is your best event, I don't want to risk overtiring you before you have to face Isabelle."

I was a little disappointed to not be able to sword fight, but I knew there would always be other tournaments where I could give it a go. That didn't stop me, however, from still practicing with the sword every evening when we were done with our jousting work. Jousting was fun but practicing with the sword just felt natural to me. Lance and Gwen were both entered to fight in the Sword, as they called it, so I would duel with them often as well. I even had the chance to duel a few others, like Cecily, who fought with two short swords, and Tristan, who preferred a longsword. On the day before the tournament, I even asked Percy if he wanted to practice dueling, when I saw him standing to the side, arms crossed, watching everyone train with the same stern expression on his face. He shook his head and stalked away.

"What is his problem?" I asked Gwen, who was sitting on a bench polishing her armor for the tournament, while we watched Lance spar with Alex and Eric at the same time. They were decent fighters, but Lance was still managing to handle them both at once.

"Who, Percy?" Gwen asked, seeing who I was looking toward. "I would say he's always like that, but he seems especially moody lately. I think he's still upset about our meeting in the Round Hall last week. A few knights insulted his family, House Igtham, and I don't think he liked that very much."

"Is he the only member of his family here in the Hollow?"

"Yeah," Gwen said. "He doesn't talk about it much, but from what I can guess, his parents sent him here to train with the knights in secret. They are a very wealthy and prominent house, and well involved in the politics outside of the Magic Hollow, so maybe they thought it would be too risky to openly show support right now while we are still in hiding. But the thing is, a lot of knights around here accuse the Igthams of being cowards because of that. They didn't want to openly abandon their castle to come to the Magic Hollow like Lady Albreda and others did after the war, but they must believe in the cause enough to send their eldest son here to become a true knight."

"And what do you think? Are the Igthams cowards? I have never seen

Percy fight, but I get the feeling that he's really good."

"Trust me. He's good. He might even be as good as Lance. Just wait and see tomorrow. Percy will be competing. I don't know about his parents, but I know Percy is no coward," Gwen said.

"When will the tournament brackets be announced, by the way?" I asked, wondering who would be dueling who.

"Those will be posted tonight, after the festival," Gwen said with a mischievous grin.

"Festival? That's the last thing I would expect the Knights of the Round Table to be doing on the night before a big tournament. Shouldn't you be sitting by the fire drinking ale and talking about honor and glory and chivalry and stuff?"

"We might be knights, but we are still kids," Gwen said pointedly. "Besides, it's a lot of fun. And its tradition. We all gather in the hot springs in Crystal Cave. You know, friendly bonding and recreation before we are at each other's throats during the tournament."

"I guess that makes sense," I said. "I don't know though; I find it hard to believe that all of the knights ever experience *friendly* bonding." I was thinking about a couple knights specifically, and Isabelle was at the top of that list.

"It's true . . ." Gwen said. "Unity isn't always our strong suit. But still, we can't give up on each other. There's always hope."

"Hope that Percy will crack a smile and Isabelle will stop being a nasty cow? Doesn't seem likely."

"Well, when you put it that way . . . you have a point," Gwen said, smiling. "To be fair though, Percy and Isabelle rarely show up to these parties. So, we should be okay."

"Yeah, as long as Tristan doesn't see me sitting in anymore cursed chairs."

"Now you're just being ridiculous," Gwen said, giving me a friendly shove. "Don't go and ruin it for everyone. It will be fun."

"All right, all right," I said, throwing up my hands in playful defense. "I'm in. It does sound fun."

Lance, who had just finished his duel with Alex and Eric, had to kick them away as they fell to the ground animatedly groveling at his feet. "We aren't worthy!" they said jokingly. "It is an honor to be beaten at your hand," one of them said, and "I will never stop this bloody nose from bleeding, as an ever reminder of your skill at smashing my face in!" the other said.

"Get up. GET UP!" Lance said, embarrassed. The two of them laughed as they walked away.

"Lance, I was just telling Hayden about the festivities in Crystal Cave tonight. Are you joining?"

Lance shuffled his feet, looking down at the ground. "Actually, I was thinking about skipping this time around. I'm tired, and I want to be rested for the tournament tomorrow."

"Are you serious?" Gwen asked, disappointed.

Lance nodded apologetically.

"Well, if Lance isn't going, there's no way I am."

"Nah, Hayden. You should go. I want you to go. It will be good for you. A chance to get to know your fellow knights and squires better."

"Friendly bonding and recreation," Gwen said. "I told you so."

I sighed. It was still hard for me to imagine the knights hanging out at a festival, which sounded a lot like a pool party to me. It was like we were normal teens. Which I guess we were, despite the extraordinary circumstances that brought us together.

Knowing that Mr. Bianco and Jack could still be in danger did make it hard to want to take a break and play. Busying myself with training every day helped take my mind off of my worries.

"Even knights need to take time off sometimes," Gwen said. "We're still teenagers, you know. If it was only work and no play all the time, we would go crazy."

"Well, crazier than we already are," Lance added. "But really, she's right. You've been working hard all week. Now you need to relax and have some fun. Besides, the warm water will be good for you."

"All right, you win. I'll go."

Gwen fist pumped. "Yes! Just wait until you meet Henrietta, our pet sea monster."

"Oh no. I forgot about her," I said, mortified.

They just laughed and slapped me on the back. "Don't worry about her. She will like you, I'm sure."

"And what if she doesn't?"

Gwen mimicked a large fish dramatically swallowing something with her hands.

"You're definitely *not* helping," I said.

We said goodbye to Gwen, who seemed disappointed about the news of Lance skipping out, but grateful that at least I would be coming. "I'll meet you at the front gate," she said to me as we waved goodbye.

As we headed to the boys' dorms, I felt like something was off with Lance. He seemed like he had a lot on his mind.

"Are you sure you don't want to come tonight?" I asked, trying to break up the silence.

"Yeah, I'm sure. I need to be ready for tomorrow. This is important to me. I have to do my best in the tournament."

"I understand," I said. "You have a big title to defend, being Defender of New Camelot and all."

"It's not about the title, or even winning," Lance said. "It's about becoming something greater. I have a lot to live up to with a title like mine, though."

I nodded, realizing what he meant. Nothing mattered to Lance more than becoming a true knight so we could step out of hiding and start making a difference in Between. I respected him even more for that.

"I think Gwen was disappointed you won't be coming."

"She understands."

"I don't know, I think she just wanted to see you in a bathing suit."

"WHAT?" Lance said. "No way. Gwen is like a little sister to me. Besides, I'm like four years older than you two."

"So, what?" I said, shrugging. "I don't think Gwen sees it that way."

"Has she ever told you she likes me?"

"Well, no. Not really. But I've seen the way she is around you. The way she looks at you and talks about you. In fact, if there is anyone Gwen talks about as much as she talks about herself, it is totally you."

"You're wrong," Lance said. "There's no way. She just looks up to me, that's all."

"All right. If that's what you want to tell yourself," I said, as we stepped into Room Three.

"What about you?" Lance asked. "Are you not excited to see any of the other girls?"

"What? Of course not," I said, embarrassed.

It's not that I wasn't attracted to any of the girls because I totally was. I just hadn't put that much thought into it. I figured someday I would date, but for now, I was okay with just being thirteen. Besides, not all that long ago in the Other Realm, I had been a total loser and could hardly get girls to notice me if I wanted them to. To be honest, even my emerging friendship with Gwen was foreign territory to me. I wasn't interested in her romantically, but I still felt nervous thinking about going to the pool party with her.

Lance must have picked up that I didn't want to talk about it anymore because he didn't push the topic any further. In fact, we didn't really talk much at all the rest of the evening. When the clock finally struck the new hour, I waved goodbye to Lance and headed down to the front of the castle to meet Gwen.

As I walked down the spiral staircase that led to our dorm tower, I saw the sun was just beginning to set behind the snowy mountains, making the snow sparkle with dazzling reds and oranges. Even the distant treetops marking the Enchanted Forest looked so much more inviting in the sunset. In fact, it was hard to think about stirring shadows, angry trolls, or any problems at all. The Magic Hollow was the most beautiful place I had ever seen. And it was my home now.

Despite my doubts earlier about being able to have a good time at the Hot Springs, now, I felt excited. Sure, I had been invited to Tiffany Peirce's party back in my old neighborhood in the Other Realm, but even that was nothing compared to tonight. For the first time in a long time, I didn't feel bothered by any of my worries because I was going to hang out with friends like any normal thirteen-year-old kid should.

# CHAPTER FOURTEEN
# AN APPARITION OF MIST

The entrance to the Crystal Cave was a large opening naturally cut out of the black lava rock. A thin, steep hallway led deep below the ground. Plumes of warm steam wafted along the ceiling of the tunnel, before expelling out the entrance and into the chilly winter night air.

The ground was slick from moisture, so Gwen held onto my shoulder to avoid slipping. I almost made a snarky comment and pushed her off me, but was in to good of a mood to mind.

As we got deeper into the cave, the air got warmer and wetter. It became humid enough that I wondered if it would be hard to keep a torch lit. Fortunately, the Hot Spring didn't need any light from fires because the same massive glowing crystals that littered the walls of the Crystal Chasm spouted out all over the walls and ceiling here too.

"Just wait until you feel the water," Gwen said. "It feels amazing. They say the water in this spring is magical because it comes from the very heart of the Lady of the Lake's dominion."

"So, basically you're saying we are partying in some old water-spirit-lady's living room?"

# CHAPTER FOURTEEN

"It's just a legend, weirdo," Gwen said. "Come on, hurry up!"

We could hear laughing and voices echoing ahead of us and when we rounded the corner, I saw the source of all the fun. The tunnel opened to an enormous cavern filled with bright crystal blue water. It was the purest, bluest, most beautiful water I had ever seen. The main pool itself looked larger than an Olympic-sized swimming pool back in the Other Realm. But I noticed there were dozens of smaller caves that connected to the main pool in almost every direction. For all I knew, the pool could be even bigger because one corner, where the ceiling got low, was completely hidden in heavy white steam.

That is when I noticed Henrietta for the first time. She was at least twenty-five feet long and looked kind of like drawings I had seen of the Loch Ness monster. Her body was blue and green, and she had big white eyes. Despite her gaping maw of shark-like teeth, she looked like she was smiling and having a blast playing in the water with a group of knights and squires, lifting them up into the air on her long tail and dropping them into the water.

Without showing any hesitation, Gwen ran and jumped into the water. She reemerged, smiling brightly as she pulled her hair back out of her face. "Come on, the water is great!"

I took one more glance at Henrietta, then swallowed my fears and went for it. As soon as I hit the water, I was immediately impressed by two things. First, she was right, the water was perfect and just warm enough; and second, I had no idea how deep this pool was. The water was super clear and blue, but I couldn't see the bottom. It looked like it just went on and on forever.

Gwen must have noticed me trying to look down into the water because she said, "It's at least one hundred feet deep in the center, but there are cracks down there that probably go even deeper. That's why the water is so warm."

Gwen turned into a breaststroke, swimming across the pool. I wasn't a great swimmer, so I more or less struggled to keep up with her, performing a special swimming technique I call the awkward fish. When we reached the other side, I realized we had swum to a group of knights playing on a small alcove on the wall that was perfect for diving and jumping from. There was Elibora, Cecily, Gale, Lucas, Cole, and the twin brothers Alex and Eric. I clung onto the wall to catch my breath, while everyone watched Alex and Eric getting ready to dive off the alcove. They walked up to the edge dramatically, stretching their limbs, then cracking their knuckles. Each in unison took a deep breath, balancing on the edge gracefully. Then, they screamed loudly and jumped clumsily off the edge in a hilarious mess that was anything but a graceful dive. They hit the water hard, sending a huge splash over all of us. Everyone laughed, then took their turn jumping off the edge.

"Let's try it," Gwen said to me, taking my hand and helping me out of the water.

Normally I probably would have been nervous about it, but right then, I was having so much fun I didn't even care. Even when we reached the ledge and I realized it was way higher than I thought, I didn't mind.

"Are you ready?" I asked Gwen.

She nodded her head nervously. "Don't make fun of me. I have to plug my nose!" She squeezed her nose closed tightly, then closed her eyes and jumped, screaming happily all the way down.

"Hey, wait for me!" I shouted, jumping off behind her, and executing what I thought was a pretty good cannonball.

I hit the warm water and sunk deep into it. I opened my eyes and realized I could see remarkably well. Ahead of me, toward the extra steamy corner of the pool, I thought I saw the Lady of the Lake herself, beckoning me to come toward her. I hadn't seen her since the time she warned me in the Other Realm, but I knew I couldn't easily forget her face. When I resurfaced, Gwen and everyone else were treading water or clinging onto the wall watching Elibora and Cecily getting ready to jump together.

I looked toward the corner where I thought I saw her. I couldn't see anyone there, but I felt like I needed to go and check. She had appeared to me before and given me helpful advice. To be honest, I don't know if I would have been as mentally prepared to accept everything I learned about my parents if it weren't for the mysterious appearance of the Lady of the Lake, even if it had been a little terrifying. Nobody was paying attention to me, so I quietly swam off, quickly disappearing into the heavy steam.

Not far in, I couldn't see even ten feet in front or behind me. It was a little eerie, as the noise from the previous cavern dulled out and then disappeared. I was alone, treading water, and hoping I was going the right direction, also thinking that this would be the perfect place for the sea monster to gobble me up.

"Hello? Lady of the Lake?" I called. "It's me, Hayden Keyes."

Suddenly, I felt my feet touch the smooth stone beneath me. I swam forward a few feet more and realized I could now touch the bottom of the pool. I stood up and inched forward. I came to a large patch of crystals that glowed brilliantly below the water, and then I noticed her. The Lady of the Lake was standing on the water in the center of the bright blue crystals. She looked exactly as I remembered seeing her, except she was a lot taller than I remembered. But maybe that's just because I first saw her in my water bottle, I'm not sure.

"Welcome to the heart of my domain, hero," she said softly. "I am the Lady of the Lake. If you are listening to this apparition, then you must have made it safely to Between, and the mission I sent Captain Jack on was a success."

There was something strange, I realized. She had said 'if you are listening to this apparition.' I stepped closer to her and waved my hands above my head. She showed no signs of noticing anything out of the ordinary. I got the feeling that this wasn't the real Lady of the Lake. She seemed like a hologram or projection, but I knew that neither of those were the right term because there wasn't exactly electricity in Between. But was it a spell? An apparition intended to pass along a message to me?

Or was it intended for the hero William Keyes instead? Jack had said they came hoping to find my dad, Sir William. Instead, they got me. His goofy, clumsy, son.

"I apologize I cannot be here to speak to you in person," the fake Lady said. "My powers have grown so weak; I have fallen into a deep sleep. With what little strength I could muster, I cast these waterspeak messages to contact you. Projecting a message to the Other Realm was not easy, and it used much of my feeble power. I was once strong and mighty, holding many dominions across the realm. But alas, this is my last. If my power fails, the protective barriers around the Magic Hollow will fail as well. This wonderful refuge would be completely exposed. So, I sleep, preserving what little power is left, hoping that we can weather the storm and survive."

I couldn't believe what I was hearing. From the sounds of it, everyone could be in far more danger than we realized. But why were her powers failing?

"The powers of darkness are growing," she continued. "Though they have yet to emerge from hiding, I have felt their presence, choking at mine. Without the sacred sword Excalibur awakened from the stone, I haven't the power to hold back the darkness that is choking our wonderful home."

# CHAPTER FOURTEEN

"What can I do? How can I help you?" I asked, knowing that it wasn't for any good because this apparition couldn't see, hear, or respond to me.

"You must unite the knights, hero. Unite the Knights of the Round Table and lead them into the light. I don't have the power to aid you in the coming fight. You must find the strength within yourself to accomplish the impossible task. I fear a great trial is coming for all of you. I have foreseen it in the water. There is a traitor in our midst, who seeks to claim an ancient right as their own."

"I don't understand," I said, but I knew it was useless.

"Unite the knights, hero, and lead them into the light," she said, as her image started to fade into the mist.

"You have the wrong person," I said. "I'm not my father! I'm not William Keyes. I'm not Lance!"

"Lead them into the light," she said, before vanishing completely into the heavy air.

I swam back the way I came, with everything that had just transpired weighing me down like a hundred extra pounds. It was a wonder that I didn't sink straight to the bottom of the pool with how heavy my head felt. I was convinced that she had the wrong person. I was not my father, who those messages must have been intended for. But she was already asleep. She wouldn't have known that it wasn't William Keyes waiting on the other side of the Other Realm. It was his kid son.

The only glimmer of hope that kept me from falling into total despair right then, was the thought that my father had left a medallion for me. The Knights, and even the Lady of the Lake, may have thought they were going to find my dad, but he alone had known the truth. He knew that in their time of need he wouldn't be there and prepared a way for his son to be there instead. My father had faith in me, long before I ever grew up.

Before, I convinced myself that my dad wanted me to find him, but now I wondered if there was more to his plan. Could he have known that someday the darkness would recoup, and the Knights would need another hero? Did he intend that hero to be me?

That thought felt warm in my heart and chased away all the doubt I had been feeling moments before. This was my home. It was where I belonged. Right then, I felt like becoming a knight truly was my destiny. It was what my father had always intended for me.

I knew I was swimming the right way when I could hear the muffled sounds of the knights and squires again. As I exited the heavy fog, I realized that the sounds I was hearing weren't the same sounds of joy I had heard when I left them. Instead, I heard a lot of angry shouting.

First, I noticed Gwen and Elibora, who were practically at each other's throats, shouting angrily. Then, I noticed Isabelle and Percy, who apparently had decided to show up after all, yelling at each other in a similar manner. Their voices were mixing and echoing making it hard to hear what anyone was saying.

I swam as quickly as I could to Gwen and Elibora. The voice of the Lady of the Lake repeating in my mind. Unite the knights and lead them into the light. I was quickly realizing that would be much harder than it sounded.

"Gwen, what's going on," I said, but she ignored me.

"Why do you have to be so cruel?" she shouted at Elibora. "If you don't want to be my friend anymore, you could just say it. You don't have to ignore me all the time!"

"You think I'm ignoring you? That is just like you, Gwen! Only thinking about yourself. You have no idea what I've been going through!"

I gently grabbed Gwen by the shoulders, but she pushed me away. "Let it go, Hayden. I want to go to bed," she said through her tears.

I looked apologetically at Cecily, while she consoled Elibora, who was just as upset as Gwen. I wrapped Gwen in a towel, and then helped her back up the cave.

On my way out, I noticed that Lucas and Gale had teamed up to get Isabelle and Percy's fight under control. Lucas had Isabelle in a tight grip, and was struggling to keep her from breaking loose, while Gale practically dragged Percy by the arm.

"That is the last time you insult my family," Percy growled. "Just you wait until tomorrow. We can settle this once and for all in the ring!"

"Bring it on, pretty boy!" Isabelle retorted, breaking free from Lucas's grasp. "I'll be ready for you." She stomped out of the cave, bumping my shoulder as she left.

"I can walk myself out, thanks," Percy said coldly as he yanked his arm free from Gale and stormed out of the cave.

I sprinted up the cavern exit, trying to catch up with Gwen. "What happened back there?" I asked.

Gwen looked like she was going to tell me to go away, but then her gaze softened as her shoulders fell into a slouch. "I—I don't know. I shouldn't have gotten so upset. I just—I hoped things would go back to normal tonight. We used to be best friends, and now she acts like I don't even exist. It just . . . hurts."

"I don't think she does it on purpose," I said.

"I don't care if she wants to be friends with Cecily . . . but why does that mean she can't be friends with me anymore? Just because I don't get along with her friend . . . doesn't mean she can't find time to hang out with me, right?"

"I—I don't know," I said. "It shouldn't. . ." I wasn't about to claim that I understood the inner mechanisms that are the female teenager, but seeing

Gwen so sad hurt, too. I didn't know how to make her feel better.

"I think Elibora will come around, just give her time," I said.

"Easier said than done. Don't get me wrong, I like hanging out with you and Lance, but no offense . . . you both are boys."

"What does that mean?" I said, laughing.

"Exactly what it sounds like. Sometimes a girl just needs a girl friend. You know because girly reasons."

"I don't know anything about girly reasons," I said solemnly. "So, I get your point."

Gwen laughed, and leaned up against my shoulder, wiping her tears. "Hayden, thank you. I'm glad I found you in that alley."

"You make it sound like I was a stray dog."

"Not that far from the truth," Gwen said. I was happy to see her smiling again. I know how much her friendship with Elibora meant to her, so I genuinely hoped they would figure it out.

"This is just a hunch," I said carefully, not wanting to reveal too much about my source, "but I feel like with everything happening outside—the trouble with Mr. Bianco, Jack, and Hal—that it is more important than ever that we find a way to unite everyone."

Gwen sighed. "We have always sat at the same round table, but that doesn't mean that we shared the same opinions or ideas. We're always fighting amongst each other over something. That's just how it is."

"King Arthur made the table round for a reason, though," I said. "I think he wanted everyone to sit together, and for no one to be at the head of the table. I think that's because King Arthur valued everyone's opinion, and he knew that one king giving all the orders couldn't be as smart as an entire room thinking together."

"Easier said than done. Trust me. We should talk to Lance about it after the tournament. He will know what to do."

"Yeah, Lance—of course," I said, feeling a little embarrassed. I was just a squire after all. Why on earth would the Lady of the Lake entrust me of all people with such an important task. "That's a good plan. Well, good luck tomorrow. In the tournament."

"You too. Don't let this exhibition stress you out. You'll do fine, I promise. Just remember everything Lance taught you," she said with a wink. "And Hayden, thanks for being there for me tonight. Goodnight."

Gwen kissed my cheek and then departed for the girls' dorms. I touched my cheek where she kissed me, then shouted after her, "Ew! Gross. Never do that again."

"Whatever, you liked it," she teased as she departed up the stairs.

I was about to turn for the quickest direction back to the boys' dorms when I noticed something in the corner of my eye. A shadowy figure slipped out of the Forest, then leaped across the stepping stones traversing the river.

Immediately, I was reminded of the words of the Lady of the Lake. There is a traitor in our midst, who seeks to claim an ancient right as their own. Right then, I was positive I knew who the traitor was. There was only one person who was grateful for Hal's absence, and loved to be in power: Baron.

Knowing I had to be sure, I slipped into the dark, chasing after the shadowy figure. For a minute, I thought I had lost him, but then I spotted him. Sure enough, Baron was just around a corner of the castle, briskly walking the grounds, looking very suspicious. It must have been him, sneaking around in the forest.

Thinking of the warning I had just heard, I wondered what ancient right he could be trying to steal. Was it the sword Excalibur? That seemed like the only reasonable answer, but I didn't see how anyone could steal that sword while it was safely trapped in the stone.

Maybe he wanted the right to rule the Magic Hollow. He had shown a certain flare for leadership and was all too excited to find out Principal Hal was gone. Would that qualify as an ancient right? The more I thought about it, the more I felt like I was in over my head.

I hid behind a bush as Baron passed, knowing it would be far too dangerous to confront him alone. Besides, I didn't have any real proof, only the tip I had received from the Lady of the Lake's apparition. If I was going to reveal Baron's plan, I would have to gather more evidence first.

When I had waited long enough, I slipped out of my hiding place, and headed toward the boys' dorms, a dozen thoughts sprinting through my mind the entire way.

# CHAPTER FIFTEEN
# THE TOURNAMENT

The morning of the tournament, I didn't need Goliath to pounce on my bed to wake me up. After everything that happened the night before, seeing the Lady of the Lake in Crystal Cave, and then spying on Baron, I could barely sleep. I spent most of the night tossing and turning in my bed, dreaming of Baron trying to take over the Magic Hollow. It only took the first light of day cracking through our window to stir me from my miserable dreams.

I realized, in all the excitement of last night, I hadn't even looked at the posted tournament bracket. I slipped out of bed, got dressed, and then hurried to the common area to see how the day would be going.

It was a chilly morning, but thankfully there were still a few burning ashes in the fireplace from last night, and it wasn't hard to get it stoked again.

With the warmth of the flames behind me, I turned my attention to the large parchment poster which had been tacked to the wall the night before.

There would be two events today. The Sword was planned first, followed by the Joust. There were two separate brackets posted on it. It looked like the Sword was scheduled first. I couldn't help but sigh in relief when I saw that. At least I had some time before the big joust with Isabelle. The matches were paired up like this:

## The Sword
**Elibora versus Gale.**
**Gwen versus Tristan.**
**Haylinelle versus Lucas.**
**Percy versus Lance.**

## Exhibition:
**Cole versus Cecily.**

## The Joust
**Isabelle versus Gale.**
**Percy versus Alex.**
**Eric versus Brandon.**
**Haylinelle versus Cassandra.**

## Exhibition:
**Hayden versus Isabelle.**

I realized that I recognized almost everyone who was competing, except for a couple names. I was as excited as everyone else for today, but part of me wished that this time around I could just be a spectator instead. Sparring with practice swords was one thing, but jousting Isabelle? What was I thinking?

I breathed deeply, willing myself to stay calm. I knew I had to focus.

Lance had taught me well, and my practice over the last week had gone smoothly. Lance believed I had a chance, so why shouldn't I? Besides, what better chance did I have to prove to everyone that I could be as good as my father than this? So, what if I wasn't the hero they had expected? My dad had enough faith in me to leave me the enchanted medallion. I just needed to have faith in myself. I was his son, so I could be like him.

Thankfully, I didn't have to worry about my match until later this afternoon. For the time being, I could just enjoy the tournament as much as everybody else. By the looks of the bracket, there would be some exciting matches today. I had only seen Gale duel a few times during our practice, and I had never seen Elibora wield a sword. She spent most of her time practicing with a bow and arrow in the archery range outside the arena, lamenting the fact that she couldn't go hunting for real in the Enchanted Forest. I knew Gwen was very skilled herself, but I had never seen Tristan duel either. Not to mention Percy, who would be facing Lance. I was certain that would be the pairing of the day. I was confident that Lance could win because he would probably win the whole tournament, but still, how good was Percy? Judging by the pompous way he walked around all the time, he seemed to think highly of himself.

Eventually Lance and Gwen met me in the commons area, and we went down to the dining hall for some breakfast. Gwen seemed like her normal chipper, prideful self. I was happy because last night had been tough for her. Lance on the other hand seemed off. We both asked him if everything was okay, but he just brushed us off saying it was pre-tournament nerves. I'll be honest, that seemed fishy to me because Lance was the last person I ever expected to get pre-tournament nerves, but I didn't press him anymore.

I wondered if I should tell Lance and Gwen about what I had seen down in the Hot Springs, and then out on the grounds when I saw Baron slipping from the forest, but I just didn't know how to tell them. There was no real way to reveal to them what I knew, without also divulging the fact that an apparition of the Lady of the Lake had appeared to me and given me the specific warning she had. Right now, the most important thing for all of us was to do well in the tournament. I decided that when all the competition was over, I would tell them everything.

When Baron walked into the room, I saw he had dark circles under his eyes, looking more miserable than ever. Now I knew why he looked so exhausted. It must be hard to sleep after staying up late into the night planning the overthrow of the Magic Hollow. I wondered if he even felt guilty for conspiring to betray Principal Hal. That's when I had the horrible realization that Baron might be working with the trolls. That would explain the letter he had been writing and tried to hide from my sight that first day I met with him for a history lesson. It made too much sense.

Lance said it seemed like the trolls knew exactly where they were going to be when they opened the portal to send Jack to the Other Realm. What if that was because Baron had tipped them off on where to go? If Baron were going to claim the right to rule the Magic Hollow, he would need Principal Hal out of the way, which made the trolls all too convenient because they had succeeded in occupying Hal for quite some time now, apparently. But how much longer would it take for Hal to find Jack and Mr. Bianco and rescue them? Principal Hal could be back any day now, and Baron's plan would be foiled. Unless he was planning to make his move soon?

"Hello? Hayden?" Gwen said, snapping me back to reality. "I asked you if you were ready to head down to the Arena."

"Oh, yeah, of course," I said, watching Baron out of the corner of my eye.

We made our way down to the Arena as the sun finally peaked over the Snowy Mountains, blanketing the Hollow in a warm yellow light. The Arena looked even more splendid today, decorated with tons of shiny purple banners all bearing the emblem of the Magic Hollow. Tons of knights, squires, soldiers, and villagers from Caerleon were pouring into the stands in droves, all chatting loudly and excitedly about the events that were about to unfold.

"Are you two ready for your events?" I asked Lance and Gwen.

Lance nodded, and Gwen said enthusiastically, "I'm going to make Tristan pay for giving you such a hard time about Siege Perilous." Then, she turned to Lance, "We are enemies for the next few hours. I better see you in the finals."

This seemed to be enough to stir Lance out of his weird daze because he smiled and clasped Gwen's hand. "You're on. But don't expect me to go easy on you because you're my friend."

"In your dreams!"

We parted ways, and I found a place to sit in the stands next to Alex, Eric, and a couple of their friends I didn't recognize. They were in the middle of an intense conversation when I sat down.

"You should have seen Percy last night when he found out."

"He was furious."

"What happened?" I asked.

"Isabelle dropped out of the Sword. Said she wanted to save all her energy for the Joust. But everyone knows that the Sword is Percy's strongest event. See, even though Percy challenged her to duel in the tournament, he never specified which event. So now, his only choice is to joust her or risk looking like a coward."

"It's true. You never back out of an event after you have challenged someone. Never."

"It's a shame," I said. "I was hoping Percy would put her in the infirmary before I have to joust her in the Exhibition."

"You poor fool," Alex and Eric said in unison.

"And what about you two. You're on the bracket to joust as well. One of you just might end up jousting Isabelle as well."

"There's a passing fair chance that might happen," one of them said. "But first, Eric has to beat our brother Brandon. And Alex has to beat Percy."

"Your brother?" I vaguely remembered the day I first met Alex and Eric. They had mentioned that they were triplets, but while they were identical, their third brother looked nothing like them. "Do you get along with Brandon?" I asked.

They both laughed obnoxiously loud. "No. Not at all. He hates us. And rightfully so. We don't really like him either."

"I'm sorry," I said.

"It's fine," one of them said.

"We've got each other," the other said.

"And now we'll have the honor of knocking him out in the first round of the tournament. It's like Christmas came early!"

"Deck the halls," the other said.

Just then a loud trumpet played, echoing through the Arena. Everyone stood and cheered as the Sword combatants stepped out into the Arena. I scanned the crowd until I found Baron sitting across the Arena from me. I made a mental note of where he was sitting, so that I could try and always keep an eye on him.

An announcer presented each combatant as they stepped forward and bowed. I noticed Gwen speaking softly to Elibora, and they both smiled. If anything came from this, I hoped that Gwen had finally gained her best friend back.

# CHAPTER FIFTEEN

When all the formalities were done, it was announced that Elibora and Gale would be fighting in the first match of the day. Everyone cleared off the Arena floor, except for Lucas who would be acting as the Knight Marshal. He stood by a simple wooden contraption that held six flags, three blue and three red. The rules were simple. For each successful strike a combatant made, a flag would be raised. First two three strikes would be the winner. Each combatant was given a colored cloth to tie to their armor corresponding to their color of flags, either red or blue. Elibora received the blue flags, and Gale the red.

"Ready?" Lucas bellowed. "Fight!"

It started faster than I was ready for. The moment Lucas had called for them to begin, Elibora was already rushing in at Gale, a double-handed sword in tow. They met in a brilliant clash of steel on steel. It was a fantastic match that lasted about fifteen minutes total. It ended three-to-two in favor of Elibora, who managed to score the final point with an expertly executed strike at Gale's leg, followed up with a finishing blow to his chest plate. Elibora was huffing audibly as Lucas raised her arm in the air and pronounced her winner. She gave Gale a tight hug, their armor clanking loudly, and he thanked her for such a good match.

I could hear a couple young squire girls crying behind us. "I can't believe Gale lost!"

The next match was between Gwen and Tristan. Even in her armor, Gwen looked tiny compared to Tristan, who was tall and skinny. Gwen held a single-handed sword, while Tristan sported a massive claymore. Despite Gwen's silver armor, I still feared for her life. One hit from Tristan's Claymore, which was practically as long as he was tall, and I was sure she would go flying.

The match began, and the two of them circled the Arena in defensive postures. The crowd cheered wildly, urging them to begin. Gwen was patient, circling around her opponent. I knew in her mind she was formulating a plan, waiting for the perfect chance to execute. Tristan didn't seem as disciplined. He dropped his guard for a moment, looking up at the crowd.

"You want to see some action?" he yelled. "I'll show you some action!"

He dropped his shoulder and charged straight for Gwen like an angry boar. She parried his strike and slid through the sand almost a foot from the impact of it, but she never once faltered or dropped her guard. Tristan may have had strength and reach on his side, but Gwen was fast. Just like that first day when I had watched her knock out two Cerise guards, she assaulted Tristan with a speedy barrage of attacks. Tristan's sword was so large, he was forced to retreat backwards quickly, doing all he could to throw his massive sword in the way of Gwen's attacks.

I couldn't believe it. Gwen was going to win. She managed to score a point striking Tristan in the back, and then after carefully waiting for the right chance, she scored a second point knocking him in the chest. Tristan yelled in defiance, then rushed Gwen with even more ferocity than before. He swung his massive sword over his head, using the momentum to strike again and again. Finally, he struck Gwen with so much force that her sword flew from her hand. He followed up with a bone crunching strike that sent Gwen rolling backwards across the sand. Everyone held their breath as Gwen came to a stop on her back. I stood up, ready to rush down if I had to. I was afraid for her. Tristan had hit her hard.

But then, Gwen stood up, her breath heaving. She drew a long knife from her belt and held it up in a defensive posture, a little blood trickling from her nose, but otherwise looking okay.

"You should have stayed down and yielded while you had the chance," Tristan yelled, charging in for another attack.

# CHAPTER FIFTEEN

He swung his sword madly, and Gwen ducked it entirely. She rolled under his guard, then leapt up, wrapping her leg around Tristan's and using his own momentum to topple him to the ground, even though he was easily twice her size. Tristan crashed down into the sand with a thud. When the dust cleared, Tristan was pinned down, his arm wrapped painfully behind his back, Gwen's dagger inches from his face. She tapped her dagger loudly on Tristan's helmet and said, "That's three."

Everyone was quiet, trying to take in what had just happened. Lucas threw up the third flag and shouted, "Gwen is the winner!" and then the crowd exploded with cheers. Gwen offered to help Tristan up, but he refused, storming out of the Arena.

I ran down to the Arena floor and threw my arms around Gwen. "I can't believe it, you did amazing!"

"What? Did you doubt me?" Gwen asked. "I knew I could win all along."

"In the next match, Lady Kaylinelle will fight Sir Lucas!" the announcer called.

Lucas unclipped his Knight Marshall's cape, and handed it to Lance, who would act as officiator during Lucas's fight.

Kaylinelle stepped forward wearing brilliant gold armor. She held a single-handed sword in one hand, and a small shield in the other. Lucas, donning silver armor, chose to fight with a halberd, a special type of spear with an ax-like blade that turned into a long point.

The match began, and Lucas was first to attack. Because of the length of the spear, he was able to attack with ease, jabbing and poking at Kaylinelle's defenses. She would block with her shield, or parry with her sword, but Lucas was such an expert with the halberd, he had a follow up move for every one of Kaylinelle's defenses. Within the first few minutes, Lucas had already scored one strike.

# THE TOURNAMENT

Kaylinelle blocked the halberd with her sword, then spun close enough to knock Lucas off-guard with her shield. It wasn't enough to score her a point, but it knocked Lucas off balance. She swung her sword around and struck Lucas square in the chest.

"One-to-one!" Lance yelled, lifting the flag to reflect Kaylinelle's successful point, as the crowd clapped and cheered.

"You go girl!" Lady Albreda shouted from the sidelines. "Knock him where it counts!"

Kaylinelle charged in confidently, striking down, up, across. Lucas secured his footing and blocked each attack with his halberd. Retreating to a safe distance, he was able to get back on the offense thrusting the spear. He knocked her sword aside, twisted the spear then thrust, catching Kaylinelle's armor in the chest.

The crowd gasped as Kaylinelle fell to the ground, clutching her gut. The wind had been knocked right out of her, leaving her gasping for air. Lucas, being such a gentleman, lowered his weapon and ran to her side.

"I'm so sorry Kay—I didn't mean to get you so hard!"

"Come on! Finish the match!" Someone shouted from the crowd.

"Oh, shut your mouth! The lad is showing some respect to a lady," Lady Albreda shouted, scolding the squire. "Like any chivalrous knight should! Hmph!"

"It's okay," Kaylinelle muttered. "Finish me off. You earned it."

"I can't do that," Lucas said. "It's not fair to strike you while you're down."

"Always such a gentleman," Kaylinelle said. "But I won't yield!" She spun, tripping Lucas with a spinning kick, then leaped to her feet, scooping up her sword on the way. She brought it down with a thud, ringing off Lucas's armor. Lucas grunted loudly as he rolled out of the way of her next strike.

Lance flipped another flag for Kaylinelle, making the score two-to-two.

Lucas picked up his spear. "Good. At least we're on a fair plane again."

"Spoken like a true Knight Marshall," Kaylinelle said, as she charged in for another series of strikes. Lucas was quick on his feet and thwarted her attack. He retaliated with a flash of jabs and strikes of his own, twisting the halberd in the air, and using the hooked side to catch the hilt of Kaylinelle's sword. One strong tug was enough to dislodge it from her grasp. A flick of his wrist, and the spear knocked her shield out of the way. He followed up with a swift strike at her chest plate, scoring the final point.

Lance raised the third and final flag to much cheers. I noticed Lady Albreda and some of the girls in the crowd frowning disappointedly. Kaylinelle had fought fiercely and bravely. It had been such a close match though; it could have been anyone's victory.

Lucas and Kaylinelle shook hands respectfully, then each bowed to the crowd. Lance gave Lucas back his place as Knight Marshall while the announcer proclaimed the final match of the round: Lance versus Percy. This got everyone especially excited.

Lance grabbed his sword and stepped out into the center of the Arena, looking calm but focused.

Percy stepped forward, drew his sword and dropped to one knee, shoving the sword into the sand. "I yield this match to Sir Lance."

Everyone went quiet. I heard a few murmurs across the crowd. "What did he say?" and "He's not going to fight?"

"Please don't hold this against my honor. I entered the Sword with one intention, and that was avenging my family's honor against Isabelle who spoke evil of me and my own. Seeing as she withdrew herself from the tournament, I am honor-bound to conserve all my energy for the joust where I intend to face her and win."

Lucas stepped forward. "As Knight Marshall and officiator of this tournament, I accept your withdrawal and wish you the best of luck later today during the joust. Arise with honor, Percy."

Everyone clapped respectively as Percy rose, then bowed to the crowd. That was just like him, I thought, yielding from a match and still finding a way to be so suave about it.

"That makes Lance the winner by default," Lucas said. He will move on to the next round! Lady Elibora shall face Lady Gwen, and Lance shall face myself. After a short recess, the matches will begin immediately."

I left my seat and went down to Lance and Gwen who were chatting down below. "Well, looks like you made it through," I said to Lance. "Shame, though. I wanted to watch you pummel Percy."

"He would have been a strong opponent," Lance said. "But I understand why he yielded. Isabelle is decent at the sword, but she is legendary at the joust. Percy will need all his energy to beat her."

"And what about you, Gwen. Are you ready to duel Elibora? This isn't going to put a greater strain on your friendship, is it?"

Gwen looked just as concerned as I was. "I don't know. I mean, we said everything was okay this morning. But who knows what will happen when we are staring each other down with weapons in hand?"

"Remember, it's just a game," Lance said. "Don't take what happens in the ring personally."

"Oh, I won't." Gwen said. "Friend or not, I'm going to give her everything I've got. And you better beat Lucas, too, Lance. I've got a date with you in the finals."

"Oh really. I always thought when I courted a girl it would be to do something nice, like walk through the gardens and pick flowers. Not hack at each other with swords."

Gwen blushed when Lance said the words "courted a girl."

# CHAPTER FIFTEEN

"Eh, I've never been into that kind of stuff. Swords sound good to me." She smiled and looked a great deal happier after Lance's comment, though.

I remembered what Lance had said the night before about Gwen being like a sister to him. I hoped she wouldn't get her hopes up too high based on his offhanded joke. Gwen and Lance went to their own seats on the sidelines, and I returned to my seat in the stands.

Elibora stepped back into the ring, stretching and jogging in place. Gwen took a deep breath, drew her sword and then stepped out as well. "Are both contestants ready?" Lucas shouted. They both nodded. "Then let the semi-finals begin!"

Gwen and Elibora both rushed each other at the same time, meeting in the center of the Arena, their swords clashing loudly. Elibora was surprisingly quick for wielding a double-handed sword, and its size clearly held some advantage over Gwen's one-handed blade. But Gwen was even quicker, and she always used the momentum of Elibora's attacks to her advantage. What Gwen lacked in size and strength, she made up for with agility and impeccable footwork. She had perfect form, sliding and stepping and dodging after every strike.

"What's wrong, Eli? Is that all you can do?" Gwen asked, neatly dodging a strike, then spinning around to right herself in a solid defensive stance.

"You're the same little squirrel as always," Elibora said. "But you can't dodge me forever!"

Maybe Gwen could. The match went on for several minutes, and still neither had scored even one point. "Come on, Gwen, come on!" I said to myself, through gritted teeth. As much as I genuinely liked Elibora, I wanted to see Gwen win, even though I knew I would never hear the end of it if she did.

And then, just like that, Gwen scored a point, having spun gracefully around Elibora's defenses and striking her in the back. Lucas raised the first flag in favor of Gwen as the crowd cheered.

"You've got this, Eli!" Cecily shouted from the sidelines, looking even more determined than Elibora was.

Elibora recomposed herself, then charged again. She swung her sword expertly, knocking down Gwen's defense, then swinging in for a strike. Gwen dodged it, barely, but was caught off balance, and could do nothing to stop the follow up strike that clanged off the armor protecting her side.

A second flag was thrown up, this time, in favor Elibora.

Gwen, who looked seriously hurt from the strike, struggled to regain her composure as Elibora struck her a second time across the front of her chest plate. Lucas raised Elibora's second flag, as Elibora continued her relentless onslaught. If Gwen didn't get up fast, she was going to lose.

"You should have known you couldn't beat me," Elibora said.

Elibora grasped her sword in two hands high above her head, then brought it down on Gwen, who rolled just in time, barely avoiding the blade. My fists were clenched so tight I couldn't believe it. Come on, Gwen, get up!

Elibora struck again, but Gwen parried it. With all her strength, she threw off Elibora's sword, then lunged at her, tackling her to the ground. Elibora dropped her sword as Gwen struck her across the helmet with a gauntleted hand. "That is for being such a jerk to me lately!" she shouted.

"Does that count?" Lance asked Lucas, who shrugged, looking nervously puzzled.

Gwen stood up then tossed Elibora her sword. "Now that's out of the way, we can finish the match."

They rushed in at each other with a flurry of blows, striking and block-ing. But Gwen fought with a new determination she hadn't shown before.

It didn't take long before she had scored another point, making it two-to-two. And then, just like that, Elibora fumbled, Gwen knocked her sword out of her hands, and followed with a quick strike to her side, scoring the third and final point. Gwen dropped her sword, beaming with excitement, She bowed to the crowd of onlookers.

Elibora fell to her knees. "I—I can't believe I lost."

Gwen took off her helmet and reached out a hand to help Elibora up, but Elibora shoved her hand away. "Thanks for the match," she said coldly, brushing past Gwen as she retreated to the stands to sit by Cecily.

I sighed disappointedly. Just when I thought everything was going to be better between them again. For Gwen's sake, I hoped they figured things out soon because I didn't want to be there when they started dueling in the halls of New Camelot instead of the regulated tournament field. I couldn't help but think of the Lady of the Lake's admonition and her call for a hero to unite the Knights of the Round Table. Part of uniting them would be figuring out how to clear up squabbles like the one between Gwen and Elibora. I couldn't help but notice that sword fighting over it was hardly the way to make friends out of enemies.

Lance and Lucas took the field, and the final match of the semi-finals began. Lucas fought with the same strategy, keeping a distance, and jabbing with the point of the halberd. Unlike Kaylinelle, Lance seemed more experienced in facing down spears. I had watched Lance spar hundreds of times, but this was something new. He was inspiring to watch. While some people let the fear or nerves of competition get to them, it seemed to fuel Lance and make him even stronger. He was simply too strong, too fast, and too precise for Lucas to break through with his spear. The match was over in minutes. Lance one three-to-one.

Lucas fell back onto his backside after the final point was earned, breathing heavily. All he could do was laugh. "And I thought I actually had a chance."

Lance helped him up to his feet, and they clasped each together around the side. "You fought well," Lance said respectively.

Lucas turned to the crowd, reassuming his role as Knight Marshal. "Lance is the winner! He will face Lady Gwen in the finals!"

The crowd stood, cheering loudly. It had been an exciting tournament, and I was sure it would be an even more exciting final round between Lance and Gwen. As they prepared for their match down below, I noticed Baron stand up and make his way to the exit of the Arena. Where was he going?

I stood up and quietly made my way out the exit after him. As I slipped out of the Arena, I looked back hesitantly. I didn't want to miss the final match between my two best friends, but I had to do this. I needed to know for sure if Baron really was the traitor in our midst as the Lady of the Lake had warned. Hiding out of sight, I watched Baron look over his shoulder and then run across the river, disappearing into the forest, confirming all my suspicions.

Baron was the traitor, and I had to stop him.

# THE JOUST

I nearly fell into the Serpentine River, trying to hop across the stones as quickly as I could. I sprinted into the forest, scanning through the trees hoping to catch sight of Baron. I was worried I lost him, when I finally caught a glimpse of him. As stealthily as I could, I followed him deep into the forest.

I kept wondering all the way about what Baron was planning, and why he kept returning to the Enchanted Forest, knowing that the Centaurs wouldn't be pleased if they caught him again.

Stomping hooves in the distance made my heart freeze, and Baron's too, by the looks of it. He dropped to the ground, and I lost sight of him completely. I crouched down, trying to stay hidden, but not wanting to lose sight of Baron. The sound of hooves past, and I waited with bated breath, hoping that he hadn't crawled out of sight while we were hiding.

Just when I was losing hope, I saw Baron's ugly head pop up into sight over some bushes. I took off quickly, closing the distance between us. Baron led me deeper into the Forest than I had ever gone before. I couldn't remember the exact way Lance and Gwen had taken me before, but I felt like we hadn't gone this far in.

# THE JOUST

Baron stopped and extracted a piece of paper from his pocket. When he unfolded it, I realized it was the hand drawn map I had seen in his office. He traced the map with his finger, stewing over it for a moment. Then he folded it back up, stuffed it back into his pocket, and continued hiking.

Several minutes later, we reached an extremely dense patch of woods, littered with massive rocks that looked to be as ancient as the forest around them. Heavy roots entangled the rocks, and some trees even grew straight out of the top of them. Wherever we were, it wasn't the magical spring where Excalibur lay.

Baron sneaked up to the large rocks and whispered something that I couldn't hear. I thought I heard someone whisper back, but I was too far away to be sure. Carefully, I made my way through the trees, being sure not to step on any twigs. I stopped when I was close enough to be able to hear what Baron was saying.

No matter how hard I tried, I couldn't see who he was speaking to, though because they were concealed behind the rocks, and Baron seemed to only be conversing with the person through a crack in between two rocks.

"The curse struck me again last night," Baron said. "Worse than ever before." He lifted his pant leg, showed something on his shin toward the gape in the rock. I caught a glimpse of something brown and rough growing on his skin.

"There has to be a way you can control it," the voice replied.

"I know . . . I know," Baron said. "I won't give up."

"And I will never give up on us," the voice said. "After everything we have been through, we deserve this."

"We deserve it more than anything," Baron said. "I will find a way to control it."

"I trust you," the voice replied.

# CHAPTER SIXTEEN

"We need to go through with the plan. Tomorrow night," Baron said.

"Really? Do you think we are ready?"

"Yes. Of course, I do. After all our planning and preparation, I know we can do it. If it won't be given to us, then we have to steal what is ours."

"Just tell me where to be, and I will be there."

I couldn't believe my ears. Baron was planning something after all. And he wasn't alone either. He had an accomplice. This was bad, and I had to warn the others. There was still time for us to intervene. We had to act soon, and I was the only one who knew the truth.

I shifted my weight, trying to get a better view of the rocks, hoping I could catch even a glimpse of Baron's accomplice. A twig snapped loudly under my shifting weight.

"Shh!" Baron hissed, ducking down and looking around frantically.

I held my breath and stayed low, counting my heart beats. Finally, Baron relaxed, and looked away. He whispered something through the rocks too quietly for me to hear, then turned, and ran away.

I leaped from my hiding spot and hurried after him. When we escaped the forest, I watched Baron cross the river, then head back toward the Arena. I followed him but ran around the Arena to the opposite entrance instead.

I stepped into the Arena and saw dozens of heads turn to look at me. Isabelle was sitting on horseback, fully armored and carrying a lance, prancing about impatiently. Lance grabbed my arm.

"Hayden—where in the two realms have you been? Everyone is waiting for you. The exhibition was supposed to begin ten minutes ago. Isabelle thought you chickened out!" He started strapping my armor onto me.

"No, wait—you don't understand," I said. "We can't do the joust. We have to stop the tournament. We have to stop the tournament!"

"What did he say?" Tristan shouted from the crowd. "Stop the tournament?"

"Hayden, what are you talking about?" Lance asked, continuing to tighten the chest plate onto me. "Showing up late like this doesn't look good for you! I did what I could to stall for you."

"We are all in danger. Baron is planning to take over the Magic Hollow—tomorrow! The Lady of the Lake warned me about it last night—and just now—I followed Baron into the forest—I heard him talking about it myself!"

"What?" Baron hissed. "What are you talking about, you foolish boy? That is the most imaginative lie I have ever heard!"

Isabelle rode up on her tall black stallion. "The Lady of the Lake warned you about something last night? The Lady hasn't appeared to anyone in over thirteen years."

"You have to believe me," I said. "We can't do this joust. We need to take Baron into custody immediately. He's planning something horrible. I know it!"

Lance looked me over with thin eyes. "Lucas, please take Baron into custody."

"What? You can't be serious. You believe this nonsense?" Baron yelled. "This is utter madness."

"Take him into custody until we can reasonably question him as to ascertain the truth or falsehood of Hayden's claims."

"I'm telling the truth, I swear!" I shouted.

"It sounds to me like an excuse to get out of our joust," Isabelle said gloatingly. "We've been waiting for a chance to see the hero's son in action. You sat in Siege Perilous, now you claim you spoke to the Lady of the Lake. You flout upon our most precious traditions and accuse our leader of treason. I say, if you're telling the truth, prove it. Prove it in combat like a true knight."

"You have to believe me!"

Lance sighed heavily, then nodded toward Lucas. Lucas drew his sword and went over by Baron.

"Get your hands off me," Baron growled. "I'm not going anywhere." Lucas stood behind him, to keep watch in case he tried anything funny.

"Are you going to fight? Or are you yielding like a coward?" Isabelle asked. "What say ye?"

"We have to stop the tournament. We don't have time for games!"

"Games?" Isabelle shouted. "Listen to the son of a hero. You sound like nothing but a coward to me. If you're telling the truth, prove it. Fight me!"

Lance continued strapping the armor onto me, then hoisted me up onto Arion. "I can't do this," I said to him. "We don't have time for this. You have to listen to me."

But Lance said nothing. He seemed cold to me now and determined to see this joust through.

"Where is Gwen?" I asked. She will believe me. She will see sense." But Lance didn't respond, and I couldn't see her anywhere.

Lance shoved the jousting lance into my hand as Isabelle smirked, lowered her helm then rode to the opposite side of the Arena.

"There isn't time for this," I complained. "I won't do this. You have to listen to me."

"Hayden, you don't have a choice. You accepted this challenge. You can't back out now. Whatever you're claiming will be verified in a proper trial. But if you ever hope to become a knight, you'll do this joust."

I looked around, trying to find someone who seemed sympathetic to my cause. The twins were silent for once, looking squeamish, but they didn't say anything. I turned to Elibora and Lady Albreda, who looked down ashamedly. I looked at Kaylinelle, Gale, everyone—but nobody would meet my gaze.

There was nothing they could do for me, even if they wanted to help. I was trapped in this joust, with no way out but forward. But I didn't even care about my honor anymore. Baron was sitting smugly in the stands, and there was a chance he was going to get away with his plans. That couldn't happen. He had to be stopped.

"BEGIN!" Lance shouted, smacking Arion's thigh, Isabelle thundering forward on her own stallion.

"Please! We have to stop! I can't do this now. You have to listen to me!" I shouted, but my voice was drowned out by the tumult of hooves as our horses raced down the Arena straight at each other.

Isabelle didn't stop, nor did Arion. I turned and saw Baron looking down at me haughtily, smiling horridly. The last thing I saw after that was Isabelle in her massive black armor lowering her lance into place, pointed straight at me.

I didn't even lower my own weapon. It happened quickly. The tip of Isabelle's lance collided into my head, sending my helmet flying off me into the air. Everything went dark and I was falling.

When I awoke, I was sitting in a bed in the infirmary, covered in white sheets. A fire was crackling in the hearth beside me. For a moment, I felt content. Safe. And then I remembered everything that had happened.

Baron's nefarious plot I uncovered in the forest, and the joust with Isabelle I hadn't been prepared to compete in. I felt my head and discovered thick bandages there. She must have hit me hard. And that meant I lost the joust.

"Oh, Hayden. Thank the stars you're awake! I was so worried."

Gwen raced forward and gripped my hand kindly. She had a large white bandage wrapped around her arm in a sling.

"Are you okay?" I asked. "You're hurt!"

"What, this?" She said, gesturing toward her bandaged arm. "This is nothing. Just a small fracture."

"Lance fractured your arm?"

"It's not his fault. Sword fighting is dangerous. These things happen. But forget about me—Hayden, this isn't good. There's something you need to know."

"What? That Baron really is trying to take over the Magic Hollow? That he did betray Hal and the others?"

Gwen frowned. "Hayden . . . I don't know where you got that idea from but Baron was proven innocent in his trial."

"WHAT! He stood trial while the prime witness of his crime was unconscious? This isn't fair. Gwen, you have to believe me. I'm not lying. I know what I heard."

"I know, I know. I believe you. I know you wouldn't make that story up just to get out of the joust, but—"

"But that is what Isabelle and Baron are saying about me?"

Gwen nodded. "The Round Counsel is meeting about it right now. Isabelle won't let it go . . . you know how she gets. She proposed that—that you be demoted from your position as a squire. She called you a coward and said so many nasty things. And Baron, he weaseled his way out of every question in the trial. There was nothing they could catch him in. There's just no proof. Only your word, which, now that Isabelle has had her say, doesn't mean much to too many of the Knights."

"And what do you and Lance think?" I asked quietly.

"I will vote in your favor, I promise! But we have to get there, right now. Can you walk?"

I strained myself getting out of bed, but I had to push through the dizziness and pain. I could hardly process what Gwen was telling me. They were going to vote against my squireship? This wasn't fair. I wasn't a coward. Why wouldn't they believe me? Baron was a threat that couldn't be trusted!

Gwen helped me along the castle passageways into the Round Hall. We threw open the door, welcoming dead silence as I limped into the room, leaning on Gwen's shoulder. The two of us must have been a peculiar sight with her fractured arm and my own bandages.

"Why did you bring him here?" Isabelle asked, pointing at me. "No squires allowed. Especially not cowards."

"I'm not a coward," I said, perhaps a little too forcefully. "Why won't any of you believe me? I know what I saw and heard. Baron is dangerous. He can't be trusted. He's planning to take over the Magic Hollow."

"This is outrageous!" Baron shouted. "Preposterous. I will not tolerate such blows to my honor!"

"We have already dealt with Baron," Lance said, emotionless. "His alibi clears. There is no evidence that what you accuse him of is true."

"But, Lance—you've got to believe me. Why would I lie? You know I wouldn't lie about this!"

"Why would you lie?" Isabelle asked. "Because you're a coward, and you didn't want the rest of us to see you for what you are. Nothing like your father. I knew from the start you didn't have what it takes to be knight. No birthright can make up for that."

I couldn't believe my ears. I wanted to run, to cry, to hide, but I knew I couldn't. That would only prove Isabelle's false accusation against me. I'm not a coward, I thought. I'm not a coward.

And then I wondered, if I wasn't a coward, why did I want to run away and hide? What if I was a coward after all? Admitting that Isabelle was right was too painful to do, but with everyone staring at me, questioning my honor and bravery, I lost the will to fight. I didn't know what I could say or do to clear my name. Everything I wanted was crashing down around me, and I didn't know what to do to stop it.

"Let us continue with the vote," Lance said stoically. I tried to meet his gaze, but it seemed like he was refusing to look at me. "Isabelle, we will start with you."

"You know what my vote is. I vote against him."

"I vote against him as well," Percy said stiffly.

"Well, I vote for him!" Gwen said. "Come on, seriously everyone! We can't really be considering this."

"I'm with Gwen," Elibora said. "I trust, Hayden. I don't think he's a coward or a liar. I vote in his favor as well."

"Me too," Kaylinelle said.

I felt my hopes rise, I now had three votes in my favor, and only two against me.

"I'm sorry, Hayden, but I'm siding with Isabelle and Percy on this one," Tristan said. "I don't think you're ready. My vote is against it. Maybe you can try again next year."

I felt my skin go cold. That meant the vote was tied three to three.

"I vote against," Lucas said, refusing to look at me. That one stung, we were roommates, and had gotten to know each other much better. "I think he needs more time as well."

"Well, I vote in his favor," Gale said. "This is ridiculous. Maybe Hayden is mistaken about what he saw, but that's no reason to kick him out of his squireship!"

I felt a sigh of relief. Gale's vote had secured my safety. By tying the vote four to four, all it would take was Lance's final vote in my favor, and everything would be okay.

The room was quiet, while everyone turned to Lance to hear his deciding vote. He cleared his throat, looked up at me, then quickly looked away. "I vote against Hayden."

I couldn't believe my ears as my entire world turned upside down. My best friend thinks I'm a coward and a liar. The knight who was training me didn't think I was ready or had what it took to become a knight.

"Does this mean I have to leave the Magic Hollow?" I asked, after an unbearably long moment of silence, the shock of what had happened still addling my brains.

Gwen's tears were falling in full force. "No, no of course not. You can stay. You can even keep training. You may not be a squire, but there's always the Captain's Guard. You could train to be a soldier. When Jack returns with Hal, you can keep training with him. He's Captain."

"You could always try again next year," Tristan said, trying to reassure me.

My heart sank. Jack and Mr. Bianco were still out there. In danger. And there was nothing I could do about it. My parents were out there somewhere. My journey to knighthood was over.

I looked up and saw Baron's wicked sneer. I turned to Lance wanting some explanation, but he refused to look at me. I felt so betrayed, I couldn't take it anymore.

"I can't stay here," I said. "I'm leaving the Magic Hollow."

"Hayden—please," Gwen pleaded, but I wouldn't listen. I threw open the door to the Round Hall and stormed down the hallway.

Gwen followed me out, grabbing my arm, trying to stop me. "Hayden—please!"

# CHAPTER SIXTEEN

"Look, Gwen—I know what it is like to be an outcast. I'm not going to have that here too. I'm leaving, and I'm never coming back. Have fun defending yourselves when Baron takes over the Magic Hollow."

"Hayden—don't go. I'm not ready to give up, neither should you. We can defend your name. Prove your innocence—prove that you aren't a coward. We can catch Baron. That would prove everything you've said is true!"

"I don't care anymore, Gwen. I don't."

With that, I stormed up the stairs into the boys' dormitory and slammed the door shut behind me. It didn't take me long to gather my few meager possessions. With everything I owned thrown into a sack, I left Room Three, without looking back, or even saying goodbye to Lance's pet drake, Goliath. On my way back down, Gwen was nowhere to be seen.

As I crossed the bridge spanning the Crystal Chasm, then exited through the front gates, the giant dragon statue didn't bother lifting its head to watch me go. I turned back, looking at New Camelot, Caerleon, and the Arena, and I was overwhelmed with countless amazing memories. The Magic Hollow was supposed to have been my true home. Feeling unwelcome here was a horrible feeling.

I turned my back on the Hollow and departed down the tunnel and out the final door. The door shut with a click, leaving me alone in the Centerra alleyway. It was over. I knew now that I had willingly left, I would never be able to open that door again. I was cut off from the Magic Hollow for good. I didn't know where I would go, but anywhere would be better than New Camelot.

I thought I could be something I wasn't. After hearing about my father, the hero, I thought I could be him. But I knew the truth.

I was not my father.

# CHAPTER SEVENTEEN
# CROSSROADS

**S**tanding alone in the dark streets of Centerra, I gripped my sack tightly, then set off randomly, thinking my first step would have to be finding somewhere to sleep. After that I would have to find a job. Anything to make enough money to support myself. Once I was stable, I could start looking for a way to travel back to the Other Realm where I belonged. It wasn't much of a plan, but it was the best I had.

I heard a familiar voice say from around a corner. "Let. Me. Go!"

I could recognize that squeaky little voice anywhere. It was Strings the mouse.

I ran to the corner and peered around it. Down a shadowed alleyway, I saw three Cerise Guards in their shining crimson samurai armor. One of them was holding a mouse that was trying very hard to wiggle free from her grasp.

"Calm down, little mouse," she said. "We just want to ask you some questions."

"I'll have you for this. Just you wait! You're lucky I'm unarmed. I'd run you through!"

The Cerise Guards laughed loudly. "You're feisty for a little mouse," she said. "Tell me, mouse, what are you doing in our streets? And awfully close to the entrance to the Hollow, at that."

"Why do you care what a mouse does in its free time? Hmm? I'm looking for food, like I always do. So, put me down, and let me on my way."

"I don't know, little mouse. My companion tells me you look familiar. Like the mouse that rides around on that pumpkin man's head."

"What? No, no, no. No way! That's not me. I swear. I can prove it. Ask me what a pumpkin even looks like. I don't know. I couldn't tell you. Never seen one. I'm a city mouse, born and raised. East Centerra, all my days. I swear."

"This mouse talks a lot," one of the guards said. "Can we just feed it to a cat or something and be done with it?"

"Oh, come on. I hate cats," Strings said.

"Then talk, mouse. What were you doing sneaking around outside of your Hollow? Trying to spy on us?"

"What no, of course not. I'm not spying. Just sniffing around. For food. That's it!"

They laughed. "Well, I guess you won't be upset to hear that we are invading the Magic Hollow. Tonight."

I froze. How could it be possible? The protective magic kept out anyone who wasn't invited. Unless . . . someone invited them. I thought back to my first lesson with Baron when he had shoved that letter into his desk drawer, obviously trying to hide it from sight. Was the accomplice he had been speaking to in the woods a Cerise Guard member?

It all made sense. Of course, Baron would need an army to accomplish his takeover. Just removing Hal from the picture wouldn't be enough. Otherwise, the knights would retaliate, beat him up and pick a new leader. But if he had an army on his side to enforce his new rule, even if Hal ever did come back, there would be nothing he could do.

# CROSSROADS

I couldn't believe Baron would stoop so low, as making a deal with the enemy. I continued listening, hoping they would reveal more information.

"If I were a mouse from the Magic Hollow, I guess that news would concern me," Strings stammered. "But I'm not, so that's cool. Good for you guys."

"It is very good for us," she said. "For too long the Magic Hollow has been resisting our rule. We own this neighborhood because we protect it. We have kept these streets safe for years. And what have they done? Stayed hidden in their safe house and harassed our guards every chance they got. The way I see it, the Magic Hollow is a threat to everyone's safety. They are loose cannons who have to be stopped!"

"Not that I would know because I'm totally not from there, but isn't the Magic Hollow like impossible to find. I mean, from what I've heard, nobody even knows if it really exists."

"Lies. I've heard the stories from the Shadow Wars. They weren't always in hiding. In fact, they were very active in the battle against Lord Marzon."

"The Marzon? He was a living nightmare," Strings said. "Not that I would know much about that, obviously. I'm just a street mouse. But not even Marzon could break into the Hollow, from what I've heard. So, how do you plan on invading, hmm?"

"We won't have to break in, mouse. We were invited in."

I knew it! The only way in was by invitation, and Baron had supplied that need. That proved it. Baron had successfully amassed an army that would fight for him, eager for a chance to squash out their enemies. This was so much bigger than I had ever imagined.

At first, I thought I no longer cared who ruled the Magic Hollow, whether it was Hal or even a scumbag like Baron. But this was different. These were my friends they were talking about. Sure, I was upset with most of them, and irritated beyond belief with their stupidity and rudeness. But even then, they didn't deserve this. An invasion would be horrible. Innocent people could get hurt, or worse.

I had to do something to warn them.

"Alright, little mouse," the Cerise Guard said, "I think it's time we find a nice hungry kitty to gobble you up."

"What? Come on, I thought we were cool? I don't want to get eaten. Just let me go and you'll never see me again. I promise. I'm a mouse of my word!"

"Enough talking. Your squeaky voice is driving me crazy."

"Put that mouse down," I said, stepping out of the shadows, and drawing my sword from its sheath at my belt.

The Cerise Guard members turned with surprise on their faces. That surprise quickly turned into smirks when they saw it was only me.

"Well, well, well. Another little mouse from the Magic Hollow," she said, dangling Strings by his tail.

"If you want him, come and get him. But choose wisely, kid, you're outnumbered three to one."

"Not anymore he's not," Gwen said, running up beside me.

"Looks like it's a fair fight now," Elibora said, arriving on my other side.

I have never felt happier and more relieved in my life. Both were wearing partial armor, which glowed radiantly in the torchlight along the otherwise grimy street.

The Cerise Guard laughed. "You're nothing but children," she said. "And what's up with you, sling?" she nodded to Gwen, whose fractured arm was still tied up in a sling.

"I only need one arm to beat you," Gwen said. "We are Knights of the Round Table. And we are going to take back that mouse."

Technically, I wasn't a knight. But I decided the Cerise Guard didn't need to know that.

"ATTACK!" the Cerise Guard yelled. The three of them rushed in, their long, thin katanas gleaming with black steel.

All three of us charged, clashing in the street. I knew I was at the most disadvantage because I wasn't wearing any armor. I also couldn't shake the thought that this was no practice duel. This was real. The sword my enemy was holding was very real and very sharp.

The guard I fought was a skilled warrior. His fighting style was very different from the traditional style I had learned from the knights. I should have known that samurai would have their own methods. Every attack he made felt so new to me, I had to guess what the best defensive maneuver would be. One wrong move, and I would be done for.

I parried an attack, and then another, scrambling to find the right foot-work and get a hold of myself. Then, I realized, he was just as inexperienced fighting a knight as I was fighting a samurai. I dodged his next attack, and then launched into the most complex series of strikes I could think of, all techniques I had practiced while training with Lance.

It worked! The samurai was used to fighting with a katana, which was much longer and thinner than the European sword I was sporting. Quick, short, and fast successions of attacks knocked him off guard, and then, just like that, I was the one in control. I managed to knock back his sword, then spun, smashing my pummel into his face. He grunted with pain as he fell over, completely knocked out.

I turned, seeing that Gwen and Elibora made quick work of the second guard but were having a harder time with the third guard. She was clearly the most skilled of the group and was easily fending them off. If only Gwen had a second hand. I would have to let Lance know how dumb he was next time I saw him. That gave me pause. Did that mean I was going to go back?

I shook off the thought. Now wasn't the time to be thinking about that sort of thing. "Gwen, I'm here," I said, taking her place in the fight. "Do something cool. You know—some magic!"

"Right," Gwen said, stepping back. She closed her eyes, concentrating, clearly trusting us to keep her safe.

After what felt like forever, Elibora said, "Anytime now, Gwen!"

"Ready!" Gwen shouted. She lifted her hands and two large embers of fire erupted just above her palms. "Look out!" she shouted. We dodged to the side as Gwen hurled the flames at the Guard, one after the other. They struck her, knocking her back onto the ground. Gwen put her hands together, wincing at the pain from moving her fractured arm. When she pushed them forward, a large swirling chunk of ice shot through the air. It struck the ground before the Cerise Guard and immediately trapped her legs.

Gwen let out a deep breath and fell to the ground, gasping for air.

"Are you okay?" I asked, dropping my sword and running to her side. I helped her up onto her feet, as she grasped her injured arm.

"Yeah, I'll be okay. It's just . . . using spells out here isn't the same as in the Magic Hollow. It's harder. Much harder."

"When all this is over, you better show me how that's done because that was incredible!"

Gwen nodded. "We'll see. It's Hal's call, I'm forbidden from teaching others."

I wondered how dangerous using magic really was. By the looks of it, Gwen was a little pale, and looked like she had just seen a ghost, but other than that she seemed fine.

The Cerise Guard struggled against the ice, pounding it with her fists. "If I get out of here, you'll pay for this! Do what you want with me. It won't stop the inevitable! We have our invitation, so there is nothing you can do to stop the invasion now! Just wait until you face our leader, Yasuke!"

Unexpectedly, a large lantern fell right on top of the guard's head, knocking her out instantly. "That's enough of that," Strings said, scuttling down from the lamppost. "She was starting to get on my nerves."

I ran forward and scooped Strings up in my hand. "Strings! I'm so glad you're here. But where's Jack and Mr. Bianco?" I'd never been so happy to see a rodent before.

Strings sighed. "Not good, kid. They're still trapped. Principal Hal, too. It was all a set up. There are more than just two trolls. The trolls have amassed an entire army of baddies. There was nothing we could do, we were surrounded. Then they lured Hal using us as bait and managed to trap him too."

Gwen gasped with shock. "It can't be!"

"It's true. All of it," Strings said. "Luckily, Jack kept me hidden from sight in his pocket. They had no idea I was there. As soon as I got the chance I escaped and made my way here. It's not easy to travel when you're legs are this small, in case you were wondering."

"But you made it!" I spoke. "Just in time to warn us about the Cerise Guard!"

"What? These clowns," Strings said, pointing his tail toward the guards. "I had no idea about them. They caught me just as I was coming down the street."

"Do you think they are working with the trolls?"

"I don't know. Seems far-fetched to me. I mean these guys hate monsters just as much as we do. They just charge outrageous sums for their services."

"What was she saying about invading the Magic Hollow?" Elibora asked. "Nobody can break through the protective spells without an invitation, but she said they have one."

"Bad news," I said. "I tried to warn everyone. But now we know it's even worse than I thought. They do have an invitation. And she said they are planning to attack the Magic Hollow tonight."

Elibora cursed in Old English. "This is bad. We have to warn everyone!"

"I think my work here is done," I said.

"Hayden. Stop. You have to come back with us. I know the knights can be infuriatingly stupid, but you were right all along. And they were wrong. Come back with us, so you can prove them wrong once and for all. Don't you see? All this time you've spent so much time comparing yourself to stories about your father, you never noticed that just being you was enough. I don't need your father, I want you, my friend, just the way you are. Even if you can be annoying. You're also kind, funny, and fiercely loyal. Please, come back."

"She's right, Hayden," Elibora said. "Noble chivalry, gentle virtue, and honest deeds, remember? If anyone deserves to be a knight, it's you. Think of all the good you could do in New Camelot, and even in all of Between. You have to come back."

"So, what do you say?" Gwen asked, grabbing my hand. "Will you come back with us?"

"Um, thanks for the kind words," I said, smiling. "I mean, wow! I had no idea you thought so highly of me. But I wasn't talking about abandoning everyone. I was going to say, I think I should go look for Sir Ector, Jack, and Principal Hal. I mean, I'm not a knight, right? So, I don't technically have to follow the order to stay in the Hollow."

Gwen shook her head, looking like she was going to punch me in the nose. Then she laughed. "That's the Hayden I hoped we'd find!"

Elibora grabbed my hand, and squeezed kindly. "I'm glad we made it in time. We would never give up on you, just like I know you won't give up on us."

"I don't know what I would do without you," I admitted.

"You would be completely lost without me," Gwen said. "You never would have survived the night in Quay and the Wharf when I first found you."

"Yeah, yeah, yeah," I teased.

"Now come on, let's get back to the Hollow," Gwen said. "I know you want to go, but we need you here. We need your help convincing everyone the truth so we can clear your name and get preparations under way. Once that is done, we can figure out what to do about Captain Lantern and Sir Ector."

I looked down the dark road longingly. Mr. Bianco was one of my closest friends and teachers. But I knew Gwen was right. Besides, Between was a dangerous place. As hard as it was to admit, I knew it wasn't the brightest idea for me to just wonder off alone, regardless of my intentions.

I turned back, smiling at Gwen and Elibora. "Thanks, you two. Seriously. Let's do this."

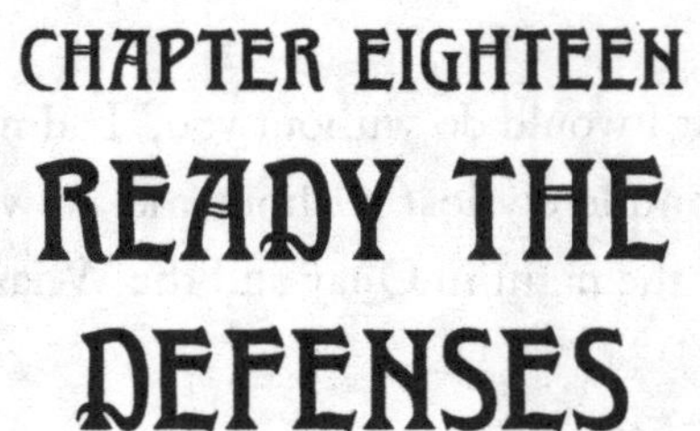

# CHAPTER EIGHTEEN
# READY THE DEFENSES

I think you all owe someone an apology," Gwen said, standing proudly before the Knights-junior of the Round Table. "Hayden, Strings, come on in."

I pushed open the door and stepped into the Round Hall. Everyone was there, except for Baron of course. Gwen and Elibora had made certain that he wasn't told about this secret meeting. For the millionth time, I watched everyone turn and look right at me. But this time, something was different. I didn't back down or look at the floor. I walked into the room confidently, Strings the Mouse sitting on top of my head.

"Hola amigos," Strings said. "Don't all jump out of your seats at once to greet me."

I think that was my favorite part: relishing in the look on everyone's faces. Kaylinelle looked pleasantly surprised. Percy looked smug as ever, but Isabelle looked like she had just lost the lottery by one digit.

"What's going on?" Lucas asked. "Strings—does that mean the others are safe?"

"Not quite," Strings said. "A lot has happened since Jack and I

234

left on our little adventure to the Other Realm. For starters, we ran into this kid, who you guys are idiots for kicking out of your club, by the way."

"Strings—" I tried to say, but he continued.

"Sure, this kid is the son of the greatest hero of our age: Sir William Keyes. But that's not why Hayden is a total boss. I watched this kid take down a troll, all on his own. That takes guts!"

"Well—it's not like it was full grown—" I tried to interrupt. I appreciated Strings speaking up for me, but I hadn't expected him to be this over the top.

"It doesn't matter how big it was. That is still more than almost every single so-called Knight-Junior in this room can say. While you were in the Magic Hollow playing war, Hayden was in the Other Realm planning an attack on three trolls with Captain Jack and Sir Ector. This kid is brave. Sure, he needs training and guidance, but who doesn't?"

"That doesn't change the fact that he's a liar," Isabelle said rudely. "We made our decision, and nothing you can say will change that."

"He's not a liar," Gwen said.

"It's true," Elibora said. "You have no idea what is coming for us. But Hayden knew, and he tried to warn us, and you were too stubborn to listen."

Lance, who had remained resolutely quiet the entire time, perked up slightly when he heard this.

"Eli and I ran after Hayden, trying to stop him from leaving the Magic Hollow. When we reached the gate, he was already outside. We ran out there to find him and Strings cornered by three Cerise Guards. We helped Hayden and together we took down the three guards."

"Hey, don't forget about me," Strings said. "I helped."

"It's true," Gwen said, sounding annoyed. "Strings helped. But we found out something in the process. There really is a traitor in our midst. Someone

# CHAPTER EIGHTEEN

gave the entire Cerise Guard an invitation into the Magic Hollow, and they are coming tonight."

Silence filled the room.

"Like I tried to say before, I overheard Baron speaking to someone in the forest," I said. "Baron said they were planning to do something tonight. I didn't know what it was, but I assumed he was going to try and take full control of the Magic Hollow. Now we know he's going to use the Cerise Guard to do it."

"He's a traitor," Tristan said loudly. "We have to arrest him. Lock him up!"

"I always knew he was a scoundrel," Percy said.

"So, we are really just going to believe this?" Isabelle said, standing up so quickly she nearly knocked over her chair.

"Yes, you are," Gwen said, standing up to Isabelle. "Why would we make this up? Elibora, Strings, and I can all attest to everything Hayden has said. It's true. And you were wrong. So back off."

Isabelle's jaw clenched iron tight as she sat back down.

"We don't have much time," Elibora said. "We need to prepare our defenses, rally the troops, send an envoy to the Centaurs and the Wolves, not to mention warn the village. Who knows how much time we have?"

"Lance—you're the Defender of New Camelot. What do you think about all this?" Gale asked, turning to Lance who was still staring at the floor.

Lance stood up, finally looking around at everyone. Then he looked at me and dropped to one knee. "Hayden, forgive me. I wronged you by voting against you when you were speaking honestly and truthfully. That is a mistake I shall carry with me the rest of my days. All of the Magic Hollow owes a great debt to you for carrying the warning message back to us, even after we had wrongfully mistreated you."

"It's okay—" I started to say, but Lance cut me off.

"No. It's not okay. We were wrong. Each and every one of us who voted against your honor. We all owe you a sincere apology. I, Lance Hawkwood, Defender of New Camelot, hereby rescind my vote against Hayden, and propose that he be reinstated as my Squire, if he will trust me again."

"Of course, I trust you," I said. "Lance, I don't blame any of you for not believing me. I know how crazy it sounded, and the timing was horrible. But all that matters now is the new threat that is coming. If we are going to win this, we have to fight as one."

"Hear, hear!" Kaylinelle said loudly, pounding the Round Table with her fist. "I hope you know, Hayden, that I never doubted you."

"I did," Tristan said bluntly. "I thought you were completely out of your mind. But I was wrong. I rescind my vote."

"Me too," Lucas said. "Forgive me, Hayden. I was a fool for not believing you. I wish I hadn't been so quick to judge you."

I expressed my forgiveness and clasped both of their hands tightly.

Percy walked up to me next and dropped to one knee beside Lance. "I only voted on the information I had. But now I see that I was wrong. There is more to you than meets the eye, Hayden. You have the makings of being a valiant knight. I beg your forgiveness and rescind my vote."

Everyone turned to Isabelle, the last and most dedicated opposition. "What are you all looking at me for?" Isabelle said, crossing her arms tightly. "Who cares what I voted for, the kid has more than enough votes to reverse our decision. But, for the record, I rescind my vote. But don't think that means I'll go easy on you next time we meet in a tournament."

"There might not be another tournament if we don't win this battle," Elibora said.

"She's right," Lance said. "We have to prepare for battle. First things first, Gwen, will you be able to ride a horse in your condition?"

"Yes, I could manage," Gwen said.

"Good. Because there is no way you're fighting in a battle like this. Strings, do you remember where Hal and the others are trapped?"

"Of course. A mouse never forgets. Well maybe normal mice, but you know, not the talking sort."

"Good. Gwen, pick any soldiers from the Captain's Guard and ride with Strings to find Hal and the others and bring them home."

"You expect her to bust them out with an arm like that?" Tristan asked. "It's too risky."

"Gwen is the best one for the job," Lance said. "She's smart, sneaky, and can use magic better than any of us."

"It's true," I said. "I just watched her pulverize a Cerise Guard without even lifting her sword once." Deep down, I wanted to be the one who went after them, but seeing Lance taking the lead was inspiring, and I knew he was right. Gwen was far better for the job than I was.

"I'm honored to accept this task," Gwen said. "Besides, I'm the one who has traveled outside of the Magic Hollow the most. It has to be me."

"Just be careful out there," Elibora said kindly. That made my heart happy. It seemed like the two of them were finally sorting out their friendship again.

"It's decided then," Lance said. "Lucas, I want you to find Weyland and make sure we have enough weapons to arm everyone. Also, see if Weyland can convince the Bunyanish Giants to join the defense. He knows them better than anybody."

Lucas nodded, then headed out the door.

"I can go and speak with my grandma," Elibora said. "Caerleon will have to be warned and prepared to defend themselves. Protecting the village has to be a top priority."

"Good idea," Lance said. "Gale, I want you to go with her and lead the defense of the village. Elibora, when you're done, I want you to come back and lead a team of archers on the main wall. We need your skill with a bow."

"Of course." Elibora hugged Gwen and wished her luck on her journey. "Good luck everyone," she said, before hurrying out of the room with Gale.

"That leaves one last hurdle," Lance said. "Hayden, if what you said about Baron is true, we can't let him join his new army. We have to capture him. Hold him prisoner if we must."

"Let me take care of that," Isabelle said.

Tristan eyed her carefully. "I don't know, Isabelle. If anyone gets along with Baron the best, it's always been you. How do we know you aren't going to let him go?"

"Are you accusing me of being a traitor, too?" Isabelle growled. "I want to go because Baron is my friend. That doesn't mean I won't do what I have to do for the Magic Hollow. If it turns out that Baron was the traitor, I will never forgive him. But until we know for certain, he deserves to be treated with respect."

"Isabelle is right, as much as I hate to admit it. Baron is still the Bailiff of New Camelot after all. Regardless, we should treat every prisoner with decency and respect—that is the Round Table's way."

"Lance—are you sure about this?" Gwen asked. "I mean, it is awfully noble of you, but we don't know what Baron is capable of. He has turned against all of us."

"We treat him with decency," Lance said. "Until we have reasonable proof of his treachery, we keep him securely locked in his office. Tristan, I want you to accompany Isabelle. Bring with you ten strong soldiers from the Captain's Guard as well. We don't want to take any chances."

"Will the Captain's Guard obey us?" Tristan asked nervously. "Baron has had them under his thumb ever since Hal left! The last thing we need is a civil war between the knights and the guards."

"I know they will," Lance said. "If they want proof, tell them to walk outside the gates and see the Cerise Guard for themselves!"

I could tell Tristan and Gwen disagreed. Even I disagreed. Baron couldn't be trusted. He deserved to be locked up in a cell. That was the only safe place for him. But Lance had a way of leading. He was so passionate, so confident, and so noble. Gwen would never question anything he commanded. She would follow him anywhere he asked. Even Tristan held his tongue and listened to Lance, and he was one of the most vocal of all the knights. That was proof that Lance was a true leader and a true knight. I knew I may never be the kind of leader that Lance was, but I was determined to become a knight that sat beside him on the Round Table. Despite the mistake he had made by voting against me, I would stand beside him and fight as his squire, and hopefully someday as a fellow knight.

"Let's get it over with then," Isabelle said to Tristan, trudging out of the room.

"The rest of you, follow me," Lance said. "We've got a lot of work to do."

Lance was so busy rallying the knights, squires, and Captain's Guard soldiers, he didn't notice me slip off with Gwen to say goodbye before she set off on her journey. Strings the Mouse sat on her shoulder, chatting away anxiously.

"Even on horseback it is going to be a long ride. We don't have time to waste. Let's go, let's go!"

Gwen had chosen a beautiful brown horse from the stables. Sitting on it, her silver armor gleaming beneath her black cloak, she looked very intimidating, even with her injured arm still wrapped in a cloth sling. Her sword hung from her belt, sheathed in black leather. I hoped she wouldn't need to use it, but deep down, I knew that was wishful thinking. The chances that she could successfully sneak Mr. Bianco, Jack, and Hal out without being seen was probably slim.

"Good luck, Gwen. And don't do anything stupid."

"I won't. That's your job," she said. "I'm the smart one, remember?"

We laughed, both trying to hide our nerves.

"This is the farthest outside of the Magic Hollow I will have ever traveled," Gwen said wistfully. "Wish me luck."

"You'll do great. I know it. Everyone is counting on you."

"That's what freaks me out. It's one thing to do little errands for Hal, but this . . . this is real. I can feel the difference. For the first time in a long time, I think I feel scared."

I was surprised Gwen was being so vulnerable with me now. She always seemed so strong and so confident. "That just means you're human," I said. "Even knights get scared. If they didn't, how could they ever be brave?"

"You know, Hayden, I think that is the wisest thing you have ever said."

"You'd be surprised. I'm chock full of wisdom. You know, like there are only rainbows after rain, or today is a gift. That's why we call it the present. Or—"

"Ugh. Please, stop. Never do that again," Gwen said, mimicking throwing up. "Remind me never to compliment your inspirational advice again."

"Aw, come on. You could use a little encouragement for what lies ahead. It's going to be tough. And you know what they say, when the going gets tough, the tough get going."

Gwen fake vomited again, shaking her head laughing. "I don't know what they say. In Between, we definitely don't say that."

"It's true. That's just horrible, kid," Strings said. "We don't even have to be from the Other Realm to know that those are cliché."

We laughed and almost forgot what trouble we were about to be in.

"Look, just be safe out there. You better make it back before all the fighting's over, too. I don't want to have to do all the hard work myself," I said.

"You? Do the hard work? I doubt that. Just do what you can to keep Lance safe, okay? As his squire, it is your duty to carry his shield and support him in battle, you know."

"I know what a squire does," I said. "And I promise, I'll do my best."

"Lance probably won't have time to stop by and say goodbye, will he?" Gwen asked solemnly, looking toward New Camelot, which was bustling with activity in preparation for the battle.

"He seems busy," I said. "I . . . I don't think he's coming."

Gwen looked brokenhearted, but that didn't stop her from mustering her courage and riding on.

"Farewell, Hayden Keyes."

"Farewell."

Gwen tugged on her horse's reins and set off at a quick gallop across the bridge then down the tunnel that led to Centerra. She sure got on my nerves sometimes, but I couldn't help but miss her as I watched her go.

When Gwen was out of sight, I took a deep breath and returned to New Camelot.

There was a large commotion in the castle as I pushed open the heavy front doors. The twin brothers Alex and Eric were dancing festively around Isabelle and Tristan, while others clapped and cheered.

"We did it!" Tristan yelled. "We captured the traitor!"

"We don't know for sure that he's a traitor yet," Isabelle said, scowling at Alex and Eric. "And will you two please shut up and get away from me. I'm not proud of what we've done."

"You did what had to be done," Lance said, approaching them. "Is he held secure?"

"Yes. Tied and gagged to his chair," Tristan said, smiling mischievously. "He didn't even see it coming."

"And is he being guarded and watched?"

"Of course. Ten of our finest soldiers. He won't be getting anywhere, anytime soon."

"Good. Tristan, it's time to bar the main gate. This castle hasn't been under siege in nearly a thousand years. If we are lucky, they may never even make it through the gates."

"You got it, boss," Tristan said.

I walked up to Isabelle cautiously because she was still sulking and looking extra cross about what had just happened. "Hey, I'm sorry you had to betray your friend," I said.

"What do you care about it?" Isabelle asked. "You're the one who accused him of being a traitor in the first place."

"Look—I know it must be hard to accept that someone you trusted could be capable of something like that. But I just remembered something. It's proof that what I said was true."

"What?"

"When I followed Baron into the Forest to see what he was up to, and I overheard him talking to someone, he showed them something on his arm. He said a curse was taking over him. Well, I may not know much about curses, but from what Gwen and Lance have told me, they happen when someone is messing with powerful magic, or harboring some serious problems."

Isabelle frowned. "Growing up around here, Baron was one of the only people who would talk to me and not look at me like I was a freak because I was so much bigger than all the other kids. No matter what he does, or what happens to him, I will never hate him. I will always be his friend because he was mine when no one else was. Curse or not, I will be there for him, and there is nothing you can say that will change that."

"So what?" I spoke. "Is that supposed to make us feel guilty for what we did? I don't care what he has done for you in the past if he's a liar and a traitor. You got me kicked out of being a squire when you suspected the same of me."

"Innocent until proven guilty," Isabelle said. "At the time, we found you guilty. But you aren't even a knight, so I wouldn't expect you to understand."

That flared my temper. "Don't you have somewhere to be or something to be doing? Everyone else is trying to get things done, and you're just moping about Baron!"

"Moping, am I? You better watch yourself, Hayden. You wouldn't want to find yourself in another joust with me. Next chance I get, I will do more than just knock you off your horse!"

With that, Isabelle turned on her heel and stomped away, leaving me shocked and fuming. Why did she have to be so aggravating, all the time? Was I supposed to feel bad for Baron like she did? In my opinion, he had brought this upon himself. In all my time in New Camelot, he had never shown me any respect, nor any of the other knights. So why should we show him respect now, when he betrayed us all?

On the other hand, I couldn't help but see Isabelle in a new light. Sure, it didn't change the fact that she was the rudest breed of bully out there, probably a close second only to Jared Phinkle. It didn't even change the fact that she had challenged me every step of my journey to becoming a squire. Or the fact that she pulverized me in our joust in front of everyone, called me a coward, and got me kicked out of New Camelot. But, despite all that, I realized that I wasn't the only kid around here who had struggled proving themselves and fitting in. Just like how everyone expected me to be a certain way because of who my father is, everyone had judged Isabelle a certain way as a child all because of her appearance.

Even Baron wasn't purely the evil villain I painted him out to be in my mind. It didn't change the fact that he had betrayed us and could be the cause of many innocent people getting hurt, but it definitely made it harder to outright hate him for his crimes. Could an evil person also be noble and honest? In all the stories I had read, the line between good and evil always seemed crystal clear. Now, I was realizing that the distinction between the two was far muddier. I still refused to accept what Isabelle said, though. The moment I started accepting bad guys as good, where would I ever draw the line between right and wrong? Or maybe, I thought, I just stubbornly want to hate Baron. But it was justified, wasn't it? He deserved it, didn't he?

"Hayden," Lance shouted across the hall, yanking me back to reality. "We've got to get outfitted in our armor, come on."

Lance led me down to the armory, where dozens of other knights and squires were getting outfitted for battle. I helped Lance with his armor first, securely tying every strap and piece one at a time, until at last, he was covered nearly head to toe in armor. I was halfway through putting on my own, when Gale entered the room. He was already wearing his plate mail and strode across the room proudly as he walked up to the quartermaster, an elderly gentleman, gray and bent with age.

"Alden, I have come for my family's sword."

I heard a few people gasp, and the room went quiet, except for a few scattered whispers.

"Of course, Sir Gale. Come with me," Alden said, bowing meekly.

"What's the big deal?" I whispered to Lance, as Alden led Gale through a locked door, which I heard lock with a click behind them.

"Gale is what some people around here call a legacy. It means he's a direct descendant from an original Knight of the Round Table."

"Are you serious? Which one?" I spoke.

"Sir Galahad. Galahad's sword has remained in the family since. It belongs to Gale."

"Wow," was all I could say, trying to wrap my mind around it. A thousand years later, and there are still people who can trace their lineage back to the original Round Table! "So, why does he keep the sword locked up down here? He never uses it?"

"Well . . ." Lance said, "it's because the sword is a legendary weapon, forged from Avalonian Gold. It won't let him wield it. At least not properly."

"That's right. I remember now. My very first day we visited Weyland in the forges, and he was trying to craft a legendary weapon, but he said he couldn't get the metal to behave properly."

"Exactly," Lance said. "Legendary weapons are temperamental like that. Not just anyone can pick them up. You have to earn their trust."

"What about Gale? Does his sword have a name?"

"Yes. Its name is Seure, treasure of Sir Galahad, one of the greatest of all the Knights of Old. I have only seen it once."

A few minutes later, Gale and the quartermaster Alden returned. In gale's hands, was a long, golden sword, adorned with a single red ruby and sheathed in polished leather and wood. There was a strange aura about it, like a magnet. I couldn't look away. I saw why Gale chose to keep it locked deep within the Armory. It was safest out of sight.

"Does that mean Seure has finally chosen you as its new wielder?" a young squire asked from the crowd.

Gale shifted nervously, looking down at the sword. "Not yet. But Seure will by the time this battle is through. The sword is mine by right. Now I only need to prove my worth in combat. The Cerise Guard will rue the day they chose us as their foes!"

Everyone clapped and cheered, rallied by the sight of the ancient weapon, even if Gale wouldn't be able to use it yet.

"Weyland," Lance said, jogging across the hall to catch the blacksmith as he was passing by. "I have to ask; how has your task been going trying to forge a legendary weapon? We could use a few of those right about now."

Weyland looked at his feet, shuffling embarrassedly. "I'm sorry, Lance. Still no progress. Our best hope is that some of the knights can win over their weapons during the fight. Otherwise, it's nothing but good old medieval steel for us."

Lance nodded, looking disappointed. "Don't lose heart, Weyland. I know you'll figure it out eventually." Lance clasped him on the shoulder, then sent him on his way with an order to secure a few barrels of exploding arrows on the battlements.

"Does anyone else have a legendary weapon I don't know about?" I asked Lance, as we finished securing my own armor.

"Well, rumor has it, Lady Albreda has one she's safekeeping for Elibora, but I'm not sure what kind of weapon it is. Percy's family has one, too, but they live outside the Magic Hollow. Isabelle has one. A spear called Rhoningan."

"Isabelle has a legendary weapon?" I asked.

Lance laughed. "Maybe you would have thought twice about challenging her if you knew, eh? I'm just kidding. She found it, but that doesn't mean it will let her wield it yet."

"Is Isabelle a legacy then? Who is her ancestor?"

# CHAPTER EIGHTEEN

"Well, she doesn't exactly descend from a knight. You see, back then, women weren't made knights. She descends from Lady Iseult, a fair maiden and wife of Sir Drustanus, who is commonly known as Tristan today."

"That's right. I've read a version of the story before. Iseult and Tristan. If I remember right, it was a tragedy."

"History proves much the same, I think," Lance said. "I don't remember the details, but that might be the case."

"How does Tristan feel about that?" I asked, chuckling. "I mean, I can't exactly picture the modern Iseult and Tristan falling in love."

Lance smiled. "I'll have to tease him about that sometime. It is a nice coincidence. As far as I know, our Tristan isn't a legacy. No relation to the Tristan—Drustanus—of old."

"Are those all of the legendary weapons then?"

"Well, don't forget the weapons I showed you in the Hall of Kings. There are several weapons in our possession that nobody holds a claim to and haven't chosen wielders. But other than those, I think that's all of them . . . no, wait. I've heard that Sir Ector has a legendary weapon. I don't know if it's true, though. Something Gwen told me she read in a book once."

"Really?" I asked excitedly. Finding out that my English teacher was a knight was one thing, but if he also wielded a legendary weapon, that would put his awesomeness level on a whole new level. "I watched him fight with the trolls, maybe he was using it? Do you know what kind of weapon it was?"

"Hmm," Lance said, "I think it was a dagger. Camwennan, they call it. The dagger of King Arthur himself."

I nearly choked. Mr. Bianco had handed me that dagger to defend myself with. I had not only held it, I used it to slay a troll. I had thought it was strange that one strike had burned the troll to ash. Was that because it was a legendary weapon? And not just any weapon, one that had been wielded by King Arthur himself? How could Mr. Bianco have let that one pass?

"What are you thinking?" Lance asked suspiciously.

"Oh, nothing. I was just trying to remember the fight. I think Mr. Bianco—Sir Ector—did have a dagger with him, but he never used it," I lied. I don't know why I didn't tell Lance the truth, I just knew how Lance felt about legendary weapons and birthrights and those kinds of things. He had been born to a small house that wasn't fabulously rich or connected to any famous knights. Everything he had achieved he had earned on his own through hard work and training, nothing else. I respected him for that. Everyone did. But I guess I didn't want him to go and think I was something special, just because I stabbed a troll in the back with a legendary dagger.

"Now you just need a shield," Lance said, selecting one from a large pile. "This one should fit you well." He handed me the shield, a large oval design, nearly as tall as me. "As my squire, it is important that you stay as close to me during the battle as possible. It is even more important that you do everything I ask, without questioning it. Do you understand?"

"Yes, of course," I said, grabbing the shield and testing it on my arm. It felt good. It would do.

"If I tell you to run, I want you to run. If I tell you to deliver a message, then you deliver it."

"Of course," I said. "I trust you with my life, Lance."

That seemed to catch Lance off guard. "Good," he finally said. "I won't let you down. I won't let any of us down."

"Lance, Gwen told me you're waiting to try and pull Excalibur from the stone. Well, I was thinking, after all our talk about legendary weapons . . . I was thinking, maybe now is your chance to go for it. You're the Defender of New Camelot. Just think."

For a moment, Lance looked like he was going to be sick, but it passed quickly. "Thank you, Hayden."

As we walked back up the stairs, though, fully clad in our armor, I couldn't help but think about Mr. Bianco's dagger and how it had felt in my hands. If I hadn't already tried to draw Excalibur and failed, I might have thought it was possible now, after finding out I had already wielded another weapon of King Arthur's.

Gwen was right. If anyone could pull Excalibur from its resting place, it was Lance Hawkwood.

# CHAPTER NINETEEN

# THE BATTLE OF THE HOLLOW

Heavy clouds fell over the Magic Hollow, and it rained for most of the evening. Two dozen archers stood along the battlements of the castle; barrels of arrows lined up behind them. Below, over two hundred knights, their squires, soldiers from the Captain's Guard, and even four Bunyanish giants dressed in makeshift armor and carrying blacksmith tools for weapons, stood at order, ready to defend the castle and their home.

Not far away, all Caerleon's villagers unable to fight and New Camelot's pages sat huddled in the town hall, quiet and waiting. They were led by Lady Albreda, who said she had survived two sieges in her day, one of them against the forces of Marzon himself during the Shadow War.

I had read about wars and battles countless times. I had seen them portrayed in movies, books, and comics, but this was nothing like I expected. So much standing and waiting after so much hurry and preparation. There was a raw anticipation that left me feeling anxious and uncertain.

I stood up straight beside Lance, following his lead, and willing myself to be brave. No number of movies or books could have prepared me for what it felt like to stand in ranks before a real battle. Honestly, I was especially grateful I went to the bathroom beforehand.

Earlier that day, I had left this wonderful place, prepared to never return. And now, here I was, ready to defend it. I hoped my father would be proud of me if he could see me now.

After what felt like ages, I was just thinking I probably should have gone to the bathroom before we took our position—Lance and I were at the back of the formation, standing on top of the garden wall to get a good view of the battlefield—when we heard loud drums echoing down the tunnel and across the bridge.

*Boom. Boom-boom-boom-boom-boom.*

I couldn't believe it. It really was going to happen. They must have filed in through the door and were now making their way down the tunnel toward the gate. A visible wave of fear passed over the ranks. "Steady," Lance said. "Don't be afraid!"

*Boom. Boom-boom-boom-boom-boom.*

"Archers, ready your arrows!" Lance shouted.

*Boom. Boom-boom-boom-boom-boom.*

The sound of the drum was getting so close, I imagined they were probably starting to cross the bridge.

*Boom. Boom-boom-boom-boom-boom.*

From our side of the gate, we watched the giant gold dragon statue raise its head, staring down at the newcomers.

Please devour them, I thought. Don't let them through. Don't let them through.

There was silence. And then the gates creaked open revealing the army of our enemy. The Cerise Guard marched in rows of five, swords in hand, their red samurai armor looking like fire in the light of the setting sun. One guard, their leader by the looks of his ornate armor, led the ranks, riding a pale white horse. His helmet looked like the head of a dragon, and his crimson red armor was decorated with ornate gold and silver shapes, like flowing flames. As he crossed the threshold of the gate, he held a piece of paper before him, for all of us to see. The letter that granted his army invitation into the Magic Hollow.

My anxiety was replaced with a pit of anger against Baron. Forget what Isabelle had said about him, in that moment, I hated him for betraying us.

*Boom. Boom-boom-boom-boom-boom.*

The drums continued as they poured in through the gate taking their own formation. When all of them, at least three hundred, had crossed the bridge and now stood in line, their leader spoke loudly, "Where is my informant? Come forward now and join our ranks and you will be given our highest level of protection!"

Fortunately, Baron was securely locked in his office. He wouldn't be joining his army today.

"No? You won't come forward?" The Cerise leader said. "Shame. My name's Yasuke. Leader of the Cerise Guard. For nearly thirteen years we've guarded Centerra from monsters, thieves, and bandits. The people accept our protection. They beg for it. But you've kept yourselves hidden from us."

"That's because we don't want, nor beg for your protection, let alone need it," Lance said boldly, his voice echoing across the field.

"Ah, a leader?" Yasuke said.

"I'm Lance Hawkwood, Knight of the Round Table and Defender of New Camelot."

"Knight, did you say?" Yasuke asked. "If I'm not mistaken, you're a knight-junior, am I correct? There isn't a single real knight in your entire army. All I see are a bunch of kids playing war."

The army of samurai laughed loudly, while members of our ranks fidgeted uncomfortably.

"So why don't you leave the monster fighting to us," Yasuke said. "And stop retaliating against our rule. Sure, our methods of protection require … *payment*, but we can work out an arrangement that works well for both of us. Say, this castle, for example. Let us set up our headquarters here, and in return, we'll offer you our protection. Easy as that."

"New Camelot was built by King Arthur himself, king of this realm. If anyone is meant to rule, it is us, by right!" Lance shouted defiantly. "We will not accept your protection, nor will we hand over our home. You're nothing but a gang of thugs, getting rich off weaker people beneath you. A bunch of cowardly thieves!"

"You think we're cowards? No. We're opportunists. We just so happen to be in the business of protective services. And don't talk to me about your right to rule!" Yasuke said. "Tell that to the kings who rule themselves fat beyond your precious little valley here. They don't honor you, nor do they respect the name of King Arthur—the fool who imprisoned us all in this realm! The Cerise Guard doesn't rule by birthright. We rule by strength. We rule because the people of Centerra let us rule. And because they know that resisting our rule is futile."

"I'll give you one chance," Lance said, "to turn back now and leave. Forget you ever came here. Do that or fight us."

"Not likely." Yasuke laughed. "Cerise Guard! Ready your swords!"

*Boom. Boom-boom-boom-boom-boom!* The drums beat loudly in response to Yasuke's call to arms.

"New Camelot, draw your weapons!" Lance shouted. "Archers, take aim!"

*Boom. Boom-boom-boom-boom-boom!*

"Hold!" Lance yelled.

Everyone went silent, on both sides of the battlefield.

"Maybe you're right, Yasuke. We are young. Many of us are inexperienced. But so are most of your warriors as well. Why waste good lives on this battlefield today?"

"So, you'll surrender after all?" Yasuke asked. "That would make this much easier."

"No. We won't surrender. Instead, I offer you a challenge. Pick your greatest champion and let them fight me. If I win, you'll swear an oath to leave and never bother us again."

Yasuke was silent, considering Lance's proposition.

"If our armies clash today, many good people will die. On both sides. Let us settle this with honor."

"Spoken like a true knight," Yasuke said. "Even we samurai of the Cerise Guard understand honor. And we, too, value the lives of our ranks. It makes no difference to me, as long as you kneel before me in the end."

"Then you'll accept the challenge?" Lance asked.

"I accept," Yasuke said, hopping off his horse. "And I'll be the Cerise Guard's champion."

"Hayden, come with me," Lance muttered.

Our ranks divided, allowing us a path through to the middle of the battlefield. I followed Lance nervously, holding my shield tightly.

"If I lose," Lance muttered. "Don't stand down. Rally everyone in my defense."

"But you made a deal—"

"I only said if I win, they must surrender. I never said anything about what happens if they win."

I nodded. "Be careful, Lance."

"I'll be okay. I know what I'm doing. This is what I've been waiting for.

This victory will be what allows me to finally become a full-fledged knight."

Lance gestured for me to stop, not too far away from the front lines of our own ranks. "Remember, if I lose, fall back and give the command to attack," Lance whispered. "After that, listen to Percy Igtham."

He continued out into the middle of the battlefield, as did Yasuke. They stopped when they were about ten yards apart from each other. Yasuke drew his sword, which flashed brilliantly. It was long and thin after the manner of most samurai swords. Something about it was beautiful and terrifying at the same time.

"Meet Kusanagi," Yasuke said. "The sword of the great hero Nagi."

I heard a few gasps from within our own ranks. "That's a legendary weapon! That's the weapon that killed the monster Orochi!"

I couldn't remember the name of the sword or the demon, but I felt like I had come across the legend somewhere in my studies. But famous or not, if that blade really was a legendary weapon, that meant Yasuke was very powerful to be able to wield it. And that made me fear for Lance. He was a skilled fighter, but he didn't have any legendary weapons.

"We fight until one of us yields, or is otherwise unable to battle," Lance said, drawing his sword.

"Very well," Yasuke said, stepping into his fighting stance. "Shall we begin?"

Lance nodded, then rushed at his opponent.

Yasuke was over a head taller than Lance, and Kusanagi was a long, thin blade, giving him far more reach compared to Lance. He blocked Lance's attack swiftly, keeping a safe distance from him at the same time. Yasuke was also quick on his feet, despite his size. With impeccable footwork, he danced around Lance, blocking his blows. I realized that in a full suit of armor, Lance had more protection than Yasuke, but he was also slower.

# THE BATTLE OF THE HOLLOW

They clashed again and again, Yasuke defending himself every time, his sword, Kusanagi, hissing through the air with each swing.

"You're a skilled fighter, Knight-junior!" Yasuke said. "Kusanagi's grateful. She hasn't faced such a challenge in a long time!"

"I don't need a fancy weapon to defeat you," Lance growled.

"Ah, but Kusanagi is far more than just a fancy weapon," Yasuke said. "Do you know what I had to do to earn her trust? I had to slay a wyvern. I did it completely on my own. The beast had been terrorizing farmers for years, until I came along. What did you do to earn the title Knight-junior, eh? Pass an exam? Win a tournament with your little friends?"

"Don't listen to him, Lance!" I shouted, knowing all too well how Yasuke's words might affect him.

"Kusanagi is said to have been born from a basilisk," Yasuke said. "Lately, I've come to believe that the legends are true. Do you want to know why?"

Lance ignored him and continued to assault him with a barrage of attacks.

"You might want to know this. Maybe you wouldn't have fought me if you had—Kusanagi is made from a magical steel that has a poisonous bite. One cut and your body will erupt in serious pain. Two or three cuts, and the poison will become potent enough to stop your heart."

"That just means you'll have to cut me first!" Lance shouted, dodging Yasuke's attack, then rallying with a barrage of his own.

It was terrifying. I'd never seen a duel like it in all my time training as Lance's squire. Gwen was right. Lance was the real deal. Unfortunately, Yasuke was very good as well. I thought Lance was better, but Yasuke had the advantage. Now that Lance knew that Kusanagi possessed a poisonous power, I could tell his attacks were slightly more reserved. He didn't want to take any big risks that might leave him exposed to Kusanagi's poison.

# CHAPTER NINETEEN

Yasuke, taking advantage of Lance's hesitation, side-stepped an attack, then successfully landed a powerful blow on Lance's shoulder. The armor protected him from Kusanagi's poisonous bite, but the force was still enough to knock him onto his knees.

Yasuke lifted his sword, ready to deal what could be a finishing blow, when a loud shriek echoed through the sky. In a flash of blue, Goliath dive bombed Yasuke, spitting and biting at his face. He yelled, grabbing madly at Goliath, trying to catch a hold of the little drake. Lance rose to his feet, steadying himself.

"Thanks for the help, Goliath," Lance said, wincing from pain, as Goliath flew up to safety, landing on top of my shield. Goliath hissed at me in a friendly sort of way, then turned to watch the fight, his wings arched, ready to take flight if needed again.

"That's not fair," Yasuke said, wiping blood from his scratched face.

"Yeah, just like how you have a poisonous sword," Lance said. "Goliath's just evening the playing field." Lance charged him again, sending another barrage of swift attacks.

Yasuke defended all of Lance's attacks, but he was hard pressed to keep his footwork right. Somehow, Lance was gaining the advantage over him. The Cerise Guard, who now looked nervous, started inching closer and closer.

"I can't take this anymore," Isabelle yelled from our side of the field. "I hate leaving it all to Lance!"

She stepped forward, and many more of our ranks followed her. Soon, Yasuke and Lance were surrounded by Cerise Guard samurai and New Camelot knights, all glaring at each other, bearing weapons. The knights and the samurai were looking like they wanted a fight. I wondered if both sides would honor their agreement.

# THE BATTLE OF THE HOLLOW

Lance dodged Yasuke's attack, then, with a fierce slash, knocked Kusanagi clean out of Yasuke's hands. The legendary weapon hissed defiantly as it spun through the air, landing with its point falling deep into the grass several yards away. Lance stepped around Yasuke, knocking him to his knees, and bringing his sword around him, holding it threateningly before him.

"Do you yield?" Lance asked.

"A samurai never yields," Yasuke said through gritted teeth. "I'd rather die than yield to you."

"Do it!" someone shouted from our side. "Finish him off!"

Lance hesitated. "How do I know your army will retreat when this duel is over?"

"You don't," Yasuke said, smiling sardonically. "Now do it. You win. Finish me off and don't disgrace me by hesitating any longer!"

Lance lifted his sword to strike, when suddenly, the sound of a deep horn echoed through the Magic Hollow.

"What?" Lance said, looking up as another horn bellowed loudly.

"Look, something is crossing the bridge," Cole shouted.

"He's right," Lucas said. "Look!"

The horns bellowed again as a small army of trolls, decked out in armor, crossed the bridge. They were ugly masses of gnarled grey skin, bulging muscles, and beady eyes. Their banner carrier lifted torn ugly flags, all bearing different colors and symbols. At the front of the army marched two very familiar faces. Even from this distance I knew it was the troll Prince Garl-Oonga, and his father the troll king Garl-Oonga-Oonga.

Lance, cursing in Old English, struck Yasuke across the helmet with the pommel of his sword. "Is this some kind of trick, samurai?"

Yasuke laughed wickedly as another deep horn bellowed. "Let's see how you fare against the army of darkness! Cerise Guard! Retreat! Pull back and retreat!"

Most of the Cerise Guard followed Yasuke's order. But others remained, watching the trolls march across the bridge, then looking back at their leader inquisitively.

"They could only come in if they were invited," Lance yelled. "What did you do, Yasuke? You've doomed us all!"

"I only did what I knew needed to be done, to ensure victory, and to be sure that the menace created by King Arthur be thoroughly destroyed from our realm. You knights are the reason we're all trapped in Between. Our ancestors were ripped from their homes and locked away in this prison! Finally, someone is bringing justice upon you. Good luck!" Yasuke ran, drawing his sword from the dirt and continuing to lead his army into a retreat.

"You coward!" Lance shouted.

"You defeated me," Yasuke said. "We had a deal, remember? You win, and we retreat, never to return. I am a man of my word. Cerise Guard—you heard me. Retreat! Pull back!"

"Wait?" I heard one of the Cerise Guards say. "*Boss* did this? He conspired with monsters?"

I heard a murmuring pass over the Cerise Guard. Many of them were hesitating to retreat. The Trolls had all crossed the bridge. There were at least one hundred of them.

"We swore an oath to defend Centerra from monsters!" another of the red-armored guards shouted. "And now we are supposed to sit back and watch them wreak havoc?"

"RETREAT!" Yasuke yelled. "THAT IS AN ORDER!"

Lance, ignoring the Cerise Guard, turned to face us. "Knights of the

Round Table—today you're all defenders of New Camelot! Our enemy is far worse than we ever imagined. More than we could ever prepare for. One troll has the strength of ten of us. But we have the courage, valor, and bravery of a dozen! Cerise Guard, trolls, whoever it is, it doesn't matter. We fight to protect our home!"

The knights screamed loudly, raising their swords and shields into the air. I felt my heart racing. I was anxious, but beneath that, I felt a strange thrill as well. I'd faced these trolls before. At least two of them. I knew they made formidable opponents. And now, seeing so many of them united against us, it was terrifying. But Lance was right. We couldn't back down. An enemy was still an enemy. We would fight just as hard.

"Brace yourselves!" Lance yelled.

The trolls, hollering and shouting with loud hoarse voices, lowered their heads and charged like angry rhinos.

# UNLIKELY ALLIES

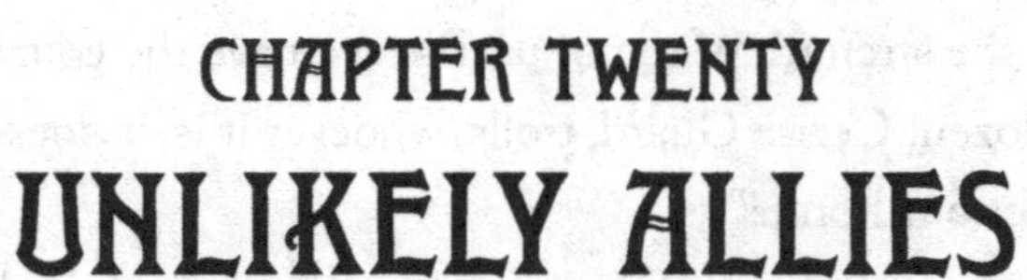

**A**s the trolls charged and the Cerise Guard fled, we readied ourselves for the battle of our lives. I stood close to Lance, flexing my sword arm, feeling very jittery. This was actually happening. I had read about a hundred battles fought by King Arthur and his knights. I never imagined I would ever be in one myself!

"Archers, ready your arrows!" Lance shouted. "Aim! Fire!"

The archers, led by Elibora, aimed their bows, then let loose, sending dozens of arrows whistling through the air. They weren't normal arrows either, these shot through the air like firecrackers, then exploded in a flash of multi-colored flames as they struck the trolls or the ground in front of them. The crackling explosions heated the air and temporarily halted the trolls' charge.

"Fire at will!" Lance yelled. Another round of exploding arrows zipped through the air. I knew we wouldn't be able to use these when the trolls got too close to our own forces, it would be too dangerous, but for now, it was a great way to slow down their charge. Their troll hide was thick, and while a little fire did seem to hurt them, it didn't stop them from stampeding onward either.

Unexpectedly, loud drums started beating from the mass of

retreating Cerise Guard, who had moved in a wide berth around the trolls, making their way for the bridge. Boom! Boom-boom-boom-boom-boom! Boom! Boom-boom-boom-boom-boom! The call of the drum was answered by several other drums calling back in response. I tore my eyes away from the charging trolls for a brief second and saw that a small garrison of Cerise Guards were flocking together at the back of their army, facing the wrong way. They weren't retreating, they were gathering at arms. They were going to stay and fight!

Even from here, I could faintly hear Yasuke barking and screaming orders, but the deserting samurai didn't seem to care. Several dozens of them had gathered and were preparing a charge. In our direction.

"Look!" I shouted. "Some of them are going to fight!" But my voice was swallowed up by the roaring sound of heavy troll feet trampling the ground as Garl-oonga-oonga's army fell upon our ranks.

"Stay beside me!" Lance shouted, as he joined in beside Lucas to face off against a nearby troll. Together, Lance and Lucas pressed back the troll and managed to injure it with several attacks at its thick tree trunk-like legs. I couldn't help but notice how this time, the troll didn't explode into ash like the troll had when I struck it with a legendary weapon.

The troll shouted with anger, swinging giant fists that left holes in the ground where it struck. Lance and Lucas dodged, trying to recoup their attack.

I watched the battle with gritted teeth. "I can't stay back and just watch this!" I shouted. Shield and sword in hand, I charged the troll.

Together, the three of us managed to stop the thing, and at last, it fell to the ground, beaten. I wanted to cheer, but I realized that this troll was only one of many. Nearly a hundred more monstrous trolls were fighting and smashing and pushing back our forces.

# CHAPTER TWENTY

A small pack of trolls turned and saw us, shouting with rage at the sight of their fallen comrade. They all rushed at us, shaking the ground as they went. I thought for sure we were goners, but out of nowhere, several Cerise Guard samurai rushed in to our aid. With their help, we were able to fend off the trolls, and somehow make it through our second skirmish alive.

"Thank you!" Lance shouted. "Thank you so much!"

One of the Samurai nodded. I could see she was a girl under her helmet. She smiled, and I quickly realized it was the same girl we had encountered earlier outside of the hollow. "There was no honor in what Yasuke did. We swore an oath to defend Centerra from monsters, and he allowed the biggest army of monsters we have ever seen to march right into the city. For this, we will set aside our differences with you knights. Today, we are allies. Even if you dropped a street lamp on my head." She glared at me.

"Er, sorry about that," I said.

"We are grateful for your honor," Lance said.

With Cerise Guard deserters by our side, we continued the battle, fighting to defend ourselves from the trolls. While only a small number of the Cerise Guard army had stayed behind to fight, I was still extremely grateful for each one of them that did. The trolls were fierce, and even though we outnumbered them, Lance was right. They fought with the strength of multiple people.

Fighting the trolls was messy work, and nothing like a one-on-one duel. On the battlefield, there were no rules. And the trolls certainly didn't play by any either. They fought ruthlessly, several trolls standing side by side, pounding and thrashing furiously, not caring if they hit one of us, or another troll. It was a mad frenzy. Our biggest advantage was teamwork. Unlike the trolls, we communicated with each other, coming to one another's aid, and trying to organize assaults. The trolls were strong, but they couldn't attack every direction at once, though they tried. Working with Lance and Lucas, together we managed to surround and take out several more trolls, one by one. It was slow and tiring work that felt like it would never end.

Amidst the fighting, just after we felled our third monster, I heard a shout from behind me. I turned and watched as Gale was struck across the chest by a massive troll's fist. The gleaming legendary weapon, Seure, fell—no, leapt—from his grip, abandoning him. Gale had tried to fight with the legendary weapon, and Seure had not allowed him to.

"Gale!" I screamed, forgetting my duty to stand beside Lance, and rushing toward him. I arrived just in time, attacking with all my strength. I blocked a punch with my shield, and the force of the blow made my arm feel like it would snap. Not allowing myself to think about the pain, I rolled to the left, slashing at the troll's leg as I passed. The troll bellowed in pain, grabbing at the wound I had made. Without hesitating, I rushed in and jabbed, hitting the troll again and again. It flung its arms madly, and I had to block with my shield, still getting knocked back from the force.

Part of me wanted to run. Part of me wondered if I could do this. The troll was so big, and I was so small. I was just a squire. And then I remembered what Gwen had told me: all this time you've spent so much time comparing yourself to stories about your father, you never noticed that just being you was enough.

Remembering her words filled me with courage. The troll attacked, but I didn't back down or flinch like the old Hayden would have. Sure, I wasn't a magnificent hero like Lance, or my father, but I was the best me I could be. And it was time to show these trolls what I was made of.

I let out my fiercest battle cry, then dodged, ducking underneath the troll. I leapt into the air, attacking with all my strength. My attack met its mark, and with one last grunt the monster fell to the ground with an earth-shattering crush.

I fell beside Gale, who was sputtering trying to find his breath. The troll must have knocked the wind right out of him when he struck. Fortunately, he was still alive.

"It didn't work," Gale moaned. "Seure wouldn't fight for me. I thought after slaying so many enemies that it would work. I thought the sword would trust me."

"It's okay," I said, grabbing Seure, which felt very hot in my hands, almost like it was trying to burn me. I quickly shoved it into its scabbard, and immediately it cooled off. I placed the scabbard across Gale's chest, and he held the sword tightly. Even if it had betrayed him, I could tell he wasn't ready to give up on it yet. Grabbing him under the armpits, I dragged him back away from the battle as far as I could, leaning him up against the castle wall. Gale winced from the pain. "Broken ribs, I think," he groaned.

"Stay here," I said. "When all this is over, we'll get you all cleaned up. I promise."

I turned my attention back to the battle. It was a huge mess. I looked and looked, but I couldn't see Lance anywhere.

I looked and saw that a garrison of trolls were making their way toward the forest. "No!" I heard Lance shout, emerging into view amidst the fray, taking off at a sprint after them.

I wondered if the trolls were heading for the sword, Excalibur. Could they possibly have known about its location, and if they did, what could they possibly want with it? Besides, if Lance took them all on alone, he would be sorely outnumbered.

Suddenly, a troll leapt at me from the side, catching me off guard. I tried to dodge, but he clipped my leg and knocked me over. Vaguely remembering Arabella in the back of my mind, I remembered her scolding me as a child for running with scissors in my hand. Well, this time, I had kind of been running with a big sharp sword in my hand. Not smart. I should have put it in its sheath.

Not wanting to stab myself, I was forced to throw the sword aside as I fell flat on my face. The troll spun around on me, and lunged, about to squash me flat.

Suddenly, two arrows exploded right in the troll's face.

I looked up to see Elibora and Cecily running to my aid. They flung their bows over their shoulders, then drew their swords. "Oh no you don't!" Elibora shouted as the two of them attacked in unison. Blinded from the exploding arrows, the troll swung around even more wildly than normal. The two girls dodged and attacked together, bringing down the troll.

"I missed the thrill of the hunt," Elibora said proudly, wiping her sword clean on the troll's tattered leather shirt before it puffed into ash.

I stood up, retrieving my sword and catching my breath. "Thanks. You really saved me there."

"No problem. But, Hayden—what's going on?" Elibora asked. "You're going the wrong way. The battle's over here."

"It's Lance!" I said, pointing ahead. He was already leaping over the stones crossing the river. "I was going to help him!"

"What is he doing running to the Forest?"

"A group of trolls went into the woods," I said. "I'm worried they are headed for Excalibur. Lance went after them alone. We have to help him!

"What about the centaurs and wolves?" Cecily asked hesitantly. "They're still upset. Will they let us enter?"

"Don't worry," Elibora said. "I've hunted with them tons of times. They know me and trust me. If the wolves notice us, I don't think they'll hurt us."

# CHAPTER TWENTY

"*Think?*" Cecily asked skeptically.

"This is no longer a battle over New Camelot," Elibora said. "The moment those trolls showed up, this became something bigger. The Cerise Guard would've been satisfied taking the castle, but not these trolls. They don't want our castle; they want to destroy everything. They'll raze the castle, burn the forest, and destroy everything in the Magic Hollow. The Centaurs and Wolves are smart. If we're lucky, they 'll see that, and join the battle."

"Let's hope so," I said. "Hang on, Lance. We're coming!"

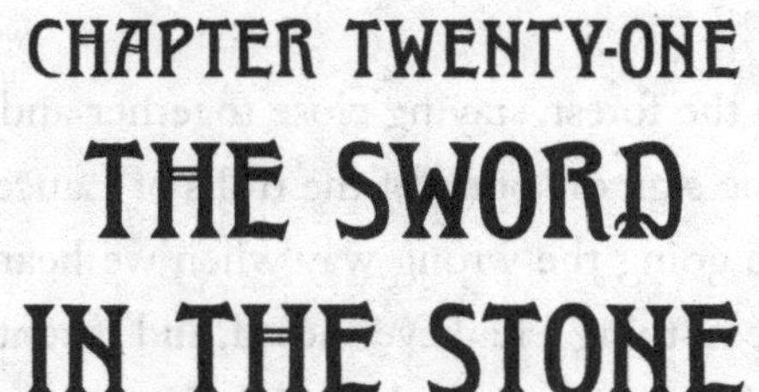

# THE SWORD IN THE STONE

The Enchanted Forest was oddly eerie and quiet. The sounds of the battle taking place before the castle were completely silent beyond the Serpentine River's roaring rapids and the forest's dense foliage. I remembered the forest was always dark, but now that the sun had set, it was unnervingly so.

"How are we supposed to see anything?" Cecily asked, as the three of us huddled close.

"One second," Elibora said. "Let me try a spell." She closed her eyes, wrinkling her brow with concentration. She took a deep breath, her eyes closed in intense concentration, then exhaled, a small glowing light appearing above her outstretched palm like a tiny star. It wasn't a great source of light, but it would do.

"I really need to learn how to do this whole magic thing!"

Elibora rubbed a bead of sweat from her forehead. "It's harder than it looks. Especially on a night like this. It's hard to explain, but when I cast the spell, it was like I could feel the despair of the battle all around us."

I wondered what she meant by that, but there was no time to ask. When all of this was over, I could have my friends teach me how to cast spells. For now, we had Lance and a gang of dangerous trolls to worry about.

We set off into the forest, staying close together and jumping at every sound. There was no sign or sound of the trolls or Lance. I was starting to wonder if we were going the wrong way when we heard wolves howling. It was a sound like nothing I had ever heard, and it sent shivers down my spine. Elibora on the other hand got excited.

"The wolves!" She exclaimed. "That was their battle cry. Hurry! We must be close!"

We started to run, weaving through the trees and pushing our way through the tangled underbrush. A loud horn echoed through the trees, followed by another howling wolf.

"That horn belongs to the Centaurs!" Elibora said. "They're close! I think they've joined the fight as well."

The trees opened, and we found ourselves in a large clearing. I had been here once before, though it looked completely different at night. Excalibur sat at the top of the rocks and fountain in the middle of the spring, glowing gently, bathing the entire clearing in a soft blue light.

It would have been a peaceful sight if it weren't for the total disarray happening around the spring. Several snow-white wolves as big as grizzly bears and Centaurs armed with bows and scimitars were fighting the band of trolls we had followed. There was no sign of Lance anywhere, which made me nervous.

"We have to help them," I said, drawing my sword and running into the fray, Elibora and Cecily trailing behind me.

I don't know what I expected, but the moment we stepped into sight, one of the trolls howled with rage. "Look, Papa! Look! Him. The one who poked Jon!"

Garl-oonga-oonga turned to look at me, roaring with rage when he saw my face. "SQUASH HIM! NO MERCY!" the troll king ordered, stomping his feet on the ground like an overgrown toddler throwing a tantrum.

Shoving two wolves aside like they were stuffed animals, their heavy bodies slamming into the trees so hard the trunks snapped loudly, the Troll Prince, Garl-oonga took off at a sprint straight for me.

"Um, Hayden. You know these guys?" Elibora asked, readying her sword.

"I'm not very popular with them," I said, stating the obvious.

"DIE!" the Troll Prince screamed, ripping a giant branch off a tree as he ran, then hurtling it right at the three of us. We all scattered trying to avoid the branch. Elibora and I escaped, but Cecily got hit in the leg, knocking her off balance.

"Ceci!" Elibora shrieked, running to her injured squire's side. "I'm so sorry . . ."

"Don't worry about me," Cecily said, limping to cover. "I'll take care of myself. Watch out—"

The Troll Prince roared in rage, charging again, joined by his father, the troll king. For a moment, I'll admit, I thought we were done for. But Elibora had different thoughts. She stabbed her sword into the ground, then drew her bow from off her shoulder with lightning dexterity. She fired off two exploding arrows like she was shooting a machine gun. The arrows hit the trolls and exploded in their faces, sending them staggering. Cecily's injury seemed to fuel Elibora with a new strength and an impressive determination to protect her squire and friend.

Seeing my chance, I rushed in with my sword and struck the Troll Prince across the kneecap. He howled with pain, kicking and thrashing about. I tried to dodge, but by sheer luck he scored a hit on me, which sent me flying backward.

"You no cut!" the troll king yelled. "I no lose son-prince to a puny runt!" Flexing his muscles, he breathed in deeply. At first, I couldn't tell if he had a stomachache or what, but then I realized the troll king was casting magic. When he opened his eyes, they were glowing purple. He raised his mammoth sized hands and a swirling black fire sprouted from his fingertips. The flames turned into shadows, and the shadows turned into writhing creatures that looked like shadowy wolves with bright yellow eyes.

"GET THEM!" he shouted. "DEADER THAN DEAD!" Even in the heat of the moment, I couldn't help but admire this guy's way with words.

"I think we're in trouble, Eli," I said, clenching my teeth. "What are these things?"

"I have no idea," Elibora said, wide eyed. "Look sharp. They're coming!" She drew her bow, firing off arrows in rapid succession. Each arrow struck a shadow monster vanquishing it into thin air, but no matter how many arrows she fired, more and more creatures continued to appear from the shadowy flames the troll king summoned with his strange magic, jutting about like lightning.

I rushed in with my sword and started attacking madly, vanquishing shadow monsters with every swing. It was like a video game, where the enemy just never stopped coming, and I was trying to get the highest score possible. Except in this game, I didn't have any extra lives. One wrong move, and it was game over.

I was so busy fighting shadow monsters, I forgot about the troll prince. I heard his maniacal laugh, kind of a stupid raspy chuckle, before I ever saw him. From the corner of my eye, I saw movement, and tried to evade, but I knew I wasn't going to be fast enough. A heavy branch whipped through the air about to hit me dead on. And then there was a flash of silver, and Lance was there, splitting the branch in midair with his sword.

"Lance!" I called out. "You're okay!"

"Don't give up, Hayden!" he said, joining the battle. "We can do this!"

Lance's arrival revitalized my courage. By his side, I felt like we were invincible. We were about to rush back into battle when the troll king yelled loudly, "STOP!" All the shadow monsters obeyed his command, encircling around us in a wide ring. "Look who joins us! The traitor!"

I gasped, looking around. But I didn't see Baron anywhere. What was he talking about? Then I realized the troll king was pointing at Lance.

"We are here thanks to you. Why you fight us?? We are your guests. No way to treat guests" He laughed moronically.

"What?" I shouted. "That can't be true. Lance is one of us—he's a knight. He wouldn't betray us!"

The troll king laughed harder. "Fool! Lance gave samurai man letter. Samurai man gave trolls letter. Trolls invade."

"Don't listen to him, Hayden. He's lying. Trying to break our courage!" Elibora shouted.

Lance lowered his sword. "It's true," he said quietly. "I penned the invitation. I invited the Cerise Guard, posing as a traitor."

"What? Why?" I asked. "How could you?"

"I had to," Lance said. "It was the only way. Nobody would listen to me, not Hal, not Baron. We can never reach our true potential if we don't leave the Magic Hollow. I staged this battle, but not because I wanted to see the Magic Hollow fail. I did it so the Magic Hollow could win. I did it to make us stronger!"

I couldn't believe my ears. But it had to be true. Lance admitted to the whole thing. I thought about Gale, injured in battle, and nearly killed. I wondered how many others were suffering the same fate. Because of Lance.

"I won't give up!" Lance shouted. "I'm not a traitor! I will fight to the death if I must! I will prove my worth!" Lance charged into the shadow monsters' ranks, hacking and slashing wildly, vaporizing dozens in seconds. He cut a path straight through them, leading up to the rock mound in the center of the spring. "I will destroy our enemies and bring peace to Between once and for all, starting with you trolls!"

Lance leaped up the rocks swiftly, then cast aside his sword. "I did it, so that I could earn the right to wield Excalibur! I only did what was necessary!" Lance clutched Excalibur's hilt tightly. "Excalibur is mine!"

Lance pulled upward with all his strength . . .

And the sword didn't budge an inch. Instead, it slid even deeper into the stone.

The troll king laughed madly as the prince rushed the rock formation. He swung his massive fist through the air, striking Lance hard in the chest. Lance's body crumpled under the impact as he fell off the rocks rolling into the shallow water.

I couldn't believe my eyes. Lance had failed.

Elibora's scream and my own were joined with another, as we watched a dozen shadow monsters pounce in the direction Lance had fallen.

"NO!" Gwen cried, running out from the trees behind me. "LANCE!"

"Gwen, stay back! It's too dangerous," I heard a man say. Gwen stopped in her tracks, falling to her knees in tears. I knew only one person could command that kind of loyalty from Gwen . . .

I turned and found myself staring at a tall, wizened man who could be none other than Principal Hal. He had a thick, burly beard of red and silver, which mixed together like a swirled ice cream cone. His bright green eyes twinkled wildly in the light of Excalibur. Hal had a glow about him, like he radiated power, but in a different way than the troll king did. Hal radiated goodness.

Jack Lantern and Mr. Bianco were standing beside him as well, armed to fight. "Hayden! I'm so glad you're okay," Mr. Bianco shouted, clasping my shoulder. "Don't worry, we can take it from here." He flipped his golden dagger in his hands, looking anxious for a fight.

I nodded, then ran to Gwen's side. I put my arm around her, trying to comfort her, but she was sobbing so hard I didn't think she could even hear me. "Lance . . ." she muttered. "Lance, how could you?"

I looked and found Elibora was kneeling beside Cecily as well, who had been struck badly by the branch that had been hurled at us. From the looks of it, she looked like she was okay. I strained my neck trying to catch sight of Lance, but I couldn't see him anywhere.

Mr. Bianco and Jack were the only things standing between us and the dozens of shadow monsters, but they fought so fiercely, not a single monster ever slipped past them. Principal Hal, on the other hand, focused all his attention on the troll prince and king.

Garl-oonga, the troll prince, didn't hesitate attacking Hal. Without even flinching, I watched Hal take a deep breath, then summon glowing golden chains from thin air. Magic. The chains swirled through the air, wrapping around the troll prince's arms and legs, tightening and then finally pinning him to the ground. The troll thrashed and struggled, but the chains held him tightly.

Garl-oonga-oonga shouted furiously.

Instead of running after Hal, however, the troll turned and ran straight for the rock formation containing Excalibur.

The troll king breathed in more swirling dark magic, then exhaled loudly, summoning even more of the black flames. The shadowy fire danced around the rock formation, twisting and writhing about it and Excalibur.

"Stand down," Hal said calmly, walking around the edge of the shallow spring. "You will not destroy the sword nor harm anyone else."

"SILENCE!" The troll king roared, sending a blast of black flames straight at Hal.

With a deep breath and a flick of his wrist, a wall of water shot up out of the spring, completely extinguishing the flames. The troll king stomped his feet angrily, looking like an oversized toddler throwing a fit.

He clenched his fists tightly, summoning dozens of swirling dark flames around his body. It looked like he was surrounded by a terrifying evil tornado. And then he released the magic, sending dozens of fiery blasts in every direction, all homed in on Hal, like rapid fire.

Hal threw up his hands in a defensive posture, summoning a large golden shield that floated in the air before him. It spun around madly, defending him from the barrage of blasts. It held, but barely. I could see the strain on Hal's face as he tried to defend himself, while Garl-oonga-oonga laughed maniacally, firing his powerful magic blasts like a machine gun.

Even Jack and Mr. Bianco were starting to be overwhelmed by all the shadow monsters. The wolves and centaurs still fought, as well, but I couldn't help but notice that we seemed to be outnumbered and losing.

If we lost, the Magic Hollow would be destroyed. Everything I had worked for would be gone. The last hope for bringing light back to Between would be extinguished like a blown-out candle.

"I won't let that happen," I muttered to myself.

I looked up, and Excalibur glowed brilliantly before me. I felt something stir in my chest. And then I realized, I was not the same person I had been several weeks ago when I first tried to pull Excalibur from the stone. That Hayden had been struggling to prove himself and live in his father's shadow. That Hayden wanted to be a hero, but didn't know how, or if he had the strength to do it.

But now, I understood. Heroes aren't born, they are made through their own choices. And I chose to stand up and fight. I wasn't going to sit back and let someone hurt my friends and threaten to destroy my true home.

I charged through the spring, then vaulted the rock formation, hacking down shadow monsters in my way. I could feel the raw pressure battering against me like an insane windstorm, coming from the magic Garl-oonga-oonga had summoned to try and break the formation and destroy the sword, but I didn't let that stop me.

I did what I knew I had to do. I gripped Excalibur and pulled.

The sword came free easily, as if I had been lifting it out of water instead of rock. I held it above my head triumphantly as a rush of glowing blue water shot out of the hole where Excalibur had been, like I had just unstopped a fountain. The water rushed down the rock, extinguishing the dark flames, and vanquishing the shadow monsters on contact.

A bright light emanated from the sword, piercing the dark forest. I felt a wave of warmth shoot out from Excalibur in a powerful ripple. Like a tidal wave sweeping through the forest, Excalibur's energy radiated in every direction, leaving behind it a trail of flowers, greenery, and light, resurrecting the forest to its true glory. I watched the forest transform in the wake of Excalibur's power. Then, millions of bright colors appeared amongst the trees as the fairies awoke.

"The fairies!" I heard Elibora shout.

Each light was actually a little sprite with beautifully colored wings like butterflies. They glowed brightly, and swirled around the spring, swarming and vanquishing the shadow monsters. One of them flew by me, a tiny winged girl with bright purple hair and a dress of bright green leaves. She winked and showed me the peace sign, before fluttering away.

I jumped off the rock formation, landing with a splash in the water,

Excalibur glowing threateningly in my hand. "You won't hurt my friends," I declared, brandishing Excalibur before him.

"NO!" he shouted, sending several large blasts of fire straight at me.

I blocked them, and Excalibur extinguished them in midair, leaving behind nothing but harmless puffs of smoke. Garl-oonga-oonga looked surprised. He turned frantically, starting to run away.

"Papa—don't leave me," his son yelled, still chained to the ground.

The Troll King summoned a large shadowy ring and jumped through it, vanishing from sight. The same ring appeared on the ground beneath his son, who fell in, vanishing as well. Similar rings appeared beside all the remaining trolls in the clearing, and I assumed the entire battlefield.

When they were gone, Hal's golden shield fell to the ground, shattering into tiny fragments. Hal fell to one knee, clutching his chest, breathing deeply. He composed himself, then stood. "Jack, Ector—are you okay?"

"A little banged up, but I'm okay," Jack said.

"Same here. Alive and well," Mr. Bianco said, leaning his hands on his knees, breathing deeply.

"I'm okay, too," Strings said. "In case anyone was wondering."

Still holding Excalibur in my hands, I stood in the water of the spring, probably looking like a total wacko. I was still processing everything that just happened.

Suddenly, Elibora and Cecily rushed into me giving me a huge hug. "Hayden! You pulled the sword from the stone!" Elibora said excitedly.

"Very impressive," Cecily said.

I looked down at the sword in my hand. The blade was long and thin, forged from a bluish-tinted material. Avalonian silver.

"I don't have a hilt," I said foolishly, realizing I didn't know what to do with the legendary sword now that the fighting was over.

"You won't need one," Hal said, beaming at me. "Watch."

I lowered Excalibur to my side, and the blade vanished into mist. "Where did it go?" I exclaimed, looking around frantically for it.

"Will it to return," Hal said.

I didn't know what he meant, but I willed the sword to return, and then, just like that it rematerialized in my hand, as real and solid as it had been before. "Wow," was all I could say.

"Lance, Gwen—did you see that?" I asked, but I realized neither of them were around. I turned about, looking for my friends. I saw Gwen, standing on the other side of the spring, examining around the spot where Lance would have fallen.

"Lance?" Gwen shouted. "Lance, where are you?"

Forgetting my new sword, which vanished into mist, I ran over to Gwen. "Where did he go?" I asked. "Did anyone see him?"

She shook her head, "I—I don't know . . . he was here. He was right here." She started to cry again.

Hal came to her side and put his arm around her in a fatherly sort of way. "It'll be okay, Gwen," he said gently. "We'll find him. Don't worry."

"And what will happen when he returns? Will we have to . . . punish him for betraying us?"

"Whatever Lance's reasoning for what he did, we all know what a true and devoted knight he is," Hal said, avoiding the question, but satisfying Gwen's curiosity for the time being.

Gwen gave me a big hug, tears still streaming down her face. "You did amazing, Hayden. I'm so proud of you!"

"Thank you," I said, partly feeling guilty about what had happened.

Lance was the hero; he was the one who was supposed to pull Excalibur from the stone. Apparently, even Lance did.

Wherever he was, I hoped he was okay.

Suddenly, I realized all the centaurs and the wolves had gathered around us. They looked at me, then bowed in respect. Ixion stepped forward from the crowd.

"Young man, you fought bravely—not only to defend your castle, but to defend our forest as well. You truly are a protector of the Magic Hollow. We thank you."

I bowed to the centaur chief, humbled by his kind words.

"Wolves and men have rarely mixed well," a tall, proud looking wolf said, who I assumed must be the leader of their pack. "But we're proud to live beside such a valiant knight."

"Thank you," I said, "but I'm no knight. I'm just a squire."

"Hayden, after this, I think it's safe to assume you are going to be made a knight," Elibora said, laughing.

The best part was, she was right.

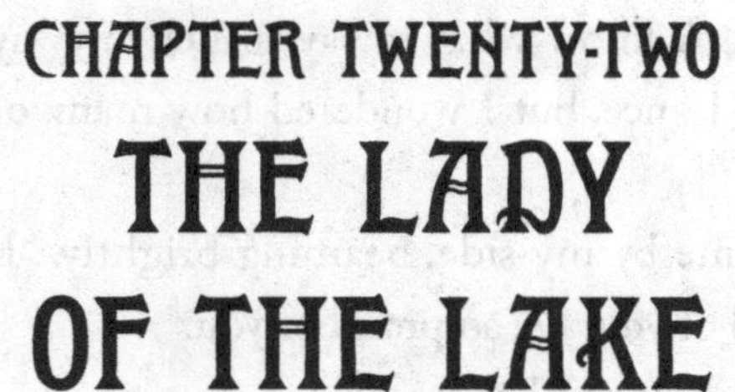

# CHAPTER TWENTY-TWO
# THE LADY OF THE LAKE

Led by a procession of centaurs and wolves, we departed the Enchanted Forest. At the front of the line, Ixion, the centaur chief, chatted animatedly with the pack leader, Fenrir, about a large hunting party he wanted to throw in honor of the day's victory and their new alliance.

"I give my word," Ixion said, "never again will a wolf be shewed away from our part of the forest. Together, we can live and hunt in harmony. In fact, my daughter is to be married soon. All of you need to be there, I won't take no for an answer."

The wolf agreed. "We would be honored," he said.

I couldn't help but feel happy knowing that the centaurs and the wolves were finally resolving their conflict. Maybe this battle really was what we all needed to come together and strengthen our bonds. That thought gave me a weird feeling in my gut. Should we be thanking Lance, or criticizing him? He put a lot of people in danger, but was he right all along about what the Magic Hollow needed to progress? If so, that made him more of a martyr for what he did, sacrificing his own honor for the greater good.

I supported Gwen under my arm, who was still crying silently as we walked. She hadn't spoken much at all since we departed the spring together, but I didn't know what to say to her, anyway. I knew she still thought highly of Lance, but I wondered how many others would share her view.

Mr. Bianco came by my side, beaming brightly. "Hayden, your dad would be so proud of you. *I'm* so proud of you."

"Thank you, Mr. Bianco," I said.

"Please, call me Ector. I'm not your middle school English teacher anymore."

"Okay, okay. I'll try. It's still just a little weird. Sir Ector," I said, smiling because it sounded so weird to address my teacher that way, "I couldn't have done it without you. When I learned that Camwennan was a legendary weapon, and I'd wielded it to slay that first troll, I realized maybe I *did* have what it takes to be a true hero all along."

Sir Ector smiled brightly. "Hayden, there's something I want you to remember. It's not the legendary weapon that gives a hero strength. *You* give the weapon strength. Without a hero, the weapon is just another piece of scrap."

"Even Excalibur?" I asked.

"Yes, even Excalibur. You're the first person to wield that sword in at least one thousand years, and not because of your birthright, fate, destiny, or anything like that. It's because of who you are—who you have become. Never forget that. Just being you was all it took."

"It wasn't easy to discover who I am," I admitted. "I almost lost my way for a minute. I was ready to leave and put all of this behind me."

"But you didn't," Jack Lantern said. "Strings told us what happened. Even when your friends had given up on you, you didn't give up on them. That is true loyalty, Hayden, and true friendship."

"But if it weren't for Lance and Gwen, I wouldn't have had the strength or courage to do what I had to do either," I pointed out. Mentioning Lance made me realize how sad I was for what happened. More than anything, I was worried about him. I knew Gwen was too.

"Wherever Lance is, he has to be brought to justice," Jack said coldly.

"We all trusted Lance," I said. "He never gave us any reason not to."

"I still trust him," Gwen said angrily. "He never meant for anyone to get hurt. And he only did what he felt like he had to do. He must have run away because he was ashamed. I wish I could tell him he doesn't have to be ashamed. I forgive him."

What I didn't tell Gwen right then was that even though she forgave him, I was certain a lot of the other knights would struggle feeling the same way when they found out what happened, just like Jack.

Jack looked like he wanted to argue, but Sir Ector eyed him sharply, shaking his head, and mouthing the words, not now.

We left the Enchanted Forest and crossed the Serpentine River, finding ourselves surrounded by a large gathering of knights, squires, soldiers, pages, and villagers from Caerleon. Everyone was there. Percy, looking stern and proud like always, even Gale, who stood clutching his wounded side, supported by Lucas and Cole, as well as Kaylinelle, smiling infectiously, and even Isabelle, arms crossed and serious as ever, still cracked a smile.

"Elibora!" Lady Albreda shouted, running from the crowd and embracing her granddaughter. "And, you, come here, too," Lady Albreda said warmly to Cecily, who looked surprised, but pleased, giving her a big hug as well."

As far as I could tell, everyone was safe. Sure, we were cut and bruised and a little broken, but miraculously, I didn't see anyone who hadn't survived the fight. Everyone was here.

Except for Lance of course.

# CHAPTER TWENTY-TWO

Principal Hal stepped forward, waving to the crowd. "I am deeply touched by the valiant way you all defended the Magic Hollow during my long absence. You all fought bravely and worthily of your roles and titles. I am honored to stand amongst such an incredible collective of knights and soldiers."

Everyone cheered loudly, celebrating the victory. I noticed, however, a small group of people at the back of the crowd, who shuffled awkwardly. It was the samurai who had deserted the Cerise Guard to stay and help fight the troll army. They all looked bashful, like they felt out of place.

Hal must have noticed them, too because he said next, "And now, I would like to give a special thanks to those few brave souls, who came as enemies, but fought as friends. You are mighty warriors, and even fiercer friends. If you desire, you are welcome to stay in the Magic Hollow."

Everyone turned, cheering for the samurai. They looked surprised but welcomed the applause. One of the former Cerise Guards stepped forward removing her helmet. She had long straight black hair, and the tattoo of a phoenix creeping up her neck.

"Thank you for your kind words. We were led to believe false accusations by Yasuke, who wanted to destroy you and steal your home, which is why we came to battle. When the troll army arrived, we realized that our leader acted without honor by consorting with monsters. Though today the Cerise Guard has lost its way, we, too, are bound by honor to fight monsters and defend the innocent. In that regard, we are no different from the Knights of the Round Table. We accept your offer to remain in the Magic Hollow, however, it is our desire to reform the Cerise Guard anew, restoring its values to what it once was. We will not join your ranks as knights or soldiers sworn to your Table."

"We offer you all that you need to accomplish this great endeavor,"

Principal Hal said, bowing to the samurai. "Now, let's hear it again for our new friends of the Cerise Guard!"

Everyone cheered happily, shaking hands and introducing themselves to the Cerise Guard.

Suddenly, amidst our celebrations, a low, warm fog rolled over us. I heard someone gasp and realized that several people were pointing at something. I turned and saw that the fog was coming from the Crystal Cave. In the middle of the fog, a tall, slender woman, wearing a silky flowing dress, walked across the mist, just a foot above the ground. I didn't need to look twice to know who it was.

The Lady of the Lake.

Everyone fell to their knees in respect, except for the Cerise Guard, who looked around confused, then decided to follow suit, and knelt as well.

As she approached, I realized she was even more beautiful in person. Her long, flowing hair nearly touched the fog beneath her. Her electric blue eyes scanned the crowd, a sweet smile on her face. Her eyes rested on me, and she grinned warmly. Just having her close by filled me with more warmth than if I had sat down inside the hot spring.

"Arise, Hayden Keyes," she said kindly. I arose, my legs shaking nervously. "You fought bravely, and honorably. When all had turned their back on you, still you returned. A true knight sets aside personal feelings for the greater good, just as you did. You did not fight for glory, you fought for friendship, but glory is still yours for what you have done. Now please, let us all see your prize."

I lifted my hand in the air above my head, willing Excalibur to return to me. In a flash, the sword materialized into my hand with a satisfying sound. Everyone gasped, oohed, and awed. The Lady of the Lake took my other hand, and it raised it above our heads.

"It was I, so long ago, who reformed the broken sword of King Arthur, and infused into it my magical power, renaming the blade Excalibur. Upon King Arthur's near death in the Other Realm, he returned the sword to me, enacting the very spell that transported all of Avalon and the magic of the world into this void we call Between. The sword was returned to the stone, waiting for a true protector of pure heart, who would be worthy to wield it again and defend us from the growing evils that beset our lands. Today, that very sword awakens, and with it, I have awakened, too! I give you, the Protector of the Magic Hollow! Wielder of Excalibur, and my champion, Hayden Keyes! Peace be unto you, knights," The Lady of the Lake said, smiling at me.

Then, with a loud splash of water, she vanished, leaving me completely shell-shocked.

Everyone cheered, even Percy and Isabelle. Tristan whistled loudly, then said, "I knew it. I told you so. I knew it, from the moment he sat in Siege Perilous, this kid was going to accomplish great things!"

Kaylinelle gave Tristan a gentle shove. "Don't be stupid, Tristan. *We're doomed*," she said, impersonating Tristan flawlessly. We all laughed, as Tristan looked sheepish.

Ector, Jack, and Principal Hal came forward and clasped me on the back. I gave Mr. Bianco a massive hug. Then, all the other knights, squires, and pages, started coming forward to congratulate me.

"Congratulations, Hayden," Elibora said, as she gave me a big hug. "You deserve it!" She gave me a gentle kiss on my cheek that left a warm spot. I made eye contact with Lady Albreda, who had a big mischievous smile.

"Uh oh," I whispered to Elibora. "I don't like the way your grandma is looking at me. Almost like she's going to try and marry us off next."

"Of course, she is," Elibora said. "You're the first wielder of Excalibur in like a thousand years. Just think of what that could do for our family legacy," Elibora said, impersonating her grandma.

"What? No way," Cecily huffed, looking back and forth between Lady Albreda and me.

"Don't worry," I said quickly. "We are just friends! We would never actually go through with it."

"So, you don't want to marry me?" Elibora asked sarcastically, which made me blush very, very badly.

"I mean, you are a great friend—and very pretty—but . . ."

Elibora laughed. "I'm just messing with you, Hayden."

Elibora turned and wrapped her arm around Cecily's waist. "Dating this girl is enough trouble for me," she said tenderly, pressing her cheek against Cecily's, winking at me when she saw the blank expression on my face.

"Wait—you mean—all this time? Don't get me wrong—I'm so happy for you two, I just didn't know. I thought Cecily liked Lance!"

Cecily shrugged, smiling brightly and beaming at Elibora. They left, holding hands, as I was bombarded with congratulations from everyone else. Alex and Eric begged to see Excalibur, then tried to smell it when it appeared in my hands. "Anything that old can't smell good," they argued. But for the record, Excalibur did not stink.

Lucas and Cole congratulated me as well, supporting Gale, who wanted to express his gratitude for helping him out on the battlefield. "You really saved my neck back there. Thank you," he said, wincing.

It was a little overwhelming, but for the first time in my life, everyone was looking at me, and not because I had done something dumb and they were laughing at me. Not because I had just gotten pulverized, bullied, or done something awkward. They were honestly acknowledging me for what I had accomplished. And that was the best feeling in the world.

# CHAPTER TWENTY-TWO

The only thing that would have made it better was if Lance had been there beside me. And if Gwen hadn't been so depressed. Everyone was happy, cheering, and celebrating the victory, but Gwen sat down alone on the banks of the Serpentine River, plucking at blades of grass. I wanted to break free from the crowd, but I was starting to realize just how exhausted I was, and it was impossible to get away from everyone. When I managed to look for Gwen again, she was gone.

Amidst the celebrations, Alex, Eric, and Weyland hoisted me up in the air. A crowd quickly gathered around us as we set back toward the castle. We had almost reached the front gate when it burst open.

Baron stood before us, looking very disheveled.

"You ingrates! You tied me up! I'll have you all in the dungeons! I'll—oh! Principal Hal. You're back!"

"I am," Principal Hal said. "You've missed the excitement."

"I heard the commotion," Baron said. "These brats tied me up in my office!"

"It was unfortunate, yes," Hal said. "But I've spoken to Gwen, and given the circumstances, I think it was warranted."

"Warranted?" Baron huffed. "This is an outrage! And what is he doing here?" Baron pointed at me.

"Hayden, pulled Excalibur from the stone and saved us all," Elibora said sharply.

Baron's jaw fell open as I summoned Excalibur in my hand. I smiled and winked. Seeing the look on his face in that moment was a memory I would never forget.

"Um, I do owe you an apology though, Baron," I said. "I was positive you were the one who . . . you know, betrayed us."

"Betray my home? I would never!"

"I saw you sneaking into the forest . . . I overheard you talking to some-one. That's what I don't understand."

Baron's face turned bright red.

"Why does it matter what I do in my own time? I didn't betray anyone, like you kept accusing me, boy! My business is my own."

"Baron," Principal Hal said. "Hayden isn't the only person who would like to get to the bottom of this final mystery."

Baron's lip curled in a sneer as he glared at me.

"I only accused you because you were always acting so suspicious!" I argued. "Plus, you were always so rude to everyone. You said yourself you were happy to run the Magic Hollow your way while Principal Hal was gone. Honestly, I'm surprised it wasn't you!"

"How dare you! I should have you thrown in the dungeons and serve you nothing but old pickle juice three times day—"

"Baron," Hal said curtly. "Enough."

The sound of hooves clicked from behind the crowd as Ixion, flanked by several smaller centaurs approached the castle. "I, too, would like to know what Baron was doing sneaking around our woods. We caught him in our village shortly after you departed, Hal."

"Is that so?" Principal Hal mused. "Baron, what's the meaning of all this?"

"I . . . I was . . ." I had never seen Baron look so nervous before. He looked like a kid who had been caught with his hand in the cookie jar. "Can't we discuss this in private?"

"It was me!" A female centaur shouted, parting the crowd of centaurs. She galloped over to Baron's aid. From the waist up, she was a woman. She had long brunette hair and warm brown eyes. She wore a blouse made of dark green ferns and beautiful blooming flowers. From the waist down her body was a dark earthy brown pony with polished black hooves.

"Luna, darling, what is the meaning of this?" Ixion roared. "What have you been doing with this human?"

"Only what we had to do to be together, father! I love this man!" Every kid in the crowd gasped, our mouths dropping to the floor. "I love him, and he loves me, too."

"It's true," Baron said, gaining confidence with Luna beside him. He raised his pant leg and revealed a patch of fur growing on his shin. "My love for Luna has started to affect me. A curse. We think Between is trying to change me into a centaur. That is what we were talking about in the forest. That is what we were planning to do together. We wanted to try and make the transformation complete."

"That is very dangerous magic, Baron," Hal said. "Very risky. Are you sure you want to go through with this?"

"Surer than anything I've ever known," Baron said.

"This can't be happening," Ixion said, massaging his forehead in clear frustration. "Luna, dear, you are my daughter . . . you could have chosen any of the riders . . . but you chose this human."

"Please, father. This is what we want. And I want your blessing."

"This is utter nonsense!" Ixion shouted. "Maybe, I can't stop you, but that doesn't mean I like it!" He turned and stormed away, the other Centaurs following him.

"This is the weirdest thing I have ever witnessed," Tristan whispered as the knights giggled.

"Awkward," Alex and Eric each mouthed.

"Well, I think it's very sweet," Elibora said proudly. "Her dad will come around."

"Now that we have reached the bottom of that mystery, I think it is safe to say we all could use some rest, or perhaps a nice warm meal," Principal

# THE LADY OF THE LAKE

Hal said. "But, Baron, I will need to see you in my office so we can discuss your treatment of the knights while I was away."

We all grinned satisfyingly as we entered New Camelot, listening to Hal scold Baron for his misbehavior during Hal's absence.

It was strange, stepping back into New Camelot, all things considered. I had pulled Excalibur from the stone. Me! The dork from the Other Realm. Everything would have been perfect if it weren't for one thing: my best friend was missing and he had betrayed us all.

I wanted Lance to come back. I wanted to yell at him. Ask him why he did what he did. But most importantly, I wanted to let him know that I was still his friend and that he wouldn't have to face his mistake alone.

I knew better than anyone how important it was to have friends who stood by my side.

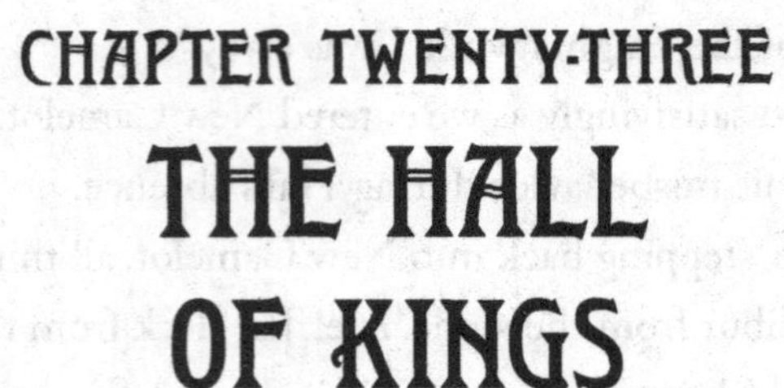

# CHAPTER TWENTY-THREE
# THE HALL OF KINGS

November passed and December came with a flurry of snow-flakes and icicles. As quickly as Excalibur had restored the Hollow to all its natural glory, the entire Hollow turned into a winter wonderland overnight, the Christmas spirit thick in the air. New Camelot looked like a colossal gingerbread mansion with snow covering its roofs like frosting and lights from the windows sparkling and glowing like gumdrop decorations.

As excited as I was for Christmas time, I was even more excited for the knighting ceremony. The Round Table had reviewed the battle and recommended several of us squires for knighthood, not to mention the advancement of several other knights from knight-junior, to full-fledged knighthood.

The ceremony was held in the Hall of Kings. When the appointed time finally came, we all gathered there, adorned in our finest tunics and clothes. I was wearing a full suit of armor, polished and gleaming in the colorful light that passed through the massive stained-glass windows. Standing beside me was Gwen, Elibora, Isabelle, Percy, Lucas, each wearing their armor as well. Percy even had a black cape draped over one shoulder.

# THE HALL OF KINGS

Principal Hal and the other Knights of the Round Table stood at the front of the hall before the golden throne. In Hal's hand, he held the pure sword Clarent, which glimmered peacefully.

"Our greatest strengths are most often discovered in the hardest and darkest of times," Hal said nobly. "As Knights and Squires of the Round Table we pledge to live with Noble Chivalry, Gentle Virtue, and by Honest Deeds. We also swear to protect those who need protecting, and to defend the realm from the evil that would see everything we love destroyed. All of you standing before me have been found worthy of the recommendations that have been given you. Your accomplishments are great, but they are not the end. With these new callings, comes an increase in responsibility and duty to your fellow knights. Isabelle, Elibora, and Gwen, please come forward."

They all did, taking one knee before Principal Hal and the throne.

"All of you successfully passed the trials and became honorary Knights-junior of the Round Table. Each of your exploits in the Battle of the Magic Hollow have been recorded in our great history and shall ever be remembered.

"Sir Percy—you single-handedly defended the gates of Caerleon from the trolls, three to one. Never has the Hollow known one so noble and true. And Lady Isabelle, your prowess in battle is unmatched. I hear your fighting was a terror and a beauty to behold.

"Lady Elibora, you alone stayed by Hayden's side when he needed a friend and companion. Even against the most terrible powers of darkness, you did not shirk in your resolve to fight for the light. Thank you for your unmatched virtue, loyalty, and strength.

"And last, but not least—Gwen. You alone rode through the dark of Between to rescue myself and my companions, Captain Jack and Sir Ector.

Were it not for you, I fear we might still be locked away in that cold and lonely cell. For that, you have my sincerest gratitude.

"All of you have been found worthy of becoming full-fledged Knights and Lady Knights of the Round Table. Now mind you, with this great honor comes a greater responsibility to live up to the titles you bear. May you all continue to lead your fellow knights and squires with honesty and respect. Now arise and join me beside the throne of Arthur."

They arose, clasping and hugging each other, whispering congratulations. Even Percy and Isabelle shook hands, albeit awkwardly.

"And now, Hayden Keyes," Hal said. "Please come forth."

I stepped forward and took one knee, my heart racing.

"Hayden, I have heard many stories about you. I even heard from a close source that you have a knack for giving motivational speeches. (I glared at Gwen, who stuck out her tongue at me.) When almost nobody believed in you, you still believed in yourself. And most importantly, you believed in each and every one of us, regardless of what had been said or done to you. We can all learn from your example, Hayden. Strength comes first from within, then from without, through unbreaking bonds of friendship. You united us, Hayden, in one cause to defend and protect each other and our home. For that, I am eternally grateful."

I felt my cheeks turning warm, and I couldn't help but smile as Principal Hal rested Clarent on my shoulder.

"Hayden Keyes, Protector of the Magic Hollow and Champion of the Lake, by the authority I bear as Warden of the Magic Hollow, I knight thee Sir Hayden, Knight of the Round Table. May Siege Perilous never be known as the empty seat again, for as long as you serve with us!"

I arose to a chorus of cheers and joined my fellow knights beside the throne of Arthur. I couldn't believe it! I was a knight. And not even a knight-junior. I was a full-fledged knight of the Round Table! I was the Champion of the Lake, and the wielder of Excalibur!

I felt an itch in my hand, and somehow knew that it was Excalibur. It was almost as if the sword were begging to be summoned so it, too, could bask in the joy of the occasion. I raised my hand above my head, and Excalibur jumped into it immediately, gleaming in the light, and basking in the glory of the Hall of Kings as everyone cheered.

Shortly after the knighting ceremony, Principal Hal called me into his office. Normally, I would have been quaking in my boots if a principal had done that, but with Hal, I wasn't worried. His office was exactly the way I remember it from my first night in New Camelot, except now that he was inhabiting it, it felt so much warmer and full of life. He offered me a seat by the fire, and a cup of tea, which I happily accepted.

"Hayden, I hope you know how grateful I am for what you have done for us," Principal Hal said. "Now that you have become a knight, and the Protector of the Magic Hollow, what next?"

"I—I guess I haven't thought about it much," I said. And it was true, with everything going on, I really hadn't put much thought into my future.

"Gwen told me that she took you to see your parent's cottage in Caerleon. You realize, as their living son, the home is yours, right?"

"I never thought of it that way," I said. "Are the Cerise Guard still looking for a place to stay? Because I'd be happy to let them stay in the cottage. We'd need to make some rearrangements, but they are welcome to it if they like."

"That is very kind of you, Hayden. I will let them know and make all the necessary arrangements."

"Also, I wanted to apologize about having Baron get tied up and locked up . . . I still feel like he deserved it, but I feel bad, too."

Principal Hal chuckled. "Don't worry about Baron, he may have a temper, but he has been a loyal servant of the Magic Hollow for many, many years. He will get past it."

"Is he going to . . . you know . . ."

"Allow the magic of Between to overcome him, in hopes that his desire to be with Luna will turn his physical form into that of a centaur?"

"Uh . . . yeah. That," I said.

"I think he has made up his mind. Nothing I say could sway him otherwise. I have convinced him to postpone the transformation, at least for a time. I will have to do more research so that I can assist with my own magic if necessary. Such transformations are very dangerous. Most end with the person becoming a monster, and we definitely don't want that to happen to Baron."

We were quiet for a moment, as I became deep in my thoughts and Principal Hal twirled his beard in his fingers. "Principal Hal?" I asked, breaking the silence.

"Yes, Hayden?"

"Am I anything like my father?"

"Yes and no," he said. "Sometimes I look at you, and I see the young man who arrived at our castle all those years ago. Sometimes I look away and I see your mother."

"Everyone talks about my father, the hero—but I never even knew him," I blurted out. "I didn't know how I could ever live up to his legacy, when he was so amazing and I was just me. To be honest, not long after coming here, I was tired of hearing everyone saying how great my dad was because I didn't know if I could ever live up to his name."

"The wonderful thing, Hayden, about parents, is that you don't have to be exactly like them, to live up to their legacy. I think you know that your parents would be passingly proud of you if they were here today. You see, Hayden, a birthright can be a very special thing. But it is important to never confuse the privilege you received from birth with your own duty to be the best knight *you* can be either.

"Never forget that for every child of noble birth, there are countless others who do not have the same advantage. It is not your birthright that makes you who you are, it is your own actions and choices. The mere fact that you failed to pull the sword from the stone proves that in the end, only finding the strength within yourself was enough to become a true hero. And that is something that no amount of right or privilege could ever have granted you."

I nodded. "I understand, sir," I said. "Besides, I know I couldn't have done it without the support of my friends either."

"Friends are another great gift many a knight has taken for granted," Hal said, smiling warmly.

"Sir, do you know where my parents are?" I asked abruptly. It was the one question that had been lingering in my mind all this time. If anyone knew the answer, it had to be Principal Hal.

"I'm sorry, Hayden, I do not. But I do know they are still alive. Of that, I am positive."

"How do you know?"

"Intuition. And, Hayden, I am rarely wrong, when it comes to my intuition."

I nodded. I wanted to trust him. "I have everything I came here for, except my parents. I want to find them."

"Do you intend to look for them, then?"

"Yes. Yes, I do," I said, deciding for the first time that is what I wanted to do. "As much as I'd hate to leave the Magic Hollow, I feel like I have to, at least for the time being. I'll be honest, though, I'm afraid. This is a whole new world for me, and, well, my Anglo-Saxon isn't great yet, either."

Principal Hal smiled. "I think I can arrange a companion for you. Jack Lantern is also searching for answers about his past and trying to recover his lost memories. He would be happy to join you on your journey. Perhaps together, you can find some clues to what you are looking for."

"That would be amazing!"

"Good. I will let him know you would like him to join you on your journey. But, first, I suppose I should let you know. You have done more for us than we ever could have asked of one young man. While this was supposed to be your home, I know it truthfully was not. You were raised in the Other Realm. You have two parents there. I imagine you miss them just as much as they miss you."

"I . . . I do miss them," I admitted. "But . . . I don't know if I'll ever see them again. That's the sacrifice I made when I came to Between."

"If I am not mistaken, Hayden, the enchanted medallion your father left you, is good for a round trip."

I reached into my pocket and pulled out the medallion, turning it over carefully in my hands, and examining it more closely. The coin vibrated gently in my hands, and I knew that Hal was right.

"You're saying I could use this to go back to the Other Realm?"

Hal nodded. "I'm afraid, though, you would have to leave the sword."

I couldn't believe it. I'd never considered being able to go back.

Deep down, I knew I could never make that trip. At least not right now. There was too much I still needed to accomplish. Wherever my parents were, they probably needed my help.

"As tempting as that is," I said. "I'm not going back. At least not yet. This is my home now. I'm the Protector of the Magic Hollow. But I'm not just staying out of duty. I'm staying for my friends. Besides, we have a lot of work to do, if we are going to prepare the knights to step out of hiding and save Between."

Principal Hal looked at me closely, and for a moment, I thought he was going to argue with me, but then he smiled. "Spoken like a true Champion of the Lake."

"Can I ask you another question," I asked, hoping I wasn't expending too much of his time.

"Of course, ask away."

"Gwen told me that you knew exactly where I was going to be when I came to Between. You told her exactly what alley to look in and even when. How did you—"

"How did I know you would be there? Well, Hayden, if I told you that it was my intuition again, would you believe me this time?"

"I don't know if I could, sir," I said honestly.

"Well, I respect your honesty. But the truth about believing, Hayden, is that it doesn't even have to be true at all to be believed in. The choice is yours, whether you want to believe or not. Perhaps someday I will be able to give you a more suitable answer. But for now, you will just have to trust me and know that I have told you enough about that."

I nodded, pretending half of what he just said hadn't gone right over the top of my head. "I do have one more question, though," I said. "When we were in the Crystal Hot Springs, I wandered off alone, and saw an apparition of the Lady of the Lake. She said that it wasn't really her, just something she called waterspeak."

"Yes, that is one of the benefits of being a water sprite. She can communicate through water, with anyone she desires, as long as there is water near them, of course."

"Well, I'm just wondering . . . do you think I could use waterspeak to communicate with my aunt and uncle in the Other Realm?"

"You should ask her, I'm sure she would kindly oblige."

The Enchanted Forest was so much more inviting after the skirmish between the Centaurs and the Wolves. I didn't feel threatened, or like I had to sneak around at all. The trees were still so dense there wasn't much light, so I summoned Excalibur, allowing its cool blue light to guide my path.

I figured I could probably have visited the Lady of the Lake in the Crystal Cave, but there were always people swimming and bathing. I figured I would get more privacy by the spring. Besides, I hadn't come back here since the day I drew the sword from the stone.

It was hard to imagine that this quiet tranquil place had been the arena for such a horrific showdown. I still got shivers remembering the strange shadow monsters that had attacked us. Whatever dark magic the troll king had found, it wasn't good.

Despite the winter chill, and the white frost that clung to all the trees around me, the warmth of the water in the spring had prevented it from freezing over. The fountain trickled loudly, falling down the rocks and into the pond. I knelt beside the water, Excalibur laying in my lap. The sword seemed to be resisting the stone like a magnet trying to be forced up against the wrong end.

"Don't worry, you don't have to go back to that stone anytime soon," I said. Strangely, that seemed to appease the sword.

I bent over the water, and, seeing my reflection in it, called for the Lady of the Lake, then asked her if she could show me Winston and Arabella in the Other Realm.

She didn't respond, and at first, nothing happened, so I started to doubt if it would work. Then, the water shimmered, and the image of my reflection changed, then grew sharper and more vivid. Suddenly, I was looking out of what appeared to be my old kitchen sink, and sure enough, Arabella was standing close by washing dishes, totally oblivious to my face that would now be visible in the water.

"Hi, Ari," I said.

She shrieked, splashing water and soap everywhere. "Hayden? What's going on—how are you doing that? I can't believe it! I can't believe it's really you! It *is* really you, right?"

"It's a long story, but at least now I know it works. As long as you have water nearby, I should be able to reach you."

"I don't care how you're doing it—I just can't believe it's really you! Let me get Winston. He just came home from work!"

She ran off from my view, leaving me with nothing to look at but what I could see of the kitchen. It only took a second to realize what was different. I could see the wall. Not a pile of boxes and junk. It looked like a normal, clean, kitchen.

Arabella came back less than a minute later, with Winston trailing behind her looking confused but excited. "Hayden? Is that you! It is you!"

"Hey, Winston," I said. "It's good to see you!"

"This is amazing! I can't believe it . . ." Winston said, looking stunned.

"There are a lot of things you wouldn't believe. Trust me."

"I'm just glad you are safe," Arabella said.

"Me too. I had a bit of a rough start here, but things are finally looking up. You'll never believe what happened." I held up Excalibur so they could see my new sword.

"That looks really sharp!" Arabella said.

"Ari, it's the legendary sword Excalibur. I pulled it from the stone."

"Is that like a party game? Or do you mean for real?"

"For real. I'm the first person to wield this sword since, well, King Arthur."

Arabella looked like she was going to pass out. "Sorry, sport," Winston said, "we are still trying to adjust to the whole monsters exist thing."

"Don't worry, though. They won't give you any trouble on your side. And I'm safe here in the Magic Hollow. Plus, I have Excalibur to look after me." I didn't tell them that I was planning on leaving the Magic Hollow. I didn't want them to worry too much.

"Have you found out anything about your parents?" Winston asked.

"Only that my dad was a really important hero around here. The problem is, nobody has seen him since he dropped me off with you two. But don't give up hope. We believe he's still alive. It's a long shot, but we'll figure it out. I will find him, and I will bring him home. Both my parents."

"Oh, Hayden. We miss you so much, but we are so proud of you," Arabella said, wiping tears from her eyes.

"What about you, two. You look like you've been busy. The kitchen—I don't see any boxes. What happened to all the stuff?"

"Well . . . after you left, we needed something to take our minds off things, so we hired a professional mover and we cleaned up the house."

"That's amazing," I said. "I'm so proud of you both!"

"It wasn't easy," Winston admitted. "And we filled sixteen storage units down at the local storage place, but it feels good. It was worth it." He wrapped his arm around Arabella and hugged her tenderly.

"We kept your room just the way you left it, for when you come home," Arabella said.

In that moment, I did feel a twinge of guilt. They had spent thirteen years waiting for my real dad to come home. Now they were waiting for me to come home. The difficult part was, I didn't know when, or if, I'd ever be coming home.

"I just wanted to let you know," I said, trying to distract all of us from that topic, "that even though you aren't my real parents, I still think of you as my mom and dad. I know I never called you mom and dad, but I just wanted you to know, I love you both, very much. Thank you for raising me. No matter what happens with my real parents, I will always love you two."

After that, Arabella was a never-ending fountain of tears, but I could tell they both appreciated hearing that from me. After a few minutes, we were able to get Arabella's tears under control enough to say our goodbyes.

When the waterspeaking communication ended, and I was staring down at my own reflection again, I couldn't help but feel a little regret. Hal was right, to a point. No matter how badly I struggled to fit in at school in the Other Realm, Winston and Arabella were still my family, and living with them had truly been my home. I missed them, but I knew I was doing the right thing. This is where I needed to be.

When Christmas finally arrived, we celebrated by having a huge festival called a carousel. Two dozen horses were dressed up colorfully, then marched around in unison to music. There were plays, singing, dancing, and lots of food. We all waved streamers in the air and had a wonderful time. It was nothing like the Christmas I knew in the Other Realm. There weren't any stories about Santa Claus, gingerbread men, or red-nosed reindeer, but it was still by far the best Christmas I'd ever had.

"Um, Hayden, can I talk to you?" Gwen asked me after the carousel had ended and several of the knights-junior started jousting for sport.

"Of course," I said, grateful for the chance to talk to Gwen. She had been so dismissive since Lance's disappearance, she was hardly the same person.

# CHAPTER TWENTY-THREE

We left the Arena and found a warm fire to sit at near the stables.

"I'm sorry for the way I've been acting. It's not your fault for what Lance did, and we're friends. Friends should rely on each other."

"Wait. You think we're friends?" I said sarcastically. "*Ah*, Gwen!" I gave her a big obnoxious hug.

She smiled but shoved me away. "Don't push it or get all sappy on me. Look, the point is, I'm sorry. I made you something to make up for it." She reached into her cloak and extracted a large book. "Sir Ector helped, but it was my idea. It's a compilation of every written thing we have from your dad. Plus, Mr. Bianco added some things from the Other Realm, too. Those nicely printed ones. I think he called them newspaper articles, or something like that."

I held the book carefully in my hands, like it was a sacred relic. For me, it really was. I flipped through the pages slowly, trying to soak in everything I was seeing. There were journal entries, history essays, research notes, newspaper clippings, and more. All bound in one place. It was like all my father's memories had been transferred into one book. I knew it wouldn't replace him or give me the perfect picture of who my father was, but somehow, I also knew this book would still help me get to know him. It was like looking into the past.

"Do you like it?" Gwen asked.

"Gwen—I love it!" I hugged her again, but this time, I was sincere. "This is the nicest thing anyone has ever done for me."

"Good. But don't get used to it."

We laughed, and I was grateful to have my friend back. Losing Lance had been difficult enough, not having Gwen around too had made it almost unbearable.

"Principal Hal told me you're going to leave the Hollow for a bit," Gwen said. "To look for clues about your dad."

"Yeah, I am," I said. "I have to find out if he's still out there."

"Just don't get killed," Gwen said. "I hope something your dad left behind in that book will help you find him. There has to be a clue somewhere. I can't help but wonder if he knew something we didn't."

"I agree. I'm positive he wanted me to come here. So there must be another piece to the puzzle. The problem is, I have no idea where to look. This book will be the perfect place to start. Thank you, Gwen."

"Hayden, while you're out there—I know you'll be busy looking for clues about your dad, but could you also keep an eye out for Lance? I'm so worried about him. If you see him, just tell him to come home, okay?"

"Of course," I said. "I promise."

"Thank you, Hayden."

We stood and returned to the Arena together, each in a much better mood than when we had first left.

When we got back to the Arena, Isabelle waved at me from the sidelines. "Hey, Champion of the Lake, what do you say we have a rematch? You know, a fair joust this time."

For once, there was no hint of venom in Isabelle's voice as she spoke to me. In fact, she was even smiling. This was new—and a little weird—but I was okay with that. Besides, it wasn't the weirdest thing that happened to me since coming to The Magic Hollow.

I couldn't help but smile. This was where I belonged.

# ACKNOWLEDGMENTS

I can hardly believe this book is finally out and in the public. I first imagined the seedlings of this story in 2009 while I was working in my Japanese teacher's farm. I was a sophomore in high school at the time. The story was almost entirely different, and I had a lot to learn as a writer (I still do, I reckon).

Since then, The Magic Hollow has been revised five times. Two of those times, I rewrote it basically entirely from start to finish. Along the way, I have received invaluable feedback and support from many. I would like to thank my brother, Kendell Clarke, for largely inspiring me to write a book for middle grade readers in the first place. Despite taking over a decade to write it (he is now married and far more mature than I am), he has always been supportive and willing to read and provide invaluable feedback.

Gaven Wood, a good friend, provided excellent feedback as he edited the manuscript. Gaven, seeing your excitement about the story encouraged me to keep going and hopefully finish strong. Thank you for your wisdom. It wouldn't be the same story without your input.

I would also like to thank Rick Margolis, the owner of Rising Bear Literary Agency. Even though, ultimately, we did not work together long term, the feedback he provided on the beginning of the story was immensely helpful and encouraged me to keep going.

A special thanks to my illustrator, Nicole Raskin, who did an amazing job creating pieces featured in the book, and without. She really brought the characters to life in her portraits.

I would also like to thank my girlfriend, Bekah, for her constant support. Thank you for listening to me ramble about all my wild thoughts and ideas.

I would like to thank the generous and supportive patrons who backed me on Indiegogo. For 30 days, friends, family, and complete strangers had the opportunity to lend their support. Together we were able to successfully fund the heftier expenses related to publishing a book. In no particular order:

Jan-Arild, thank you dear friend. As you know, "Nobody can stop the clock!" Tori Clarke, thanks, sis!  Britley Clarke, sister, friend, and teacher extraordinaire! Kendell Clarke; Judy Heaton; Trisha Headman; Hannah Headman; Michael Oncken; Brian Bates; Mason Wilkes; Jacy Anderson; Luan and Ron Stephens; Skyler Drage; Travis Empey; Stanislav Todorov; Randee Carns; Sarah Hipp; Esther Kekauoha; Carissa Bell-Chase; Jamilla Barstow; Gaven Wood; and, Chris and Jen Clarke (my supportive and inspiring parents! I love you.)

Finally, I would like to thank my readers. If you made it this far, wow! Thank you for embarking on this journey. If you enjoyed this story, please consider taking a moment to leave a review or recommend it to a friend you think might like it as well. I can't wait to meet again when the adventure continues in book two!

THE ADVENTURE CONTINUES. . .

# HAYDEN AND THE KNIGHTS

# THE QUESTING BEAST

## COMING SOON!

### ENJOY A SNEAK PREVIEW! ☞

# ON THE ROAD

I'm not saying everyone needs to pull a legendary sword from stone—I totally get it, not for everyone—but let me tell you, ever since I pulled Excalibur from the stone during the Battle for the Magic Hollow last year, my life has seriously changed. I would love to say it's been nothing but awesome, and don't get me wrong, it's been great, but I have also faced a number of challenges since as well. It turns out basically every monster in Between kind of hates and fears my guts and will do anything to make sure I die a horrible and painful death. So that's fun!

Just a year ago, I was an average kid, leading an average life. I was also a major dweeb, just trying my best to fit in at school and make friends. Now I can look back at that time with fondness. At the time, though, it seemed like I was doomed to an eternity of geekhood. Turns out, my English teacher and sincere friend, Mr. Bianco, is actually a knight, Sir Ector, who was sent to the real world to watch over me by my father.

And then Jack Lantern showed up, and the trolls, Jon, rest in peace, and Prince Garl Oonga-whatever. I discovered my dad's enchanted medallion that was hidden in my foster parents' (or aunt and uncle—still getting used to that) house. The rest, as they say, is history. I traveled to Between, the magical realm that was banished out of the real world like a thousand years ago, had an epic heroic struggle to win over my new friends in the Magic Hollow, fought to save Excalibur, united the Knights of the Round Table, and of course, drew Excalibur from the Stone. I was also betrayed by my best friend, Lance.

I still missed Lance. But the sting from his betrayal hadn't lightened either. I kept hoping I would find him. Jack and I had traveled pretty far since we left the Magic Hollow, tracking the troll army and the Cerise Guard's movements as well, but I had yet to see a single sign of Lance.

Being Defender of the Magic Hollow, and Champion of the Lady of the Lake definitely comes with its perks, though. Forget the fact that are zero bars of cell service in all of Between, thanks to my new powers, I can use waterspeak to essentially video chat anyone I want, whenever I want— as long as they are close to water of course. That's how Jack and I had been keeping in touch with everyone back home during our journey.

We have been traveling for over three months now and still not a single clue about my parent's whereabouts, Jack's mysterious lost memories, or any hint of where Lance ran off to. We followed the Trolls for a while, they peaced out North after the Battle of the Hollow and eventually settled in the shadow of some mountains Jack called the Howling Hills. They seemed to have gotten nice and cozy, so eventually we decided to leave them be for now.

Next came tracking the Cerise Guard, the Samurai gang that ruled the streets of Centerra for years before they got bold and tried to take over the Magic Hollow. Their leader took a gamble when he sicked the troll army on us, because we totally won. He had no choice but to get out of the city and find a new place to set up shop. They've been traveling around Between like nomadic puppies looking for a home, and beating up monsters and baddies along the way. While I'm not a fan, I also can't condemn them for their actions at this point. I hate to admit it, but they are doing more for Between then the Knights of the Round Table right now. That thought made me think of Lance, and deep down I knew he was right. The Knights shouldn't stay in hiding. We should be out fighting monsters and trying to make life better for everyone else.

If my travels with Jack have taught me one thing, it's how massive Between is. There are dozens of cities, villages, and country sides in Between, home to thousands and thousands of people, and unfortunately, nearly just as many monsters. Whether the monsters are naturally born or created by people losing themselves to the raw magic of Between, it makes no difference. They are a problem, and they make life extremely difficult for the average person.

I can't tell you how many farms I've passed from a distance that are completely walled in, and at night, guarded carefully by weapons and torchlight. We've stayed at a fair share of inns, and every time they are thrilled to see travelers. "Aye, business is slow. Dark days, dark days," they would always say as they led us to a room. I always left a tip, something that irritated Jack. I thought he was being stiff, but once we had been fresh out of gold for over a week, I started to see his point.

It had rained late into the night, making it hard to keep a fire going. I hadn't slept well, lying on the rocky ground and all. Jack was snoring loudly, the light within his pumpkin head flickering to the rhythm of the noise, as he cradled his big iron shield like it was a stuffed bear. Strings, the armor-clad talking mouse, was kicking his legs and squirming, probably lost in a dream.

I stared up at the sky thinking about New Camelot and how in just a few hours everyone would be waking up and gathering for breakfast. That thought made my tummy rumble and miss my friends. I tried not to think about how disappointed Gwen was going to be when I told her I hadn't found any news about Lance.

I watched the last trace of stars fade into a cool dark blue sky, hints of orange far off in the horizon as the sun began to peak over the Howling Hills in the distance. My stomach growled and I tried not to think too hard about the fact that I wouldn't be eating a big breakfast.

I was lost in a daydream (dawn dream?) when suddenly I heard a young boy scream. "Help! Help me, please!"

"CLICK! Get back here, CLICK CLICK boy! CLICK!" came an odd scraping voice that sounded like scraping metal.

More clicks, followed by another voice, this one of a slightly different pitch. "You might not be the Excalibur boy, but we are so hungry so this will have to do for now!" Great, whatever it was, there were two.

I didn't need to know what the source was, to know that it was a monster, and this kid was in serious trouble. He was close by the sounds of it, just down the other side of the ravine from where we had made camp. I leaped up to my fight and started to run, then stopped turning back toward Jack and Strings. The two of them were snoring loudly, completely oblivious to the danger.

"Jack—Strings—wake up! Someone's in trouble!"

Strings rolled over and opened his eyes lazily. "That's nice, mommy."

Jack continued to lie there completely unfazed.

"*Heeeeeeelp!*" the boy screamed.

"You two are useless, you know that!" I turned, running toward the ravine and the sound of the boy's cries.

Sure, I was storming in blindly to a fight against two who-knows-what monsters completely alone. But hey, that's basically my life now.

I leaped down the ravine, landing in a roll to diffuse the force of my fall, stopping right in front of the boy, and one really big centipede. Like, huge. Like, ten feet tall huge, and as wide as a tree trunk. It has a million little legs, hard black armor and two heads, one on each side of its body, with fang-like mandibles and glaring purple eyes.

"What's this?" asked one head.

"Looks like we don't have to share after all, brother."

"Who, slow down there, bug brains," I said. "Nobody is eating anybody."

The Centipede twins laughed, which was more a weird cacophony of clicking and scraping mandibles mixed with intermittent wheezing than actual laughter. So, on second thought, maybe they weren't laughing. Maybe they were just feeling ill.

"Who's gonna stop us. You?" Lefty said, baring his mandibles.

"T-that's right," I said, pretending to be nervous. I slowly reached down and picked up a stick. I winked at the boy on my way down, who looked back at me confused.

"Don't make us laugh, boy," said the head on the right.

"Let's get him, Chuck," said Lefty.

"Wait, your name is Chuck?" I asked. "Really? And what's your name?"

"Charlie."

"Huh. Right on"

The centipede twins hesitated. "You don't like our names?"

"No, no, it's not like that. I love your names. I guess I just expected something more menacing, you know?"

Chuck hesitated. "Hmm. You know what, Charlie, the kid does have a point. I mean, in centipede the name—" Chuck let out an odd series of hisses and clicks, "—sounds so much cooler, but it just doesn't really translate, you know?"

"Oh, the confines of the English language," Charlie bemoaned.

"Wait—Chuck, look!"

I grinned guiltily as I helped the little boy slip behind some large boulders.

"Stay there," I whispered. "Don't worry, I'm a knight!" The little boy's eyes lit up with wild excitement. He nodded eagerly.

I turned around to face the centipedes. "I won't let you hurt him," I said, purposely trying to sound unsure of myself.

The centipedes laughed, or coughed, I really couldn't tell.

Charlie bared his mandibles and Chuck bit a large branch tightly, then pulled down powerfully, breaking off the branch with a large echoing crunch. He tossed it to the side like it was a plaything.

"See what I did there, kid? And you think you are going to beat us up with that little stick?"

"Stick?" I asked. I willed Excalibur to appear. "Oh, you mean this?" I dropped the stick just as Excalibur materialized into my hand, it's blue light glowing brightly in the morning dusk.

"It's him!" Charlie growled. "That's him, Chuck. That's the kid!"

Chuck roared angrily, charging right at me, yanking Charlie in tow.

I dodged, rolling to the side, then slashing at Chuck or Charlie. I don't really know. Let's just say I slashed at the centipede. Excalibur sparked as it bounced off their armor like exoskeleton.

"You can't cut us, boy!" Chuck yelled amidst the sound of his scraping and clicking mandibles.

Chuck's side turned and lunged at me, but I sidestepped, avoiding his bite by several feet.

"Too slow—" I started to say, but then I noticed the ploy. I had stepped right into Charlie's range. The centipede's body flipped wildly, Charlie's gaping maw coming right for me. I dropped to the ground, feeling the wind rush past my head as Charlie barely missed my head.

Before I could think, the centipede was twisting around and Chuck was coming right at me. I had hoped being conjoined at the center would make them move more clumsily, but they were well practiced at fighting together. When they moved, it was almost like they weren't even two separate minds. I threw up Excalibur just in time, bracing with my left hand as Chuck crashed into me. Excalibur deflected his mandibles, but the force still sent me sliding backward through the dirt.

I knew this wasn't going to work forever. I couldn't just stay on the defensive. I needed to find a weak spot and strike.

Charlie struck next, as I knew he would. Of course, I thought. You know what they will do. Despite being in the thrill of the moment, it seemed silly that I hadn't thought about it before. Because they were conjoined, they were limited in reach, and how far apart they could be from each other. Not only that, they always rotated who attacked.

Ready for Chuck's next attack, and judging where he would be, I flipped Excalibur in my hands, then threw it as hard as I could, as if it were a spear. Chuck, mouth open, struck exactly where I expected and, to his surprise, Excalibur soared right in between his mandibles, lodging in a place that swords really shouldn't be in a healthy centipede monster thing.

I sprinted toward the center of the centipede, as Chuck thrashed in pain. I counted in my head. One. Two. I leaped into the air. Three. Excalibur rematerialized in my hands as I brought it down with a powerful slash. I aimed for the space in between the centipede's armor and, just as I suspected, Excalibur passed straight through.

The two sides writhed in pain, Chuck's end fading into ash. Charlie however, remained, very much alive. I hadn't been expecting that.

Charlie laughed. Again, I think, it was a laugh. Can you choke on your own spit exaltingly? Give me a break, I'm taking some liberty here, okay?

"I'm free!" Charlie shouted. "Finally free from that controlling ingrate of a brother!"

"Yeah, but . . . you're kind of . . . gushing," I said, disgusted, pointing at the back end of Charlie which was leaking a nasty yellow ooze. "Not a good look for you, bud."

"Bah," Charlie said. "It will heal. Now, how can I ever repay you?"

"You could just give up and let me turn you to ash," I said, maybe a little too hopefully.

"Not a chance," Charlie said, lunging at me. He moved way to well for someone who just got chopped in half, but then again, he did still have like half a million legs.

I rolled to the side, slashing Excalibur, but Charlie swerved, changing the angle of the crack between his armor plates. Excalibur bounced off his armor with a loud clang. I had to roll to the side, dodging another attack as Charlie whipped around.

Charlie was smart, I'll give him that. He never struck head on, making it impossible for me to hurl Excalibur down his throat. Not only that, he kept twisting his body, making it nearly impossible for me to get in a strike between his armor-like exoskeleton.

"I used to be human, once, you know," Charlie said. "A long time ago. I was born conjoined to my brother's hip. Everyone in our village laughed and made fun of us. And then one day, we had enough. We wandered out into Between and let all of that anger fuel our transformation. And look at me now! I got my revenge. Just like I will do to you, boy!"

I dodged his attack, slashing with several of my own, but Charlie was too quick, and his armor kept him safe. "Cool story, bro," I said. "I'd love to write a biography about you. Is now a good time?"

"What? No!" Charlie shouted, striking ferociously.

"It's been nice getting to know you, but I've got better things to be doing," I said, skirting to the side of Charlie's next strike. This time, instead of trying to slash through a crack in his armor, I slid Excalibur across the flat of his back, point first, with all my strength. "Sorry, this is going to hurt, bud." Excalibur slid under the armor plate, and I yanked up, tearing it up.

Charlie screamed in pain. He thrashed to the side, knocking me in the gut and sending me rolling backward in a tumbled mess. Excalibur, thankfully disappeared, so I avoided getting skewered on my own legendary blade, as I slammed into a tree trunk.

"You'll pay for that one, kid!" Charlie yelled as he lunged at me.

I rolled to the side just in time. Charlie slammed into the tree, snapping it in two with his powerful bite. I leaped to my feet. One. Two. Three. Excalibur reappeared in my hand just as I brought it down on the weak exposed spot I had opened in his armor. Charlie screamed as the magical blade turned him to ash.

I sat down with a sigh, as one does after a life-threatening battle with a killer monster. "Gross," I mumbled as I wiped Excalibur clean on the grass. And then, I remembered a little sheepishly, that I could just banish it. Excalibur would return spotless, leaving the centipede ooze behind when it disappeared.

I did a good job of not appearing unnerved during the battle, but thinking about what Charlie said made me shiver. I mean, I always knew that a lot of the monsters strolling Between these days were once normal people who lost themselves to the raw magic of Between, but hearing it directly from the source was chilling. It reminded me of the strange power I sensed the day I stepped out of the Magic hollow alone for the first time. That thought made a cold sweat drip down my neck. Had I let that feeling of anger and frustration overcome me, would I, too, have turned into a monster?

The boy started coming out of his hiding place, but hesitated when a loud clapping sounded from up on the ravine, both of which helped to distract me from my thoughts.

"Good show, Hayden. Smashingly well done!" Jack said, clapping his hands enthusiastically.

"Look who decided to wake up," I said, annoyed. "How long were you watching?"

"The whole time," Jack said.

"Yeah, we woke up when that idiot snapped that tree branch," Strings said from his favorite perch atop Jack's pumpkin head. "But you looked like you were having fun, so we just enjoyed the show."

"Thanks, for the help, guys."

"We were sending you good vibes the entire show—I mean battle," Jack said with a wry smile. After traveling so many months him, I was pretty good at reading the subtle shifts in his jack-o-lantern. They weren't as pronounced as normal people's expressions, but they were certainly there. "Besides, you know I'd step in if I thought you actually needed the help," he added.

When we first started our journey together, something like this would have really set me off. After everything we had been through, Jack and I were pretty good friends, all things considered.

I turned toward the boy, cowering in the rocks. "It's okay," I said. "You can come out now, it's safe."

The boy shook his head, looking nervously up at Jack Lantern. "Oh, him?" I said, realization dawning on me. "He's nothing to be afraid of. He's my friend."

"B-but he's a morph," the boy said nervously.

"A morph?" I asked.

"It's what they call people like me," Jack said. "Outside of Centerra my kind aren't exactly considered acceptable, you know."

Suddenly, it all made sense. I wondered why Jack had been so shy around others, and nervous about entering highly populated areas during our trip. He had always preferred sleeping outside in the dirt if it meant avoiding a hamlet or town.

I looked back at the boy, holding out my hand. "He's not just a morph. He's the last Lantern. He fought beside the Knights of the Round Table in the Shadow War, and he has fought beside me, too."

"Did you fight in the Shadow War?" the boy asked. "I wasn't born yet, but my dad fought in it."

"I didn't fight in it," I said, "but my dad did, too."

"A-Are you . . . King Arthur?" The boy asked, blushing.

I laughed. "Nah. My name is Hayden." I held out my hand and summoned Excalibur. "And this, well, you know what this is don't you?"

The boy's eyes lit up with excitement as he ran out of his hiding place. "It's Excalibur, isn't it?"

I nodded, smiling at his visible excitement. Excalibur really was a beautiful sword. It's blade, which for me always appeared leaf-shaped and slightly shorter than most two-handed swords, was a polished pale blue, which glowed softly in the morning light; it was made from a special type of metal, sanctified silver, which had been imbued with the powers of the Lady of the Lake. The cross-guard was silver, ornamented with deep blue jewels, the grip wrapped in fine brown leather, and the pommel shaped like a fish tail.

"I knew it was when I saw it," he said admiringly. "I've heard all the stories about it. This sword must be a million years old!"

I laughed, urging Excalibur to disappear. Immediately it vanished into mist.

"Wow," the boy said. "I have to tell my dad. Please, please can we show him?"

"Hayden," Jack said warningly, taking a step closer.

I ignored him. "Of course. Let's get you home, okay? What's your name, by the way?"

"Vlad!" the boy said with excitement. "Our house is just over the hill there, not far from here. I was picking berries I was when that monster showed up and scared me off! I'm not supposed to go this far from home. I don't want to get in trouble. But when dad sees this, he will forget all about it, I'm sure he will!"

"Hayden," Jack repeated, "Do we have time for this?"

"Of course, we do," I said. "Come on, this is the most exciting thing that has happened in weeks. Besides, he's just a kid, barely even old enough to be a Paige. Let's get him home safe, and maybe his dad will even give us a real meal in return. What do you say?"

"Fine," Jack said. "But you go on your own, I'll watch over camp. Bring me some food if you can spare it, but don't worry about me. And don't be too long."

I wanted to argue with him, but I could tell he wasn't going to bend easily. I felt bad for spending so long with Jack and never realizing until now how hard it was for him being what he was.

"Suit yourself, Jack," Strings said, sprinting down his leg, then hopping through the grass toward me. "I'm going with them. I'm starving!"

"This way!" Vlad said excitedly, gesturing for me to follow him up the hill.

I waved bye to Jack, wishing there was something more I could say, then turned and followed Vlad to his home.

TO BE CONTINUED ...